To
Sarah,

With Lots of Love,

Joanne Hall

BristolCon 2015

The Art of Forgetting

Book Two : Nomad

Joanne Hall

www.kristell-ink.com

Praise for The Art of Forgetting : Nomad

". . . an excellent 'rites-of-passage' story set in a well thought out fantasy world."

Andy Fairchild – The Cult Den

"Joanne Hall's world creating skills are absolutely beautiful. I followed the characters so closely that I felt a bond with some of them…"

IA Book Reviews

"When the story does move, it's a hell of a ride. We meet demons and royalty and see both Rhodri and other characters come into their own. Morality is questioned, bravery is tested and tribulations endured . . ."

Alex Shepherd – Fantasy Faction

"This is a good book that pulls the reader along at a cracking pace."

Cheryl Morgan

"Joanne Hall has created a richly developed world, where she has taken careful consideration of not only the majestic a fantasy world can offer, but also its flaws and political instabilities . . . But it's the little intricacies of the characters – none are perfect – and the plot, that show the author to be a master of observation."

Gillian O'Rourke – The Reluctant Prophet

"Joanne Hall is a wonderful writer and has done a beautiful job in crafting a fantasy story that almost feels like a historical novel."

Michelle Randall – Reader's Favourite

"The Art of Forgetting is a compelling read, with an intriguing young hero struggling to discover the truth about his past. It's not a book I'll be forgetting any time soon!"

Emma Pass – ACID

ISBN 978-1-909845-36-7

Cover art by Evelinn Enoksen
Design by Ken Dawson

Kristell Ink
An Imprint of Grimbold Books
4 Woodhall Drive
Banbury
Oxfordshire
OX16 9TY
United Kingdom

www.kristell-ink.com

For Heather and Colin, and for Claire.

Chapter One

I T WASN'T LONG before Rhodri heard the sound of pursuit. He said nothing, but his arms tightened around the girl. If they wanted to take her, it would be over his bloodied corpse. He was sure Drusain would be keen to make that a reality.

"Head to the river," she said with no hint of fear, "it will hide our tracks."

He steered Liberty towards the water. It was deep here, the northern banks overhanging steeply. The opposite shore was churned into soupy mud by the hooves of the goats that fled bleating as the mare leapt from the bank and splashed into the river. Rhodri had an idea.

"We'll be safe here," he whispered, to reassure himself as much as the girl. He didn't feel safe. It was too much to hope Drusain would give them a quick, merciful death. With luck, Liberty might get away. He hoped she wouldn't come snuffling back to reveal their hiding place.

He slipped from Liberty's back into the cold, swift-flowing river, taking the girl with him. With much cursing and floundering, he removed Liberty's tack and pushed her towards the muddy shore. "Go on, Lib!" She looked back at him, flicking a curious ear. "You love rolling in the mud, you silly mare! Go on, quickly now!" She wanted to play, but there was no time to waste with the King's Third hard on their heels. He slapped her rump, and Liberty needed no further prompting; she dropped to her knees, then rolled and squirmed on her back, staining her dapple-grey coat

1

dingy brown. She heaved to her feet again with a snort, glancing at him for further instruction. He waved her away. "Go!"

It would not withstand close inspection, but from a distance, she was one brown horse among hundreds. With a sigh, he let her tack fall to the bottom of the river. Riding bareback for a while was a small discomfort if it would save their lives. He swam back to the Atrathene girl, who trod water beneath the overhanging bank. She had pulled trailing fronds of grass down to form a curtain that might conceal them from searching eyes, if they were lucky and those eyes were blind. It wouldn't fool a determined hunter for a moment. The river was cold, and even stretching down with his toes Rhodri couldn't feel the bottom. He clutched hold of a protruding root beside his head, and kept as still as he could.

They hid in silence, shivering and afraid. Rhodri tried to judge the passing of time, but the sun was masked by thick, grey clouds and the waving strands of green offered the fugitives fragile concealment. They could have stayed there a few minutes, or a few hours, with no sound from above to tell them if their pursuers were near or far.

"Come find us, Dru, if you're coming," Rhodri muttered through teeth clenched against the chill that seeped into his bones. It made it hard to think straight. Maybe he should send the girl on her way, go back, try and pass off taking her from Drusain's tent as a prank that had got out of hand. He doubted Dru, once he recovered from his bruising, would see it that way. And the summary justice he liked to mete out, with no captain to rein him in, was vicious.

"It's all gone to shit now, hasn't it?" The girl looked at him curiously. "I wish this would end," he added in Atrathene.

She nodded. "Me too. Rhodri?" she asked, as if wrestling with some internal dilemma. "That's your name, isn't it? Rhodri?"

"It is."

She extended a hesitant hand towards him. "My name is Nasira."

Her fingertips felt like an old woman's, wrinkled with cold. "Why didn't you tell me before?"

"I wanted to be sure I could trust you. My tribe keeps our names close."

"Then I'm honoured. Thank you." He hoped he would live long enough to be worthy of her trust.

She drew closer to him. Her skin had a greenish hue, either due to the light falling through the leaves, or genuine sickness. He felt grinding nausea in his own gut at the sound of approaching hoof beats.

"Iron feet," Nasira mouthed, with a grimace of fear. He squeezed her hand. He didn't need her to tell him. If the ringing of metal horseshoes on the stony ground hadn't beaten out a warning, Drusain's cold tone assured him death stood mere inches away. With his free hand, he groped for his sword.

"Damn it, what do you mean? The tracks can't just vanish!"

Luk's voice, still sour: "They must have gone into the river."

Rhodri glanced at Nasira. Her hand was clamped over her mouth, her dark eyes massive with terror.

"Off this height?" Dru's tone admitted grudging respect. "He's a fearless little bastard, I'll grant him that."

"I'd say reckless."

"He always was, the short-arsed bugger. Why didn't you stop him?"

"I didn't know what he'd done! He told me he'd had the woman and he was taking a swim to cool off. I didn't see the horse-bitch. If I'd known he'd punched you sideways—"

"Drop it now, Luk. That's not something everyone needs to know."

"Yes, Corporal. Sorry, Corporal."

Rhodri heard men shifting about on the bank above. He could picture Dru, one blue eye blazing, the other hidden under a drooping eyelid, a permanent reminder of the last time he and Rhodri had come to blows. It was inevitable, that their years of service together would end in bloodshed.

"Can we ford it?" Luk asked

"Not here. Let's spread out along the bank. Bloody Rhodri, I'll gut him for this!" He raised his voice: "Men! Fan out along the river, find a place to cross. I don't want to waste any more time today."

The sound of hooves echoed away in either direction. Rhodri released the breath he was holding, and opened his mouth to speak. Nasira pressed a warning hand to his lips. Drusain's men may have gone, but the corporal lingered on the bank, along with his companion.

"Is it worth it?" Luk said. "They could be miles away by now."

"Most likely, but what kind of leader would I be if I didn't try to find him? He's a traitor to his unit, and to the Crown. If I had the chance, I'd hunt him down like a dog." Drusain sighed. "We'll search until nightfall, but tomorrow we need to move on. Curse him! I tell you, Luk, if I ever see him again, I'll unleash all the demons of hell on him!"

Rhodri heard them moving off. Nasira lowered her hand. "What did they say?"

"We have to stay hidden until dark. They'll stop looking then."

She shuddered. "It's a long time until night. I'm cold."

"Come here." He wrapped his arms around her slender frame, hoping to warm them both. "Sunset will come sooner than you think. If we stay here, we'll be fine. I promised to protect you, and I meant it."

"On your name?"

"Is that an oath?" He tried to smile. "On my name, then." He wondered privately how much his name was worth. His father's disgraced name probably had more value now.

The light was growing dim when a cry broke out on the far side on the river. Nasira tightened her grip on his arm. Her fingers were blue. He hushed her, holding still as death and trying to listen.

"A shod horse! Small feet. The tracks go off in this direction!"

Rhodri breathed a quiet curse. *No! Not Liberty* . . . she was all he had left.

"The lance-corporal's ride is a dappled grey mare. Find her and he won't be far away."

His former troop moved off, following Liberty's hoof prints away from the river. In the fading light, with a sheen of mud plastering her coat, the trick might work. But he couldn't relax; if he lost her, he might as well tie stones to his feet and sink to the bottom of the river to lie with her bridle.

"Will they come back?" Nasira shuddered. "My legs ache. I'm so tired . . ." Rhodri supported her with his arm. His own limbs were heavy as iron, dragging him down through the water.

"Not much longer. The moons are up now."

She shook her head. "You can't see the moons from here."

"Do you call me a liar?"

Nasira smiled weakly. "It's a great crime to lie, Rhodri."

"A greater crime to punch your . . ." He sought the word. ". . . your *leader* in the face, then run away!"

She chuckled. "I don't know why I trust you."

"Do you have any choice?"

She had no answer to that, leaning back against his shoulder while he trod water for both of them, until it was so dark he couldn't make out the opposite bank. "Do you think you can swim?" he asked. He wasn't sure he could, numbed in his legs and lower body.

Nasira nodded. "I can keep going as long as you," she said.

"That won't be long, if I don't find my horse!" He swam across the river with leaden arms, struggling against the current. It took an eternity, and as he pulled himself up on the muddy shore he gasped for breath. Beside him, Nasira groaned.

"Come on!" He scrambled to his feet, then collapsed again as his knees gave way beneath him. "Shit!"

"Was that a curse?" Nasira sat, trying to massage the feeling back into her calves.

"I fear so." He followed her example, slapping his numb legs until they tingled. "I hope we don't have to walk far!"

"Is that your horse?"

Rhodri couldn't see anything in the darkness, but he heard the soft clop of approaching hooves. Nasira must have the eyes of an owl. He wasn't sure, until the moment Liberty nudged him in the chest with her long nose, that it was her. Her coat was crusted with dried mud, which prickled as he threw his arms around her neck. She snorted in his ear, and nibbled him affectionately as he gave her a smacking kiss. Below the mud, she smelled of home—the home he had left behind; the sea port; the barracks. Of Keir. He had not thought of Keir in too long, and the memory, sharp and tangible as all his memories were, was a painful lump beneath his breastbone. It was hard to swallow, and he kept his face turned to Liberty's neck for a moment, concealing himself from the Atrathene girl he had saved.

"I'm glad they didn't find you, my girl. Let's get out of here." He turned back to Nasira, who stood with her arms folded and a wry expression on her face. "What's funny?" he asked her.

"Your horse. You act like she's a woman. What's the point in kissing a horse?"

"Liberty's my best girl." He fondled her ears. "Her kisses are sweeter than some women, too."

"Liberty? She has a name? What does it mean?"

"It means 'Freedom'. Don't you name horses in your tribe?"

Nasira shook her head as she mounted. "A horse is a tool. Like a cooking pot, or a blade. Have you named your sword, too?"

"Of course not, that would be foolish."

Riding bareback, the spikes of dried mud on Liberty's coat dug painfully into his thighs, even through the thick winter breeches he had been wearing since the mountain crossing that had claimed so many lives.

"Is it far to your tribe?"

"Dawn," she told him. "At good speed. And if they haven't moved on. They may think me lost."

"What if they have moved on?"

She patted his arm. "We find them. You saved my life, I owe you welcome in my home, if you need shelter."

The choice was a night alone on the steppes, with the prowling wildcats and the bitter winds scouring his skin, or a return to his unit, to face Dru, most likely to face death for his betrayal. Dru was not known for mercy. Beside those choices, spending a few days with Nasira's tribe did not seem a bad alternative, if they would protect him. And he could always walk away in time, ride his own trail while he decided what he would do with the rest of his life.

*

As dawn unfurled, Rhodri could see the smoke from the Atrathene camp a few miles away. Their progress was steady rather than swift, but he felt far enough from the King's Third to begin to relax and look around, instead of into the darkness behind them. The land had not changed, still open and flat, with low, wind-gnarled bushes and the occasional stand of twisted trees to break the monotony of the steppe. No buildings at all, not a hamlet or even a farmhouse. He missed the sturdy grey stone of Northpoint, and even, before that, the one-roomed wooden house where his foster-father had given him to the King's cavalry. If he'd known then that he would end up a traitor, a murderer, would he have ridden the same course? He told himself he'd had no choice, but there was always that niggling voice at the back of his mind, asking him if that was the excuse his father had used.

He dismounted to give Liberty a break, and walked beside her head, trying without success to brush the mud from her hide. His own clothes were crusted and stinking, and there was a raw tickle in the back of his throat. Nasira sneezed.

"Are you all right?" Rhodri asked. He had been about to suggest they stop and bathe in the river, but the girl looked so sick and miserable huddled against his horse's neck that he changed his mind. "We're nearly there, look!"

Nasira frowned, and sneezed again. "Let's walk with care," she said. "Your tribe and mine have a long story behind us."

"What do you mean?"

There was a rustle, a whisper of wind in the tall grasses. A moment before, the steppe had been empty; now they were surrounded by long-haired Atrathene warriors, bristling with bows and savage curved knives, every weapon aimed at Rhodri. Liberty bucked, snorting with alarm, and he calmed her with a pat to the neck.

"Throw down your weapons!" the leader commanded. Locking eyes with him, Rhodri let his sabre fall, followed by his belt knife and mercy blade. Nasira slipped from Liberty's back into the embrace of a young warrior.

"Temion!" she cried.

"Are you hurt?" The warrior stepped in front of her, blade drawn, and made a slashing gesture at Rhodri. "Did he hurt you? I'll have his eyes!"

Rhodri dropped into a fighting crouch as the warrior advanced. Nasira seized his arm. "Temion, wait!"

"What is it, sister?"

"You don't understand." She spoke quickly; Rhodri couldn't catch all her words. "He saved me. The short-hairs wanted to force me to their bed, and he helped me escape. He risked his life. I know his name, and he . . . he knows mine."

Her brother rounded on her, furious. "You told a short-hair your name? What were you thinking?"

"I trust him. I'm here, alive and unhurt, thanks to him—"

"Did he do anything to you?" Her brother seized her wrist. "Did you let him?"

"No I didn't!" Rhodri lunged at Temion, halted by the clash of steel an inch from his throat. "Let go of her. She's done nothing wrong."

Temion let his hand drop. "He speaks our tongue. That's different." He turned to the leader. "Maybe we can use him."

"Make use of me as you will." Rhodri fought to keep his voice steady. "But don't punish Nasira, and don't hurt my horse."

"Your horse is more valuable than your skin!" Temion gave him a sharp prod in the back with the handle of his blade. "Start walking!"

As the group approached the camp there was a stir of excitement. Children ran out to stare at the pale stranger, before their mothers snatched them away. Older ones ringed around, firing questions, held back by the warriors of the tribe. He was pushed and prodded into the centre of the village, and Temion lashed his wrists to the fence that contained the horses. Rhodri twisted in his bonds, trying to see where Liberty had gone. A stone, hurled by a hostile onlooker, struck his upper arm a glancing blow. He flinched, and heard laughter as a second missile caught him on the hip.

"Stop that!" The jeering, jostling crowd parted at the command of a tall, slim man, with greying hair pulled back into long braids. He was dressed in horsehide jerkin and breeches, richly decorated with beads and small, polished stones that jingled as he moved. He stood a sword's length from Rhodri and surveyed him.

"Why is this short-hair here?" he demanded. "Is the tribe in danger?"

Rhodri stood as straight and proud as the ropes that held him would allow. "I mean you no harm," he said in careful Atrathene. "I brought the woman back. Release me, and you'll never see me again. My tribe won't hurt you, I swear on my name."

The leader's eyes were slits. "You speak well, and you know our customs. Are you a spy?"

"No, I—"

Temion butted in: "I found him with Nasira. Her dress was ripped and she was bruised. She claims he didn't hurt her—"

"I didn't!" Rhodri kicked the post, tugging the ropes in an effort to break free. "Listen to her! She told you what happened!"

The older man tugged one of his braids thoughtfully. "We should have full moon council," he declared. "Nasira should tell her tale."

"A woman addressing council? Even if she's my sister—"

"Silence, nephew!" The leader cut him off. "I have spoken. Nasira will address the council at full moon. This short-hair's fate will be decided then."

Rhodri decided to speak up. "Full moon is days away. Will you leave me tied like a hog until then? Nasira said I was welcome in her home."

"You're lucky you've been allowed this chance," the tribal leader told him. "Our welcome is to let you live among us, at least until your fate is decided."

Rhodri thrashed, but the ropes held firm. "Cut me loose then, so I can repay your trust."

The old man snorted. "You must think me a fool." He turned to Nasira's brother. "Temion, bring the forge."

The forge was a small folding anvil heated over a campfire. The Atrathenes may not have shod their horses, but they fired metal for pots and pans, and for the jewellery they wore in their ears and hair. Whatever welcome they offered Rhodri would be made over the fire, and by Temion's grim expression, it wouldn't be pleasant. He renewed his fight against the ropes as Temion beat and twisted metal over the flames.

"You can't do this, uncle!" Nasira pleaded with the old man. "I promised him welcome! He laid no hand on me!"

"You'll have your chance to speak in council," the leader snapped. "Unless you'd rather I slit his throat now? Temion, is it ready?"

"Is what ready?" Rhodri lapsed into his native tongue. "What are you doing?" He struggled as the men of the tribe descended, calloused hands seizing his arms and legs, pressing him flat to the

10

ground. Temion advanced, links of yellow-hot metal held at arm's length in a pair of tongs. The colour was so bright Rhodri screwed up his eyes. Were they going to brand him like his own people branded cattle? "Let go of me!"

The heat was agonising. Rhodri's skin crackled as the chain dropped over his feet. Searing, raw pain clenched around his ankles and raced up his legs like flames. He screamed, choking on vomit, dizzy enough to pass out. There was a smell like a pork joint fallen in the fire and, far above, a woman cried out. His world was a blur of hands and fire and pain. He would welcome death, to make it stop, and there was a word to bring about death.

"Mercy! Mercy, by the hells! Father, help me!"

No mercy for Rhodri, just the burning that went on and on. He screamed and kicked, trying to pull his feet away from the fire, but the pain travelled with him. He felt himself lifted and carried, and the blessed shock of cold water, engulfing him to his knees. His head spun, and the world crashed into darkness and forgetting.

*

It was dark when Rhodri came round, but it was the familiar brown dimness of a tent in shadow, not the crushing blackness of oblivion. There was a rare, disturbing gap in his memory. His legs throbbed, and when he tried to move, spears of pain raced up his calves, making him gasp. His feet were leaden. What had Temion done to him?

"Stay quiet!" Nasira's voice cracked as she pressed a pungent drink into his hand. "This is for the pain."

"I don't know why you bother." Rhodri recognised Temion's throaty tones. "He's likely to die before you speak at council."

"Then his death will bring shame on Trogir's soul. What he did, what you did today, was barbaric, Temion."

"Because what the short-hairs do to our people is just ill fortune? If it was my choice, I would have cut his throat on the steppe. You asked for mercy, and mercy was given. Stop complaining about it."

Rhodri's hands shook so violently he spilled most of the warm drink over his chest. Nasira was at his side at once, mopping him down with a damp rag. "I'll make some more," she assured him. "You lie quiet."

He caught her wrist. "What's wrong with my legs? What happened to me?"

She looked away. It was wrong to lie, but the truth could be evaded. "I'm doing all I can for the pain."

"Show him, sister," Temion said. "A fighting man needs to know his limitations."

She rounded on him. "You get out! I'm sick of you. You pretend innocence and virtue, but you were the man who swung the hammer. If he dies, it won't just be Trogir's soul walking in eternal shame, but yours!"

He backed away before her fury. "Do you want me to fetch the shaman, if he'll treat him?"

"That would be a start. Then you can stay out of my sight."

He hesitated in the entrance. "Will you be safe, alone with him?"

"He can't walk. He's hardly going to throw me down and ravish me. Out!"

She pushed him outside and turned back to Rhodri, who struggled to sit up. Every movement brought fresh waves of pain. Nasira shook her head. "I told you to lie still. What happened to you is shameful, but fighting it won't help."

"What have they done to me? Why won't you tell me? And why are my legs chained? Do you think I'll run away?"

"Oh Rhodri!" Her voice was heavy with sorrow. "I don't want to show you . . ."

"I need to know what they did. It unsettles me to forget . . ." He bit his lip as she approached.

"Are you sure?"

He nodded. Nasira gently lifted the blanket concealing the lower half of his body. Rhodri looked at his legs, unsure at first what he was seeing. Below his knees, his breeches were cut open and peeled back, like flayed skin. Swollen blisters and crimson welts scored his legs like tongues of flame, while the unmarked skin was corpse-pale. His ankles were bloated, and around each leg, sunk into his flesh, were shackles. A short, stout length of chain linked them together.

"Get these chains off me!"

"I wish I could." Nasira picked up a soaking rag and laid it across his calf, bringing momentary relief.

"Where's the key?"

"There is no key."

"What do you mean, no key?" The iron rings embraced his ankles, smooth and seamless as a wedding band, with no lock or fastening. He could walk, but he couldn't run, and he couldn't ride. Sealed in, welded to the tribe. He felt sick. "What have you done?"

"Rhodri, I'm sorry—"

"You caused this!" He clawed the shackles with a howl of frustration, unleashing a fresh wave of torment. "Cut me loose!"

"I can't—"

"Cut me loose, damn you!" He tried to rise, flinging himself out of bed and onto the floor. Fire exploded through his lower limbs, and he screamed and choked, rolling in agony as Nasira fled before his rage. Helpless and alone, he crawled beneath the bed, pulling a blanket after him, a wounded animal seeking a solitary spot to die.

*

Rhodri drifted in and out of the world, every tiny movement bringing fresh hurt. Even the vibration of footsteps on the floor set a tremor through his tortured body. He whimpered, dragging himself away from the flare of torchlight. Nasira's voice was too loud. "I left him right here. He couldn't have run away."

Lying under the bed, he saw her bare feet and delicate ankles only inches away. With them was a second pair of feet, bigger and dirtier, with a gold ring piercing each heel. *That must hurt*, he thought, dizzy and confused. *How can he walk with rings in his heels? Is it a wedding band?*

"Am I married now?"

He must have spoken aloud. Nasira dropped to her haunches beside the bed and reached out a hand to him. "Rhodri? Why are you under there?"

Even in his delirium, Rhodri knew he must speak in Atrathene. His father would be angry if he didn't, and then Valery might kill. His anger had never been directed at Rhodri, but it had always been cold and terrible.

"It hurts," he whispered.

"I know it does. I'm sorry."

"Where's my father?"

"Your father?" She took his hand and drew him by slow and careful inches back into the light. "Your father's not here. This is our shaman. He wants to help you."

"Am I being punished?" Rhodri pulled his knees up to his chin and wrapped his hands protectively around his blistered calves. "I tried to forget the things he told me to, but it won't go away! What can I do?"

Nasira exchanged a long glance with the shaman. "Can you reach him, Kilujen?"

"I can try. His spirit is as damaged as his legs. Neither will heal without scars. Help me lift him onto the bed."

They moved him as gently as they could, Rhodri flinching at every touch. The shaman bent over his feet, nostrils flaring as he inhaled.

"Where's Liberty?"

"She's safe," Nasira said. "No one in the tribe would harm a fine mare like that."

"What is he doing?" Rhodri tried to sit up, and she pushed him flat.

"He wants to help you. Keep still."

Kilujen transferred his attention from Rhodri's legs to his head. He checked the pulse in his neck, massaged his temples, and stared deep into his eyes. His skin was unlined, and he wore more gold hoops though his nose, earlobes and lower lip. Some had chains running between them, and Rhodri reached out to rub them between his fingers.

"Are you being punished too?"

Ignoring his question, the shaman turned to Nasira. "His spirit was troubled long before the chaining," he declared. "But there's power, too, behind his eyes. I want him, if he lives."

Nasira frowned. "His mind is broken, I think."

"It will mend. He's stronger than he looks."

She chewed her lip. "If he survives with mind and body intact, the moon council will decide his fate. They may declare him too dangerous to live."

"I will speak for him," Kilujen promised. "Why has his care fallen to you?"

"He saved me from the short-hairs. I owe him my life."

"From his own tribe?"

She nodded. "The ones who came over the mountains to harry the lands near here. I was tied up in one of their tents, and he cut me free. He fought with his own leader to get me out. He can't go back, they'll kill him."

"More proof of his strength. I have herbs and powders to ease his suffering. I'll bring them before morning. I can ease his physical pain, but his spirit lies in your hands."

*

The care of Rhodri's spirit fell not only to Nasira, but to her grandmother and younger sister, who all shared her tent. Between them they tended his burns, and supported him as he hobbled about. As his physical pain eased, the torment in his head became more bearable. He was deeply ashamed of his childish outburst, and regretted the mention of his father. Nasira said nothing about it, but her pitying glances filled him with resentment.

A quarter-moon passed. Rhodri only left the tent in that time to use the latrine trench, a humiliating experience when he needed help to stand. His blisters burst, oozing foul-smelling liquid, and they itched like the pox. The swelling in his ankles went down, but his skin was raw and chafed, mottled with infection despite the salves the shaman brought. He experimented with the shackles, twisting them as far as the thick chain allowed in his search for a weak spot, a release that wasn't there. With the chain attached, he could only take short, limping steps, and when he tried to take a full stride, he fell on his face. He felt the tribe was taunting him, testing to see how far they could push him before he snapped. He wouldn't give them that pleasure.

"Here!" He looked up from his fruitless clawing at the shackles. Nasira stood before him, hands on hips. "Come with me," she commanded. "It's time you saw your horse."

"What's the point? I can't ride. Your tribe have stolen everything from me." He kicked the wooden frame of the bed, setting the chain rattling.

"We move from here after moon council. You might come with us—"

"Or I might be dead at your brother's hand. Better than living as a slave."

Her dark brows knit at the Western word. "A slave? I don't know the word . . . What is that?"

"A man forced to work for another with no reward. A man kept in chains."

Her mouth fell open. "Is that what you think of us? Has anyone made you lift a hand to help them?"

"What difference does it make? You keep me chained. I'm no better than a dog to your tribe."

"If you were a dog," she told him with a dismissive flick of her braids, "you'd be dead by now. Do you want me to help you to your horse, or would you rather sit here and wallow in misery?"

He stood, wobbly on his feet. "Take me to my horse."

Liberty was corralled with the other steeds, attracting attention and admiring glances for the pale sheen of her coat. It was strange, Rhodri reflected, that while Atrathene bays and chestnuts were so valued in his own country, here the position was reversed, and Liberty was the rare prize.

He leaned on the fence and called to her. She trotted over, head and tail held high, snorting a welcome. He rubbed down the length of her nose and blew softly in her ear, while she closed her eyes and swished her tail in glee. He rested his head against her neck. He needed to ride more than life itself. If he could no longer ride, he'd rather be put to death.

Nasira rested a gentle hand on his shoulder. "You'll ride again," she said. "Trust me."

*

Adeamus neared fullness, increment by increment. Every night Rhodri watched the moons rise, often shrouded by cloud, waiting for the evening when the tribe gathered to pass judgement on him. The threat pressed down on his shoulders, and although Nasira tried to occupy him with minor chores, he was restless and morose.

The night before the full moon, Nasira joined him in his vigil. They sat in silence, side by side at the edge of the slow-moving river. There was a frosty nip in the air, and she dragged thick blankets from the tent to huddle under as they watched Adeamus, fat and yellow as a gold coin, breach the horizon with the smaller moon Calarian nipping at his heels.

"It's a good moon for hunting," Nasira remarked.

Rhodri smoothed his fingers over the cold metal of the locket around his neck, the one Amerie had pressed into his hand the night his world crashed down around him. It contained tiny, perfect portraits of his parents. His real parents—the ones he couldn't remember. Amerie had proved to him his life was based on a lie, but there was strange comfort in the touch of silver. It told him that he might not belong here, or even with the King's Third anymore, but there was somewhere he did belong. If the tribe let him go, he would return to Hierath, even if he had to walk over the mountains to get there. But first he had to survive his trial.

"What happens tomorrow night?"

"You'll tell your story, and I'll tell mine. At least, that's what I've been told. Unmarried women aren't usually permitted to speak at important councils. The men of the tribe will speak for you, or against you, and Trogir will decide your fate."

"I'm glad you'll speak for me." Rhodri pulled a fold of the blanket over his head like an old woman's headscarf. Shielded, he could no longer see his companion, only the steppes, the river, and the brooding yellow moon. Calarian was a sickle, barely visible in the shadow of his dominant brother, but the stars gleamed bright and steady through gaps in the cloud. "What do you think he'll decide?"

"My uncle is not a cruel man—"

Rhodri snorted, rattling the chain between his ankles.

"He's not!" she insisted. "Everything he does is for the good of the tribe, even shackling your feet. He could have caged you—"

"I'd rather he had—"

"Or killed you on the spot. He's given you a chance, and bartered himself time to think." Her hand crept under the blanket to clasp his. "If you can't ride, you're good as dead. I don't think he'll kill you."

"How can I ride again?" Rhodri scratched the itchy, flaking skin on his left ankle. "Unless I ride side-saddle, like a woman. That's no style for a fighting man!"

"Would you rather ride like a woman, or not at all?"

Rhodri had no answer to that. How could he explain the humiliation, when the cavalry had been his life? He sighed, and sucked the fresh blood from his fingers.

"Talk to me. Tell me what I can say that might help you. I know you're a good man, but my tribe fears you. Help me convince Trogir you're no threat."

Her voice was as low and calm as a ripple on the water. Rhodri couldn't see her face, did not have to shy from any judgement in her eyes. They were alone on the plain, and he might die tomorrow. Her gentle encouragement released the catch on the locked chest that was his spirit, and everything came tumbling out. Dallow and his loathing for the child he had saved from the forest, Drusain, Astan's unveiling, and her death. He told her about Keir, and Valery, and the shock of discovering his true parentage. The murders on Dragon Pass, and his refusal to join in with Drusain's savage destruction of the Atrathene camp. By the time he fell silent, the moon was far above the horizon, and a bitter wind whipped around them.

"You can take from that what you will," he concluded. "I'm not a good man, but I'm trying my best. Trying to be a better man than Valery."

"You called out to him, when . . . your feet . . ." Nasira trailed off, twisting her hands delicately. "I think he's not as far in your past as you'd like."

Rhodri said nothing. His life was entwined with Valery. Some deep-buried part of him still called the man his father, though it shamed him to admit it.

"You're a good man, Rhodri, a noble of your tribe. You might not be able to forget what you've done, but I think you forget to believe in yourself." Her hand snaked up under the blanket to caress his cheek, and she drew his mouth down to hers in the briefest of kisses. It caught him by surprise, and he tried to hold on to her, but she slipped from his arms. Quick and silver as a minnow, she darted away towards the camp, leaving him to struggle to his feet alone. By the time he hobbled back to the tent, she was nowhere to be found.

Chapter Two

CLANGING BELLS INDICATED the beginning of the council to decide Rhodri's fate. The encampment was lit by torches, and the Atrathenes gathered next to the central corral. It seemed everybody in the tribe was there, from tiny babies balanced on their mother's hips, to a toothless old woman who was carried in and set down in the front ranks with great respect. Her empty gums worked a piece of leathery meat as she stared at him with eyes that glittered like onyx.

With a murmur that could equally have been apology or contempt, Temion bound Rhodri's hands to one of the upright posts of the corral. He wondered at the precaution. He couldn't run away, and he would struggle to put up much fight against the horde of savages come out to judge him. But it was part of the ritual, Nasira told him, and ritual seemed to be everything in tribal life, so he submitted with the best grace he could.

As the rising sphere of Adeamus balanced precisely between the three poles that crowned Trogir's tent, the bell stopped ringing. A hush descended as the tent flaps swept open. Trogir was carried on a litter, supported on the shoulders of the four strongest men of the tribe. As they laid it down in the clear space, the leader rose. In ceremonial dress, haloed by the moon, he was an intimidating sight, taller than Rhodri remembered. He took a deep breath to calm his singing nerves. This man had already mutilated him, and now he held his life in his hands. Rhodri had not left his lover and ridden halfway across the world to die at the whim of an Atrathene council. The fates owed him better.

Trogir wore a long cloak of horsehide, richly decorated with feathers, long sleeves draped over his hands. He raised an arm to point at Rhodri, the dangling pinions like claws. "Tell your story," he commanded.

Rhodri licked his lips. He recited the tale, from the moment he heard the disturbance outside his tent, to his capture by Temion on the steppe, a mile outside the village. "You know what happened from there," he finished. "Everything I've told you is the truth. Nasira will speak for me."

Trogir turned to Nasira, who sat bolt-upright and cross-legged in the front row. "Niece?"

There was a ripple through the crowd, but no one dared question Trogir's right to call the girl to speak before the council. She rose, lantern light rippling across her long, lean limbs, and bowed towards her uncle. "Thank you, Leader, for letting me speak in council. Everything Rhodri the short-hair says is true, but he does not mention his courage in rescuing me. Without him, my soul would ride the Spirit Trail. Uncle, I urge you to free him from his bonds and accept him as a member of our tribe. He saved my life, and I owe it to him to return the honour." There was a mutter of agreement, but Nasira had not finished speaking. "If you cannot accept him, at least allow him to live. I will stay behind with him, and we will form our own tribe."

She was forced to shout over the chaos her words caused. Rhodri stared at her in surprise. Her jaw was set, and only a faint tremble hinted at the anxiety she must feel. He had never expected such an offer, and he wasn't sure he wanted it. Her life, her body, was not part of her obligation to him, however they did things in the tribes. He would have to try and explain that to her without offending her.

"May I speak?" Kilujen the shaman strode through the seated crowd, who watched him with keen interest. He bowed to Trogir,

22

who returned the gesture, a meeting of equals.

"I welcome you to our council, Kilujen. Do you speak as our shaman, or as a member of our tribe?"

"A little of both. I am here to speak for the short-hair who names himself Rhodri of Pencarith."

Trogir stepped back. "Speak then."

"Your niece asked me to see the short-hair after he was shackled. In truth, I expected him to die. He is stronger than his small frame suggests. Both the strength he has shown in his bonds, and his courage in rescuing Nasira from his own people, would be an asset to the tribe. But there is something else, more than physical strength and courage. There is power in his spirit, the power of memory. It is a shamanic gift, and I'd like to train him to use that gift to benefit us all."

Temion sprang to his feet. "He's a short-hair! He can't be trusted. I say we slit his throat and have done with all this talk."

Rhodri heard Nasira's hiss of indrawn breath; she had not expected this attack. As if Temion had fired a beacon, chaos broke out. Some were on their feet yelling for Rhodri, others, the young warriors and most of the elders of the tribe, were against him. Turning his back on them all, Trogir strolled over to the fence and regarded his prisoner with mild curiosity.

"Can you be trusted?" he mused. "You turned against your own people to help my niece, and she has pleaded for your life, both before the council and to me, privately."

"I did not know that." Rhodri felt he should be grateful for her interference, but he felt only irritation. "I don't need a woman to defend me. I would prefer to speak for myself."

"A fine trait. You have borne your suffering with dignity and honour. Perhaps I was too hasty, but I acted for the good of my tribe. Do you condemn me?"

"In your place, I might have done the same."

Trogir tugged his braids. "The shaman is rarely wrong. I don't know about spirit-strength, but I know when I'm looking at a good man. You will live." He glanced back at his bickering tribe. "Let them talk it out, and they'll see things the way I do. It's wise to let a man think he's made up his own mind, even when the choice was made long ago. I've no doubt you'll remember that, Rhodri." He winked.

Warming to the leader, Rhodri plucked up the courage to ask the question that had worried him most about the trial. "My feet—will I be able to ride again?"

"To stop you riding would condemn you to death. We are not a cruel people."

The talk behind was turning in Rhodri's favour, and even Nasira wore a faint, anxious smile. Trogir snatched up one of the lanterns. Holding it high, he addressed his tribe:

"I have chosen!" he announced, in a deep, booming voice that carried across the camp. As one, the tribe fell silent. "People of the Plains Hawk, I have come to a decision about this man. He will live, and Kilujen the shaman will train him in his magic art. He is one of us now, part of our family, and will be treated as such. At least until trading season, when he may leave us for another tribe. Temion! Strike his chains!"

Temion's expression was black as thunder as he walked slowly from the audience towards Rhodri, swinging a sturdy hammer between his hands. He looked him hard in the eye before kneeling at his feet, and there was no friendship in his gaze.

The first blow of the hammer smashed down on the inner bone of Rhodri's right ankle. He yelped and jerked away. "Sorry," Temion muttered. Rhodri glowered down at him, sure the assault was deliberate, but what could he do?

"Hold still," Nasira's brother went on with a grim, humourless smile, hefting the hammer. "I'd hate to hurt you again."

It took many hammer blows to the chain, and a few more against Rhodri's bones, before the link between the shackles fell broken to the ground, leaving behind the sealed iron bonds that wedded him, for good or ill, to the tribe. He flexed and stretched his legs, groaning with relief. His feet still felt heavy, but now he could walk normally, and he would be able to ride.

"Cut him loose," Trogir commanded. "He's one of us now."

The upward slash of Temion's blade sliced through Rhodri's bonds, nicking the skin of his wrist. He shook off the ropes as Temion stepped back, regarding him through narrowed eyes, expecting him to comment. Rhodri inclined his head. "Thank you," he said, "it's good to be free."

Trogir turned back to his tribe, and moved on to other business. Rhodri sank to the ground next to Nasira, still getting used to moving his legs freely. She squeezed his hand, her whisper a tickle against his ear. "I'm glad you're with us now. Do you want a drink?"

The ale she brought to him was stronger than he was used to, with a pleasant fruity taste. One of the Atrathenes beat out a rhythm on a drum, singing with a throaty warble words Rhodri couldn't make out. Nasira hummed along, tapping her foot. Her thigh pressed close against his, and the movement sent an enjoyable thrill up his spine. By the end of his second mug he felt bold enough to slip an arm around her waist, and she rested her head against his shoulder.

He had missed this, the warmth, the closeness. The scent of horse that clung to her skin like a fine lady's perfume reminded him of Keir. The horse master had urged him to take his happiness where he could find it; he closed his eyes and breathed her in, fingers drifting across softly yielding flesh where once he had found hard muscle. He pulled away, and wondered if he should get another drink to cool the sudden heat in his skin.

Some of the tribe were dancing; the shaman brought out a set of pipes and whistled a high, uplifting tune.

Maybe dancing was a better idea. The unexpected closeness, the shifting shadows, the drums, combined to confuse his senses. "Do you want to dance?" He caught her hand, ready to tug her to her feet.

She turned her head so her lips met his. "I'd rather stay here with you."

She was all invitation, and he was only flesh, after all. He backed away from her embrace to fill the flagons from the barrel that stood nearby, taking a moment to try and cool his head, and his ardour. If she was behaving like this out of obligation, he didn't want it. He would rather go down to the river and take matters into his own hands.

He returned to her, holding the drinks before him like a foaming shield. "Nasira, before you have another drink . . . you don't have to stay with me, you know. You could go and dance with your friends."

She held his gaze. Her eyes were clear, unclouded by drink. "What if I don't want to dance with them?"

He passed her the flagon. "I just thought—"

"What? That because I owe you my life, I feel I have to take you to my bed?" Her lip curled in derision. "I make my own choices, short-hair. Come, sit next to me. You worry too much, and it makes your face hard."

She nestled into his embrace once more. She was watching the dancing, but her fingers beat a delicate tattoo on his thigh; it was hard to withstand their demand.

His hand slipped under her shirt, fingers brushing the soft curve at the underside of her breast. She wrestled his hand down, gentle but firm, surprising him with her change in direction.

"Hold a moment. My brother is watching."

Temion stood apart from the dancers, arms folded, lips pinched into a disapproving frown. Rhodri raised his flagon in mocking salute. Goading Temion made his desire to bed Nasira even sweeter. "If not here, where?"

"Too keen, short-hair!" She extracted his hand once more with a giggle that let him know she was teasing, leading him on a rein until the last possible moment. The anticipation only fanned the

26

flames. "Have another drink," she suggested. "Or that dance you spoke of?"

Dancing might carry them away from Temion's scrutiny. "Come on then." He caught her hand, brought it to his lips. "Let's dance like they do in my country."

"Lying down, you mean?"

Rhodri laughed at Nasira's mock-innocence as he twirled her in his arms, enjoying the feel of her body close to his. Away from her brother's gaze, she relaxed, allowing his hands to wander. She nibbled his earlobe. "Let's get away from all these people."

"Will we miss anything important?"

"You might, if you don't come with me." Her laughter swept aside the last of his doubts, and he chuckled.

"Come on then." Together they slipped away from the dancers. "Do you think Temion will notice we're gone?"

Nasira shrugged. "I don't care. He'll drink himself to sleep. The day after tomorrow we move to the winter grounds at Kharikan. The other tribes will be there. We should arrive before the snows come. I'm glad you can ride again . . . I'm talking too much, aren't I?"

He smiled. "I like to hear you talk about your people. Especially now they're my people too." The night wind was bitter, and he wrapped his arm around her as they walked, stroking her upper arm with the flat of his hand. Her breath came in gasps, steaming in the air. "Are you warm enough?"

"I'm fine." The tent was empty. Nasira lit the lantern that hung from the central pole, casting a friendly circle of light. "It's good to be alone."

She sat next to him on the bed, hands clasped tightly in her lap. Whatever invitation she offered him had evaporated in the cold night air. She shivered in his embrace, and it dawned on him that what they were doing might be unacceptable in her tribe. Was she breaking a taboo letting him touch her like this?

"Nasira? Is something wrong?"

She started at the question. "Not at all! Why would you think that?"

"It looked like you might have changed your mind. If your tribe value purity . . . I won't do anything that would bring a scandal down on you." He wanted nothing more, at that moment, than to cause a scandal that would knock the breath from Temion's lungs, but he wouldn't use Nasira like that.

"Purity?" She laughed, and some of the tension lifted. "No, my tribe prize fertility, not purity. I was late coming into womanhood, and my moon-bleeds are erratic." She said it without a blush, and Rhodri caught himself admiring her candour. Western women were more delicate about such subjects, at least around men.

"That's why I was allowed to stay and care for my little sister after our mother died," Nasira went on. "Most girls are traded out quite young. But—" She hesitated, as if debating whether to go on.

"But what?"

Her fingers picked at the blanket. "I never thought I'd go with a short-hair."

"You don't need to be nervous around me. I might not be shackled any more, but you know I'd never hurt a woman."

"I know. You're not like this Valery you speak of."

He cradled her cheek in his hand, brushing his lips against hers. He was surprised by her ardent response, the way her long fingers traced fire up his spine. He lifted her so she sat on his lap, legs wrapped around his waist. He released the buttons on her jacket deftly, one handed. His other hand caressed her back and the nape of her neck as they kissed, her mouth warm and yielding against his.

Beneath the jacket, Nasira wore a loose fitting leather vest. He slid a hand up beneath it, seeking her nipples, enjoying her sharp intake of breath as his fingers brushed over them. This time, she didn't push his hand away.

"You like that? Tell me what you like." He pushed her vest up over her head, mouth working eagerly across her pert breasts, looping his tongue around her nipples. She moaned, arching her back as he traced light kisses over the curve of her belly. He slipped a hand inside her breeches, and at once she tensed, sitting upright and taking hold of his wrist.

"What's wrong?" He ached to be inside her, to tumble her down on the bed and make her cry out in pleasure, but Nasira shook her head.

"Too fast," she said. "Let me catch my breath."

"Don't tell me you don't want to." He had felt her, just for a second, open and yielding beneath his fingers. She wanted this as much as he did. He smiled, trying to make her feel better. "Remember, it's a great wrong to lie."

Her eyelashes fluttered, and she folded an arm over her bare breasts.

Rhodri stroked her back. "There's no need to be shy."

"I'm not shy. But I don't want to rush things with you. You're not like the men of my tribe. I don't know you well, and I don't want to make a mistake."

"Does this feel like a mistake?" His tongue flicked over her earlobe, and she shuddered. "I can stop any time, on your word."

In truth, he wasn't sure he could. With her legs around him, her hips against his, the smooth warmth of her bare back under his urgent hands, it would be difficult to walk away. She made him so hard it was painful. His hand crept towards her waistband once more.

She closed her eyes. "No. Don't stop."

She gasped, and he felt her tense, then relax, as he pushed his hand between her legs, seeking the spot that brought her pleasure. She reached down to guide him, her fingers entwining with his and slipping inside her. He laughed.

"What's funny?"

"You've done this before." He felt a twinge of jealousy at the thought of her in another man's bed. "You seem to know what you like, but I hope there's a thing or two I can show you."

He pulled his hand free of her grip, and rolled her over so she lay face down. She was touching herself, and he found the sight powerfully arousing. He swept his tongue over her rounded buttocks, wrapped his hands around her hips and pulled her against him so she rested on her knees and elbows. She uttered a little cry at the unexpected move.

"Don't be scared. I promise I won't hurt you," he whispered in her ear, one hand curved around her breast, the other brushing the tangle of hair between her legs as he slid inside her. Long strokes, slow and gentle. Her thighs quivered beneath his touch, and she groaned. The lantern light rippled across her bare skin. He tried to hold back, to prolong her enjoyment as long as he could, but the feel of her backside against him was too much. She cried out in pleasure, collapsing face-down on the bed and carrying him with her over the edge.

Rhodri woke at the sound of a soft footfall. The lantern burned low, casting a golden glow over Nasira's bare skin. She slept face down, one arm flung out. Her legs tangled around his, her right foot resting on the metal band that clasped his left ankle. His arm draped around her waist, and his cheek was cradled on her shoulder. He felt the draft from the open tent flap brush his skin, raising goose pimples. Someone stood there, staring down at them. From the soft clearing of his throat, Rhodri knew it was Temion. He held himself still, hardly daring to breathe, aware that his pocket knife lay on his belt, several feet away on the floor. His arm tightened protectively around Nasira, who sighed and murmured in her sleep. There was a soft swish as the tent flap fell, and the draft was cut off. Temion left, without saying a word, but his fury was palpable in the still night air.

*

Rhodri slipped away before dawn. Nasira's reputation might be destroyed in her brother's eyes, but he would not embarrass her before the other women in her family. She rolled over as he was leaving, and stretched her arms out in a sleepy gesture. "Stay?"

"I would if I could." He kissed her goodbye, lingering over the moment, and let himself out into the silent camp. Temion slept sprawled, right outside the tent. Rhodri stepped over him, wondering if Nasira's brother had stationed himself there to pick a fight. If so, the empty flask in his hand would have damaged his chances. Leaving him snoring, Rhodri hurried to the corral through the debris of last night's festivities. Empty flagons and splayed bodies lay everywhere; people seemed to have dropped where they passed out drunk in ones and twos. The horses were restive and hungry, and there was no one to tend to them. He took a couple of bales of fodder from the store and threw them into the corral, leaning on the fence and watching the horses eat. The breeze was stiff this morning, the grass frosty, but the sky was high and pale blue, the colour of Valery's eyes. He felt very far from home, out here in this quiet, wide landscape, but the isolation of the last half-moon was gone. The memory of Nasira's skin against his made him tingle.

Liberty raised her head from her fodder and snorted her pleasure at seeing him. Time for a ride, her eager stance suggested, front legs shifting in restless anticipation. He had neither reins nor saddle, but that didn't matter. He mounted from the fence, swinging one leg over her back and gripping a firm handful of her mane. "Let's go!"

She bucked lightly, keen to be off, and he calmed her with a pat to the side of her neck. He knew how she was feeling; the playful spirit swept through him too, and once away from the camp they cantered for the joy of it. Rhodri didn't care where he wandered, emptying his mind of everything but the rhythmic pounding of Liberty's hooves against the turf, the cries of birds from far above, the chuckle and gurgle of streams as he vaulted them. It was a perfect day for riding, for solitude, for aimless thought. But his thoughts couldn't wander forever, and as he found himself drifting further from the Atrathene camp, Rhodri realised he had to make a choice.

Stay, Nasira had said, reaching out to him. In that one entreaty, he knew, she meant more than just stay until the sun came up, and she had spoken not just for herself. She wanted him in her life, but to stay with Nasira meant embracing the ways of the Atrathenes. Until now, Rhodri realised, there had always been a tiny thought in the back of his mind that he could return. If not to the King's Third, then at least to the New Kingdom, to claim his birthright and the recognition he deserved from his sister, Serren. He could ride south, find Captain Garrod and throw himself on his mercy, explain that Drusain's ways were abhorrent to him, and hope to avoid harsh punishment. Or he could try and cross the mountains and find his way back to the Estmarch, and from there to Northpoint. Back to Keir. They could run away together, take a couple of horses or even a boat, and make a new life for themselves far from the disapproving eyes of the King's Third. But Keir was half a world away, and braving the mountain passes this close to winter was suicide. Returning to the King's Third might not be a better option. And then there was Nasira. She trusted him when she had little reason to, interceded with her uncle on his behalf without prompting, listened to him spill his heart on the ground without judgement or condemnation. Since he arrived at the camp, she had stood quietly at his shoulder, backing him up, listening to him, and tending his wounds. All she asked in return was that he stay, and her soft plea was truly all he needed. It might not last, and he hoped he wouldn't come to regret it, but for now staying with her seemed the safest course.

In high spirits, he swung Liberty round and galloped back towards the camp. He let her pick the route; she seemed to know where they were going.

Kilujen met him before he reached the circle of tents. The young shaman was bleary eyed but cheerful, and heralded him with a raised flagon. "I hoped you'd be back!" he said. "Did you make your choice?"

"As you said, I'm back." Rhodri dismounted and sent Liberty back into the corral with a friendly slap. "What does that tell you?"

Kilujen shrugged. "Either you had nothing worth returning to your own tribe for, or you've found something here that makes you want to stay. I hope it's the second one."

"Me too." Rhodri took a mouthful from the flagon. "You want to train me as a shaman. What does that involve?"

"You mean, what will you have to give up?" Kilujen's laugh set the jewellery in his face jingling. He wrapped an arm around Rhodri's shoulders and steered him towards the river. "If it's my little cousin you worry about, there's no need. You can be a shaman and marry, raise a family if you want to. In fact, it's useful to be married. Ginamor helps me with my work. You don't have to give up bedding women. Or men, for that matter."

Rhodri thought it wise to ignore this last comment, at least until he knew the taboos of the tribe a little better. "Nasira is your cousin?"

"So you have been bedding her!" Kilujen squealed in amusement, slapping his knee in delight. "Don't worry, I won't tell Grandmother. We're all cousins here, or half-cousins. Nieces and nephews. It's rare to get new seed in the tribe. That's part of the reason Trogir let you live."

"For my . . . seed?"

"Don't look so alarmed, my friend! Anyone would think we wanted to put you out to stud!" He doubled up with laughter, tears rolling down his cheeks. Rhodri couldn't help but smile at his playful nature, hidden beneath the serious robes of a shaman.

He stretched out on the bank, resting on his elbows. "What makes you think I'd be a good shaman?"

Kilujen sat up, back straight, arms wrapped around his knees. "Nasira tells me you remember well."

Rhodri smiled wryly. "I have a very unusual memory."

"That intrigued me, even before I saw the strength of your spirit. One of the most important duties of a shaman is to keep the history of the tribe. Our story is passed down from mother to daughter, father to son, and it must be remembered properly. Everything we do is part of the story. You, and me, and Nasira's liking for a short-haired stranger . . ." He winked. "All are strands woven into our fabric. You, with your unique memory, you could be our record keeper."

Rhodri nodded. "I think I could do that."

"There are other things. Healings, magic, talking to the spirits. Your mind must be open to everything. But don't worry," he added at Rhodri's mutter of alarm, "we start small. There's plenty of time. For now,"—he drew a tangled length of twine from his pocket—"we will practice the noble art of fishing. Do you fish, Rhodri?"

"Not since I left the sea." Fish had never interested Rhodri as much as horses, but Astan and Niklaus liked fishing from the sea wall in Northpoint, and he had often joined them. It was a companionable activity, a quiet, friendly way to waste a few hours. He caught the twine Kilujen tossed to him, and settled in for a lazy spell on the riverbank.

*

As Nasira predicted, the tribe began packing up late that afternoon, ready to move to their winter grounds. Rhodri was kept busy, dismantling tents and checking the mounts. Each tent converted, ingeniously, into a covered wagon pulled by a pair of sturdy horses, and every wagon was stuffed with the possessions of the tribe. It was a feat carried out with remarkable speed and efficiency, and in almost total silence by the people of the Plains Hawk, many of whom still suffered from last night's drinking binge. He didn't see Nasira, who had her own errands, but as the sky darkened he felt a tug on his arm and turned to see her wide-eyed younger sister.

34

Odval stared up at him. Her hair was loose and curled around her ears, and she sucked one long strand as she stared at him. She was too young yet for the braids of a warrior.

"What is it, Odval?"

She spat out the hair and pouted. "Grandmother says you're not to share our tent while we travel. She says it's not proper."

He wasn't surprised by this. Nasira's grandmother was a perceptive old woman. Even if Temion said nothing, she was bound to have guessed something was going on. "Tell her that's fine. Thank her for her hospitality."

Odval shrugged. "She says you can sleep under the wagon at night, but you're not to make noise with my sister and upset Temion. Don't know why Temion cares if you make noise, he's not even riding in our wagon!"

Rhodri felt a slow grin spread over his face as he realised the old lady had given him her tacit blessing to sleep with Nasira, as long as they were discreet. "Don't worry, I'll be as quiet as a sleeping beetle! I don't want your brother angry with me!"

Odval scowled, and dug one bare toe into the dusty ground. "You grown-ups are all weird. If Grandmother doesn't want you bedding my sister in the tent, why doesn't she just say so?"

*

The convoy of covered wagons wound eastwards, following the course of the river as the weather grew colder and the first snow flurries began to fall. Rhodri spent his days learning the stories of the tribe with Kilujen, and his nights curled up below the wagon with Nasira. He was surprised the first night she crawled under the wagon and pressed up against his side. It had crossed his mind that perhaps she was embarrassed at what had passed between them, or was keeping her head down because she feared Temion's wrath, but as he watched her by day and listened to her at night, he realised that she wasn't one to be intimidated by her brother, or anyone else. She hadn't slept in her own bed since the tribe moved on. Her grandmother refused to relent, even though, as Nasira herself pointed out, there was no point trying to protect her honour against the invading short-hair when everyone else in the tribe knew what was going on between them. Rhodri was subject to much good-natured ribbing, which he took with a cheerful heart. The only people who had a problem with the liaison were Nasira's grandmother, who glared at him with disdain every time he ventured into her sight, and Temion.

Temion had barely spoken to Rhodri since the moon council, and Rhodri knew it must be eating him up to see his sister fraternising with a man he regarded as an enemy. All he could do was stay out of his way while they travelled, but that wouldn't be an option forever; sooner or later the two men would collide, and Rhodri was prepared for the confrontation.

He trotted along, musing on a story Kilujen had told him; the shaman would often tell him stories, and then ask him to puzzle out the meaning behind them. He said it was a way of expanding the mind. He said this so often Rhodri wondered how wide he wanted his mind to be. As wide as the plains, maybe, or the sky. He didn't think he had enough knowledge to fill a space that vast. So much land lying empty, while the houses of Northpoint teetered three stories high with a family in every room. No wonder his sister coveted this land. He was sure the savages could share some of it, if they wanted to.

He rode alongside Sudak, an angular boy some years his junior, yet to grow into his muscle and with braids that reached no further than his shoulders. Sudak seemed disinclined to chat, but he watched Rhodri with sharp eyes, staying constant by his shoulder. He was friendly with Temion, and Rhodri suspected Nasira's brother had sent the young tribesman to keep an eye on him in case he caused trouble.

They followed the course of a wide stream, too shallow to be called a river, and as the horses stopped to drink and wait for the wagons, Sudak straightened in the saddle, scanning the horizon with eager eyes. His nostrils twitched, and he sprang up in one easy movement to stand on the back of his mount, one hand held high to block the afternoon sunlight that streamed at a low angle across the steppe. His upper lip drew back in a snarl.

"What can you see?" Rhodri asked.

Sudak spat. "Fire and metal."

"What does that mean?" But the young warrior had already wheeled his horse around and was riding hard for Temion, who had gone back to check on the progress of the wagons. Rhodri decided to follow him. Sudak's face told him that what he had seen was serious, perhaps a threat to the tribe. If he could fight, he could prove he was on their side, and erase some of their lingering doubts.

Sudak was already in close conversation with Temion when Rhodri arrived, leaning over in his saddle to talk in urgent, hushed tones. Temion looked beyond him, caught Rhodri's eye, and glowered.

"I'll deal with it," he said, suddenly speaking in a normal voice that seemed too loud. "Find Trogir, get him to circle the wagons. We'll try and head them off before—" He broke off, and turned abruptly to Rhodri. "What do you want? Why are you here?"

"It looked like there was trouble." Rhodri tried to keep his voice affable. "Can I help?"

"You can keep your face out of it," Temion snapped. He was about to turn away when Sudak laid a daring hand on his arm.

"He can fight," he said. "Why not give him a blade?"

"It's who he's fighting for that troubles me."

"At least a dagger," Sudak persisted. "Let him defend himself, if it comes to blood. Trogir says he's of the tribe now—"

"I don't care what Trogir says!"

Sudak hissed at this open rebellion, and Temion backed up a pace. "He's not of the tribe. He has yet to prove himself worthy of us."

"Give me a knife then," Rhodri pressed. "How can I prove anything if you won't let me fight?"

Temion snarled, but he drew a blade and threw it in the dust before Liberty's front hooves. She startled and tossed her head before the sudden movement.

"I'm watching you, short-hair. Any tricks and that blade will be in your back. And we won't wait for you if you fall behind."

"I won't." Rhodri slipped from the saddle to retrieve the blade. It was Temion's belt-knife; the hooked point was sharp enough, but the edge was blunted and it was too light to use as a club. Still, it was more of a weapon than his bare hands. He remounted, holding it between his teeth. Temion was already galloping back towards the scouts, his big roan's heels throwing up the dust of his passage. Rhodri transferred the knife to his hand and set off after him.

By the time he arrived, Temion had his warriors gathered around him, and Sudak was pointing in the direction of the threat. Rhodri was surprised to see women among the small band of warriors. He had seen them hunting, admired the way Nasira could take down a hawk or a wild goat with her bow, but he had not expected these women to fight alongside the men. How easily Astan would have fitted in here, fighting for the tribe, and the thought was a dull kick in his gut.

"We don't want blood," Temion said, his eyes flicking over Rhodri and dismissing him. "We want to scare them away from the wagons. If it comes to a fight we know we're outmatched, so let's set them running."

"Who are we fighting?" Rhodri asked. Temion ignored him, raising his hand for his warriors to fall in behind him as he nudged his ride into a trot that swiftly became a canter. The fighters of the Plains Hawk fanned out across the steppe and Rhodri was swept up with them, feeling the thrill of battle quicken his breath and constrict his stomach as Liberty stretched her legs beneath him. They had no armour, they were barely armed, and he didn't know who they were fighting, but that surge of adrenaline was still addictive, and he realised he had missed it since he crossed over the mountains.

The Atrathene mounts were swift and long-legged, and Liberty laboured to keep up. They fell behind as from every throat came the long, ululating war cry of the tribes. Rhodri had heard that cry before, in the tent he shared with Dru as they were hounded across the plains by an invisible enemy. It had raised the hairs on his neck then, and it was no less chilling now under the afternoon sun on the barren steppe.

They were headed for a low line of stunted trees, dull green, and as they neared, metal flashed in the warriors' hands. Temion might not want blood, but he was ready for it. Rhodri tightened his grip on his own dull knife and urged his big-hearted mare to greater efforts to keep up.

There was movement in the trees, a sudden stirring that sent little birds up in a black, twittering cloud. The war cry pitched a note higher, and the enemy broke left and right, so quickly it caught Rhodri by surprise. They were mounted on light-coloured horses, and it took a moment for him to realise what that meant. The Atrathenes rode bays and chestnuts, roans and sorrels. They never rode greys. The sturdy little greys like Liberty were Western horses.

Liberty whinnied an eager welcome as he pulled her up in confusion. It couldn't be Dru's troop, not here, not so far out. At a sweeping glance he saw that the strangers were better armed, better fed than Dru's men, and their insignia was the sky-blue of the Royal household, not the black and crimson of the King's Third. Men from Hierath, deep in the heart of the tribal lands. His sister's men.

They scattered before the blades and arrows of Temion's warriors, and Rhodri kicked Liberty into action once more, wondering where they had come from—and if there were more of them hiding behind the trees. He plunged between the leaves, hearing the sounds of pursuit race away on either side of him, and pulled up sharply as the ground dropped away beneath Lib's front hooves. The trees lined, and concealed, the steep bank of a deep, swift-flowing river. From upstream came a scream, swiftly and brutally cut short, and even as he watched, the water darkened to crimson.

So much for not wanting blood.

Putting the sullied river behind him, Rhodri trotted out from beneath the shadow of the trees into the waning sunlight. The invaders had scattered, and the victorious warriors were returning. Sudak rode slowly, one hand clamped to a deep slash in his upper arm, and one of the women had a swelling to her eye that was rapidly darkening to a bruise, but they were otherwise uninjured and in high spirits. Sudak even offered Rhodri a wan smile as he pulled up alongside him.

Temion was the last to return, coming from upriver with a scarlet streak of blood splashed up his jerkin and across his face. He led his horse, and marched straight up to Rhodri, hauled him from the saddle and pushed him up against Liberty's flank.

"Hey!" Rhodri shoved his hands away. "What's wrong with you?"

"Sudak, hold his horse."

Sudak shrugged, but it was the woman with the black eye who leaned over and took Liberty's bridle, throwing Rhodri a filthy glare. She backed off a few paces and joined the rest of the warriors circling Temion and Rhodri. Rhodri's back felt very exposed, and his fingers tightened around the useless knife.

"You knew they were there, didn't you?"

"What are you talking about?"

"You've been signalling to them." Temion pushed him again, forcing him a step backwards. "That's why you fell back. You hoped they'd catch us by surprise and hack us to ribbons."

"Temion, I swear—"

"What were you going to do?" Another shove, and Rhodri felt a sword level cold and cruel between his shoulders. He didn't dare look behind him to see who wielded it. "Go back to the tribe as the lone survivor? Convince my sister you were a hero, when all the while you plotted to lead them down our throats?"

"Why would I do that?" Rhodri shoved Temion's arm away again, striking him across the forearm with the back of the knife. "I left them for a reason!"

"You're a spy for the Westerners, admit it!" Temion lunged forward, and Rhodri let him inside his reach, hooking a nimble foot around his ankle, trying to dump him on the ground. Temion was too quick for him. His elbow took Rhodri in the gut, and as he doubled up, air exploding from his lungs, Temion's fist connected with the underside of Rhodri's jaw, sending him spinning to the ground. He tried to rise, tasting blood on his lips, and a boot crunched against his ribs, knocking him sprawling.

"Temion, I think he's had enough." Sudak's voice came from some distance. Rhodri lay in the dirt, biding his time, steeling himself for another blow. A hand fell on the back of his neck. Temion was so close Rhodri could smell the blood on his face, and see the droplets of sweat on his lips.

"You should leave," he said, in a voice meant for Rhodri's ears alone. "Leave my sister, leave my tribe. Clear out and don't come back. Or I'll kill you." He let Rhodri's head fall and straightened, turning away.

"Leave him here," he said. "Let's go home."

Rhodri gathered his strength as he heard Temion walk away, waiting for him to let his guard down. His muscles bunched, and he sprang to his feet, lunging after his enemy with a roar that came from deep in his gut. Temion, caught off guard, fell back before a flurry of punches and kicks. Rhodri didn't waste his breath cursing or trying to make excuses; he went in hard and fast. Teeth scraped his knuckles, bone crunched under his fists. Hard hands seized his wrists, his shoulders, dragging him away before he could grind Temion's face to a bloody pulp. Sudak flung him back on the ground and stood over him, breathing heavily, one hand resting on his belt knife.

Temion sat up, groping on the ground for a lost tooth. He shoved it back into the hole in his gums, pressing it with his thumb to be sure it held.

"Do you want me to finish him?" Doubt flashed across Sudak's face. "Trogir won't like it."

Temion rubbed his jaw. "I said leave him. We'll take the mare. If he chooses, he can walk back to camp. Or he can follow the Western rats fleeing to their holes, I don't care." He mounted, moving stiffly, and took Liberty's rein from the bruised woman. He glared down at Rhodri. "I doubt we'll see you again, short-hair. But if we do, I'll make sure to kill you."

Rhodri remained sitting until the sound of hoof beats faded away. With a grunt, he forced himself to his feet, probing his bruises with hard fingers. Nothing appeared to be broken, except his pride. He didn't relish explaining the damage to Nasira, but he had to go back. Not just for Liberty, but for himself. He had nowhere else to go, and he wasn't going to let Temion win another hand. If he walked away, it was as good as admitting he had led Serren's men to the camp, and he would find himself branded a traitor by both sides.

With a sigh, he trudged back towards the camp, following the hoof prints in the dust.

*

Days passed, bruises faded, but the resentment still simmered between Rhodri and Temion. Nasira tried to keep the peace between her brother and her lover, but the strain showed on her face and in her sharp retorts when the subject came up. Rhodri thought it might be easier if she didn't come to him at night, but on the nights when she left him alone, the space beneath the wagon was too cold, and too empty.

He found himself thinking more and more of Keir. His relationship with the horse master had been secretive out of necessity;

they had been teacher and pupil, after all, and the King's Third frowned on their love. It seemed he was destined to spend his life sneaking around with the people he slept with, hiding from condemnation. His whole life was shrouded in secrets and lies. With his memory, it was easy to keep a secret, to hold together a lie, but he didn't want to do that for the rest of his life.

"What are you thinking about?" Nasira rode up beside him, her hair gathered into a rough knot at the back of her neck. She carried a stout hunting bow, a clutch of small birds dangling from the pommel of her saddle.

He shook himself out of mournful reverie. "I was thinking what a fine shot my girl is." He forced a grin, for her benefit, and she laughed.

"Who says I'm your girl? And if you think I'm a fine shot now, you should see me hunt short-hairs."

"You couldn't bring down a short-hair," he told her.

She winked. "I got you, didn't I? Follow me!" She dug her heels into the sides of her big liver chestnut, and raced off. Rhodri nudged Liberty after her. His mare might have shorter legs, but she was bred for speed and agility, and he quickly caught up.

"Where are we going?" he called.

"You'll see."

He hoped that meant they were heading far enough from the tribe for a quick, uninterrupted tumble in the frost-bitten grass. More to spite Temion than from any sudden, urgent desire. But Nasira had other ideas. She led him to the top of a small rise and reined in, pointing. "There you are."

Across the horizon, as far as he could see, was a towering ridge of stone, a breezeblock flung down by the hand of Adeamus. In its looming shadow, horses grazed. Hundreds of them, more even than the stables at Northpoint. Flocking across the plain towards the edifice from every direction were covered wagons, identical to the ones used by the people of the Plains Hawk. The tribes gathered for winter, he realised. Dark hollows cut deep into the side of the rock, rope ladders and bridges crisscrossing its facade.

Rhodri glanced at Nasira. Her eyes shone as she stared at the rock formation.

"What is this place?" he asked.

"This will be our home for the next four moons. This is Kharikan."

Chapter Three

KHARIKAN TOWERED TWO thousand feet into the sky. It took a day and a half to ride all the way round the base of the rock, which was pitted with holes and hollows, and long cracks where rainwater flowed like streams. Ropes ran across the face of the edifice, an immense tangled web of walkways and ladders. Every family had a cave, and there were more caves in Kharikan than stars in the sky. Tunnels ran deep into the heart of the rock and emerged in unexpected places, or ended abruptly in blank walls. Goats scampered up and down the sheer cliffs, and the horse herds of the Atrathenes grazed the plains around the slow, wandering river that kissed the root of the stone city.

The people of the Plains Hawk occupied caves in which their ancestors had wintered for centuries. They were halfway up, near the southern end of the rock, a precipitous scramble up trembling ladders and across walkways abandoned since last winter. Rhodri found the climb exhilarating, but Nasira trembled as she dumped her belongings in the tribe's communal cave, and groped for a drink.

"I've got no head for heights," she admitted. "Walking across those ropes makes me feel sick. Every winter we leave just as I get used to it, and I forget how bad it is until we come back."

Rhodri touched her elbow lightly "I won't let you fall," he promised.

She narrowed her eyes. "Really?" She turned away before he could ask what she meant, heaving her bag onto her back. "Where will you sleep?"

"Where am I allowed to sleep? What does your grandmother say? And your brother?" Rhodri had let Temion go ahead of them across the narrow rope walkways. It would be too easy to stage an accident at this height, and his broken body might never be retrieved from the slopes of the mountain.

"This is Kharikan. The rules are different here. Even Temion agrees to that, however much he dislikes it." An enigmatic smile played across her lips. "Where you sleep is your own choice, although I'd like it to be with me."

He grinned and caught her hand. "I think I could endure that for a few moons."

"Glad to hear it," she said. "Come with me. I know a good spot."

She led him through a network of tunnels. It was easy enough for Rhodri to find his way through this warren, but he wondered how others managed it. He asked Nasira, who smiled.

"I've come here every winter since I was born," she said. "I know these tunnels like my own face in a glass. Mind you, so has Kilujen, and he still gets lost. Although he'll tell you he's exploring—expanding his mind or some foolish talk like that."

"You don't believe in shamanism?"

"Of course I do! But sometimes Kilujen . . . he's like a horse that's eaten too many green mushrooms, wandering around in a daze." She did an alarmingly accurate impression of a mushroom-addled horse, stiff-legged, with wide, rolling eyes. "If you follow his path, don't come to me talking nonsense about it."

"I wouldn't dare!" Rhodri laughed, but she had a point. Nasira was the closest thing he had to a lead rein. If he chose to walk with the spirits, he would need her there to draw him back to the real world.

Nasira rounded a boulder in the path. "Here we are. Our little stone tent." She snorted in mock-indignation. "And you can get right out of it!"

"Who, me?" He rounded the stone; she stood, hands on hips, glaring at a large plant. It was round, deep blood-red, with waving tentacles instead of leaves. As Nasira took a threatening step towards it, it rolled and bounced away, fluttering its arms.

"Not that way, you silly thing!"

"What is it?" Rhodri asked.

"A tumbler. The rock is full of them. They're not plants, but they're not really animals either." She flapped the tumbler away, and it rolled end-over-end towards the exit. "They roll about in here. You can break off their fronds and fry them in oil. It's good eating, but you might be sick of it after four moons! And they cry, so you might not want to do it often."

"Cry?"

"Like a babe. I'll show you!" She snapped off one of the tumbler's brittle fronds. The creature uttered a piteous wail and rolled away in trembling agitation. Nasira gave it a push and it bounced away down the corridor.

Rhodri shuddered. "What a horrible noise! Does it hurt them?"

"Not really. You know when a hound gets underfoot and you step on his paw? It's more a cry of protest than of pain. See, it's fine now." The tumbler had come to a halt and stretched probing fronds up the face of the rock, pulling itself up into a crevice and vanishing with a wriggle and a rustle. "The noise is the worst thing about them. They're harmless otherwise. The little ones like to tease them."

From inside the rock came a faint rustle, almost of agreement, or protest, that made Rhodri smile.

"You haven't told me what you think of your winter quarters. Do you like them?"

Rhodri looked around the cave. It was oval, with an arched roof. The sandy floor sloped gently upwards to an opening like an iris that allowed the light in. The floor was warm beneath his feet, and water trickled on the edge of his hearing. Nasira hung back as he walked to the iris and looked out.

The cliff fell away below his feet, a dizzying drop of a hundred feet to a rough patch of boulders that looked like pebbles from this distance. Below that, the south flank of Kharikan flowed towards the broad, treeless plain. He could see tiny dots that must be horses, and a flurry of activity near the river. A small tumbler floated past, caught on the breeze, and he ducked to avoid the brush of tentacles against his face.

"I don't know how you can stand there looking out." Nasira was on her knees, unpacking the bedroll. "That drop makes me feel sick. Come away from the edge."

He lingered, leaning out, the wind tugging his hair.

"Rhodri, please! You make me nervous."

"I'm sorry." He stepped back from the brink and wrapped his arms around her, burying his face in the curve of her neck, breathing in her scent. But at the echo of running feet in the passage outside, she squirmed out of his embrace.

Odval burst into the cave, skidding to a halt in a flurry of sand. She stuck out her tongue. "You're not at it *again*, are you? That's disgusting!"

Nasira frowned. "Did you want something, Odval?"

"Kilujen wants to see Rhodri first thing tomorrow."

"The maindy run starts tomorrow. We'll need all hands."

"Shaman's privilege." Odval shrugged. "I want to be a shaman. You get out of all the work."

"Odval, button your mouth." Nasira gripped her shoulders, spun her around, and gave her a shove towards the exit. "If you can't be polite to Rhodri, say nothing."

Odval frowned, but didn't apologise. Rhodri felt he should defend her.

"She wasn't being rude," he said, "just blunt. And being a shaman is better than gutting fish!"

Odval threw him a grateful look. He was glad at least one of Nasira's family was on his side.

Nasira sighed. "Go chase tumblers," she told her sister. "Tell Kilujen Rhodri will meet him by the river at dawn."

*

The riverbank was crowded at sunrise, the air crackling with anticipation. Kilujen stood at the end of a shabby jetty, dressed in his white ceremonial robes. Trogir walked through the gathered tribe towards him, and his people fell silent.

Nasira nudged Rhodri, and pointed. The same scene was being enacted further down the bank, and on the far side of the river. The leaders of all the tribes of Atrath came together with their spiritual guides to begin the maindy run.

Trogir held his hand out, palm upwards. Kilujen brandished a black blade, hewn of pure jet. He slashed across Trogir's palm, and raised his arm in a gesture of triumph, letting the leader's blood drip into the water. As one, the tribes of Atrath erupted into applause, and thronged towards the river, unfurling their nets.

"What was that about?" Rhodri asked Nasira.

"The maindy run demands a blood price. Better to pay now, than a higher price later." She kissed him on the cheek. "Go talk to Kilujen. I'll see you later." She waded into the river and took a corner of the net that spread over the surface of the water. Everywhere people were dredging the river, hauling the nets with their slippery, silver cargo up the banks, to be gutted and packed into barrels filled with salt.

Feeling redundant, Rhodri picked his way over ground already slippery with fish scales to Kilujen, who sat cross-legged on a rock, washing the blood from his knife. It swirled into the swift, flowing water in a delicate red bloom, reminding Rhodri of the red-running river the day he had fought Temion. He shuddered at the memory.

Kilujen patted the stone beside him. "Join me, cousin."

Rhodri climbed on to the rock. "I feel I should be helping with the fishing," he said.

"You're learning. You could hardly swim with your iron feet, could you?"

"I miss swimming." Rhodri regarded his ankles ruefully.

"Be grateful you can ride. And bed women! If Trogir realised you were to become Nasira's bedmate, he might have clapped the shackles higher up!"

Rhodri winced. "Temion would have, I'm sure. Don't make a joke of it. I can't." He looked downstream. Temion waded thigh-deep in the river, wrestling with the nets, pitching in with the rest of the tribe. As Rhodri should be. Sitting up here talking to Kilujen would win him no respect.

Kilujen tilted his head, like a bird, regarding him with keen interest. "What's it like?"

"Being shackled?"

"Being unable to forget. I can't imagine anything worse. It must be as fresh today as when they held your legs over the forge . . ."

"It is." Rhodri would not be drawn. His pain, the unfading memory, was private. Nasira understood a fraction of it, but there were black depths in his mind even she could not reach. "Tell me about the maindy run, if you want me to learn."

Kilujen watched his tribe work with an air of paternal indulgence. "You must understand the maindy run to understand our people, how we live in tune with the seasons. Every year the maindy gather here, to lay their eggs and die. The eggs float downriver on the current, hundreds of miles, further than any man knows. The maindy hatch, and spend the rest of their lives swimming back up the river, to the place they were spawned. They arrive at the same time every year, and so do we."

"How do you know when to come?"

"How do we know? How do we know the sun will rise in the morning, or the seasons will turn? It's always been this way. We

50

arrive at Kharikan, and the maindy come a few days later. We catch the fish before they die, and the maindy feed us through the winter. If we arrived too late, we would starve. Too early, and the maindy wouldn't have time to lay. The maindy and the tribes depend on each other. That's why tradition is so important to us. It maintains the balance between the land and the people. Without it we wouldn't be able to live the way we do."

"How long does the run go on for?" Rhodri asked.

"A moon. By the next moon we'll have enough fish to last the winter, and the snows will be falling." Kilujen smiled slyly at Rhodri. "There are many rites that happen at Kharikan. The maindy run is only the first of them. Come on!" He jumped down from the rock. "We have work to do. I'll show you the herbs that grow here, and their uses. I'm sure you're a quick learner."

The next few days were a blur. In the mornings, Kilujen took Rhodri around the rock, showing him the best places to gather medicinal plants, telling him how to prepare and use them. The young shaman knew everyone, and Rhodri discovered his tribe's reluctance to share their names was common. People were happy to give up their names to Kilujen, who carried powerful magic in his soul. They were less keen to share them with Rhodri.

"Maybe it's your hair?" Kilujen suggested, twisting his waist-length braids around his fingers.

Rhodri ran a hand through his own dishevelled mop. "I prefer it short," he said. "It's my face they don't like."

Kilujen frowned. "Your tribe have done terrible things to my people. You can't change your face, so we'll have to try and change their hearts. It might take a long time."

In the afternoons Rhodri helped with the maindy run. The gore of gutting and filleting was left to the women, laughing and gossiping as their knives darted in and out amid the falling scales. Rhodri's job was to pack the fillets into barrels and seal them closed, ready for transport to the rock. It was hard, tedious work that left his hands raw and chapped. At night all he could do was collapse into bed beside Nasira, the stink from the maindy lingering on their skin despite their efforts to wash it away.

The maindy swept down the river in their thousands as the run wore on. The surface of the water was clouded with eggs, clumped together like white, trembling rafts, sticking to the bodies of the fishers. The wet, slippery ground made the job even more difficult. Rhodri stretched, easing his hands against the small of his back. He made a futile effort to wipe the grease from his palms and looked for Nasira, who sat with a group of women further up the bank. They giggled, heads close together. Her blade flashed like sunlight through the mound of fish. He could watch her easy movement all day.

Nasira looked up, flicking her hair back over her shoulder. Catching his eye, she smiled. She set aside her knife and rose with easy grace, heading for a dense patch of scrub. He assumed she was taking a break to relieve herself, but the look she threw him, the inclination of her head, implied he should follow.

"Stop dreaming!" Temion dumped another load of fish at his feet, making him jump. His eyes were cold. "You can lust after my sister when the fish are salted. You've got all winter."

Rhodri thrust his knife into his belt. "I need to piss. I might be a while."

"Leave her alone, short-hair."

"Or what? You'll punch me again?" From the water, Trogir was calling Temion to his aid, and Nasira's brother couldn't ignore his leader's call. He scowled.

"I've got my eye on you. Stay away from my sister, or I'll slit you open." He lowered his voice. "I'm going to make sure she's traded out this season, to get her away from you. Enjoy it while it lasts!"

"I intend to."

Temion snarled, rounding impatiently at Trogir's call. Rhodri strode towards the spot where Nasira had vanished, trying not to appear too eager. As he reached the bushes, the peace of the afternoon was shattered by a high, terrified scream that stopped his heart. Without stopping to think, he dived into the scrub, knife in hand.

Nasira lay sprawled on the ground, her back striped with scarlet. A large feline, fur patched tawny and black, crouched over her fallen body. Its lips were pulled back over snarling teeth. One paw pinned Nasira to the floor, razor claws digging into the flesh of her hip. The cat lashed its tail and wriggled its haunches, ready to spring.

With a howl, Rhodri flung himself at the beast, slashing with his short blade. His blow tore open the cat's shoulder. It snarled, thrashing around, sinking vicious teeth into his calf. His grip weakened with the pain, and the cat wrenched free. Warm blood splashed into Rhodri's eyes as he lashed out, blinded, blade striking flesh and glancing off. The cat shrieked, leapt forward, not to attack, but to flee. Thrown back, Rhodri had a blurred vision of claws and teeth. By the time he scrambled to his feet, the beast was gone.

Rhodri dropped to his knees beside Nasira, gathering her in his arms. Her skin was grey, except for those three terrible bands of exposed flesh, torn open from spine to hip. Her breathing was ragged, and as he pressed her to him he felt her heart racing.

Nasira! Nasira, stay with me!

He couldn't speak, choked with fear. He was aware of running feet around him, people shouting, but the sound came from leagues away. His world was Nasira, her fluttering breath, her blood pumping warm and thick over his hands. All he could do was hold her against his chest and try to staunch the flow.

Hands fell on his shoulders, pulling him away. He fought the grip, cursing, as Kilujen shoved him aside and knelt beside his cousin.

"Take her back to the rock," the shaman commanded with quiet authority. "There's nothing I can do here. Temion?"

"Here!" It was Nasira's brother who held Rhodri, fingers digging into his biceps. "I'll bring her. Someone fetch a horse!" He spun Rhodri round to face him. "This is your doing. If she dies . . ."

"She won't die." The blood was thick and sticky on his hands. Too much blood, harsh and bright under the winter sun. Astan's blood had covered his hands like this, as he struggled to stem the tide flowing from her wounds. Wounds that had been carved by his betrayal, as much as by her own hand. Her life had flickered out in his arms, and he couldn't save her. But he could save Nasira. He had to. Saving her wouldn't bring Astan back, or the men who had died under his knife in the mountains, but it would be a step towards redemption. A step away from turning into his father.

"I can give your sister my strength. Help me move her."

Still Temion hesitated, but now his expression of loathing was tempered with doubt, and fear. "What can you do?"

Kilujen butted in. "Rhodri is a shaman, or he will be. I have taught him some of my art. Between us, we can save her."

"No Western medicine?"

Kilujen shook his head. "I swear."

Temion relented, helping Rhodri carry the limp body of his sister out of the bushes. They draped her over a horse, the same way Rhodri had brought Astan back from the black isle. Every step of that hideous journey rushed to the front of his mind, sending him reeling. He cradling Nasira's head as he limped beside her, back to Kharikan with her blood staining a trail on the ground.

Kilujen's healing rooms were in a cave at the base of the rock. Temion and Rhodri lifted Nasira onto the bed. Rhodri peeled the shredded, bloody remnants of her dress away from her back as Temion stepped back, hand pressed against his mouth. "I can't watch this," he muttered.

"You're a warrior, aren't you?" Rhodri felt his anger flare at this display of weakness, just when Nasira needed those around her to be strong.

"It's different when it's one of your family. I wouldn't expect a short-hair to understand that."

"Your sister is in the hands of the spirits," Kilujen told him. "I'll watch over her. Rhodri will help me. You don't need to be here."

Temion looked from Rhodri to the shaman, stricken. "You will bring her back, won't you?"

Rhodri was reluctant to let Temion see that he was feeling the same vulnerability, the same fear. He bent his head over Nasira, brushing the nape of her neck with a shaking hand, feeling her ragged pulse. There was so much in his life he had lost: his father, his home, Astan, Keir, the King's Third. Was he destined to lose Nasira too? Was this his fate, the price he paid for his memory, that those he cared for could live on only in his mind?

Kilujen's hand fell on his shoulder. "Are you going to help me?" the shaman asked, quiet and respectful.

Rhodri stroked Nasira's cheek. "The tribe would never have accepted me without her, Kilujen. She saved my life, as much as I saved hers. I can't lose her."

The shaman's face was grave. "You won't. We can bring her back. Light the healing candles. They will help us see, and think."

Rhodri tore himself away from the bedside and Kilujen took his place. He rested his hand on Nasira's shoulder and made a low rumble in the back of his throat. Nasira's eyelashes fluttered, and she rumbled back.

"What's happening?" Rhodri demanded. "Why is she making that noise?"

"The spirit of the patchcat is inside her. It must be driven out before she can heal, and quickly. She's still losing blood. Look at her hands."

Rhodri took Nasira's hands between his own. Her nails, normally short and blunt, were elongated and twisted into sharp points. Her fingers twitched, raking her nails against the back of his hand and drawing blood. He let go with a gasp of pain. "What's happening to her?"

"Her nails and teeth will grow long and savage, and then her eyes will change, become feline. If that happens, she will wake, but she won't be Nasira. All she will desire is to tear and kill."

"How do we stop it?"

"We need to draw the spirit out, to banish it. Wait with her, but be careful. I'll be back as soon as I can."

Kilujen dashed from the cave, bare feet slapping against stone. Rhodri was left alone with Nasira. He stroked the hair from her forehead, and wiped away the beads of sweat on her temples. Her lips fluttered, and she ran her tongue over teeth that had grown pointed and sharp.

Talk to me, Nasira! How can I bring you back?

Her eyes flickered open, dark irises flecked with amber.

"I'm here. I'm right here." He slipped an arm under her shoulders, her head pressed against his chest. "I won't leave your side."

Tears squeezed from between her eyelids.

"Kilujen's going to help you. Try to hold on a bit longer." He rocked her back and forth, and she squirmed in his embrace, stretching up so her lips brushed against his throat. He held back from her, though his nerves cried out to pull her close and protect her. "Lie still," he urged. "You'll make it worse." For a moment she relaxed. He felt her warm breath against his neck as he stroked her hair. "It'll be all right," he promised.

With a snarl, she twisted in his arms, lunging for his throat. Sharp teeth snapped against his skin. He jerked away. "What are you doing?"

She drew back her top lip, exposing long, lethal canines. The growl came from deep in her chest, an ugly, primal sound, devoid of humanity. Her eyes, more amber than black now, flicked over him without recognition.

"Nasira!"

She sprang. Her speed caught Rhodri by surprise. He threw up an arm to defend his throat as she struck, and her teeth met in the flesh of his forearm. The weight of her body threw him off the bed onto the stone floor, slamming the breath from his lungs. Nasira raked his flesh with her nails, snarling, teeth snapping as he struggled to hold her off.

Feet pounded outside the cave, Kilujen's voice yelling for help, but all Rhodri saw was Nasira. Her face was inches from his, eyes wild as her mouth sought his throat. There was nothing there of the girl he knew. Her soul walked in shadow, and in its place was this beast, intent on taking his life.

Kilujen threw his arms around Nasira, pinning her arms to her sides. She thrashed and growled, a sickening sound. Rhodri could only watch helpless as Kilujen and two other men lashed her, face down, to the bed, bucking and twisting. She cried out in pain, the sound a blade driven deep inside him. He seized Kilujen's arm. "You're hurting her! Leave her alone!"

"Your arm's bleeding." The shaman pushed him into a seat and handed him a cloth to cleanse the wound. "I told you to be careful!"

"Never mind my arm!" Rhodri flung the cloth aside. "Bring her back to me! I need her!"

Kilujen caught him as he staggered. "Did you hit your head when you fell?"

"Why do you care? Nasira needs help! She—" His knees dissolved, and he sagged against the shaman's arm.

"She needs you, Rhodri." Kilujen turned to his helpers and bowed, supporting Rhodri with one arm. "Thank you," he said. "The spirits smile on you. Now bring me all the firewood you can find. And a horsewhip. Listen,"—He took hold of the older man's arm—"if the worst should happen, if I command it, seal the cave."

"With you in it? And the short-hair? What about the girl?"

"If something goes wrong, the girl will be lost anyway. Do as I bid. Don't question it, unless you want to unleash death on the tribes. Do you understand me?" The man nodded. "Then go!"

They left, and Kilujen pressed Rhodri into the chair, and took his face in both hands. "You can't help her," he said, "unless you look after yourself. She needs you as much as you need her."

Nasira groaned and squealed, arching her back against the straps holding her down. Rhodri buried his head in his hands, unable to witness her suffering. Kilujen cleared his throat. "You love her, don't you?"

Rhodri nodded. "I didn't know I did, until now. I saw her dying, I imagined my life without her and it was just . . . a void. Empty. I was stupid not to realise it." He groaned. "There was a man, before. Back in the west. I didn't think a woman could make me feel the way he did . . . Not this soon."

Kilujen expressed no surprise at the revelation. "You're a fool. If you love her, help me bring her back. Take this!"

He handed Rhodri a slab of raw meat, still warm. "Put it near her mouth," he instructed. "The patchcat spirit will be drawn to the scent, and lured from her body. At least, I hope it will."

Rhodri placed the bloody chunk of horseflesh on the bed. Nasira snarled weakly. "And if it doesn't?" he asked. "What then?"

Kilujen placed more meat at points around the room, and blew out all but two of the candles, which he set on either side of the cave entrance. "Then . . . I believe your tribe call it mercy. It would be merciful, to take her—"

"No! I'm not doing that. Never again."

Kilujen hushed him. "It may not come to that. Sit quiet and watch. The spirit won't come out if it hears us talking."

The two men sat in silence, Rhodri near Nasira's head, Kilujen at her feet, only rising to lay a fresh bandage on her back when the blood soaked through. Kilujen's helpers returned with the wood, and the whip, which the shaman lashed to his belt. He piled the tinder-dry wood in a rough circle around the perimeter of the cave, enclosed the bed, and himself and Rhodri, within its confines.

Nasira twitched, asleep or unconscious, and the room grew dim. The smell of fresh meat grew more pungent in the still air. The candles by the entrance burned lower. Kilujen's head tilted back, and every now and then he snored, but Rhodri couldn't sleep. He kept his eyes fixed on Nasira, waiting for the spirit that had taken her to emerge.

A faint wisp of smoke—at first, his eyes tired and stinging, he thought he'd imagined it—trickling from between Nasira's parted lips. He sat straighter, not daring to make a sound.

The smoke solidified into the shape of a probing paw, bristling with unsheathed claws, groping tentatively towards the meat. Rhodri looked around in alarm, unsure what to do.

"Move the meat away. Very slowly." Kilujen's voice was a breath in the darkness, and Rhodri heard the soft swish as he unfurled the whip. Rhodri took the slab of horseflesh by the edges and pulled it across the bed a few inches, leaving a bloody smear. The probing paw froze, lifted inquisitively. He retreated a step.

A leg formed from the smoke, then a second paw. Nasira yawned, and the patchcat spirit tumbled from her lips, growing larger and more definite in form, pale and grey as the smoke that birthed it. It scented the meat, wide nose snuffling. Its ears flicked, and it looked up, freezing at the sight of Rhodri. Its body was a swirling mass of smoke, but its eyes were alive, solid amber. Its lashing tail swept over Nasira's face.

Another step backwards. "Can it hurt me?" Rhodri drew his knife, a slow careful movement. How could he fight a creature fashioned purely of spirit?

"I think so, yes." Kilujen picked up one of the candles and moved towards the circle of wood.

"You're not sure? I thought you knew all about this!" As Rhodri backed away from the patchcat spirit, Kilujen lit the wood. There was a crackle, and Rhodri felt the heat of flame on his skin as the circle ignited, enclosing them in a wall of fire and smoke. It was hard to breathe, hard to see with his own fire-shadow thrown before him across the spirit-body of the patchcat, flames reflected in its liquid amber eyes. The cat flinched at the roar of the fire, stretching its jaws in a silent snarl. It crouched on its hind legs, muscles tensed, tail whipping. Rhodri tightened his grip on the knife, and dropped into a fighting stance.

"Come and get me then, you bastard!"

The spirit cat leapt. Rhodri sprang forward to meet the rush, but it never came. In mid air, the creature twisted, snapping at its flank. It crashed to the cave floor on its side, paws scuffling against the rock. The shaft of an arrow, misty and grey as the beast itself, trembled in its side. The cat squirmed in silent agony as the mist around it thickened and changed form to reveal a young warrior, crouched over the creature.

"Kilujen, what's happening? Is that Temion?"

It was hard to distinguish mist from smoke. The heat was suffocating, and it was painful to draw breath. Rhodri groped for Nasira's hand, and it was cold.

The beast twitched as Temion sliced open its throat, spilling a grey cloud of blood that was swiftly lost in the choking blackness. Rhodri doubted what he had seen, but there was no time to wonder. His throat was closing; Nasira would die if he didn't get her out of here soon.

"Kilujen! Let's go!"

The shaman coughed and spluttered. Rhodri fumbled with the leather straps that held Nasira down, freeing her and snatching her up from the bed. She cried out in pain as he flung her over his shoulder. He staggered under the weight, the heat, the churning smoke. There was a hiss as Kilujen threw water on the fire, and a gap opened in the wall of flame, but it wasn't enough. Rhodri felt his skin crackle as he leapt over the burning barricade and stumbled out into the merciful light and air of a cold winter dawn.

Kilujen was at his heels, overtaking him on the way down the slope as smoke billowed from the mouth of the cave. He shouted to anyone who would listen:

"Seal the cave! We don't know if it's dead yet!"

Rhodri didn't care about the cave. He cared about Nasira, ash-streaked and bleeding again. She groaned, but it was a human sound, not the predatory snarl of before. Rhodri dropped to his knees, weakness sluicing over him as Kilujen hauled him back to his feet. The shaman's face and hands were streaked with black, and he was breathing heavily. He held out a skin filled with water, and Rhodri snatched it and drank deeply. Every gulp felt like he was swallowing gravel.

"Is that it?" he croaked. "Is she safe now?"

"You're not done yet, my friend. We've brought back her spirit. Now we must heal her body."

Rhodri shook his aching head, bewildered. "What happened?"

"Temion avenged himself on the patchcat that attacked his sister."

"In the real world, or the spirit one? Is Temion dead?"

"The real world and that of the spirits are closer than you think. What you saw was the shade of Temion as he killed the cat in this world. Temion lives, and Nasira too. She needs you now." He knelt beside her on the frosty grass, which was darkening under the warmth of the blood flowing from her wounds.

Nasira's eyelids fluttered. "Rhodri?"

"I'm here." He held her close against him, feeling her heart beat.

"I did terrible things," she whispered. "I knew I was doing them, but I couldn't stop myself. I didn't hurt you, did I?"

"Don't worry about it."

Between them, Kilujen and Rhodri lifted her and laid her face down on a blanket on the grass. She winced as Kilujen inspected her back. "I feel sick . . ." Her eyes rolled back in her head, and her body sagged.

"Kilujen!" Rhodri shook her, panicking. "She fainted! What do I do?"

"She's still bleeding." Kilujen frowned. "It should have stopped by now."

"Can't you stitch the wounds?"

He shook his head. "Patchcat claws carry sickness on them. If I stitch her wounds, they'll fester and go bad. We could still lose her, unless . . ."

"Unless what?"

"It's dangerous. She could die from the cure."

Rhodri rubbed a filthy hand across his face. "Is she going to die anyway?"

"Without the cure, certainly. With it, she may have a chance. She needs blood from another's veins, to replace what she's lost."

"She can have mine." Rhodri rolled up his sleeve. The chill air made the fine hairs on his arms stand on end, and he shivered. On the slope above, a curious crowd gathered to watch. Kilujen turned his back on them and spoke in a low voice.

"I hoped you'd say that. You two are bonded. She has already taken you into her body, so your blood won't be foreign to her. It's the best chance she has."

"What do I have to do?"

"Sit down beside her. I'll set it up."

Kilujen fastened a strap tightly round Rhodri's upper arm, and tapped the inside of his elbow, seeking a vein. When he brought up a raised blue thread, he took a knife, fashioned like a tiny mercy blade, and laid it against the inside of his arm. "This might hurt."

A sharp scratch. Rhodri felt his skin break open, and the warm trickle of blood down his forearm. He turned his face away, focussing on the delicate tracery of a frozen leaf as Kilujen took a long, thin tube and pushed it into the incision. "Hold this in your left hand," he said. "When I tell you, raise your arm and open and close your fist until I tell you to stop."

He made an identical cut in Nasira's arm. Rhodri had no trouble looking at his own blood being spilt, but seeing Nasira's was hard. Kilujen tapped him on the head. "Close your eyes if you feel sick," he urged.

Eyes closed, arm aloft, fist clenching and unclenching, Rhodri could feel the blood draining from him, transferring his own life to Nasira. It seemed to be taking a long time, and the ground he sat on was hard, the cold soaking through his breeches and numbing his flesh.

Temion pushed through the crowd, carrying a steaming flagon. He was sweaty, dirty and bloodied from the fight with the patchcat. His fingers clenched around the cup were crusted red, and his braids were tangled.

"What's going on?" he demanded. "What is he doing to my sister?"

Rhodri opened his mouth to reply, but he was too exhausted to frame words that would make sense. Kilujen caught Temion's arm before he could come any closer. "Rhodri's giving her his blood," he said. "He offered. It might save her life, and it's the only way."

"It didn't work last time, did it? With Wanval?"

"Don't talk about her." Kilujen turned away, a cloud crossing his hardened features. "It will work this time. It has to."

"She could have my blood. Why does she need his?"

"You weren't here. Would you have her die before you'd see her saved with short-hair blood?"

"No, but . . ." Temion's lips tightened, but he bent down and pressed the mug of warm ale into Rhodri's hands. "Just . . . don't let her die."

Rhodri's lips were numb. "I'll try not to." He locked eyes with Temion for a long second, and then Nasira's brother turned away, the crowd parting respectfully before him.

Kilujen watched him leave. "There will be trouble there, before too long," he muttered.

"There's already trouble," Rhodri said. "Even if I gave every drop of my blood to save his sister, he wouldn't have any friendship for me." His tongue felt thick, and his words slurred. "Much longer?"

"Not much. Don't worry about Temion. I'll work on him for you."

By the time Kilujen told him to rest, and withdrew the tube from his arm, Rhodri's head was spinning. He lay down on the ground while the shaman spooned honey into his mouth.

"You've done well," Kilujen told him. "Nasira sleeps. Her colour is better, and her back has stopped bleeding. I think she'll recover, thanks to you." Rhodri tried to sit up, but Kilujen pushed him back down. "You can see her tomorrow. Rest now. I'm worn out from healing her. I'm not taking care of you as well."

*

In a few days, Rhodri was fit to return to the maindy run. Kilujen had found another empty cave, but he was mourning the loss of his supplies, and the length of time it was taking to restock with the ground frozen and nothing growing. Nasira stayed in the healing cave for a moon, while the flesh on her back knit into long, pink scars. Rhodri longed for her at night. Waking up beside a cold empty space made him realise how much he missed her.

Dawn thrust long fingers through the iris as he dressed, and over the bulk of Kharikan as he picked his way down the outside of the mound to the new healing cave, where Kilujen greeted him with a cheery wave. "You're up early!" he observed.

Rhodri shrugged. "Trogir says it's the last day of the maindy run. You said I could have Nasira back today."

"When she wakes, you're welcome to her! I should warn you,"— Kilujen lowered his voice—"there's still something of the patchcat in her. Watch out for it."

"Something of the patchcat? What do you mean?"

"You'll see." He smiled. "Now the maindy run is over, so is the hard work. Trading season will be easy, at least for you!"

"Trading season?"

Kilujen winked. "I'm going to take some time to teach you the skills you need to become a true shaman. I sense a longing in you, to talk to those who ride the spirit trail. Am I right?"

"I don't know." Rhodri's hand crept to the chain around his neck. "I have questions, but I'm not sure I want to know the answers."

"The last day of trading season is the Dawn of New Blood. Then we have a feast, to eat the last of the maindy. After that,"—Nasira stirred, and Kilujen hurried over to her—"after that, the tribes ride their separate trails. How are you feeling, little cousin?"

"Is Rhodri here?" she asked. "I heard you talk about trading season. Has Trogir—?"

"Nothing has been said. Temion asks for a meeting of the Plains Hawk at sunset. Both of you, take the day for yourselves. The maindy can be brought in without you, and you need time. If Trogir questions it, tell him it's my order. Rhodri, walk with me while Nasira dresses."

The two men strolled out to the rock near the river, where Kilujen liked to watch the maindy run and play his flute. A carnival atmosphere prevailed. The tribes sang as they pulled in the nets, lighter now the bulk of the maindy swarm had passed. Work proceeded at a leisurely pace, and the children were let off their chores. A small gang raced past, squealing and rolling a helpless tumbler between them. Rhodri pulled his tattered cloak tight against the frosty nip of the wind.

Kilujen sniffed the air. "Snow's coming," he announced. "In the next few days. Can you smell it?"

Rhodri sniffed, then shrugged. "My nose isn't that good."

"You'll learn in other ways too. The way the twigs snap under your fingers, or the horses herd closer together. A hundred tiny ways to tell you trading season is here. There's one."

He pointed to the river bank. The tribal leaders gathered, deep in conversation. Trogir glanced their way, and nodded. His face suggested Rhodri was one of the subjects under discussion. "What happens at trading season?" he asked.

"Nasira will tell you about it. Here she comes now."

The sight of Nasira striding confidently along the riverbank, a smile playing across her lips, snatched Rhodri's breath away.

Kilujen whispered in his ear. "You should tell her!"

"What?"

"It will benefit you. Tell her!"

He moved away as Nasira approached, hands on her hips. "What are you two whispering about?" she asked.

"Shaman business." Rhodri slipped down from the rock. "Want to go for a ride? Just you and me?"

"Watch out for ferocious beasts!" Kilujen warned him with a chuckle.

Rhodri patted the sword at his hip. "It's me the patchcats should watch out for! I'm not letting it happen again. I've missed my girl too much!"

Nasira slapped him lightly on the chest. "Who says I'm yours, Rhodri Short-hair? It's trading season, anything could happen! I might trade you for a barrel of smoked fish heads."

"You'd miss me too much." Rhodri turned to Kilujen. "I'll do what you ask," he promised, "but in my own way, and at a time I choose."

"Don't leave it to long," the shaman said. "Be back by sunset, or Temion will tear into you more fiercely than any patchcat. You don't want scars from his claws."

*

Rhodri and Nasira rode away from Kharikan. Neither spoke much, content to enjoy the ride and each other's company. The chill wind stole any spare breath Rhodri had for talking, and the sound of Liberty's hooves thudding on the frozen ground comforted and lulled him. He could have ridden at this easy pace forever.

To the north was a small clump of trees, and it cheered Rhodri to see them. Since he left Pencarith there had been few trees around him, and he missed the scent of rain on leaves, the feel of rough bark beneath his hands. In silent accord, the lovers guided their horses towards the copse.

Dismounting at the edge of the wood, they lashed their horses, keeping a wary eye out for patchcats and the screaming eagles that hovered above. The two horses set to work cropping the short grass and ignoring each other. Rhodri smoothed Liberty's nose and glanced at Nasira. "Will they be safe here?"

"We won't go far," she promised. "You have your blade, I have my bow. No matter what happened to me, it's rare for patchcats to hunt while the sun is up, and an eagle won't take a living horse when it can find carrion."

Reassured, Rhodri followed her into the trees. The thick trunks shielded them from the wind. Nasira spread her cloak on the ground and rummaged in her bag for food. Rhodri curled up beside her, slipping a hand under her jerkin to feel the three parallel scars that seared her back.

She pushed his hand away. "Don't."

"Why not?"

"I saw it in the glass. It's ugly."

"Nothing about you is ugly." Lying on his side, he pushed up her top, and kissed each of the broad pink lines in turn. "They're part of you, part of your story. Our story."

Nasira stiffened. He heard her breathing, but he couldn't see her face. "*Our* story?"

"Yours and mine. If you want to join your story with mine . . . ?" He kissed the marked skin again. "If you think you can put up with me, I'd like you to be my woman. My wife."

She twisted around and rolled him over in one lithe move, pinning him to the ground. There were flecks of amber in her dark eyes, and he remembered Kilujen's warning.

"Was I wrong to ask?"

"Of course not!" She kissed him, and he wrapped his arms around her, luxuriating in her warmth.

"Is that an answer?"

She rested her head on his chest, and he twisted her long braids around his fingers. "I'd like nothing more." She sighed. "If it was up to me, I'd say yes right now."

"It's not up to you?"

"What about Keir? What if there are other beautiful boys who want to lie down with you, and you with them? It wouldn't be fair to deprive you of that kind of love—but I don't think I could share you!"

"You wouldn't have to," he assured her. "I haven't looked at anyone else since I met you. Man or woman!"

"Liar!" She punched him gently in the chest. "I've seen you looking!"

He squirmed, his lie exposed. "Yes, I might have looked. But I haven't touched! I can't pretend I'm not attracted to some of the men of the tribe. Some of the women, too. I can't help that. But I don't want to spend my nights with anyone else. I hate waking up to find you're not there. I thought I'd lost you, and it half killed me. Why would I risk that for a quick tumble?"

"Your woman, Bianca, the girl who sold her body to you—"

"Keir knew about Bianca. I was younger then. I wasn't sure what I wanted. Now I am."

She was silent. He felt the rise and fall of her breathing as he waited for her to speak.

"It's trading season, Rhodri. Do you know what that means?"

"Kilujen said you'd tell me."

She snuggled closer, her arm tightening round his waist. "Trading season is when the tribes exchange blood. Horse blood, and human blood."

"You've spilt enough blood this season," he said, softly.

"Not like that. Every tribe needs fresh horses, to keep the bloodline strong. The same applies to women. Even women who might be barren, like me. We're still useful, in our way. Temion wants to trade me out, to get me away from you."

68

"Kilujen said Trogir kept me alive for my seed." He kissed the crown of her head. "I think I understand what he meant."

"The tribes barter, for horses and new mates. If a man from another tribe makes a good offer for me, Trogir would have to consider it. Other leaders will offer their women in exchange for what we have. There's a lot of gift giving, and negotiation. It goes on all winter. On the last day—"

"The Dawn of New Blood?"

Nasira nodded. "On that day, horses and women are handed over to their new tribes. It's meant to be a celebration." She pulled a face. "I've been lucky. I was allowed to stay to take care of Odval. But Odval will be a woman soon, and ready to be traded herself."

Rhodri felt slow-burning anger in his chest. "You don't have any say in this? You, or Odval, could just be sent away and you might never see each other again?" The idea of a child being sent away from her parents brought it all back, the flight through the forest, Padraig's voice telling him to run, Dallow's calloused hands plucking him from the tangled roots of the tree where he hid as darkness gathered and the wolves howled. No child should be sent away like that, forced into exile with strangers.

"If a woman finds a man she likes, even if he doesn't have the best goods or horses, a kind leader might permit the union. Happy couples make stronger babies."

He stroked her back. "It's not right. Women shouldn't be treated like horses."

"You treat your horse like a woman," Nasira pointed out.

"That's the way of my people."

"This is the way of mine. If you want me for your wife, you must convince Trogir that a terrible short-haired boy like you would be a valuable husband, and persuade Temion to let me stay."

He groaned. "I'll need luck with that!"

Her lips brushed his forehead. "You already have me, and I don't want anyone else. I think that's a promising start."

*

It was dark before sunset; storm clouds rolled in from the west, carrying sleety rain and angry gusts that sent the tumblers bouncing down the slopes of Kharikan. The Plains Hawk cave was crowded when Rhodri and Nasira arrived. They slipped in at the back of the room, trying not to attract attention. Rhodri suspected most people there were hiding from the rain, rather than driven by interest in what Temion had to say.

Distracted by the closeness of Nasira, he listened with only half an ear, until he heard his name called and she nudged him in the ribs.

"Temion wants you," she urged. "Try not to offend him. We need him on our side!"

Rhodri worked his way through the crowd. Many wanted to shake his hand or pat him on the back, and it took a while to reach the natural dais where Temion held court. Trogir leaned against the wall, a wry smile tugging his lips, but this was Temion's show, and the leader would not interfere.

Rhodri stepped on to the dais to a murmur of approval. Temion held a flat, cloth-wrapped bundle in his arms. He inclined his head at Rhodri's approach, but he didn't crack a smile.

"I haven't always treated you with the honour you deserve," Temion said, his clear voice carrying to every corner of the room. "I thought you were my enemy, and the enemy of my tribe. I may have been wrong."

"Thank you." If it was an apology, it was half-hearted and delivered with ill grace, but it was better than nothing. Temion must have had to swallow a lot of pride to get even these grudging words out in front of the people he aspired to lead. Rhodri knew when to fold his cards. "I accept your apology."

"I want to thank you for saving my sister's life, and to give you this gift. I hope you'll accept it." He held out the bundle, and a rustle went through the audience. Uncomfortable with the scrutiny,

Rhodri unwrapped the gift. He brushed the shiny fur, black and tawny, and shook it out. A cloak—

"Is this—?" His eyes sought Nasira, who had followed him to the stage. She watched him with shining eyes.

Temion nodded. "I took its life. I have the right to wear the skin. I choose to give it to you. Will you accept it, and join our family?" His eyes were wide, eager for the acceptance. It was a rich gift to come from a man who despised him, and Rhodri wasn't about to turn it down. He swung the cloak around his shoulders, and grinned.

"I accept gladly, *brother.*"

The tribe cheered as Temion stepped forward to embrace him. "You might have saved her," he said, in a low voice, "but that doesn't make us friends. I'll do everything in my power to make sure you don't get to marry her, this trading season or any other."

Trogir strode up to the dais and placed a hand on both their shoulders. His face was grave. "Will this be an end to it?" he asked softly. "I can't have infighting in the tribe. I'd sooner trade you both out. Do you understand?"

Rhodri nodded and, after a second, so did Temion. Trogir straightened. "Remember my words," he said, then, in a louder voice, he addressed his tribe as a whole. "I welcome Rhodri as Temion's brother," he said with a low bow. "He will become a fine shaman. Now, let trading season begin!"

Chapter Four

R HODRI HAD NOTHING to trade for Nasira's hand but his
new cloak, his unstinting hard work, and his memory.
She might let everyone in the tribe know who she wanted,
but he feared it wasn't enough, especially when Temion confided
with a triumphant sneer that a man from another tribe had offered
a string of horses in exchange for her.

"Your shamanic skills might win this for you," Kilujen told
him. "But you need to learn fast."

They worked together in the healing cave, Kilujen teaching his
apprentice how to brew potions for sickness and fever with his
limited supplies. The pungent herbs scorched his nostrils and set
his eyes watering. As he sniffed, the shaman took pity on him.

"Leave that," he said. "It needs to stew for a few hours. It's time
you walked the spirit trail. It takes practice. I've asked Nasira and
Ginamor to meet us here. My woman has brought me back from
the spirit trail many times, and she'll guide Nasira, as I guide you."

"I know you said Ginamor helped you. I didn't realise women
were so closely involved in shamanism," Rhodri said.

Kilujen chuckled. "There's no reason a woman can't be a shaman.
Often they're more skilled than men—their bodies are more in tune
with the rhythm of the earth, and the moons. It's a different form
of magic, but just as potent." He chalked a circle in the middle of
the room, and set candles at the four main compass points. "It's
not necessary," he said when Rhodri asked. "All you need is a rope
and somewhere to tie it, in an emergency. Having a lead rein to

pull you back helps, and you must draw your protective circle if you don't want to bring something"—he shuddered—"back with you. But don't think that taking the spirit trail is an easy ride. It's dangerous. That's why we need our women."

"Is it dangerous for them?" Rhodri had come so close to losing Nasira, he wasn't prepared to risk her again.

"No, but if you wander the spirit world you need someone to bring you back," Kilujen said. "Who better than your woman?"

"Are you talking about us?" Nasira appeared in the cave entrance, accompanied by Ginamor. Kilujen's quiet, petite wife carried a stout coil of rope over her shoulder.

Kilujen smiled. "Always! No man talks of anything but horses and women during trading season!"

She groaned. "Must you remind me? How many horses is my body worth again?"

"More horses than Rhodri owns, I'll wager. That's why he needs my help." Kilujen took the ropes from Ginamor, and lashed his right wrist to Rhodri's left. "It's easy to get lost on the spirit trail. I don't want you to stray from my side."

He fastened a second, longer rope around Rhodri's waist, and handed the other end to Nasira. "Are you happy to do this?" he asked. "There's no one else I'd trust more to guide Rhodri home."

Seeing Nasira's anxiety, and hearing Kilujen's words and the precautions he took, it dawned on Rhodri for the first time that those who ventured into the Spirit Realm did not always come back.

Kilujen bound his own waist, and gave Ginamor a kiss, wrapping his arms around her and holding her against his heart for a so long that Rhodri had to swallow the urge to clear his throat to separate them.

The two women stood outside the circle, feeding out the ropes, while Kilujen and Rhodri sat cross-legged in the centre, so close their knees touched. Kilujen's face was sober. "Do you have any questions?"

"So many I don't know where to start," Rhodri admitted. "You'll have to guide me."

"That's my sacred duty on this walk."

"Can I talk to anyone? Anyone who's gone North . . . who rides the spirit trail, I mean?"

Kilujen shook his head. "Only people who live in your memory. That's why I thought you'd be skilled at this. Your memory is stronger than any I've known."

Rhodri bit his lip. "So I couldn't talk to my real parents?"

"Is that what you hoped? I'm sorry to disappoint you. But Nasira told me of your friend, the girl who was a boy? You could find him and talk to him. Or the man who said he was your father . . ."

Rhodri shuddered, not ready for that confrontation. "I'd like to talk to Astan, if I can."

Kilujen nodded at Ginamor, who lit the candles. The rising smoke was heavily scented, and it made Rhodri's head spin, his eyelids heavy. "Take my hands and close your eyes," Kilujen instructed. Rhodri did as he was bid. "Now reach back into your past. Think of a powerful memory of your friend, and focus on it . . ."

A cursed island, the chill of water against his skin, blood on the flagstones . . .

"Not there!" The rope jerked against Rhodri's wrist. He opened his eyes. Beyond the candlelit circle, everything was black, and women's voices chanted a soft, wordless rhythm. He and Kilujen could have been alone in the world.

"That was powerful," the shaman said with a shudder. "You have remarkable skill, but you wander in dark places, Rhodri. Try to find a happier memory."

"I'll try." Rhodri forced away the image of the island, thinking instead of the day Astan chose her ride, the sun shining on the green field, the smell of horses and chewing herb. Keir's laughing eyes. The thought of Keir sent a jolt through him, of pleasure and longing. Those eyes had shone in the dark of the hayloft, those fingers had traced fire across his skin. How could he have left?

"Remember who you're looking for." Kilujen stood at his shoulder, looking around with interest. In this spirit version of Northpoint, buildings and trees looked flattened, like paper cut-outs. The grass was glass-smooth, and the fence was blurred at the edges, as if seen through the bottom of a glass. Rhodri spun round slowly. There were the stables, and the garrison block behind them, the King's flag hanging limp on the highest tower. He half-expected, longed, for Keir to stride across the field towards him, the secret smile he saved for Rhodri dancing on his lips.

"The living aren't here, Rhodri," Kilujen reminded him. "You seek one who went before his time. Is that him?"

The approaching rider was as real and solid as she had been in life. *He*, Rhodri reminded himself. Astan had identified as a man. Only men could fight in the King's Third, and Astan had fought as hard as anyone. He deserved the honour in death that he had been denied in life. And he, or his spirit, was undoubtedly male. More than male; Astan had an identical shadow that mirrored his every move, and the shadow, Rhodri knew without having to look closely, was female. The girl who had been hidden for so long. He could only stare, marvelling that Astan rode before him as if the island had been no more than a hideous, bloody dream.

Astan, and his shadow, dismounted, watching Rhodri with a wistful smile. Kilujen gave him a nudge. "Talk to him," he said. "This is your chance. That's why you're here."

Rhodri stepped forward, and the fence dissolved before him; he passed through the solid wood like a phantom, then looked back at Kilujen in alarm. "Was that meant to happen?"

"You appear as a spirit to those who ride the trail, just as they appear as spirits to you. You can't touch anything here, but you can see and be seen, hear and be heard. Talk to your twin-spirited friend."

Kilujen hung back as far as the rope joining their wrists allowed as Astan spread his arms in welcome to Rhodri.

"I'd hug you," he said, "but I know your slutty ways. You'd only try and take advantage of me!"

Rhodri's eyes flickered to Astan's wrists. The wounds he had carved there lay open and raw. Astan let his hands fall. "I know it looks bad, but it doesn't hurt any more. Try not to think about that night. It was a mess, I know . . ."

"The rest of you doesn't look too bad." Rhodri grinned. "'Fat as ever, I see!"

"As least I don't have to put up with Dedruh's shit cooking any more." Astan's brow creased at the mention of his mother, who had kept his secret for all the years they had served. He shuffled his feet in the still grass. "How's Liberty?"

"She likes it here. She gets on well with the other horses, she enjoys the freedom, I think . . . Shit, it's good to see you again! There's so much I need to say, I—"

"Don't start by saying sorry. What happened to me was never your fault. I'm glad you were with me, at the end."

He longed to embrace Astan, not as he had held him in dying on the tower, but as two old friends reunited. "Who's your shade?"

Astan smiled at his shadow. "My friend is me. Everything's so clear now, Rhodri. When I was alive, I had two spirits inside me, tangled up together so it was hard to tell where I ended and she began. I knew I was me, but all anyone ever saw was her. Sometimes I hated her. I wanted to cut her away, let people see the real me underneath. Now my spirits have been untangled, and we can live in harmony." He smiled wryly. "Relative harmony, at least. It's hard to see someone outside of you that you always resented."

Rhodri stared at the female version of Astan, trying to understand. "Does she talk?"

"She talks to me. She won't talk to you. She's part of me that's walking around outside my body, and I feel better for that."

"How does that make you feel better?"

"I had to die to find the peace I never had in life. Everything makes sense here. And I've still got a horse!" He patted the grey, who looked as solid as Astan himself, almost too real against the paper cut-out background of the stables. "He's not Starshine, but he'll do."

An awkward silence fell between them. All the questions Rhodri wanted to ask dried up in his throat. Kilujen fidgeted. "We shouldn't tarry too long, Rhodri," he said.

Astan winked. "Got to get back to your lady, Rhodri? She's pretty—tell her I envy her!"

"For being pretty? You can see her?"

"Not for being pretty, no. I can see your thoughts. I know what you've been up to." His face clouded. "I know what Dru made you do in the mountains. That was wrong. You need to watch out for him, Rhodri. Your story with him isn't finished."

"I will." There was a tug at Rhodri's waist. He couldn't see the rope binding him to the realm of the living, but he felt its insistent pull. He looked at Kilujen. "Is that Nasira?"

"Our women are calling us home."

"But we just got here!"

"Time flows differently in the Spirit Realm." Kilujen bowed to Astan. "It is an honour to meet you at last. Rhodri speaks of you often. May both your souls ride the trail in harmony."

Astan returned the bow. "Take care of him," he said. "I'm very fond of him, the little bastard."

The tugging against Rhodri's waist grew urgent. The Spirit Realm blurred.

"Kilujen!"

The shaman grabbed Rhodri's wrist. "Don't fight it," he urged. "Just relax. If you struggle, she might let go and you could be lost. Go limp."

Rhodri sagged against the rope. There was a sharp, sickening sensation in his gut as he was whisked from his feet and spun around, the wind whirling against his face. He closed his eyes against the draft, and felt a hard bump, then cold stone beneath his hands.

"Rhodri? Rhodri, can you hear me?"

"Nasira?" He opened his eyes. Her face, an inch from his, radiated concern.

"Are you back? You've been gone all afternoon!"

"I'm back, I think." He felt down his torso to check he was actually here, in the world of the living. His mouth was gritty. "Could I have some ale?"

Nasira rounded on Kilujen with a spiteful, feline hiss. "Don't ever make me do that again! I thought he was dead!"

Kilujen sat up, trying to maintain his dignity, though his hands trembled. Rhodri remained flat on the floor, too dizzy to rise. Ginamor pressed a water skin into his hand. Travelling between worlds felt like being kicked in the chest by an angry horse.

"Travelling in the Spirit Realm is a vital duty for a shaman, little cousin. Rhodri has a natural talent for it. He was never in danger."

"That's not the point! I can't stand to see him like that. I won't be part of it again. It frightened me."

"Nasira, I'm all right." Rhodri tried to reassure her. "If I want to be a shaman, I must do this. I have to make myself worth more to Trogir, and to the tribe—" He broke off, coughing.

She dropped to her knees beside him and took his hands. Her nails were sharp and pointed. "My bride-price is not worth your death—"

"I'm hardly dying—"

"—and it cuts me up inside to see you as one dead." Tears welled in her eyes. "I don't want to be your lead rope again, Rhodri. I would do it, but I beg you not to ask me."

"Then I won't." Behind Nasira's back, Kilujen shook his head in warning. "I promise I won't. I wouldn't put you through that."

"It will be harder to travel in the Spirit Realm without Nasira as your lead rein," Kilujen said.

"Then I won't travel there, unless I have to." Rhodri curled his arm around Nasira's waist. "Nasira doesn't want to do it, and I respect her wishes. I'm sure there are other ways to make myself valuable."

*

On the darkest midwinter days, the snow lay three feet thick on the ground outside. The strongest men broke the ice on the river and hauled barrels of water back to Kharikan. Every rope bridge carried a tinkling compliment of icicles, which jingled and sparkled as they moved. Even the goats ceased their restless scamper up and down the rock and huddled together miserably, bleating as they were turned out of any cave they ventured into. But in the warm heart of Kharikan, campfires burned, and old songs and stories were handed down through the generations, while the women mended tents and patched old hides. The tribes mingled freely, sounding each other out, trading, jockeying for advantage in a good-natured fashion. The women, Rhodri was surprised to see, were most adept at this. The leaders might think they led the negotiations, but the women had subtle ways of letting their menfolk know what they wanted. Mothers and daughters conspired to prod their leaders into the right choices. He hoped Nasira was employing the same wily feminine pressure on her uncle, but she would not be drawn on the subject, artfully dissembling every time he mentioned the Dawn of New Blood.

The moon changed, the snow on the ground began to melt; in the air it gave way to wet sleet. The scent of new life growing pushed through the earth. The tumblers shed the offspring they had carried in their fronds all winter, and the children tied string around them and bounced them up and down the corridors, callously indifferent to their cries. Nasira wore a secretive smile, and whispered in corners with her cousins, whispers that broke off if Rhodri ventured too near. The people of the Plains Hawk packed up, preparing for spring, and the return to the road. The

Dawn of New Blood approached, and even a shaman couldn't stop the progress of the moons across the sky.

Rhodri lay in his cave, watching the passage of Adeamus drifting past the iris-shaped opening. The moon had a faint pink tinge—an ill omen.

"Have I done enough?" he wondered aloud.

Nasira yawned, nuzzling his side. "Quite enough for one night. I need to sleep sometimes!"

"That's not what I meant!" He laughed. "I'm glad I've satisfied you, little patchcat." He massaged the back of her head, behind the ear, and she butted his hand playfully.

Since the spirit of the patchcat had been driven from her body, Rhodri had seen a subtle change in Nasira. In moments of anger or passion, her eyes flashed amber, and the scratches down his back were a reminder of her claws. The feline spirit remained inside her, dangerous, seeking release. Nasira was aware of it, but when he brought up the subject she laughed it off, not at all troubled.

She joined in with his laughter. "For now, short-hair. But what did you mean, if not that?"

"Have I convinced Trogir I'm worth more than a string of horses? Or even a barrel of mouldy fish heads?"

"I believe so." She rested her head on his chest. "We find out tomorrow, for good or ill."

"Tomorrow?" He started up. "The Dawn of New Blood is tomorrow? *Shit!*"

"Why do you always curse in that foreign tongue?" She pushed him back down. "If you haven't won over my uncle by now, then his soul is not for winning. It's too late to worry. Besides,"—she gave him a playful pinch—"all the women in the tribe have approached Trogir on your behalf. None of us want to lose such a handsome boy!"

"What about Temion? He wants rid of me."

She sniffed dismissively. "My brother does not lead the Plains Hawk. He only thinks he does, and Trogir will have to put him in his place soon."

"But there must be something more—"

"Quiet!" Nasira laid a hand over his mouth. "Sleep now. We must be up with the dawn. You don't want the new year to start without you, do you?"

She rolled over, and went back to sleep, but Rhodri lay awake long into the night, ruminating on what the new day would bring. He resolved not to be parted from Nasira for the sake of a string of horses, or goats. If he had to run away with her, he would. He knew her value as well as Trogir did, knew she was worth far more than a wandering short-hair who had abandoned his own people.

As the pink glow of dawn crept through the cave, Rhodri rose. Careful not to disturb Nasira, he pulled on his clothes and walked to the opening, looking out over the slopes of Kharikan. In the misty light, the rope ladders swarmed with people, hurrying towards the river bank. Many of them were laden with items to trade, and he marvelled at their agility. He watched one elderly woman make her way, slow but determined, down a rope ladder with a live goat slung across her shoulders.

"Is it busy out there?" Nasira asked, in sleepy tones.

"Everyone's heading to the river. I'm in no rush to join them."

"They're excited." She sat up, reaching for her comb. "The Dawn of New Blood is a day of celebration. Pass me my dress."

She wriggled into her shift, flicking out her plaits with a coquettish glance. "Don't look so worried. Everything will be fine. I've seen enough of these ceremonies to know—" Her last words were drowned out by the mewling cry of a tumbler, bouncing into the cave with Odval in pursuit. Her pout was so deep she could have balanced a saucer on her lower lip.

Rhodri caught the tumbler on his instep and booted it back to her. Odval ignored it as it crashed into the wall before Nasira scooped up the tormented creature and batted it gently out through

82

the iris, to be caught and swept along by the tender morning breeze. "What's the matter, Odval?" she asked as the girl flounced onto the bedroll.

"Nothing." Odval's eyes were brimming. Rhodri retreated towards the exit, sensing he should leave the sisters alone. His escape was thwarted by a glare from Nasira.

"Odval, do you want Rhodri to go?"

"I don't want *you* to go!" Odval threw her arms around her sister. "Why can't I be traded with you?"

"That's not how it works, little one. Why are you so sure I'm going to be traded?"

"I heard Grandmother tell Trogir that Rhodri wasn't worth your bride-price. That he was a foreign dog and unworthy of you, whether he saved your life or not." She sniffed, and wiped her nose on her palm with an apologetic glance at him. "Sorry, Rhodri."

He shrugged. "It's not your fault, Odval. Your grandmother has no love for me."

Nasira raised her eyebrows. "Tribal politics, my love. This bodes well for us."

"It does?" Rhodri and Odval asked the question simultaneously.

"Grandmother is very smart." She kissed the crown of Odval's head. "She and Trogir rub together like burrs. If she tells him not to do something, she knows he will do it, simply to spite her." She wiped Odval's eyes with her sleeve. "Let's show them we're united. I don't want to go, and you and Rhodri don't want me to go. It seems Grandmother is on our side."

She led the way out of the cave with a proud, determined stride. Odval hung back, plucking Rhodri's elbow.

"What is it?" he asked.

"If you and Nasira run away, can I come with you?"

"It won't come to that," he said, with more confidence than he felt.

"But if it did, could I? I only want to know."

He linked an arm through hers. "How would you like to be shaman in our new tribe?"

Odval grinned. "I'd rather be a warrior!"

"I'm sure you would. But it won't happen, so you don't need to worry."

Odval sighed. "I wouldn't mind if I was being traded too. When you join a new tribe everyone makes a fuss of you, because they know how much you're worth. It's an honour to be wanted."

Rhodri shrugged. "It seems like slavery to me."

"That's because you're a short-hair." Odval snorted. "You don't understand our ways at all." She squeezed his arm in a rare moment of affection. "My sister likes you though, so you can't be all bad."

"For a short-hair, you mean?"

"I suppose. I hope she gets to stay with you."

Rhodri squeezed her in return. "So do I."

*

The tribal leaders and their shamans stood before the excited crowd. They held down a goat between them, and it squealed and thrashed as a tall woman in an elaborate headdress pinned it between her knees and expertly slashed its throat. The blood splashed over the broken semicircle of rocks that formed a backdrop to the ceremony, and the woman who wielded the knife held up her bloodstained hands. Rhodri and Nasira, with Odval who would not let them out of her sight, sat on the cold, damp ground near the edge of the crowd, too far away to hear her words, no matter how hard Rhodri tried to follow the ceremony.

The tribal leaders flanked the woman who had sacrificed the goat, like a collection of ostentatious statues. The shamans orchestrated the elaborate dance, as a young man entered through a break in the rocks with a pair of fine mares, laden with goods; he led the horses to the woman. She made a show of inspecting the gift, and at length, she nodded, and gestured for Kilujen to bring a girl from the Plains Hawk into the circle. She called Trogir forward to clasp the couple's hands together, muttered a blessing, and there was a smattering of applause. That seemed to be it. A simple ceremony, repeated over and over.

Odval sprawled on her stomach, picking at the grass and looking bored, until a disruption broken out in the hemisphere of rocks. Her eyes brightened, and she sat up. "Oho! Fun! Let's go closer!"

Nasira caught her arm. "We're not going closer. Sit quiet and listen."

A hush fell over the crowd. Nasira leaned over and whispered in Rhodri's ear:

"Two men have made equal offers for the same woman, and the silly girl hasn't expressed a preference. A girl usually knows who she wants, but this one doesn't care either way. She hasn't negotiated very well."

The presiding woman had a terse discussion with the leaders of the three tribes involved, and pointed to a cleared space, a patch of bare ground in front of the circle. The rival claimants stripped to the waist and squared off.

"They wrestle now," Nasira went on. "The winner is the first to pin his opponent."

"Pin?"

The crowd, sensing blood, sprang to their feet and surged forward. Rhodri lost sight of the circle behind a sea of enthusiastic onlookers. Nasira bobbed up and down on her toes, craning her neck. "I can't see!" she cried in frustration, pushing at the wall of backs blocking her view. "Let me look! They—oh!"

A moan of disappointment rippled through the audience. The bout was over in seconds, the victor raising his arm in triumph, pinning his vanquished foe to the ground with the weight of his body. As he released his rival, who shook his hand and walked away without a backward glance, a shaman brought the girl in question into the arena. Moon-faced and bored, she showed no emotion as her leader linked her hand with her new husband's. Nasira sniffed in disapproval.

"She should have worked harder," she muttered. "That won't be a happy union."

"Have you been working hard?" Rhodri asked. "I doubt I could win a wrestling bout for you."

Before Nasira could reply, Rhodri was tapped on the shoulder by a boy of the tribe, hopping from foot to foot, puffed up with importance. "Rhodri Short-hair, Nasira, you're to go to Kilujen now."

"Time for our show." Nasira was calm, almost placid. "Are you ready?"

"I think so."

She seemed to enjoy his discomfort, but Rhodri felt sick as they pushed through the crowds and down to the riverbank where Kilujen waited. He had two men with him. One led three beautiful mares, and was taller than Rhodri by almost a foot although his hair was solid iron-grey and his face was heavily lined. The other was only a little shorter, but younger, bulky and well-muscled. Rhodri didn't fancy wrestling either of them.

Nasira slipped her hand into his. "I'm yours," she whispered. "I've made sure everybody knows it. I won't go willingly to another man."

"Will Trogir make you go, even if you're not willing?"

She smiled, her teeth sharp. "Who would argue with a woman who carries the spirit of a patchcat within her? He would have to be courageous, or very foolish."

Kilujen had dark hollows under his eyes, and the eagle feathers decorating his braids were askew. "I hate ceremonies," he muttered to Rhodri. "It's like rounding up tumblers. People are never where they're meant to be when you need them. You can do this next time."

"Kilujen, I don't stand a chance against these two!"

"Of course you don't." Kilujen grinned. "But I won't have my apprentice shamed before the tribes. And I'll keep an eye on Temion too, make sure he doesn't disrupt things."

"I don't think he will," Rhodri said. Nasira's brother had been strangely polite whenever the subject of trading season came up. Rhodri hoped he wasn't plotting any uncomfortable surprises.

Kilujen winked. "Maybe I whispered in his ear. You wait here. Nasira, come with me."

He took her arm and led her away, leaving Rhodri alone with his rivals. He shuffled his feet and stared at the eddies on the river. One of the mares whinnied, nudging him with her nose. He raised his hand in an absent caress. "Nice rides."

"Thank you."

Another aching silence. The shorter tribesman cracked his knuckles, a sound like the lash of tiny whips, and muttered a low curse.

"Is something wrong, friend?"

"You're the short-hair." A blunt statement, followed by a long pause. Rhodri wondered if he should reply. "You saved Nasira of the Plains Hawk from the patchcat. You gave her your blood."

Rhodri nodded.

"You've been fucking her for moons."

The man with the mares looked at him with new respect. "That's you, is it?"

"It is." Tribal gossip spread like fire.

"Shit on this!" the knuckle-cracker spat. "I can't compete, can I? Tell the shaman I withdraw." He turned on his heel and stormed away.

The horseman shrugged. "I'm going nowhere, friend," he said. "She's a fine girl. I've much to offer for her hand."

But she wants me. Rhodri hoped that was enough to win Trogir over. Looking at the mares, he doubted it. "You know she might be barren?" It was a slim chance, but it might put the older man off.

"I've got eight colts by my first woman. She died in summer. I want someone to warm my bed and take care of my hurts. I've done my share of breeding."

It had been worth a shot, at least. They lingered in uncomfortable silence until Kilujen returned, straightening the feathers in his hair. He flashed Rhodri a smile as he addressed his rival. "You have the better gift. You go first."

The man looked triumphant as Kilujen led him into the circle. Rhodri sat on the riverbank, knees pulled up to his chin, waiting miserably for the applause. The thought of Nasira in bed with her arrogant suitor made the blood pound in his skull. He dug angry holes in the turf with the point of his knife. Let his rival touch her, and the blade would strike deep into his heart. What was taking so long?

He raised his head at the crunch of hooves on gravel. The older tribesman left the arena, leading his rides; he turned his head as he passed, and spat.

"Hey!" Rhodri sprang to his feet, brandishing the knife. "What was that for?"

"It seems eastern mares aren't as valuable as Western cock."

"What are you talking about?"

Kilujen stepped between them. "Rhodri, you're needed in the circle." He seized his arm and dragged him away.

"What happened?"

"Trogir turned down his offer. You have your chance."

Before Rhodri could gather his jumbled thoughts, the shaman pushed him firmly into the circle of bloodstained rocks. He dropped to his knees before Trogir and the tall woman, as he had seen others kneel, head lowered in respect. Behind the ceremonial mask, Trogir's eyes glittered like frost. The woman offered a smile and extended a large hand to help him to his feet. Up close, he could see the lightest brush of stubble on her chin, and there was a hardness to her jaw. She quirked her eyebrows at him as if daring him to say something. He thought it wise to keep quiet.

If he offended her, they might give Nasira to the iron-haired man after all.

"You're the short-hair who has been living with the Plains Hawk?" Her voice was pitched deeper than he was expecting.

Rhodri swallowed, his mouth suddenly dry. "I am."

"You had a friend who was a twin-spirit, Kilujen tells me."

"I do . . . I did . . ."

"A shame. He would have done well here." *Better than you*, her eyes suggested. "Twin-spirits make good shamans. We understand men and women from both sides. You aspire to be a shaman?"

"I'm doing my best," Rhodri said.

"Maybe you'll do well." Her eyes softened. "Let's get on. You request the hand of a woman of the Plains Hawk tribe. What name does she carry?"

"Nasira."

"Your leader asks what you offer in return?"

"Tell my leader I have little to offer. I have neither a string of mares, nor polished gems. I was a leader in my own kingdom, but a leader without home or tribe. I have only myself, my horse, and my memory. I've trained as a shaman, and walked the Spirit Realm, and I gave my own blood to save his niece. I hope that will be enough."

He wished he could see Trogir's expression. Listed before Nasira's uncle, his assets were meagre. If Trogir had already turned down three beautiful mares, what hope did he have?

Trogir took a step forward "You forgot to mention something you have, that no other man can own," he said, solemnly.

"What's that, my leader?"

"The love of my niece. I do not know why, but she bargained for this bonding with more fire and passion than I have ever seen. Short-hair, I hope you will make her a worthy mate. I had to persuade her brother of the wisdom of this union, and he has yet to be convinced."

Rhodri kept his head bowed, sure the smile spreading across his face was inappropriate for the occasion. "I'll do the best I can," he promised.

Trogir laid his hand over Rhodri's. The hand of the twin-spirit woman enclosed them both. "Then the proposal is accepted," she announced in a voice intended to carry to the crowd.

Rhodri was aware of movement behind him, but he kept his eyes on the clasped hands, waiting to be told he could let go. Trogir tapped him on the shoulder.

"Stand together and be bonded," the woman commanded. "I hope your union brings happiness, and many fine sons!" She clasped his hand in Nasira's as she came up to stand beside him, quiet and demure, but her eyes gleaming in triumph. Rhodri flinched at the sting in his palm. Looking down, he saw blood welling between their linked fingers. Trogir raised their joined hands high, and the crowd cheered. Odval, who had pushed to the front, jumped up and down. He winked at her.

Trogir let their hands go. "Walk the trail together, and be at peace."

Nasira bowed, pulling Rhodri down with her. *Thank you*, she mouthed over her shoulder as Kilujen steered them out of the circle, an arm around each of their shoulders. "Congratulations!" he said. "Are you all right, Rhodri? You look dizzy!"

"I need to sit down." He sank onto a nearby rock and traced the star-shaped cut in his palm, which mirrored the wound in Nasira's. "Is that it? Are we married now?"

Nasira giggled. "It's done. You didn't even have to wrestle anyone."

Rhodri shook his head. "It's very different from the way my people celebrate marriage." He stroked the locket he wore around his neck, and pondered. "Come with me a moment." He held out his bleeding hand to his wife. "Somewhere private."

Kilujen shot him a knowing look. "I know you couldn't hold back before you were bonded, but give her time to catch her breath."

"Nothing like that!" He caught Nasira's hand and ran with her, down the river, away from the celebrating crowds and their curious eyes. The low winter sun was setting, casting long shadows across the dark surface of the water. A fish splashed, and in the distance a patchcat coughed and snarled. Nasira lifted Rhodri's arm and snuggled underneath it, and he leant against her, savouring the warmth of her body against his side.

"Are you happy?" she asked. "Is this what you wanted?"

"Yes. It took me a while to realise it, though. I was blind, or stupid. Here, I have a gift for you."

He lifted the locket from his neck, running the chain through his fingers. It was the first time he had taken it off since he left Hierath, running from an uncomfortable truth. "In my culture, a husband gives his wife a necklace to wear as a symbol of marriage. We are married in the eyes of your tribe. I'd like us to be married in the way of mine too. I want you to have this."

He pressed the locket into her hand. She hesitated. "But it's precious to you . . ."

"That's why I want you to have it. Open it."

She fumbled with the catch, until he took it from her and flicked it open. "There's a knack to it," he said. "These are my parents. My real parents."

Nasira twisted the locket, studying the portraits, comparing them to Rhodri's face. "You look like your father," she said. "But I can see your mother in you too, around the chin. They would have been proud of you."

He fastened the chain around her neck, the locket falling down between her breasts. "They should have been my family," he said. "I never got that chance. But now you are my family."

She kissed him, long and lingering. "My whole tribe are your family now." Her nose wrinkled, and she sniffed. "They're cooking tumbler fronds. Can you smell them?"

All Rhodri could smell was campfire smoke, but the prospect of food made his mouth water. He helped Nasira to her feet, and slipped his arm around her waist, and together they strolled back towards the feast.

Chapter Five

THE NEXT FEW days were a blur of post-celebration exhaustion, and then of activity as the tribes packed up and prepared to leave Kharikan, abandoning the rock to the tumblers, the patchcats, and the fearless little goats. Rhodri was so busy he barely saw Nasira, but as the tribe rolled out, her grandmother leaned out of the cart and nodded at him.

"Good job you've got your own wagon now, short-hair! You won't keep me awake at night!" She pulled her head in before he could reply. Rhodri sighed as he urged Liberty into a trot. Nasira assured him he was part of her family, but her fearsome grandmother clearly didn't feel the same way.

The people of the Plains Hawk headed south, following a tributary of the river. It was a different route from the one which brought them to Kharikan, but Rhodri, expecting a change in scenery, was disappointed. Mile after mile, day after day, the endless flat steppe rolled out before them with barely a break in the skyline for trees and hills.

If the scenery was dull, life with Nasira was the opposite. Trogir had given them a wagon as a wedding gift; Nasira was adept at driving, and Rhodri rode alongside on Liberty, watching his wife work the team of placid cart-horses. They were big, lumbering beats, towering over his nimble little Lib, but they were good natured and hard working, and he secretly gave them names of their own. It didn't seem right that they should miss out on having names.

Ten days out of Kharikan, in a region bordered to the east by haphazard piles of rocks, Trogir called a halt. The grasslands were lush and green, and the river coiled like a snake. Tents were struck, the horses corralled, and life continued as it had for centuries, a peaceful tribe making a slow crossing of the great plains. Rhodri spent his days hunting, fishing, and studying with Kilujen, and his nights wrapped in Nasira's arms.

It was early morning. The sunshine lighting the tent promised a warm day. Nasira yawned and stretched as Rhodri swept her hair aside to kiss the nape of her neck. He pulled her close, his arms creeping around her. She gasped.

"What's wrong?"

She caught his hand, flattened it out, and laid it gently on her stomach. He felt a strange flutter beneath his fingers.

"What's that? Are you ill?"

"Far from it. This is the first time I've felt him move. Now I can tell you."

"Felt who move? What are you talking about?"

"You can feel it too, Rhodri. That's our baby moving in my belly. Yours and mine."

Rhodri snatched his hand away. "You can't be. You said you couldn't—"

"I didn't think I could." Her smile dimmed. "Maybe Western seed is stronger, I don't know."

"How long have you known about this? Why didn't you tell me?"

"Since before we were bonded. It convinced Trogir to let me stay with you."

"Trogir knows? You told him, but not me?" He knew he sounded harsh, but he couldn't help it.

"I had to tell him, or he would have sent me away." Nasira's voice trembled. "I couldn't tell you before, tradition forbids it. I thought you'd be happy."

The air inside the tent was close and humid. Rhodri felt strangled. He struggled to his feet and groped for his clothes.

"Rhodri? Talk to me! What's wrong?"

Nasira reached out and he pushed her hand away. "I'm not ready for this."

"Not ready for what? To be a father? You don't have a choice."

"I don't know how to be a father." Rhodri shoved his feet into his boots, catching his finger on the edge of one of the iron bands. "Shit!"

"Don't curse at me!" Nasira sat up. "What do you mean, you don't know how to be a father? You just learn. Do you think I know how to be a mother?"

"I can't think about this now. I need air." He threw back the entrance to the tent, heedless of her pleas, and strode towards the corral.

Kilujen caught up with him as he saddled Liberty. "Rhodri? I heard shouting—"

"Mind your own business, shaman." Rhodri mounted, wheeled the little mare around and vaulted the fence with an easy stride.

"Rhodri, stop!" Nasira stood in the doorway of their tent, clasping a blanket to hide her nudity. He didn't want to see her. He crouched low over Liberty's neck, easing her into a canter, charging through the camp in a blur of whirling dust. Out on to the barren, empty steppe, looking for a place to be alone.

He found it in the warren of rocks a few miles west of the camp. Leaving Liberty to wander, he began to climb. The rising sun beat down on his shoulders and back as he hauled himself hand-over-hand, seeking toeholds in the rocks, losing himself in the physical challenge. He was almost disappointed when he reached the summit of his chosen spire, a flat plateau twenty feet in diameter. He collapsed on his stomach, sweaty and breathless, letting the breeze cool him. Far below, Liberty looked like a toy horse, a child's plaything, and as he thought that, everything he had climbed here to escape flooded back.

"Seven hells, what now?" He cursed, the echo bouncing off the surrounding peaks, and smacked his fist against the unyielding rock. Nasira deserved a man who knew what he was doing. Dallow had been distant with all his blood-children, but it was only Rhodri, the foundling, who felt the lash of his belt buckle. As for Valery . . .

The thought of Valery made him shudder. Once he had been Rhodri's world, but he had committed such appalling acts. Crimes the child couldn't understand, but as a man, Rhodri could see clearly; Valery was everything he hated, but he was the only loving parent he knew. The father he remembered was a good man, gentle in his discipline. There had been many disquieting things about his interactions with other adults, but Rhodri had been a child, had seen with a child's eyes, and not fully understood. He had no idea if Valery had brought him up well. He suspected not, knowing what he knew now about the man. But he was the only example Rhodri had. How could he learn to be a father, and not be like Valery? He had been toying with a loose piece of shale, and at this thought he hurled it away, off the edge of the spire to tumble into empty air. He should leave. Nasira would be better off without his bad influence on their child. But where could he run? There was no one in this desolate land who would open their arms to him.

He sat up, careful to avoid being seen against the skyline, the ingrained habit of caution. On the southern horizon a thin column of smoke rose, marking the campsite of another tribe. He could see his own camp nestled by the river, and it tugged his heart. What would happen to Nasira if he left?

A horse cantered away from the settlement, heading towards his retreat. Rhodri flattened himself against the rock, hoping it was coincidence, that the rider would turn off or pass by. He cursed his luck as Liberty trotted out to greet them.

Lib, you've betrayed me! Not you as well! He buried his head in his arms with a groan. It seemed he couldn't run without fighting first.

"Rhodri Short-hair!" The shout from below was distorted by the rocks, but there was no mistaking the tone of command. "Get down here now! Don't make me climb up after you!"

Nasira's grandmother, iron-grey braids twisted into a bun on top of her head, dismounted awkwardly. Waving her cane, she stumped towards the rocks.

"I mean it!" she hollered. "I'll climb up there, and curse you if I fall and break my back!" She set hands and foot on the bottom of the spire, and glared up. "Must I kill myself to get you down?"

"Stop!" he cried. She let go and stepped back, arms folded, stick beating a tattoo on the ground. "I'll come down."

"You'd better!"

By the time Rhodri slithered and shimmied down the tower of rocks, scraping hands and calves, Nasira's grandmother had spread a blanket over a nearby rock and settled comfortably, chewing a strip of dried horsemeat. She nodded at him. "Decided to be a man, then?"

"What are you talking about?"

She patted the space beside her. "Nasira told me what happened. You've upset her, running off like that over a baby. I measured you as many things, but not a coward. Sit!"

No one argued with the old lady when she used that tone. The only one who dared was Odval, who could get away with much where her grandmother was concerned. She offered him a strip of meat to chew on. "My name is Borta," she said.

It took a moment for Rhodri to register that she had given up her name to him. "Thank you," he said with a solemn nod. "I'm not sure I deserve your trust, but I'm honoured."

"You'll be the father of my great-grandchild. We need trust between us." She stared into the middle distance, weak eyes glazing. "It's hard for me to trust you. The short-hairs slaughtered my tribe the summer before I was traded to the Plains Hawk. Seeing Nasira with a short-hair sets a frost on my heart."

"I'm sorry," Rhodri said. "I didn't know."

"Not many do. Trogir knows, and the shaman. Nasira doesn't, and I'll thank you to keep it that way."

"Of course." Rhodri chewed the salty meat, uncomfortable with the revelation. It must have been over fifty summers ago, but the hurt was still there in Borta's eyes.

"Besides," the old lady snapped, "I didn't ride all this way to talk about me. I came to drag your cowardly backside back to your wife."

"I can't go back. Don't try and persuade me, Borta. I'd just make a mess of it."

She arched her eyebrows. She must have been a lot like Nasira, in her youth. "Make a mess of what, young man?"

"Being a father."

She nodded, sucking on her gums. "No man is born with the skills to be a father. What makes you think you'd be so terrible at it?"

Rhodri sighed. "My father—well, he wasn't my real father, but he brought me up as his son from the earliest I can remember. He was the sun in my sky. He could do nothing wrong."

"So where's the problem?"

"Everything he did was wrong! I couldn't see it because I was a child, and he didn't seem to care, or even notice . . . He killed people in front of me, and I thought that was normal. He had sex with women across the end of my bed while I was asleep, and if he saw I was awake, he would press his finger to his lips and carry on. I grew up surrounded by sex and aggression, thinking everything was fine, that this was all normal. He was a crazed, violent man who could have turned on me at any moment. But the only model I have as a father is him. What if I do the same to my son without realising it?"

"Do you intend to do those things? To kill people and bed women in front of your child?"

"Of course not!"

"Then what makes you think you're like this man who raised you? It strikes me that if you behave in the opposite way to him, you'll make a very good father."

98

"Valery thought he was a good father! He was proud of it. I thought he was too, until I understood . . . I don't want to hurt my son, believing I'm doing a good job. I'd rather have nothing to do with him than have him suffer the pain Valery caused me."

Borta frowned. "You don't speak of your mother. Where was she when this was going on?"

"I never knew my mother." An aching loss opened within him, for the life he should have had, the life Valery had stolen.

"But your child will have a mother," Borta pointed out. "A good girl who knows right from wrong, and who can put a wayward, confused boy in his place. She'll help you. With her, you can build the family you missed when you were a foal." Her wrinkled hand clasped his knee in a gesture of affection. "You have the whole tribe with you. You won't be bringing up your baby alone, everyone pitches in. There's no need to be scared."

Rhodri sighed. "I wish I understood what went on in Valery's head, so I don't make the same mistakes."

"It doesn't sound like a mind you want to look at too closely." Borta heaved herself to her feet. "Are you coming back of your own will, or do I have to beat you with my cane and drag you behind my horse? I will, you know."

"I don't doubt it!" Rhodri laughed at her fearsome expression.

"It's not funny, young man." Borta brandished her cane.

"No, it's not. Sorry, Borta." Rhodri turned away to hide his smile.

"Go back to calling me Grandmother. No one uses my name anyway."

Rhodri helped her onto her horse, and handed up her stick. She delivered him a sharp crack across the head. "That's for making me come after you. I'm sure you won't forget it in a hurry."

He rode beside her back to camp, skull stinging from the rebuke, determined to make amends with Nasira and be the best father he could. But Borta had planted the seed of an idea in his mind, and over the next few days it sprouted and grew, until he could no longer ignore it.

*

After a week of rumination, Rhodri's mind was set. He said nothing to Nasira, or Kilujen. What he planned was dangerous, but private. He couldn't do it with the shaman standing at his shoulder. He took a long rope and looped it around his waist, throwing on his patchcat-skin cloak to conceal it.

He wouldn't stray too far, in case anything went wrong. He found a patch of stunted, twisted trees, none of them taller than he was, around two miles to the east. He scanned the ground for hoof prints, but the only ones he found were old. People rarely came here; it suited his purpose well.

He scratched the protective circle into the dirt with a stick, making sure there were no breaks. If the circle was broken, a determined spirit could cross over into the world of the living. He wanted to keep the restless soul he sought confined to his own realm.

With the circle drawn and the candles lit, pale in the morning light, he fastened one end of the rope to a sturdy tree, and secured the other around his waist. Taking a deep breath, gathering his courage, he closed his eyes and stepped into the circle.

The jolt of recognition, of memory, was so powerful it snatched his breath away. He stood in the Great Hall of Hierath Castle, an empty, echoing room that should have bustled with life. Tapestries hung from the walls, blurry in the corners of his vision. A chill hung over the room, and he shuddered, pulled his cloak tight to ward off the cold as he walked towards the throne, and the lounging, indolent figure of the man he once called his father.

Valery Northpoint rose as Rhodri approached, and inclined his head. "You've grown since we last met," he remarked, jumping down from the dais to land with catlike grace. "I didn't expect to see you again, I must admit." Rhodri backed off as Valery approached, watching him through narrowed eyes. Valery opened his arms. "Don't look at me like you hate me. If you feel that way, why did you seek me out?"

Rhodri swallowed, torn between longing for the security of his father's embrace, and the terrible knowledge that had set him on this path.

"You're not my father."

Valery shrugged. "Not by blood, true. But I taught you to hunt and fish. I held your hand when you were sick, and hugged you when you had nightmares. I did everything a father should, while your own father failed you. Alex chose to abandon you. You owe me your life, Rhodri. I understand that's important to your chosen tribe."

"My father didn't abandon me. You stole me from him!" Rhodri retreated another step, groping for his sword.

"Do you think you can hurt me? You're a little fool, Rhodri." Valery snorted. "Did you come here to whine about how your parents didn't want you? Or is it more than that?" His lip curled. "That's a fine girl you've settled down with—"

"Don't talk about her!" Rhodri's sword flashed in the hazy light. "You leave her alone! I don't want you even *thinking* about her, after what you did!"

Valery roared with laughter. "I wish I could do more than think! You've got your mother's fiery spirit about you. I could never tame her, and you've gone the same way. Lower your sword, it's no use here."

Rhodri instinctively obeyed the quiet command.

"That's better." Valery hitched himself up on the edge of the dais, long legs swinging. His pale blue eyes were piercing. "You came here to talk, so talk. You know I'm not a patient man."

"Nasira's pregnant."

"Congratulations." Valery raised a sardonic eyebrow. "I trust that's what you wanted. If not, there are ways around it—"

"I don't want to know!"

"What do you want to know, Rhodri? Why I took you into my home? Why I brought you up as mine?"

Rhodri hung his head. "I want to be a good father. I don't want to be . . ."

"Don't want to be like me, is that it?" Valery's eyes narrowed. "Don't be so bloody self-righteous, Rhodri. I know what you did on the mountain. You're no better than me. Worse, in fact."

"Worse? How can I be worse than you?"

"You tried to run out on your own son, just like your father did to you. I was a better father than Alex. You never wanted for anything while you were with me. The only reason you're against me now is the stories you've heard. Bloody Lydia!" He slammed his fist against the wooden dais. "Even now she's gone North she taunts me. She's turned you against me. I knew she would . . ." He sighed and shook his head. "I was a fool to let her live. I never told you about my own father, did I?"

Rhodri shook his head, hurt and confused.

"He killed my sister. Threw her down a flight of stairs when she was a babe in arms. My mother sent me away to keep me safe. That's what I did for you, Rhodri. Protected you from your mother, from her lies and schemes. She would have used you to get at me, I know."

"But *I* don't know. You took me away from her. You never let me know her."

"You want to know her, do you?" Valery laughed as he jumped down from the dais. "I can see your memories, you know. All of them. Such a crowded little head, but no room for your poor mother? What a pity. Do you know why you can't remember her? Do you want me to tell you what happened to you?"

"You know—?" Another surge of sickening hate. "What happened to me? Was it your doing?"

"I'll show you. Follow me."

Valery led the way out of the hall with long strides, Rhodri followed at his heels. The hall faded to grey behind them, as if they travelled in a bubble, a bubble fabricated from Rhodri's memories. The walls were flat, the features smoothed from hewn stone, but every stain, every crack was just as he remembered it, and the corridor unveiled before them out of greyness like a picture coming to life before his eyes. There was a door at the end of it, and he knew it led to the great courtyard that was the heart of life in Hierath. Beyond it were the stables, the forge, and the infirmary. It had been his kingdom once, where he had chased and played with Amerie. Now it all belonged to Serren, everything that should have been his.

"It should have been yours, you know." Valery voiced Rhodri's own thoughts. "I meant to leave it to you. You can blame your mother for that, too. She never wanted you to inherit. Thought you were too much like me." His chuckle was bitter.

"I'm not like you."

"Are you sure about that?" Valery eyed him, then changed the subject abruptly. "You see that wall there?" He pointed at an area of the castle wall, no different from any other as far as Rhodri could see.

"What about it?"

"You used to have a pony—I forget what it was called—but one day it threw you and you hit your head, just there. You were never the same after that. The slate was erased, wiped clean and started anew. You couldn't remember anything that had come before, but it didn't take me long to realise that now you remembered everything with perfect clarity." He shuddered. "It wasn't natural. It chilled me, if I'm honest, even as I realised I could make use of your new talent."

Rhodri stared hard at the spot on the wall. It looked no different to the rest of the building; there was no mark there. But the impact had affected his entire life. It seemed such a trivial thing. Too trivial.

"That's it? A bloody riding accident left me the way I am? Not magic, not a curse, just me falling off my horse?"

"Did you think you were special, Rhodri?" Valery's tone was openly mocking. "Did you think a mage came down and blessed you when you were a baby? Lydia always laboured under the delusion that she was special too. I can see too much of her in you, and I don't like it."

"I can't see anything of her in me." Rhodri spoke dully, wrenching his eyes away from the wall. "How could I, when I never knew her?"

Valery closed his hands over Rhodri's shoulders with the chill of mist. His voice was soft, no breath to disturb the hair over his ears as he leaned in. "You want to know your mother? Know her like I did? She's right here, in my memories. I can give my memories of her to you, if you want them . . ."

His hand drifted towards Rhodri's forehead. His smile was cold, devoid of humour, of warmth. In the chilly depths of his eyes something savage glittered, and Rhodri knew that whatever Valery could teach him about his mother, it wouldn't be something he wanted to know.

He backed away, raising his hands in instinctive defence. "What are you doing? Leave me alone!" His blow passed through Valery's insubstantial flesh like mist, leaving the frost of death on Rhodri's skin.

"I told you, you can't hurt me here." The air between them crackled with the menacing energy of an approaching storm.

Valery pressed forward, fingertips brushing Rhodri's temple. "I thought this was what you wanted? All you ever wanted, right here in my hand, and only I have the power to give it to you—"

"Get away from me!" Rhodri tried to push him away, but it was like fighting frosty air.

"You want to know your mother. Every moment we spent together. The way she cried out when I made love to her . . . Don't you long to hear it?"

Valery's slender fingers sent icy tendrils into his skull. Rhodri caught a flash of pain and fear, and an overwhelming sense of betrayal. He felt a wrenching jolt against his waist, jerking him from his feet away from his father and that cold, intrusive touch. He lost his footing, stumbling away across the paved courtyard.

A sound like thunder, and the sky above him ripped open like a wound. The snarling shape of a patchcat tumbled through empty air, twisting as she fell, to launch herself at Valery. He threw up his arm in defence. "Call it off!"

"Nasira!"

The patchcat pulled up in mid-leap, landing awkwardly, one hind paw raking Rhodri's stomach. She lowered her head, lips curled back over wicked teeth. Rhodri wrapped a restraining arm around her neck.

Valery's eyes widened. "This is your woman? And I thought *I* had some unusual habits in the bedroom!"

Nasira butted Rhodri with her head, pawing his chest with sheathed claws. He felt the rope clench around his waist, tugging him back to the realm of the living.

He braced his feet against the ground, and gripped the fur at the nape of Nasira's neck. "I know what you did to my mother," he said, "and what you just tried to do to me. My memories are my own, but of all the people I remember, I've never hated anyone as much as I hate you."

Valery shrugged. His smile was disarming, and it did not reach his eyes. "That's your choice," he said. "I never abandoned you, until now—"

"You sent me away. I was five years old, and you never came back for me."

"I would have come for you, if things had turned out differently. You can believe me or not, but I cared about you once."

"Liar!"

Valery's face began to blur, the grey mist descending as the lead rein pulled Rhodri back between the worlds. Then there was only

Nasira, her rough fur beneath his hand, as Valery's final words fell through the void with him.

"You've lost my love, Rhodri. Just like you drove away your mother. You're alone now . . ."

Alone . . . Rhodri gasped for breath, hugging Nasira's slender, human waist. She shuddered as she struggled to her feet, dragging him with her. "Get up! They've taken Odval! We need you!"

"Who's taken her? What's going on?" Rhodri felt sick. Nasira's face was ravaged, tears rolling down her cheeks. Kilujen hacked at the rope binding Rhodri to the tree with shaking hands. His skin was grey, and his breath came in tight, pained gasps.

"The short-hairs came," he said. "You can smell the smoke. Convenient you were walking the spirit trail, when your tribe decided to attack . . ."

"Kilujen, not now!" Nasira cried. "They took my sister, you have to get her back!"

Rhodri caught her hands. "I'll find her," he swore. "Tell me what happened."

"Kilujen and I were looking for you. I thought you might try to walk the Spirit Realm alone, to find your father. We heard the iron feet coming, so we hid. They passed so close I could smell the sweat and blood on them, and they had Odval. She was screaming, Rhodri! There was nothing I could do!" She burst into fresh tears and burrowed her head into his shoulder.

"We'll get her back," he promised again. Kilujen shook his head, his eyes cold.

"We all know what your tribe do to our women."

"Not Odval. Not while I breathe. Where's Temion?"

Nasira gave a heaving sob. "I don't know."

"Can you walk back to camp?"

She leaned on his arm. The acrid smoke blew across the steppe. A light drizzle fell, turning heavier as they neared the ruined camp. Nasira's step faltered. "I can't look, Rhodri. Don't make me."

"I'll stay with her." Kilujen's voice was sharp as he took Nasira's arm. "Go and see what they did."

Rhodri held his sleeve over his mouth to ward off the smoke, the taint of blood and the taste of wet ash. Every tent lay in ruins, ripped open and torched. He stumbled over the body of a young woman, still clutching her bow, run through the belly in the wreckage of the home she died defending. But there weren't as many bodies as there should be, and many of the dead wore the scarlet flash of the King's Third. There were familiar faces on both sides, and he grieved.

He found Trogir on the wooden gate of the empty corral; it creaked as it swung, an eerie sound amid the stillness of death and the faint hiss of dying flame. The leader was on his knees, arms spread wide as if in supplication. Nails were driven through his hands deep into the top bar of the gate, his head tilted back. The handle of a blade protruded from his open mouth, forced through the back of his throat. Rhodri wrenched it free. From the blood soaking the front of Trogir's jerkin, Rhodri guessed it had taken him a long time to die.

Sickened, he used the bloodied blade to pry the nails from Trogir's palms. He caught the old man's body as he toppled forward, and laid him on the ground, closing the leader's staring eyes.

"They think they've got away with this," he whispered, "but they're wrong. As long as you live in my memory, I will hunt them down and make them pay. Serren, the King's Third, the whole Kingdom will suffer for what happened today." He pressed his forehead to Trogir's. "Ride in peace in the Spirit Realm, my friend, my uncle. Your death will not be forgotten."

"Rhodri?"

"Stay back, Nasira!" With a swift movement, he covered Trogir's body with his cloak. Nasira's hand was pressed to her mouth, and she swayed as she looked around at the devastation. He stood and caught her by the upper arms. "Why didn't you stay with Kilujen? I would have spared you this."

She pointed at the covered body. "Is that . . . Temion? Did they kill my brother?"

He shook his head. "It's Trogir. I'm so sorry, Nasira."

"Trogir! Oh no! *No!*" She pushed past, wrenching free as he tried to hold her back. She flew to her uncle's body and gathered him in her arms, pushing aside the cloak.

"Nasira, don't!"

"What have they done? How can they do this?" She rocked back and forth, holding Trogir to her chest.

Rhodri glared at Kilujen, picking his way through the broken settlement. "Why did you let her follow me?"

"She insisted. Have you found Temion? Or Grandmother?"

"No, but I haven't found any dead horses either. Could they have escaped? Did you see if the raiders had any prisoners, apart from Odval?"

"I was flat to the ground. I didn't *see* anything. Nasira recognised Odval's cries."

"If there are survivors, they might be hurt. They'll need your skills. We need to find them quickly. Can you track?"

"I can track." Nasira rose. Her shirt was smeared with blood, and the tears rolled down her soot-stained cheeks, but she held herself proudly.

"You don't need—"

"I can track," she repeated. "Let me do something. I feel so helpless . . ."

"Let her track, Rhodri," Kilujen said. "Patchcat senses can help us now."

"But . . . Trogir, the rest of them—?" Rhodri felt he should do something for the fallen, cover their faces at least. It felt disrespectful to leave dead eyes staring blankly at the empty sky.

"Help the living. Then we can tend the dead."

Rhodri retrieved his cloak, replacing it with a shroud ripped from a ruined tent. The rain fell in sheets, transforming the ash-strewn ground into a bloody mire. Nasira walked away from the corral, head down, studying tracks in the mud. "This way." She pointed. "They went north."

"Don't say that!" Rhodri shuddered. "Where I come from it means something else."

"Where you come from putting women to the sword is an acceptable way of doing battle," Kilujen snapped.

"Not for me. Not ever. Why are you angry with me? I didn't do this." Rhodri watched Nasira track across the camp, and called out to her. "Are you tracking men, or horses?"

"Some of these horses had riders. The prints are deeper. Bare feet ran this way, horse and human. Quiet now, I need to think."

Rhodri and Kilujen followed her in silence, away from the camp, up a slight incline. The hoof prints were spread wide in open country, but Nasira found a set and followed them, weaving from side to side, until she came to a halt and indicated a cluster of low scrub. "There."

"Are you sure?" Rhodri asked. There was no sign of life.

"That's the way the tracks go. Where else could they hide?"

"They might be running."

"They're not running. They wouldn't abandon Trogir. It's not our way."

But there was no need to search for the tribe; as they approached, the bushes rustled, and a man emerged. He was limping, and his face was haggard, aged with sorrow and anger—it took a second glace before Rhodri realised it was Temion.

"Temion!" Nasira raced towards her brother, and he hugged her fiercely, but his eyes were fixed on Rhodri with the same cold stare Kilujen wore.

"We need to talk," Temion said.

Rhodri nodded. "More than talk. How many survivors?"

"Twenty-seven. Some hurt. Kilujen, Ginamor's here. She's wounded, but not badly. She keeps asking for you."

"Where is she?" Temion pointed, and Kilujen took off at a run.

Nasira glanced at Rhodri. "I should help him," she said. "I have a little skill . . ."

"Go on." He was reluctant to part with her, watching her back until she vanished into the scrub, leaving Temion eyeing him warily.

Nasira's brother broke the silence. "Where were you?"

"Walking the Spirit Trail. I should have been there, I know. You can't make me feel more guilt than I already do, Temion."

"Did you know what they were planning?" Temion's fist closed around his knife. "Did you?"

"Is that what you think? Shit, Temion!" Rhodri was staggered by the accusation. "That's what Kilujen thinks too! Nasira carries my child, why would I betray her?"

"You weren't too pleased when you heard about the babe. Are you a spy? You've already betrayed one tribe . . . but perhaps you never betrayed them at all."

"You stood before me in the cave at Kharikan and accepted me as your brother. You have no idea—" *Alone* . . . Rhodri turned away, not caring about the knife. Let Temion strike him between the shoulder blades rather than think him a traitor. "You don't know what that meant, to be accepted into a family. To have a real brother. You think I'd throw it away for a tribe that had already cast me out?"

"But the babe—"

"Any problem I had with being a father, I've dealt with. It has nothing to do with my loyalty to the tribe!"

"I want to believe you, Rhodri—"

"You want me to prove it? Ride with me. We'll cut down the dogs who took Odval, and bring her back."

Temion took a step back, hand clasping his throat. "They took Odval?"

"You didn't know? Nasira heard her screaming—"

Temion sank to the ground. "I can't bear this. My baby sister . . ."

"You have to bear this." Rhodri stood over him. "Trogir is dead. You lead the tribe. What will you do?"

"Trogir dead too? No!" Temion buried his head in his arms. "I thought, I hoped— He stayed behind to defend the camp."

"All those who defended the camp are dead or captured. The camp was burned to the ground. You did well to get anyone away."

"I fled like a coward! I should have stayed to protect my uncle, my people . . ."

"There was nothing you could have done. If you'd stayed, you would have died with the rest of your tribe. Come on." Rhodri helped Temion to his feet. "We live, and we can fight. How many warriors do we have who can ride, and draw a bow?"

"Maybe nine?" Temion shook his head. "Some of them are just children. I tried to get the mothers and the youngest children away . . ."

"What about horses?"

"I let the horses go. Most of them are here, or can be rounded up. The short-hairs took a couple, I think, but it wasn't horses they came for. Your mare is safe, I made sure of that." He smiled weakly. "Rode her here myself."

Rhodri gave Temion a thump on the back, touched by this unexpected kindness in the midst of horror. "Get your warriors out here, those that can ride."

"You want to go after the short-hairs now?" Temion's eyes widened.

"I promised Nasira I'd get Odval back. The sooner we move, the better. Are you with me?"

*

Rhodri rode shoulder to shoulder with Temion, leading the small band of warriors back past the smouldering wreckage of their home. They skirted the camp. Temion wanted to honour the dead, but the risk to Odval increased by the moment. They pulled up by the river to consider their strategy.

"Their camp could be anywhere," Temion said. "They came out of nowhere, hit us from three directions at once. I've seen no fires on the horizon."

"I have," Rhodri said softly.

Temion rounded on him. "Where? When? Why didn't you tell me?" His eyes narrowed. "What do you know about this?"

"I thought it was another tribe. I climbed one of the Spire Rocks, the day Nasira told me about the baby. I saw smoke, but it was far to the south . . . How was I to know?"

"You didn't think to tell me?" Temion ground his teeth. "You could have spared us much pain, if you chose to— What?"

He rounded on Sudak, who was beckoning to him. The youth seemed to have escaped serious injury. "I found a blood trail on the ground." He pointed. "It leads west. Should we follow it?"

"Temion?" Rhodri urged as Nasira's brother hesitated. "Don't you think we should go after them? The longer we wait the more danger to Odval . . ."

Temion nodded. "Yes, of course. Sudak, you've got a keen eye for the trail, you take the lead. We'll follow."

After only a mile, it was obvious the raiders were heading for Spire Rocks. "Why would they go there?" Rhodri asked.

"Riding on rock leaves no prints. If they hide there, they could leave in any direction, and we'll lose Odval. We should hurry."

"Temion!" Up ahead, Sudak threw his hand up. "I think our trail ends here."

Rhodri trotted up to him, Temion at his heels. The ground was scuffed and churned with prints. A Kingdom soldier lay face down in the mud, a tribal blade protruding from his lower back. A few feet away, Trogir's wife Kediri sprawled on her back, throat slashed to ribbons. It was her blade embedded in the soldier's flesh.

Temion dropped to his knees beside her. "Beloved aunt," he said in a low voice. "Trogir would be proud. May you ride in peace at his side." He aimed a vicious kick at the dead soldier as he rose. "If they've killed Odval—"

"If they've killed Odval, may the seven hells take them!" Rhodri swung Liberty around with a savage jerk. "To Spire Rocks!"

As they neared the pillars, Temion gestured for caution. "We hunt vermin now," he said, his voice soft and deadly. "Don't let them escape. Find the prisoners, cut down any man who stands in your way."

The moment they entered the maze of rocks and boulders, Rhodri felt an uncomfortable prickle up the back of his neck. It reminded him of the narrow alleys of Northpoint. "This is the perfect place for an ambush," he muttered. "If I was fighting on their side, I'd set one up."

"What do you suggest?"

"Climb one of the spires and see how the land lies." Rhodri slipped from the saddle, removed his shirt and tore it into strips. "We have an advantage," he said, tapping Liberty's legs. She lifted her feet in turn so he could muffle her hooves. "Iron-shod hooves echo on stone. Bare feet don't. If I judge my former tribe right, they won't have considered that."

"So if we spot them, we can sneak up on them?" Temion nodded, answering his own question. "Sudak, shin up the spire and see what you can find out."

"Take your bow," Rhodri added. "You might be able to pick them off from that height."

The warrior band waited, still as the stone around them, while Sudak scrambled up the rock. Rhodri looped his arm round Liberty's neck, her muzzle against his chest, trying to swallow his fears for Odval. Nasira had been terrified by her ordeal at the hands of the King's Third, but Odval would be angry, and when she was angry she acted without thinking. He thought of Kediri, lying in the mud with her throat torn open. Had Odval seen that? Would she have the sense to stay calm and quiet?

Sudak slithered back down the spire, bringing with him a shower of pebbles and grit. "I can see them," he said. "They're about a quarter-mile to the north-west. They look as nervous as goats at a sacrifice."

"Was Odval with them?" Temion demanded.

"I couldn't see her."

Temion scowled. "Let's give them reason to be nervous."

"We'd best move quickly if you want to catch them in the rocks," Sudak said. "They'll be back on open ground soon."

"Lead the way." The war band trotted behind Sudak single file as he guided them through the labyrinthine columns of rock. "There's a canyon ahead," he whispered. "They were entering it when I saw them. If they're moving at the same speed, they should be halfway down by now."

"Steep sides?" Rhodri asked.

"The north face is sheer. The canyon runs east to west. The southern slope is steep, but we can ride it."

"Could we chase them the length of the canyon, send someone round to block the far end?" Temion asked. "That's not what you're thinking, is it?"

"There aren't enough of us. If they're trapped, they'll kill the prisoners. They won't expect us to come over the southern slope. I hope they'll scatter, or be pinned against the north escarpment. If we panic them, they might drop Odval and run. Is it the prisoners we want, or blood?"

"I want my sister back. If it takes killing, so be it."

"Take me to the slope." Rhodri followed Sudak on foot around to the edge of the canyon. The slope was treacherous, but a bold horse could take it. Far below, the New Kingdom soldiers crept along, jumping at shadows. There were around fifty of them, but he couldn't pick out faces at this height. Nor could he see Odval.

Are we chasing a phantom? Maybe Odval was already dead, her body discarded in a gulley. He had to find out.

He reported back to Temion as he stripped the bindings from Liberty's feet. The vengeful Atrathenes gathered at the edge of the slope, Liberty jogging her front feet as she sensed Rhodri's anticipation. He patted her neck. "Are you ready, girl? Time to go to work!"

At Temion's war cry, his warriors poured over the edge, whooping and hollering, making the noise of a party ten times their size. Arrows seared down amongst the panicked Westerners. Rhodri took out three with his bow before he reached the foot of the slope, and whipped out his blade. His old comrades, caught by surprise, had no time to draw before the tribe crashed down among them. Some fled, only to be brought low by Atrathene arrows.

Rhodri heard a voice yelling orders, a core of resistance forming, backs against the sheer northern wall. He pirouetted Liberty on her hind legs, slashing either side to bring down the men who tried to grapple his legs. This was not about Odval now. It was about revenge.

"*You!*" His sabre met another, a jarring crash that numbed his arm. Beneath his assailant's helm, blue eyes glittered, the left beneath a drooping eyelid. He had known those eyes for years.

Dru charged him, swinging his blade two handed. Rhodri flattened himself to Liberty's neck as it whistled through his hair.

"You back-stabbing shit! Have you gone native?"

Liberty danced back as Dru lunged, steel grinding against steel as their horses pressed shoulder to shoulder, Killer forcing the mare towards the wall, her hooves scrabbling on the rocky ground.

"You bastard! Where's my sister?"

Rhodri yelped as his leg crunched against the wall. Pinned. His leg would snap like a twig under any more pressure. Liberty's eyes rolled and she twisted to sink her teeth into Killer's neck.

The gelding squealed, rearing to shake her off, and Rhodri ducked under Dru's guard and smashed his blade down on the mailed forearm.

"Your sister?" Dru fumbled his grip on his sabre as Killer backed away from Liberty's clashing teeth and hooves. "I bloody knew it! You *have* gone native! No mercy for traitors, Rhodri."

"Found your honour up your horse's arse, did you?" Free of the wall, right leg on fire, Rhodri swung around to ward off Dru's feeble blow. "I know where my loyalty lies, and it's not with you."

"You're dead, you little bastard!"

Dru switched his blade to his left arm, a swing that struck Liberty's muzzle a glancing blow. She shook her head, whinnying in fear, but Rhodri had the advantage now that Dru fought with his weaker hand. He feinted, striking with darting moves that pushed Dru out into the canyon, away from his men, into the shower of arrows. Killer had the weight, but Liberty was nimble, dodging his hooves.

"Look around, Dru. Your men are broken. It's not my life that's over."

Killer backed against a rock. Dru uttered a command, and he reared, hooves flashing. Liberty sprang back, a loose stone turning under her foot. Rhodri felt her slip, a sickening jerk, and Killer's iron-shod hoof crashed down on her shoulder.

She squealed and pulled away. Rhodri fought her, determined not to let her bolt. Killer barged the little mare aside, racing for the canyon entrance. Liberty, desperate to obey, tried to follow, but blood poured down her leg. Rhodri pulled up.

"Shit!"

Dru glanced over his shoulder, saw the pursuit had failed, and slowed. "Fuck you, Rhodri! I know who you are, and who your father was. I'll make sure everyone knows you're the Northpoint bastard! You set foot over the border again—" He ducked as an arrow whirred overhead, turned, and fled for his life. His surviving men, seeing their leader in flight, broke their resistance and followed.

"I missed him." Temion rode up as Rhodri dismounted. "Is your mare hurt?"

Liberty had a long gash in her shoulder, and the surrounding flesh was swollen. She shied away from Rhodri's touch. He shook his head. "I can't ride her like this. Did you find Odval?"

"I saw her." Sudak bent double, hands on his knees, a thin stream of blood running down his face. "She ran up the canyon. I tried to follow her . . ."

"I'll find her," Rhodri said at once. "You did your best, Sudak. Were there any other prisoners?"

"Ask him." One of the New Kingdom casualties groaned as Temion kicked him. As he lifted his head, struggling to focus, Rhodri recognised Luk. Temion dragged him into a sitting position. He cradled his right arm, wrist drooping in his lap.

Luk blinked at Rhodri. "What are you doing here? The sergeant said to kill you on sight . . ." His head dropped. Temion pulled it up by the hair. "What's he saying, Rhodri? You speak their tongue."

"He says they were meant to kill me on sight. Let his head down, Temion. He can't talk with you stretching his neck."

"Why would they want to kill you? How do I know you're not lying?"

"He's not lying." One of the warriors, a scarred older woman, rested her hand on Temion's arm. "I can make out some of their talk. What Rhodri says is true."

Temion released his hold on Luk's hair. "Find out about the prisoners."

Rhodri crouched on his haunches before his former comrade. "You took prisoners from the savage camp. How many?"

"Two." Luk shook his head, blinking. "A woman and a girl. We killed the woman. These savages fight like demons. Did the sergeant send you to ask me?"

"If you like." Rhodri looked at Temion and held up two fingers.

The Atrathene nodded. "Ask him where their camp is. How many men?"

"I know what to ask, Temion. I had to interrogate your sister once."

117

A spasm of pain crossed Temion's face. "If it wasn't for you, she'd be where Odval is now . . ."

"Or worse," the scarred woman added. "I was with them a moon before I escaped. I was a girl then, but we don't forget, do we Rhodri?"

"No, we don't forget." He had to demand the information twice. Luk had trouble understanding his words. Blood trickled from his nose and ears. "You know where the camp is, Lance-corporal. You were with us. Weren't you?"

"I got lost. Help me find my way back."

Luk sniggered, sagging against Temion. "You never get lost. You're special. That's what the sergeant says, why he told us to kill you . . ."

"What does he say, Rhodri?" Temion asked.

"Nothing of any use. His mind is broken."

"Then what good is he?" Temion threw Luk to the ground, exposing the gaping wound in the back of his skull; they had been lucky to get anything from him. "Finish him. We need to find my sister. I would leave him for the patchcats and carrion-birds, but he's your tribe. If you want to be merciful . . ."

With a heavy heart, Rhodri drew his mercy blade. Luk whimpered at the sight. His mind might be fractured, but years of conditioning at Northpoint held strong. He knew what he was looking at.

"It's just a headache, Rhodri! You ask the sergeant. He'll tell you! You should listen to Drusain, Rhodri. He knows what's best . . ."

"I wish that were true." Rhodri caught him by the hair, stretching his head back until the skin on his neck was taut. Luk's life vein pulsed below his jaw.

"You can't stick me, Rhodri!" His eyes rolled in fear. "I'm on your side! I won't tell him I saw you—"

"I'm sorry." Biting his lip, Rhodri pierced Luk's throat, life draining away under his hands. He pulled the blade free as Luk's eyes glazed, letting his victim's head fall. He wiped the blade and slammed it back into the hilt. They called it mercy, but in his mind it was vengeance. So why did it feel like murder?

He rose with a shudder of disgust. "Let's find Odval."

The warriors spread out, leaving the bodies of the fallen where they lay, insects buzzing in their open wounds. Rhodri had little hope of finding Odval unhurt, but Sudak said she was running, and if she had the strength and will to run, there was a chance she would survive. Climbing onto a rock to survey the landscape, his eye was drawn to a fluttering piece of cloth caught in a crevice. At first he thought it was a torn rag from her dress, until he saw a small, bare foot, dirty and bleeding, ill-concealed in the crack.

"Odval?" A shuffling sound, the clatter of falling pebbles as the foot vanished. "Odval, it's Rhodri. Are you hurt?"

Silence. He gestured to Temion as he scrambled up to the crevice, head-height from the ground. "Odval?"

The girl was crammed into the gap where the columns split like forked tree branches. Her eyes were rimmed with red, her mouth bound with a filthy, blood-stained rag. She raised her hands, trussed at the wrists, trying to push him away, kicking out with her feet.

"Odval, it's me! Don't you know me?" Rhodri drew his dagger to slash her bonds. She whimpered, pressing back against the rocks.

"I won't hurt you." He gripped her hands to free her wrists. She struggled so violently he feared he would cut her by accident. He sliced through the rag muffling her mouth, and as it fell away she screamed, beating his chest with balled fists.

"Leave me alone! Don't touch me! *I hate you!*"

"What's going on?" Temion, breathless, clambered up the rocks to join them. "Why is she screaming?"

"Temion!" She threw herself into his arms. "The short-hair, he wanted to hurt me, like the others . . ." Her words were lost beneath a flood of sobbing.

"That's not a short-hair, it's Rhodri. You know Rhodri." Their eyes met over her head.

"You know Rhodri," Temion repeated. "He's our brother."

She said nothing, only wailed and burrowed her head into Temion's shoulder as he carried her to the ground. Her dress was ripped down the front, rucked up to reveal ugly purple bruises on her thighs. Her budding breasts were stained with bloody handprints.

Temion set her down and swathed her frail form with his own cloak. She clutched his arm as he turned on Rhodri. "Your tribe did this."

"They're not my tribe." Rhodri clenched his fists. He would kill Dru for this. "They will never be my tribe again. They came here looking for a war, and I swear on my name, I'll bring them their war."

Chapter Six

TEMION STARED AT Rhodri, as if weighing up whether he could trust him. "You want to chase them now? What about Odval?"

"I'll take her back," Sudak offered. "I can carry her, and lead the little mare, if Rhodri doesn't mind."

Rhodri turned his attention to Liberty, running shaking hands across her shoulder, probing the wound as she snorted and backed away. It wasn't as deep as he feared, and her muscles felt sound. He had needle and thread in his saddlebag, and he sluiced out the cut with ale and stitched it while Sudak held a twitch to the mare's upper lip to keep her calm. The care he had to apply to the task calmed him to the point where he could eventually speak again. If Dru had been within reach, he would have run him through, slowly, twisting the blade in his gut so it took him many bells to die. The way it had taken Astan. There was no justice under the stars, that Astan had fallen while Dru still lived to taunt him.

"Do you want me to take her?" Sudak asked as the silence stretched unbearably between them. "You can have my ride."

Rhodri found his voice. "Yes, take her," he said. "Take Odval straight to Kilujen. Don't let Nasira see her like this, it won't be good for the baby."

"As you wish." Sudak handed over the reins of his mount.

Temion lifted Odval into Sudak's arms, carrying her like a rare, fragile treasure. He watched Sudak lead the mare out of the canyon, and turned to Rhodri. "You say they're no longer your tribe, but can you hunt them down? If not, go back to Nasira—"

"I can hunt them down, and I can kill them. I *will* kill them." Rhodri mounted Sudak's roan gelding. "Let's hunt."

The landscape beyond Spire Rocks was empty, but the trail led south. The warrior party cantered after their prey, Rhodri growing accustomed to the longer stride of a horse taller than Liberty. They rode until it was too dark to see, waking with the dawn to hunt again. The trail was fading, but still Temion led them south, unwavering. Rhodri rode silent and grim at his shoulder. With every passing mile, the ball of fury in his gut grew hotter.

Temion pulled up, pointing. "Fire on the horizon. Ride with care."

The roiling brown cloud stretched across the sky, too much smoke for a single fire. Rhodri clutched Temion's bridle with a feeling of dread. "We should walk from here," he warned. "Just you and me. This smells like trouble."

Temion nodded, calling his riders to halt. He slipped from the saddle and followed Rhodri across the steppe, keeping low, using every scrap of cover.

The source of the fire lay beyond a low hill, but even before they reached it, the rising stench made Rhodri gag. The smells of sweat, horses, open latrine pits and too many men living close together mingled with the smoke from the fires. On his belly, he wormed his way to the brow of the hill and looked down with a sharp intake of breath.

The camp covered the floor of the valley, stretching into the distance as far as he could see. Row upon row of tents, brown and green, with flags fluttering. Endless picket lines, supply wagons, festering fly-blown middens, a thousand campfires burning. He laid his forehead on the ground and groaned. Beside him, Temion whistled a bird call. "Where did they come from?"

"My sister sent them, the bitch."

"Your sister?"

"Never mind." Rhodri stared down at the massed armies of the west, willing them to be an illusion. But the stink rising from the camp was impossible to deny.

Temion's brow furrowed. "I never knew there were so many short-hairs in the world! How can we fight them?"

"We can't. There must be twenty thousand men down there, maybe more." He retreated on hands and knees. "We need to get back. Move the tribe far from here."

"You think they'll come hunting us?" Temion panted at his heels.

"I'm sure of it. We—*they*—were sent here for one reason: to wipe the tribes of Atrath from the earth, or die trying. That's what Serren—my sister—ordered. I didn't know it had gone this far."

"But where can we go?"

"Anywhere!" Far enough from the camp, Rhodri scrambled to his feet, and ran back to the horses. Temion outpaced him on his longer legs.

"Why would she do this, your sister?"

"I don't know, I don't know her!"

"You don't know your own sister?"

Rhodri swung into the saddle. "It's too complicated to explain. We have to get back!"

Temion fielded questions from his war band with an abrupt gesture. Rhodri was right, there was no time to talk. As one, they thundered north, with many anxious glances behind to see if they were followed.

Rhodri was so intent on keeping watch behind him, he was unprepared for trouble ahead. The first he knew of it was Temion barging him aside as an arrow flashed past his ear. At once, the air was full of missiles.

"Down! Get down!"

Rhodri flattened himself in the saddle, stretching across his back for his bow. A horse screamed, but he couldn't look up, could only see pounding hooves and the ground whizzing past underfoot. He hung on grimly with his knees, nocking an arrow as the horse veered left. Risking a glance, he counted four Kingdom soldiers, one bowman and three wielding sabres, charging towards the Atrathenes as they scattered in alarm.

Years of training conditioned him to fight by instinct, even on an unfamiliar horse. He loosed an arrow, ducking before he could see it strike, and heard a strangled cry. He circled round behind the swordsmen. The archer lay on his back on the ground, legs kicking. Temion yelled to rally his troops, unleashing a storm that took down the rest of the patrol as they scattered, but the rider closest to Rhodri spun his horse around to face him. Their eyes met as Rhodri unsheathed his sword.

"Rhodri? Rhodri of Pencarith? I thought you were dead!"

"Beron?" Rhodri had patrolled with this man, got drunk and whored together with him in Northpoint.

"What are you doing here? Captain Garrod will be pleased—" Beron broke off. Rhodri kept a tight grip on his blade. None of the patrol would live to report to the captain.

Beron paled as he raised his own sword. "So it's true. I didn't want to believe it, not of you—"

"Were you there?"

"Was I where?"

"When Drusain slaughtered my tribe! Were you there, you bastard? Did you fuck my little sister?"

"Rhodri, I don't know what you're talking about—"

"Liar!" Rhodri charged to meet him. Beron flung up his sword, warding him off with a jarring clash of metal. His horse slipped, staggering under the ferocity of the assault, hooves scrabbling on the muddy ground.

Beron didn't waste his breath on taunts. He galloped in, sabre low, aiming at Rhodri's unarmoured horse. The gelding reared in alarm, ears flat, nostrils flaring. Rhodri fought, one handed, to bring him under control. Liberty had been bred and trained for these situations, but Sudak's ride was terrified, muscles bunched to bolt.

124

Beron never reached his target. Outstretched blade a hair's reach from Rhodri, intent on his victim, he never saw Temion barrelling in from the side to knock him from the saddle. He rolled as he fell, coming up with blade in hand. Abandoning his frightened mount, Rhodri leapt to the ground to confront him. His head was full of the image of Odval, brutalised and afraid. Maybe Beron had nothing to do with the assault, but he was one of Serren's men. The army that had cast him out, slaughtered his tribe. By the hells, they would pay in blood.

Beron put up a desperate defence, gasping, slithering in the mud, but his longer reach was no protection from Rhodri's fury. As his ankle turned on the treacherous ground, a low blow knocked his from his feet. Twisting, Rhodri drove the tip of his blade down into an unprotected spot at the base of his throat. Beron's lips moved silently, blood bubbling up between them, and Rhodri saw the confusion and betrayal in his eyes. He yanked the blade free in a spurt of crimson. "Hells!"

"Well done, brother." Temion slapped him on the shoulder, but Rhodri hardly felt it. He stared down at Beron's glazed eyes, remembering the times they had spent together as boys. He stumbled away, fighting the onslaught of memory, and dropped to his knees in the mud to vomit. Behind him, he heard whoops of victory, but in his ears they were hollow, and he could not join in.

*

Temion's warriors met no further opposition. He set a fast pace home, and Rhodri was grateful. He longed for the sanctuary of Nasira's arms, away from the bloodshed and guilt.

The remains of the tribe camped in the scrubland north of the river. Salvaging what they could from their ruined settlement, they had improvised shelters from ripped canvas and sheets, fluttering brave defiance. The Plains Hawk are still here, those flapping banners said. They endure.

The twenty thousand men camped a few miles to the south were determined to crush that fantasy. Temion nudged Rhodri aside as they approached the camp.

"What should I tell them?" he asked, shaking the raindrops from his braids.

"Why ask me? You're their leader." Rhodri knew he was irritable, but Nasira was there, behind those frail canvas walls. He needed to be with her, to protect her from what was coming.

"Because I'm not ready to lead. I'm asking your advice, brother. What would you do?"

"How are you not ready to lead? You don't have a choice."

Temion turned away, but Rhodri had already guessed the truth, had seen it on the journey back. 'Pasture-bound', Astan had derisively referred to it, this shattering of nerves in the face of conflict or battle-trauma. There had been hardened soldiers back in the garrison at Northpoint, men who had fought in the war, or in keeping the uneasy peace that came after, who were fit for nothing more now than tending horses or growing crops. Temion's confidence in his own ability had taken a beating, and it would take time for him to get it back, if he ever did.

"If it was up to me, I'd take them back to Kharikan," Rhodri said.

"Kharikan? But it's summer. The maindy won't be running."

"There's more to eat at Kharikan than fish."

Temion scratched his head. "Kharikan is the winter place. No one goes there in summer. It's against tradition."

"This is no time to worry about tradition. If you want the tribe to survive, you'll have to break with the routine of generations. Can you do that?"

"I think so." Temion nodded. "Yes. If you and Kilujen say it's all right . . . But the tribe might find it hard to accept."

"Make them listen. They look to you for leadership, so lead. Bring them together and tell them we have to leave. I'll help you spread the word. But first I'm going to find my wife."

126

Rhodri found Nasira tending the sick and wounded, shaded by a tattered sheet spread between two trees. It let in light, but also rain, and the ground beneath her feet was churned to soup. It was no place to keep wounds clean. Watching her move between her patients, he saw the deep lines of strain on her face. Odval trotted at her heels, never venturing out of her shadow, constantly touching her for reassurance. It sickened Rhodri to see the vivacious girl reduced to this.

He cleared his throat, reluctant to draw attention to himself when Nasira was so busy. She looked up, saw him, and a cloud lifted from her eyes.

"Rhodri!" She ran to him, throwing her arms around him. "I'm so glad you're back! It's been awful here without you. Ginamor died, and Odval—"

"I know about Odval," he said, softly. "What happened to Ginamor?"

"She was bleeding inside. She didn't say anything. By the time we found out, it was too late."

Rhodri blinked back the tears. Another friend taken from him. "Kilujen must be devastated."

"I haven't seen him. He won't come here . . ." She leaned against him, and he felt her trembling. It was as if the strength that had kept her going over the last few days had leached from her limbs. "To lose another wife . . . I couldn't bear it."

"Another wife?"

"Kilujen was married before, when he was very young. This must be so hard for him."

"Even so, he shouldn't have left you alone with all this. Especially not when you're carrying a baby. When did you last sleep?"

"I wasn't alone. I had Odval to help me." Nasira stretched her arm out to her sister, who hung back, scowling at Rhodri. As their eyes met, she turned and ran.

"Don't be upset." Nasira sensed his hurt at the rejection. "She's in pain, body and spirit. I gave her a herb to stop any babies coming, but I can't make her feel better. When she looks at you, she sees *them*—" She uttered a little sob. "What will we do, Rhodri?"

"We're going away from here. All of us, tonight."

"Going away? Where? Where can we go?"

"To Kharikan." He saw doubt in her face. "Temion agrees with me. There's shelter there, and food. I don't want my son born in the mud. And there's more." He lowered his voice. "The short-hairs are here. Not just a raiding party, but more men than there are grasses on the plain. We ran into a patrol on the way back. We killed them, but it won't be long before they come after us, to finish what they started. That's why we have to get away."

"But to Kharikan? Will we live in caves all summer?"

"My people have always defended themselves behind stone walls. If it works for them, why not for us?" He laid a hand on her belly. "I want you to be safe. How's our little one?"

"He kicks like an angry colt. I think he missed you."

"He'll be a strong one." At his words, the baby gave a vigorous kick. Nasira winced. "He knows his father's voice too."

"I wish he'd listen to his mother telling him to stop kicking her." She sighed. "He'll need his strength, won't he?"

"I hope not." Rhodri hugged her close. "I hope we have enough strength between us to carry him. Come on, Temion wants us at a meeting. Then you can rest. I'll take over here."

The meeting was in full spate when they arrived, and Temion had trouble making his voice heard over the howls of protest. A return to Kharikan in summer was an unacceptable break with sacred tradition. Rhodri sat and listened to him plead with them. Nasira pressed against his side. "This was your idea," she said, in a soft voice. "Why does Temion claim it's his?"

"No one wants to listen to me after what happened. You saw Odval. Temion is our leader. He can take the credit if it keeps us alive."

But Temion was losing the tribe. Kilujen, red-eyed and shrunken, staggered to his feet to denounce him, Rhodri, and the whole world. No one, not even the dead, escaped his ire. Rhodri felt he should step in and say something, but before he could offer Nasira pushed to her feet, one hand pressed into the small of her back. "May I speak, brother?"

Temion frowned, but nodded. "If you feel you have something to contribute. As I said, it's time to put aside old traditions."

"Thank you." She inclined her head. "What Temion says is true. We need to leave for Kharikan, and we're wasting time discussing it."

Kilujen sprang up, eyes blazing. "You only speak for Temion because your iron-foot tells you to. He herds us into a trap!"

"I speak as I choose, Kilujen. I know you're in pain, but hear me out." There was a dangerous rumble in Nasira's throat. Rhodri reached up to catch her hand, and felt her nails dig into his wrist. He willed her to calm down, before more harm came from her anger. She took a deep breath.

"I speak as I choose, not for the short-hairs. Rhodri—"

"Where was Rhodri when we were attacked? He says he walked the Spirit trail, but how do you know he wasn't lighting signal fires for his friends?"

There were mutters of agreement. Rhodri clenched his fists. Fighting would do no good.

"Because I followed him into the Spirit Realm, as you know. I saw him grieve for Trogir, and ride to save Odval. He took arms for us against his old tribe, and cut them down to buy us time. Time *you*"—she stabbed a long-clawed finger at the shaman—"waste with these accusations! I ride to Kharikan tonight, with Temion and Rhodri. You can stay here and wait for the short-hairs." Her voice lowered. "Because they *are* coming, and when they get here, they will show no mercy. Have you ever known them grant mercy to any but their own kind? If Rhodri says twenty thousand men are racing to fall on us with upraised swords, I believe him. I say we waste no more time."

129

"I agree." Borta struggled to her feet, leaning heavily on her cane. Her wrinkled face was streaked with tears. "I have known Rhodri Short-hair as long as any of you. I told him there must be trust between us, and I show that trust now. I don't believe he wishes harm on this tribe, on the family of his unborn child. Why would he? We are bonded by blood—"

"His blood is Western!" Kilujen spat his contempt.

"His son will ride between two worlds. It's a hard road to travel, and he'll need our support. I have no love for short-hairs, but I won't sit here and wait to be trampled under their hooves. I'm with Temion, I say we leave, and leave now. Besides,"—she thumped her stick into the ground—"what is there to stay here for? Poor shelter, no food, and if we don't leave, soon we'll have no tribe!" The old lady staggered, and sank back to the ground, shaking off hands that offered assistance. "I've said my piece," she declared, glaring around with hawk eyes, daring anyone to argue with her.

Once Nasira's grandmother threw her lot in, the discussion was over. There was little to pack, no evidence the tribe had lived here but footprints and broken branches. Bareback, without reins or bridles, defeated but not destroyed, the last of the Plains Hawk tribe set out under the moonlight, following the path of the river back to Kharikan.

*

Temion pushed his people hard, fearing pursuit. Nasira was tired and in pain, Odval sunk into her silent sorrow, and Kilujen would not speak to Rhodri. They were no longer a tribe, but individuals forced to travel in the same direction, thrown together by circumstance. Only Nasira's indefatigable grandmother kept them going, riding up and down the line, cajoling the stragglers, handing out treats from her limited supply. She prodded them onwards when even Temion sagged against the neck of his horse in fatigue.

After over a moon of hard travel, Temion halted his horse and pointed. The rock lay on the horizon, ancient as time, solid as a fortress. A ragged cheer rose from the throats of the tribe at the thought of food, and sleep between walls, no longer exposed to the sky. Temion nudged his horse over to Rhodri and clapped him on the shoulder. "I thought we'd never get here. I hope your idea keeps us safe."

"It'll be hard," Rhodri admitted. The grass hadn't had time to recover from winter grazing, there were no stores in the rock, and the maindy wouldn't spawn for moons. But they were alive, and that was a small victory.

Nasira looked around. "Where's Grandmother? She should see this. Grandmother!"

"Maybe she fell behind," Rhodri said. "I'll go back and look for her."

He found Borta's horse ambling along a few hundred feet behind the rest, snatching at strands of grass. There was no sign of the old lady. He didn't want to call out in case he alarmed Nasira, but his anxiety increased as he followed the trail back the way they had come.

Borta sat on the side on the track, huddled in her ragged cloak, head resting on her knees. Rhodri knew she was dead before he reached her. She looked as if she had dropped off, and would wake at any minute. She had a smile on her lips, and he wondered if she knew they had reached Kharikan, if that was why she had held on to life for this past moon.

With a sorrowful sigh, he lifted her body on to Liberty's back, marvelling at how light she was, and returned to break the sad news to her family.

*

Despite Borta's death, life went on. The horses were fenced in a mobile corral, moved from one skimpy patch of grass to another, further and further from the rock. There was little food; if the whole tribe had been there they would have starved, but between fish, tumblers and the occasional goat, the survivors struggled through the summer months of famine. Rhodri gave most of his food to Nasira. Always slender, now he could count his ribs when he breathed in. The gnawing in his belly kept him awake at night, and hunger and fatigue played tricks with his mind. There was too much time to think, lying awake staring into the dark, his unborn child kicking at his side.

It was late summer, a stifling night. In two moons, the other tribes would return to Kharikan in time for the maindy run. Rhodri would be a father by then. Nasira suffered with her pregnancy in the heat, showing the same quiet forbearance that carried her through the famine and the death of her beloved grandmother. He loved her dignity, her unflinching grace in the face of adversity. Without her, he would have given in to despair long ago.

Restless, he rolled away from the warmth of her sleeping body. They slept in the cave they had shared the previous winter, and he walked to the opening and sat on the lip, legs dangling over hundreds of feet of empty air. A wisp of a breeze played over his bare skin, not enough to cool him. The moons poured silver light down the slopes, and the tumblers darted in and out of the shadows in a mysterious game of their own. Everything was peaceful. His chosen people had endured, and survived.

So why does my heart feel so sick?

He buried his head in his hands, trying, as he had tried and failed so many times, to blot out the memories. Odval's screams rang in his ears; he only had to close his eyes to see Trogir, nailed to a fence, bleeding to death, Luk falling to his knees, Beron. Beron was the worst. His old friend was blameless, but he had forced the blade through his throat, tried to justify his actions with accusations he knew were false, to make himself feel better.

In his ears, he could hear the echo of Valery's voice, calling across the barrier between life and death . . .

You drove away your mother. You're alone now . . .

"Come back to bed." Nasira's words slurred with sleep. "Don't make me come over there, terrible boy."

"I can't sleep." Below his feet, the rocks were swallowed in shadow. It was easy to pretend it was only a few feet down.

"You sit there every night. I miss you. Come back to me, my Rhodri."

"I'm right here," he told her, staring into the chasm.

"You're not. You're far away in your head." She padded across the stone floor of the cave, and her hand brushed the back of his neck. Short nails, he noted. "It's not so bad when you can't see the bottom," she observed.

"That's what I thought."

"You thought you could hop off the ledge, and all this guilt you carry would go away? Is that it?"

"No—"

"Because it won't. You will walk in shame in the Spirit Realm, carrying not only the guilt you feel now, but the burden of leaving me here alone, with our child." She sighed. "Why don't you talk to me? I know your thoughts better than anyone."

He leant back against the solid curve of her stomach, stretching a hand to caress the bump. "You know me too well, Nasira."

She lowered herself beside him with a lot of puffing. He drew her head down to his shoulder.

"You feel bad because you were looking for your father when you should have been defending the tribe. Am I right?"

Rhodri sighed. "Actually, I was thinking about Beron."

"Who is Beron?"

"He was my friend. We used to drink together, and chase women. We weren't close, but I knew him well enough—" He broke off, choked.

"Why do you think about him now?"

"I killed him. He was in the patrol we ran into. He knew me, he was pleased to see me . . . and I stabbed him in the throat. I watched him die while he stared right into my eyes. How do I forget that?" He massaged his temples. "Tell me how you forget. Teach me. There's so much in my head I don't want to remember! My father, Odval . . . all of it. How can I make it go away?"

"My love, I wish I knew." Nasira cradled his head against her breast. "If I had the power, I'd take these memories from your mind. But even a person with a normal memory finds some things impossible to forget." She kissed him, comforting him like a child. "We will make new memories, you and I. Good memories, to drive the bad ones to the back of your head. Weave the pattern of our story into your mind."

"I can't. Our story is full of pain and blood."

"It won't always be like that." She held him close, her bare skin warm in the humid air. Rhodri was beginning to drop off when he heard her gasp.

"What's wrong?"

"I don't know. A pain. Help me stand up."

He struggled to lift her to her feet. She had been having pains, on and off, for a few days. "Is it the same as before?"

"I don't think so." Nasira winced. "No, it's not. Help me down to the main cave."

"It's the middle of the night. Wouldn't you rather stay here?"

"No I would not!" He stepped back as she snapped, wary of her claws.

"What can I do to help?" He hated seeing her in pain. It made him feel so helpless.

"Pass me the blanket." She snatched it from him as he tried to drape it round her shoulders. "Don't fuss. I don't need— ah!" Rhodri steadied her as she doubled up in pain. "It's time, I know it."

"Time for what?" Belated realisation dawned. "Is the baby coming?"

134

"Coming soon, I think. Take me down to the cave. Wake Kilujen and Temion. Odval might want to know . . ."

"I don't want Kilujen there," Rhodri said flatly. "He hates me, and he hates our babe."

"What are you talking about?" Nasira clung to his arm as they walked.

"The things he said, about Western blood . . . I don't want Kilujen near our baby."

"Well, I do." There was a dangerous glint in Nasira's eyes. "He's our shaman. He has to be there in case anything goes wrong."

"You think things might go wrong?" The thought hadn't occurred to him. "You don't have to be scared. I won't leave your side."

"That's what you think." The communal cave echoed to the sound of their voices. Rhodri spread the blanket on the floor.

"Do you want to lie down?"

"Not yet." She paced back and forth, hands pressed into her back, panting like a dog on a hot day. "It's coming again. Hold on to me!" She dug her nails into Rhodri's arm as he held her until the contraction passed. "Get help," she said. "Wake them up. I don't want to do this on my own."

"You won't be on your own—"

"Do as I say, Rhodri! Please!"

Rhodri raced through the maze of caves in panic, calling for Kilujen, rousing the tribe. The shaman's sleeping cave was up a tight spiral of rock, and he smashed his knee as he ascended. "Kilujen! I need you!"

He skidded into the cave, stumbling over his own feet. Kilujen's sleeping mat was empty, candlelight falling on a bed that hadn't been slept in. Kilujen lay on the floor, breath coming in shallow gasps. The rope tethering him to the world of the living stretched taut from beneath his body, lashed around a stalagmite.

Rhodri hesitated. He had never brought anyone back from the Spirit realm, only watched Ginamor do it for her husband. Love brought you back, but Kilujen had lost his soulmate, and he had

135

no love for Rhodri, not any more. But he had to try, for Nasira, and for the sake of their baby.

He took the rope in both hands, feeling it quiver, and closed his eyes. He thought of Nasira, in pain, and how much she needed Kilujen, and pictured himself drawing the shaman back into the world, hand over hand. The rope fought him, he felt it sliding through his palms, and clutched it tighter.

"Kilujen, come back! Nasira needs your help!"

He didn't know if he spoke aloud, or in his mind. All he knew was that he had to keep hauling the lifeline. He gave it a sharp jerk, and with a sound like fabric tearing, the air above the circle ripped in two. Kilujen twitched and choked, clutching at his head.

He threw Rhodri an evil look. "Why have you called me back? I was with my wife!"

"I nearly fell under a curse last time I walked the Spirit Trail alone," Rhodri reminded him. "It's too dangerous. That's what you told me."

"What's dangerous for you is less so for me." Kilujen sat up, retching. "Fetch my flask." Rhodri did as he was bid, and the shaman took a long draft. "What do you want? It's not even dawn."

"Nasira needs you. She's having her baby."

"Why does she want me?" Kilujen turned away in disgust. "I don't care about your mongrel brat."

Rhodri grabbed him by the shoulder and spun him around, seizing his throat and forcing him back against the wall. "That's my child you're talking about!"

Kilujen's eyes bulged, and he scrabbled at Rhodri's hand. Rhodri tightened his grip until the shaman's face purpled.

"I'm sorry you lost your woman. If I could go back and change what happened, I would. I have to live with my guilt, but Nasira is *my* wife, and I won't let anything happen to her." He twisted the skin of Kilujen's throat. Drool bubbled at the corners of his mouth as his lips worked soundlessly. "Whatever you think of me, and my son, Nasira is your cousin. Help her, or I'll kill you."

He let go and stepped back. Kilujen dropped to the floor, breath rasping, clutching his neck. Rhodri prodded him with his foot. "Get up."

The shaman struggled to his feet, shaking his head. "You short-hairs are all the same," he croaked. "Thugs and animals."

"Go and help my wife." Rhodri caught Kilujen by the shoulders, and shoved him towards the exit, following to ensure he arrived in the cave. They were intercepted by Temion at the bottom of the spiral. His hair hung loose and dishevelled down his back.

"What's going on?" he asked.

"Nasira's having her baby. I have to get back to her."

"Not so fast." Temion grabbed his arm. "She doesn't want you with her."

Rhodri shook him off. "What are you talking about?"

"Come with me, brother." Temion wrapped an arm around Rhodri's shoulders and steered him away. "Leave the birthing to the women. We'll hunt wild game for the feast!"

"But Nasira—" Rhodri glanced over his shoulder. Kilujen vanished into the cave. He hoped the shaman would take care of Nasira, regardless of his troubled feelings.

"She's well looked after. You'd get in the way. You don't want to see her in pain, do you?"

"No, but—"

"Then come on!"

Dawn was a faint glow below the eastern horizon as Temion and Rhodri mounted and rode away from the rock, hunting bows slung over their shoulders. They cantered a long time with little sign of game, and the further they travelled, the greater Rhodri's anxiety grew, until eventually he pulled up.

"Let's go back," he said. "I'm worried."

"Do you want a break?" Temion dismounted and let his horse run loose, squatting on his haunches in the long grass. "This is good grazing. We should bring the herds out this way."

"Why can't we go back? Are you hiding something from me?"

"Come down here, my brother. Share a drink with me." As Rhodri hesitated, he added, "They won't let you see her, even if we go back. You might as well enjoy the sunshine, and the hunt."

He spoke so reasonably Rhodri was persuaded he was right. He let Liberty run free and joined Temion in the grass. The Atrathene warrior sat cross-legged, braiding his waist-length hair, which he had dragged into a loose horse-tail as they left the rock. Rhodri lay watching him, admiring the quick, supple movement of his fingers. He had a brief vision of those fingers stroking his spine, holding him close, and he pushed it away. Temion wasn't the type of man he was normally attracted to, and besides, he was Nasira's brother. Was it baby-madness making him think this way? He groaned and tried to focus on the yellow insect industriously climbing up the grass stem in front of him.

"Don't fret. Nasira will be fine."

Temion was so calm, so solid, like a rock rising from the plain. His stoic form helped ease Rhodri's anxiety.

He glanced at the sun. "Do you think it's over yet?"

"It took Siralane over a day to have our first," Temion told him. "The babe will be born when it's ready. That's when the fun starts."

"Do you like being a father?"

"It's better than hunting!". This was high praise; Temion lived for the hunt.

"Talking of hunting." Rhodri rolled onto his belly. "We're not making much effort. I thought you wanted to bring home enough for a feast."

Temion shrugged. "It would be fine to have a feast, but I brought you here to keep you out of the way. It's traditional. The women flutter over the birthing, the men make themselves scarce. Especially the anxious father!" He grinned. "The last thing they need is you panicking and getting in the way. Trogir took me fishing when I first became a father. I didn't even realise Siralane was labouring until I came back and she put my son in my arms."

138

"What happened to him?" Rhodri asked, quietly. Temion had two little girls, and Siralane was expecting a third child.

"He caught a winter fever." Temion's eyes clouded. "I'm sure he rides a little pony on the Spirit Trail, but it still hurts."

"I'm sorry. I didn't know . . ." Silence fell, and in the void Rhodri sought to change the subject. "We have to do something about the short-hairs."

"What can we do but run? We can't fight the whole of the west. There aren't enough of us."

"If we don't fight, they won't stop coming. We've lost grazing land to the south, and east. If Serren keeps sending men at this rate, they'll reach Kharikan in a couple of summers."

"Do you and Serren have the same parents? You said you didn't know her . . ." Temion brightened. "Does she ride with her men?"

"No. She sends them to fight in her name."

"Then she's no leader. If she rode with her army, you could find her, talk to her. Tell her she's wrong to take our land—"

"She doesn't recognise me as her brother. She wouldn't listen."

"You short-hairs have a strange idea of family." Temion shook his head. "Talking of family, we should hunt.—just to keep up the pretence." He winked at Rhodri. "My sister will tear a strip off us if we don't come back with food."

He whistled, and his horse trotted back to him. Liberty followed, a few blades of grass sticking out of her mouth. She snorted and nudged Rhodri with her nose as he swung a leg over her bare back. "Temion? Will we be able to trade for saddles this winter?"

Temion nodded. "Saddles, tents, the lot. We won't have any new brides when we leave Kharikan. I might have to trade Odval, though it will break Nasira's heart."

Rhodri chilled at the thought. "Isn't she too young?"

"Before, I would have said so." Temion scanned the horizon for game. "But Nasira tells me she's a woman now. And she knows the ways of men, thanks to your tribe. Young girls make better trade, and we need all the supplies we can get." He pointed. "That way. It's a good spot for deer."

"They're not my bloody tribe." Rhodri cursed in his native tongue as he thumped Liberty with his heels, following Nasira's brother in the direction he indicated. Odval had been taken by men, but that didn't mean she knew their ways, and she was terrified of being traded. No matter what goods Temion thought he could get for her, Rhodri would not let it happen. He suppressed a shudder at the thought, and readied his bow for the hunt.

*

Rhodri and Temion returned to Kharikan at sunset, carrying the bodies of two fleet, spiral-horned deer that hadn't been quick enough to evade them. The tribe would eat well for a few days, and the excitement of the chase had pushed Rhodri's worry for Nasira to the back of his mind. They were nearing the rock when Temion pointed out a lone rider, cantering to meet them. As he drew closer, Rhodri saw it was Sudak, and raised a hand. "Good hunting, Sudak!"

"Not so good, cousin." The young warrior's braids were awry, and his horse was foaming. "I've been looking for you."

"What's wrong?" Rhodri tasted bile in his throat. "Has something happened to the babe?"

"The babe is fine. Nasira—"

Rhodri didn't wait to hear. He dug his heels into Liberty's flanks, crouched low against her neck and thundered towards the rock, wind rushing in his ears and the blood pounding in his veins.

He threw himself from the mare's back and scrambled up the rope ladders and across the swaying bridges, back to the cavern. The rings around his ankles clattered and jarred against the bare rock face, and he was panting as he stumbled into the passage leading to the cave. Odval barred his way, catching his arm with shaking hands. "You can't go in there."

"Let me see Nasira!"

She dug her heels in and hung on to him. "She had the baby and it was fine, but then she started bleeding and Kilujen had to fight to stop it. He doesn't know if she'll live."

"Get out of my way!"

"You wait here." Odval gave him a hard shove, and ran back into the cave. She returned with a bundle, thrust it into his arms. "Take her. She needs you."

"What?"

She fled without replying. Rhodri twitched the blanket away from the face of the child in his arms. She was scarlet, with a shock of black hair and an angry, screwed-up face. His daughter.

A shadow fell over him. Temion was breathless from the climb. "Sudak told me what happened," he said. "Is that your babe? Boy or girl?"

"A girl. She looks like her mother." Rhodri stared down at her in wonder, through tear-blurred eyes.

"Have you named her yet?"

"Nasira said not to talk about names until she was born. I thought she would choose . . ."

"You have to give her a name. The spirits won't recognise her without one. Our names are everything we are."

Rhodri nodded.

"A good Atrathene name. None of your Western rubbish, that means nothing." Temion smiled, but his grin was forced, and he twitched towards the mouth of the cave. "You think about it while I check on Nasira. I'll find out if you can see her."

He left Rhodri alone in the passage studying his infant daughter. She blinked at him, slowly, with deep blue eyes. She had a squashy nose, like his—and his father's. "A royal nose, baby girl."

She yawned, not caring about the shape of her nose.

"Look at you, not a worry in the world." He smiled. "I've got the perfect name for you, little one. In honour of someone I loved, a long time ago."

"Have you decided?" Temion stood in the doorway. "Nasira's awake. She asks for you. Although I warn you,"—he caught Rhodri's shoulder—"don't be upset by what you see. It was done for everyone's protection."

Cradling the baby against his chest, Rhodri followed Temion into the cave. Nasira lay spread-eagled on the floor, a blanket draped over her to protect her dignity. Her hands and feet were shackled to iron bars, and her mouth was bound tightly with a cloth. Tears squeezed from between her closed eyelids.

Kilujen knelt beside her. Rhodri took a menacing stride towards him, but Temion held him back.

"What have you done to her?" he demanded.

The shaman concentrated on stitching a long gash in his forearm, breaking the thin gut with his teeth before he replied. "If I hadn't bound her, she would have killed me," he said, "and the Spirit Trail would have three new riders. She lives, and so does your little one. The price was not too high."

He raised his head to reveal a bleeding bite wound on his cheek, and staggered to his feet. "Free her, if you dare," he spat. "I've done my duty, but I'll do no more. I don't deserve this. The mongrel child should have died."

Ignoring his barbs, Rhodri dropped to Nasira's side, fumbling one-handed with the straps that held her down. She smiled faintly. "Rhodri?"

"I'm here, little patchcat. What did you do to Kilujen?"

"He was hurting me. The beast took over."

"You made a mess of his face. He won't love you for that."

"His heart bleeds for Ginamor. Give him time to heal." She tried to sit up. "Can I hold our babe?"

Rhodri settled the baby on her chest, and Nasira cradled her as he released her feet. Other members of the tribe moved around them, cleaning up the mess of birthing, but he wasted no attention on them. Wincing, Nasira shuffled into a sitting position to let the babe suckle. Rhodri stroked her soft skull as she fed, overwhelmed by the rush of love she brought out in him.

"Did you give her a name?" Nasira asked, her voice heavy with regret. "I should have been there for her naming . . ."

"It wasn't your fault. Temion told me to give her a good Atrathene name. Not like mine." He grinned.

"You never told me what your name means. Is it rare, among your people?"

"I don't know what it means, whether I'm named after someone." Rhodri felt a pang of regret. Something else he had lost along the trail. "I might be, it's a common enough name. There were other boys where I learned to be a warrior who shared my name."

Nasira frowned. "A man should know what his name means. As long as you've given this little one a name that means something, I don't mind what it is. What did you call her?"

"Asta. I'm not sure what it means—"

"Asta? After your friend with the twin spirits? I like that. It means, you would say,"—she made a face, trying out the unfamiliar Western word—"*precious*. Like a gem. Did I get that right? It is a good choice, my short-haired boy."

"I'm glad you think so." He slipped an arm around her and watched their daughter feed. He had given her a fine name, and he would make sure he was a good father. He would remember Valery's mistakes, and learn from them. His little girl would never feel abandoned. She would always have a home.

Chapter Seven

RHODRI SAT ON the highest summit of Kharikan. He had dragged a blanket with him, and his two-moon-old daughter lay on her belly, cuddled close beside a doll Nasira had made her. He kept a close watch to ensure she didn't get cold, and his bow was ready to protect her from the circling eagles. She was tiny, so helpless, and he loved her so much.

"Look!" He picked her up and pointed to the wagons rolling across the plains, converging on the rock. "Mummy's people are coming back for winter. They're going to love you, my little dot!"

Asta yawned. Her head lolled against his chest as Rhodri watched the wagons approach. So many tribes, working together to survive. But there were few arriving from the west, and none from the south-west, and that troubled him. Thousands of people, following the rhythms of nature as they had for centuries, but Serren could wipe it all away in a few years. Did she realise what she had set out to destroy?

An idea squirmed in the back of his mind. It had been growing there a while, bubbling like stew in a pot, and now it rattled too loudly to be ignored. He needed to talk to Temion. Tucking Asta into the leather sling he wore across his chest, he kissed the crown of her head. Moving with care, he lowered himself down the nearest ladder, determined to find Nasira. He would need every ounce of her support to turn his idea into a reality.

*

"No. Absolutely not. It'll never happen."

Rhodri knew it would be hard to talk Temion round, but he hadn't anticipated such outright refusal. Nasira's brother folded his arms and stared into the middle distance, lips clamped tight. As far as he was concerned, the discussion was over.

"Why not?" Rhodri persisted. Beside him, Nasira bounced Asta on her knee. She, at least, had offered cautious support when he put the proposal to her.

"Because it's against all tradition. What happens if we fail?"

"If we don't try, what happens?" Rhodri flashed back. "Serren's army isn't going away. You don't know her—"

"Nor do you!"

"I served in her army for years. They're not going to turn around and leave. Serren sent them here to break the tribes of Atrath so they can never threaten her eastern border. That means they're going to push out from the mountains. Maybe even settle here, take grazing land for their farms, and raise their families. You're spirit-walking, Temion. One day you're going to open your eyes and wonder where your country went."

Nasira hushed him as Asta fretted, upset at his raised voice. He carried on in less heated tones.

"If you can think of another way to fight back, let me hear it. All I see are frightened tribes, fighting a hit-and-miss war they can't win, terrified of what Serren's men will do to their women and children."

"Your men can't win either," Temion insisted. "They can't hold this land while we live here."

"They're not my men. And they *are* winning. This summer they drove us back to Kharikan. By the time we recover, and ride out again, they'll have taken another swathe of the grasslands. They'll keep cutting us down until there's no one left to fight them. Already this winter there are whole tribes who haven't come back from the west. What do you think happened to them?" He sighed in frustration. "They don't want to defeat us, Temion. They want to *destroy* us. Trust me, I know."

"But what you suggest—- It's never been done before!" Persuading the tribes to break with ancient tradition was the hardest part of Rhodri's plan. If he could talk Temion into it, the rest might follow.

Nasira leant forward. "You say that, brother," she said, "but think of the maindy run."

"What does that have to do with it?"

"For one moon, all the tribes work together, for the good of everyone. We achieve so much more working together than we would if we were competing. If we can work together for a moon, why not for longer?"

"Serren thinks the tribes are fragmented," Rhodri added. "That's why she pushes her men east. If we stand together she might back down."

"What if she doesn't?"

"We'll lose everything if we don't try!" Asta grizzled, and Nasira glared at Rhodri. "Sorry. But I'm fighting for her, and for Temion's little ones. For the children of Atrath who will be driven from the lands that should be theirs by birth. And for Odval."

Silence fell across the trio, broken only by Asta's grumbling. Odval had been changed forever by her ordeal at the hands of Drusain's men. The confident, funny girl was lost behind a veil of shadow, and no one knew how to bring her back.

"I would do whatever it takes," he said in a soft voice, "to protect Asta from that. I know you'd do the same for your girls. Tell me you're with me, brother."

Temion nodded, slow and thoughtful. "I'm with you," he said at length, "for all the good it will do us. But you're right, we have to try."

"And you have to lead us."

"Me?" Temion looked startled. "Why me?"

"You got us through the summer alive, even if you doubted yourself at times. You listen to advice, but you're your own man." Rhodri hoped his support would help Temion settle more easily under the leader's robes. He might not be pasture-bound yet.

"You're one of our own," Nasira added. "I mean no ill by this, Rhodri, but to most of the tribes you're an outsider, the enemy. They won't follow you."

"I'm not asking them to. I'm asking them to follow Temion, if he'll lead them."

"Lead the tribes of Atrath to war with the west?" Temion sighed. "It's a heavy burden you lay across my saddle, Rhodri. I'm not sure I can take the weight."

"I'll be at your side," Rhodri promised. "I know the best ways to fight them. But it will take everybody, all the tribes, working together."

Nasira rose, raising her voice over Asta's wailing. "I'm taking this kitten off to bed. If you can get all the tribes to work together, you boys can achieve anything!"

*

Rhodri knew how manipulative his clever wife could be when she wanted something badly, but he had never witnessed her devious practices first hand. She would find a receptive mind, plant an idea, and watch it spread like fire on the grassland. Temion was more direct, but Nasira had the ear of the women. And the women held the balance of power of the tribes, unacknowledged, but always there in the background. Win over the women, and he hoped the men would follow. He watched her slip from group to group during the maindy run, chatting idly. When she caught his eye she would give a little nod, or wink.

"How's it working out?" he asked her as they lay in bed, listening to Asta snuffle in her sleep.

She stroked a long, elegant finger along his collarbone. "Kilujen stands against us. He's powerful, and he'll be hard to win over."

Rhodri sighed, trying to resist the temptation of her exploring hands. "I wish I could make things right with him. I let him down. I can only imagine how much he's suffering."

"He spends too much time walking in the Spirit Realm, with Ginamor, and not enough being our shaman." Nasira's voice was disapproving. "I wish he'd come back to how he used to be. He grows cold and bitter, especially towards you."

"Don't be hard on him. If I lost you, I wouldn't want to come back to the real world."

"But he has responsibilities." Her mouth set in a thin line. "It's wrong of him to blame you."

"It might be beyond even your skills to make Kilujen warm to me again."

"Do you doubt my skills, short-hair? Shall I show you how persuasive I can be?" Her hand slipped down under the blanket, and her mouth followed, leaving a trail of kisses down his chest and over his stomach, and Rhodri, who had hoped to get some sleep before Asta woke up with a noisy demand for food, was persuaded to stay awake a while longer.

He awoke to his daughter's gurgling laugh, as Nasira put her down on his chest while she dressed and braided her hair. He held her up before the iris and studied her, kissing her stomach as she chortled and kicked her plump legs. "Nasira, have you seen this?" he asked.

"Her being sick because you've waved her around too much? Many times. I don't need to see it again."

"I meant, have you seen her eyes?"

"What about her eyes?"

"They're darker. Take a look." He handed the baby to Nasira. "See?"

It wasn't a trick of the light. Asta's eyes had darkened from blue to a rich brown. Nasira looked from her daughter to her husband, and muttered a curse.

"What's wrong?"

"She looks like you."

"Is that so terrible?" Rhodri pouted in mock hurt. "You always told me I looked good!"

"She's my little girl. I hoped she'd look like me."

Her distress was so comical he couldn't help laughing. She slapped him on the chest. "It's not funny!"

"I don't know why you're so upset. She's beautiful. That comes from you."

"Flatterer!" A smile tugged the corners of her mouth. "Keep saying things like that, and I might forgive you."

"We'll have a dozen more daughters, and they'll all look like you. How does that sound?"

"Exhausting!" She nudged him. "Come on. We've only got a few more days to spread your message. Let's not waste time."

As they were leaving, Rhodri and Nasira ran into Kilujen, hurrying up the passage with a dark look on his face. He seized Rhodri's arm.

"What are you and Temion planning?" he demanded. "I hear rumours, but they're so far against tradition I can't believe they're true. Are you trying to kill us all?"

Nasira hesitated, and Rhodri waved her on, wanting to deal with the shaman on his own. Her narrowed eyes told him she wasn't happy, but she didn't make a fuss. Rhodri drew Kilujen into his cave.

"Kilujen," he said. "This is going to be hard enough. We need your support. Temion plans to unite the tribes behind him and launch an attack on the army of the west. Is that so wrong?"

Kilujen glared. "What part do you play in this?"

"Temion is my brother now. I support him. I know how the short-hairs think, how they react."

"You're not trying to take over?"

"The tribes would never follow me, and I don't want them to. I want to live in peace. What happened to Odval, to Ginamor, should never have happened, and must never happen to anyone else. I want this settled, and if the only way to do that is to fight, then that's what we must do." He sighed. "Say you're with us, Kilujen, for the friendship we once had."

The shaman shook his head. "I used to trust you, but now? I don't know . . . The chill on my spine tells me this course of action will only lead to disaster. The world will be thrown out of balance, and we'll all suffer for your recklessness."

"We're already suffering," Rhodri pressed. "I've seen too much death. It needs to stop. Temion doesn't want to lead us to war, but there's no other choice."

"Temion might not want a war, but you do! Don't drag my people into your feud with your sister, and don't use us to try and regain power in your own land. If you do that, you're no better than any other short-hair. That's why you want this battle, isn't it?"

"I don't want any battle—" But Kilujen cut him off with a gesture and swept out of the cave, leaving Rhodri troubled, and uncertain. When he talked to Temion, everything was simple, but the shaman forced him to question himself, to travel to dark places in his mind, places he would rather not go.

*

Temion's meeting took place four days later. The last maindy had laid their plumes of eggs and been swept up into nets, gutted, salted and stored. The snow clouds gathered over Kharikan, and the tumblers abandoned the blustery slopes for shelter inside the rock. It was the eve of trading season, but this year, no one spoke of unions and prices. They were all talking about Temion's plan. Nasira had sown the seeds of a radical idea on fertile ground.

The sharp nip of ice was in the air as the tribes gathered beside the river shortly after noon. The ground was still slippery with fish innards. It was against tradition to start trading until the season was declared, so with little to do until the next day it was the perfect time to sell Rhodri's plan to the tribes. He expected interest from the people of the Plains Hawk, and that others might pass and be netted. What he had not expected was a vast, excitable crowd.

"What have you done?" he asked Nasira, as he steadied her arm. Most of the population of Kharikan had turned out to hear Temion speak. Rhodri hoped his brother didn't let his nerves overwhelm him.

Nasira smiled. "Never underestimate a woman's power to spread rumour." She shifted Asta's weight on her hip. "Let's go down the front. We'll be able to hear better."

The crowd was loose at the fringes, and it was easy to make their way to the front, to the right of the stone semicircle that Temion chose as his stage. Nasira tightened her grip on Rhodri's arm as her brother stepped out to address the audience.

Trogir's ceremonial garb was lost when the Plains Hawk camp was destroyed, and Temion had spent long evenings during the maindy run fashioning a new headdress from feathers, scraps of fur, shiny stones, and whatever else he found lying around. It was ragged and thin, but it did the job. Rhodri watched him shuffle his feet. "He doesn't look like a leader, Nasira. Are you sure they'll follow him?"

"Be quiet and listen." She pinched his elbow.

Temion put forward his plan, quiet and hesitant at first, but growing in confidence, pacing up and down, stopping to gesticulate or elaborate on a point. Rhodri felt the mood of the audience change, from sceptical curiosity to enthusiasm, excitement growing in waves. He looked around to see nodding heads, clenched fists, and small groups in fevered discussion. It was going to work; the tribes would agree to follow Temion, fight under him as a single leader, and Temion would lead them well. He felt his grin spreading.

"This is going to give Serren a fright," he muttered, proud of his tribe, his chosen people. They were willing to listen, and try something different. Willing to fight for their homeland.

And then Temion turned the world on its head.

"Rhodri! My brother, come up here! Where's Rhodri?"

Nasira gave him a shove towards the stage, a smile playing across her lips. "Get up there and support your leader," she hissed. As the crowd parted, leaving him exposed, Rhodri had no choice. He forced a smile as Temion welcomed him into the circle.

"What's going on?" he mouthed, beneath the cheering. Behind the mask, Temion's eyes were large and pleading.

He dropped to one knee before Rhodri and bowed his head, arms sweeping wide. "I'm sorry," he muttered. "Nasira and I thought this was the only way you'd agree to it."

"Agree to what? Stand up, you're embarrassing me!"

Temion rose. "Forgive me," he murmured again, turning to address the spectators. Slowly, with great significance, he lifted the mask from his head.

"I must make a confession," he announced, as renewed hush fell. "You have agreed to everything I've suggested today, and I'm proud to have you stand behind me. But the words I've spoken are not mine. I am the mouthpiece for another—a modest man, but a true leader. It is Rhodri's vision you follow, and it is my brother who should lead you into the storm."

"What?" Rhodri retreated a step as Temion held out the mask.

"Put it on."

"I'm not putting it on!"

Temion addressed the crowd. "See how heavy my brother's heart is, that he must lead you to war? Are you behind him?"

The tribes roared their approval. Beneath the crescendo of sound, the chant of his name that began somewhere near Nasira and spread like a ripple across a lake, Temion pleaded with Rhodri. "Please take it. I can't do this, but you can." He thrust the headdress into Rhodri's hands. "For all our sakes, brother, will you lead?"

Battling his reluctance, Rhodri lifted the mask. It was heavy, too big for his head. He balanced it carefully, knowing any sudden movements would drop it over his eyes. Looking over the crowd that bayed his name, he spotted Kilujen. The shaman stood alone, arms folded, mouth set firm, and as he caught Rhodri's gaze he shook his head in a gesture of bitter disappointment.

*

"Why didn't you tell me what you planned?" Rhodri flung the headdress across Temion's cave at his brother. It smashed against the wall, stones bursting off and bouncing on the floor.

"Because you would have refused." Temion offered him a drink. "Sit down, we'll talk—"

"I don't *want* to talk!" The swipe of his hand dashed the flagon from Temion's grip. Asta howled, and Rhodri rounded on Nasira. "Get her out of here. I need to hear myself think!"

"It's not her fault. Stop yelling around her!"

"I'll yell where I please!" Asta's cries grew louder, and Nasira gathered her daughter on her shoulder and hurried from the cave, throwing Rhodri an amber glare over her shoulder. He cursed. "Now I've let the cat out. This is your fault, Temion!"

"Will you hear me out?" Temion caught Rhodri's arms and dragged him into a sitting position, while Siralane fussed over the spilt ale. He snapped his fingers at her. "Out, woman! This is male talk."

Her glare lacked the feline intensity of Nasira's eyes, but it was no less ferocious. Temion shook his head as she left. "I'll pay for that later," he said, pressing a fresh flagon into Rhodri's hands. "Drink, brother. Ale makes the world a better place."

There was a statement that couldn't be argued with. Rhodri took a long draught, and it eased the trembling in his hands. "Talk, then," he said. "I'll finish my drink before I decide whether to kick you from here to the mountains."

154

Temion refused to meet his eye. "I'm no leader," he said. "I hate to admit it, but it's true. Ever since Trogir died, I've looked to you for guidance, taken your words as my own."

"I don't mind," Rhodri assured him. "If it's for the good of the tribe . . ."

"But *I* mind." Temion swirled the ale in his cup. "If I can only lead as the puppet of another man, I'd rather not lead at all." He sighed. "I thought I was ready for this. I was wrong."

"What makes you think I'm ready?"

"You don't see it?" Temion's eyes widened. "I do. Nasira does. This was her idea. If you're angry with anyone, let it be her."

"What do you and Nasira see in me, that I don't?"

"You inspire loyalty. Men want to follow you, because you give them hope. Didn't you find that, in Serren's army?"

Rhodri shrugged. "Not really. There were other men more suited to leadership than I. I was just a—" he sought for the word, "—a warrior who walks with the others. Not a leader."

"But your friends have always been loyal, am I right?" Temion pressed.

Rhodri stared into the brown depths of his ale and thought of Astan, and Niklaus, who had lied to Captain Garrod to protect his friend. "I just thought I had very loyal friends."

"It's more than that. Lead us and you'll see."

"Do you think the tribes will follow me? Even though I'm a short-hair?"

"I can't speak for the tribes." Temion gripped Rhodri's wrist. "But I'd follow you through blood and fire, little brother!"

"That's the least you can do, as you dropped this on me!" Rhodri laughed, and the tension was broken. "So what happens now?"

"We carry on with the plan. *Your* plan. We have the winter to learn to work together as one tribe, and we ride with the first of spring."

"It means no trading season. Will the elders accept that?"

155

Temion snorted. "They'll accept it or be left out in the snow! Most of us, the ones you called the warriors who walk, are behind you." He tapped his belt knife and bared his teeth. "My steel will talk to those who don't agree."

Rhodri shook his head. "No violence. It makes us no better than those we fight. People have to follow with willing hearts."

Temion chuckled. "I knew you were better at this than me. Drink up, brother, we have much work to do!"

*

It had been years since Rhodri led drill, back in the cold, windy courtyard of the garrison at Northpoint. The Atrathenes, while full of enthusiasm for the fight, did not take well to Kingdom discipline. It went against tradition, after all, and while he could break one huge, sacred tradition, there were hundreds of smaller ones that held firm. Temion joined him towards the end of one fractious session to explain why he was having trouble.

All the drill sessions took place in a massive cave at the bottom of the rock. The snow was waist-height outside, and riding was impossible. But training indoors had its disadvantages, and Rhodri sighed as he took up a broom to sweep up the mess the horses left behind. "If you've come to tell me what I'm doing wrong, grab a broom," he said. "You can shovel shit while you lecture me."

Temion began to sweep in long, smooth strokes. "You're trying to turn them into the army you came from," he said. "You're not letting them use their own strengths."

Rhodri leant on his broom while he mulled over Temion's words. "Go on."

"We've fought our own way for a thousand generations, and now you're trying to make us fight differently. You should combine the best of what you know with the skills we already have. I've seen the Western armies in battle. They're strong, but slow. We may be small, but we're fleet, and ruthless in the hunt. They have power, but we have speed . . ."

"We need to combine speed and power . . ." Rhodri nodded. "Yes, I can see that. Use what the tribes are already good at, and make it better. Good thinking."

Temion grinned. "Of course, we have our secret weapon."

"Which is?"

"You. We can use your knowledge of your old ways against them."

"And you say you're no leader." Rhodri laughed, but broke off as the glowering figure of Kilujen swept into the cave and beckoned to him. "Here comes trouble," he muttered. "Can you finish up here and take the next session?"

"A fine way to reward me for my wisdom," Temion grumbled, but with good humour.

"You'll recover." Rhodri propped his broom against the wall and approached the shaman, touching the knife at his belt for reassurance. "Did you want to talk to me?"

"Walk with me, *Leader*." Rhodri chose to ignore the unpleasant inflection he put on the title.

"I'd rather not. There's nothing you can say to me that I wouldn't trust Temion to hear." *And walking lonely corridors with you could lead to in a knife in my guts.*

Kilujen's mouth turned down. He closed his eyes as a spasm of pain crossed his face.

"Kilujen? Are you ill?"

"If I am, it's not a sickness of the body. Let's sit down and talk. Can we go to your cave? I promise I won't knife you."

Rhodri wasn't convinced by this flash of the shaman's old humour. "I'd rather not have you in my cave. I don't want you around my daughter."

"Would you rather come to mine?" Kilujen's face was strained. "I'm offering you this ground. All I want is to offer some advice, in private. You don't have to listen, if you want to be stubborn . . ."

"I'll hear you out," Rhodri conceded, "but I keep my own counsel, and Nasira's. Can you live with that?"

Kilujen nodded, and followed Rhodri as they made their way up the side of the rock, via ladders and bridges that glittered and chimed with icicles. Every step sent a shower of icy shards tumbling into the depths. Looking down, with Kilujen breathing at his heels, Rhodri knew it would take only a push from the unhappy shaman to send him spiralling after them. He caught Kilujen's eye, cold as frost, and knew the shaman was thinking along the same track. He tried not to think of his body slamming against the rocks, bouncing like Asta's rag doll when she flung it in temper. He longed for a free hand to draw his knife against assault, and the tension gathered in his neck and shoulders. He began to see why Nasira hated heights.

He hesitated on a small plateau below the Plains Hawk caves. One more ladder and they would be home. If Kilujen moved against him, he would have to do it now. Backing up against the rock wall, he whispered his knife from its leather sheath. As Kilujen scrambled over the parapet, Rhodri dropped to one knee and pressed the blade hard against the shaman's throat.

"All I have to do is push," he said, in a low voice. Kilujen froze, hands clenching so hard against the ladder his knuckles were bloodless.

He swallowed. "You said you weren't a man of violence."

"I am when my family is threatened. What do you want of me?"

"Let me up. I've done everything for your family. Why do you think I'd harm them?"

"Why do you want to talk to me in my cave?" Rhodri countered. "You said my daughter was a mongrel brat, that she should have died. How can I trust you around her?" He relented enough to let Kilujen clamber onto the plateau, the edge of the blade scraping his throat. "If you want to talk," he said, "talk here. I don't trust you, and you're not getting near my little girl." He made a slashing motion with the knife. "Start talking!"

"I came to warn you. The spirits are unsettled by what you're doing."

"The spirits are unsettled? Or you are?"

Kilujen shook his head, careful of the blade. "You've turned away from your training, Rhodri. You can't see the right path any more."

"I didn't turn away from my training. You cast me aside."

"You walked a dangerous path, and look what happened."

"If I hadn't been walking the Spirit Realm that day, what would have happened? I've asked myself that question a thousand times, and the spirits don't have any answer for me. You can't forget Ginamor, but I can't forget any of it. Trogir, Odval, all of them . . . I close my eyes and every hurt is as fresh as if it happened yesterday." Rhodri let the knife drop and turned away in grief. "It happens over and over in my head. I can't stop it . . . When I think of it, I burn with anger for what was done to our people."

"You want revenge," Kilujen said. "This path will only lead to violence and death. Fighting between the tribes took Wanval from me, and your men took Ginamor. All we gain from war is blood and pain. We can't win."

"Wanval . . . you gave her blood, and she died."

"I gave her *my* blood! She was my wife, it should have worked. It had worked before . . ." He choked. "She was wounded in a tribal fight. I tried to help, but my blood fought with hers and she died screaming. I was nineteen, and I was broken. Ginamor saved me, the way Nasira saved you. And now I've lost her too."

Rhodri caught his arms. "I want this to stop, as much as you do. The killing, the rapes, the burning camps . . . all of it. If I can stop it by walking this path, then stars help me, I will."

"Do you think this course will heal your mind?"

"I don't know. But if we don't fight back, we'll be slaughtered. If not this summer, then the next, or the one after. Our whole way of life is under threat. You must be able to see that."

Kilujen shook his head. "I see a boy. A boy gifted with too much power. Wield it wisely, Rhodri. The stars stir in their courses, and the spirits watch closely. You walk on the cliff edge, and I'd hate you to slip and fall. You might carry us all down with you."

"I know what I'm doing."

"Do you really? You break traditions that have been held sacred for generations, with no heed to the consequences, and think that you can walk away without paying a blood-price? Nasira will pay, as Ginamor paid. The spirits won't let her live."

Rhodri narrowed his eyes. "Your advice isn't welcome, Kilujen. Stay away from me and my family. If I want help from the spirits, I'll seek you out."

"I just thought you—"

"Go!" Rhodri lashed out, his blade whistling an inch from Kilujen's face. The shaman stepped back, teetering on the narrow ledge.

"You see what I'm talking about?" he yelled. "It's happening already!"

"Get out of my sight!"

Kilujen vanished down the ladder, scuttling hand over hand like a massive cloaked insect. Rhodri sank against the wall, fighting the shudders that kicked him deep inside. In his head he heard Valery's mocking laughter, taunting him. Even when he crammed his hands tight over his ears, he couldn't make it stop.

Chapter Eight

SPRING DAWNED BRIGHT and gusty. The first grass of the season struggled towards the sun through dwindling patches of snow. An air of nervous anticipation hung over Kharikan, as it had on this day for countless generations. But today was different. There would be no long marriage ceremony; no celebratory drinking until the early hours. If there was blood, it would be spilt, not joined.

Rhodri carried Asta to the iris for a last look out at the plains surrounding Kharikan. A year ago, his daughter was no more than a secret in her mother's belly, and Rhodri had been sick with nerves at the prospect of marriage. It seemed he was fated to begin every year in a state of anxiety.

"Not next year," he swore. "Next year there will be peace. I'm going to make a better world for you, baby girl. For you and your little brothers and sisters." He caught Nasira's eye, and winked, feigning innocence. "What?"

"Don't count your maindy before they're netted, terrible boy." She knelt on the bed roll to hold it in place while she bound it, and rose to look around the cave. It was neatly swept, their few personal belongings piled against the far wall. Only Rhodri's clothes lay where he had abandoned them to crawl into bed, exhausted. They would leave no evidence that a family had lived and grown here, and soon the tumblers and the goats would take over once more.

"I wish you'd change your mind," he said; they had argued long into the night, but Nasira could be as mulish and stubborn as he was, when her heart was set.

She joined them at the iris, avoided looking at the sickening drop. "I wish you wouldn't hold her so near the edge."

"Don't change the subject. Odval will miss you."

Nasira leant her head against the stone wall, and sighed. "Don't use Odval to make me feel bad. I'm coming with you, because I can't stand being left behind. Besides,"—she forced a giggle, high and false, but her lips trembled—"I don't trust Temion to keep you out of trouble!"

"You're not crying, are you?" He hugged her close, Asta pressed between them, and kissed her, the salt taste of her tears creeping into the corners of his mouth. "We'll be fine. We'll raise our daughter in a safe home, where she'll never know fear. I know you want that."

"I don't want to ride to war to get it!"

Asta's face reddened, and she began to cry.

"Nor do I, but we have no choice." He let his arms drop. "You can stay here—"

"No, I can't."

Rhodri looked out of the iris. His people gathered outside the rock, waiting for him to lead them to an uncertain fate. He bit his lip. "I have a job to do. Will you follow me down?"

"I want to say goodbye to Odval first, and settle the little one." She gathered Asta to her breast, and bowed her head, her unbound hair falling like a dark curtain over her face. He knew that behind it, Nasira wept.

*

There should have been a rousing speech, a goat sacrificed to ensure the success of their mission. Rhodri had expected all that, but had given little thought to what he should say. In the event, he needed to say nothing. Temion, with quiet efficiency, had organised everyone into one great tribe. Only a few, the elderly, younger children, and warriors injured in previous conflicts stayed behind. Temion mixed up the tribes, ensuring the convoy wasn't split on family lines, bringing out the elders and their shamans to speak to Rhodri in private before they left. Kilujen hung back, wearing the same hooded look of warning he had when the desperate venture was first proposed and accepted. No sacrificial blood stained his forearms, and Rhodri regarded him with cynicism. "It seems Kilujen wants us to fail," he said in an undertone. "His hands are very clean."

Temion shrugged. "You don't believe sacrificing a goat will bring us luck anyway, you've said so dozens of times."

"I might not believe it, but Kilujen does. It's a deliberate insult."

"Let it drop. Enough goats have died today. What's one more or less?"

Rhodri merely shook his head, tucking the offence to the back of his mind. There was no point confronting Kilujen in front of everyone. Instead he moved down the line of elders, receiving their blessings, letting them mark his face and arms with the fresh, warm, blood. The woman who had officiated at Rhodri's marriage offered him a wan smile. "I hope you know what you're doing," she said in a low voice as she smeared his cheeks with scarlet, right and then left.

"So do I," he muttered back.

"Not all of the tribes are fully with you. Watch your back." She pushed him on down the line, but he was grateful for her warning. Some of the shamans frowned, or hesitated in the gesture of blessing, and he made a mental note of their names and faces. Temion walked behind him, his right hand never far from his blade. If the holy men and women had any doubts to express, they died on their lips.

At the head of the line, Sudak held Liberty, keeping a tight grip on her reins. She tossed her head and flared her nostrils at the scent of blood on Rhodri's skin.

"It's me, you daft mare!" The gore was sticky on his face and hands, but he couldn't wash it off until the long march west began. Liberty snuffled him, flicking her ears to let him know she wasn't impressed with his face paint. Even when he mounted, she cast him an ill-tempered look over her shoulder. He hoped she got used to the smell quickly, though he wasn't sure he would himself the way it turned his stomach.

Temion rode up beside him. "You look a little grey," he observed. "How do you feel?"

"Like I'm swimming, and I just felt the bottom drop away under my feet."

"Me too." Temion flashed his teeth, almost a grin, but his face reminded Rhodri of a smiling skull. "Too late to stop it now!"

With the sickness settling at the pit of his stomach, Rhodri raised his arm and gave the signal to move out. There was a tremendous jingle of harness, and the wooden wagons creaked as the tribes of Atrath left Kharikan, taking the first steps on their long road to war.

*

The convoy made slow progress over the steppes, following the course of the river, south and west towards the mountains. Every morning, Rhodri scanned the horizon for campfire smoke, and every day it was clear. There was no sign of Serren's forces. It was as if the ground had opened up and swallowed them, men, horses and tents, in one greedy gulp. But Rhodri knew they were out there, waiting beyond the horizon, sharpening their blades and thirsting for Atrathene blood.

He was sitting outside his wagon with Nasira, mending a harness and enjoying Asta's valiant attempts to pull herself up by the running board. She could crawl with alarming speed, and was intent on taking her first wobbly steps as soon as possible. And she loved riding; when he carried her in front of him on his saddle she giggled and waved her arms about as the wind tugged her dark, curly hair.

"Just like her father," Nasira observed. "She's happiest on horseback!" She ladled out a bowl of spicy stew and handed it to him. "Get this down you."

As Rhodri ate, a shadow fell across him. He looked up to see Kilujen, backed by two of the other tribal leaders. Rhodri's heart sank. *What now?* He forced a smile as he caught Nasira's eye. Saying nothing, she scooped up Asta and vanished behind the wagon. Rhodri set aside his bowl and motioned for his visitors to sit by the fire. "You're not here to join me for dinner. What's wrong?"

His two companions glanced sidelong at Kilujen. Whatever they wanted was at the shaman's instigation. He crouched beside the fire, feeding it scraps of wood and grass. "We want to go back," he said.

"Back to Kharikan?"

"Back to how we used to be. We want the tribes to ride their own paths again."

"We want, or you want?"

Kilujen stared into the flames. One of his companions, a tall woman with greying braids, cleared her throat and twisted her hands. "Kilujen thinks you've led us on a phantom quest," she said. "I mean no insult by that . . ."

"I take none," Rhodri told him, "but I think Kilujen can speak for himself."

"We've ridden three moons," the shaman said, "and we've had no sight or smell of your Western army. We think they've gone."

"Gone?"

"Back over the mountains. They found no one to fight, and they've given up."

Rhodri folded his arms. "I don't believe that for a heartbeat."

"Why not?" Kilujen leaned forward, suddenly eager. "Have you seen anyone?"

"No. But I took the King's coin when I was fourteen summers old, and from that moment I was taught that the King's Third stay until their job is done, or until the leader changes her mind. I don't believe their current leader is one to change her mind." He allowed himself a smile. "She has stubbornness in her blood."

"Like you," Kilujen snapped. "Will you consider it? The tribes grow restive."

"Seeds of unrest have been sown among them." Temion stepped from behind the wagon, arms folded across his broad chest. "Rumours grow like vines, and I wonder who plants them. Do you know, Kilujen?"

Kilujen scowled at this intrusion. "I might have known you'd be lurking in the shadows, Temion. Can't your sister's husband fight his own battles?"

Temion let one hand fall to his blade. "I support our leader in every way. It shames you that you don't."

"You ride a different coloured horse now, don't you? There was a time you would have agreed with me. It's no shame to question the sanity of this plan!"

Kilujen's companions backed away, leaving him alone beside the fire as Temion bristled. Rhodri held up his hands.

"Stop it, both of you," he commanded. "I won't tolerate infighting. You're as bad as children." He turned to the shaman. The effort of trying to be polite set his temples throbbing. "Kilujen, I concede to your beliefs, although I don't share them. If we find no evidence of the invading army a moon from now, the tribes will ride their separate trails again. Does that satisfy you?"

For a moment it looked as if Kilujen was going to argue. He gave the fire a final savage prod and scrambled to his feet. "I have work to do," he said grimly. "One moon. No longer."

"I swear." Rhodri watched him lead his companions away and turned to Temion, who watched with a frown. "Did you hear all of that?"

"Enough. Nasira came to find me. She thought you might need my muscle in a fight."

Rhodri shrugged. "I could take Kilujen."

"And all of his followers?"

He chuckled. "I fought half the boys in my village, when I was little. Used to get the blue beaten out of me, too! I'd like to think I was brighter than that now, but there are days when I'm not sure."

Temion joined him beside the fire. "Will you do what he says? He makes a good point. The tribes won't stay together without good reason."

Rhodri nodded. "We'll keep pushing towards the mountains. Have a word with our more trusted warriors, and send them out on wider patrols." He inhaled the smoke from the fire, and frowned. "They're out there, Temion. I can sense it. They wouldn't leave. We need to find them and drive them out before we split and go our separate ways. That way lies ruin."

"I'll talk to Sudak," Temion promised. "We'll find your old tribe. They'll pay for what they've done."

"I hope so." Rhodri looked up at the moons, placid in their endless course across the night sky, heedless of the turmoil the passing of time caused to the world below. He sighed. "Why is there never enough time?"

*

Time weighed on Rhodri like the heavy iron bands around his ankles, dragging his spirit down. The ponderous journey of moons and sun was unstoppable, their pitiless gaze mocking the tiny figures that played out their game of strategy on the vast plains below. With every day that passed, Kilujen's gaze grew more disapproving, and Rhodri sent his patrols wider and wider, seeking something that wasn't there.

"Even Temion thinks you should let it go," Nasira told him as she changed Asta before breakfast. "He doesn't doubt you, but he thinks you're obsessed."

"Obsessed?"

"He knows how stubborn you are, how you hate to be wrong."

"I'm not wrong," Rhodri insisted. "You'll see."

She was silent, staring over Asta's head.

"Something's bothering you, little cat. Spill the soup."

"What if we've missed them completely? Oh, Rhodri!" Nasira pressed her hand to her mouth in horror. "What if they've got to Kharikan? What about Odval?"

"That's why we must find them." He hated the way she lent voice to his unspoken fears. "If we don't, they'll reach Kharikan, and then we'll never get them out. Even if the tribes split, I won't stop hunting them. I'm going to be a splinter under Drusain's skin until one of us is dead for what he did to Odval. I swore on my name I wouldn't let him live, and I intend to keep that promise."

"I'll hunt with you." She gave him a squeeze. "I'm good at hunting short-hairs."

"If they make you angry, they've got no chance, my fierce little patchcat!"

"The cub is fierce too. Do you want to feed her? She bit me last night. Only three teeth, and every one savage!"

"Pass her here." He sat on the wooden steps, holding his daughter on his knee, cradled in his right arm. He blew on a spoonful of milk, and poured it into Asta's mouth, while she kicked her legs and giggled and tried to grab the spoon. It was already pitted with marks from her teeth. Some of the other women of the tribe had already complained that they wouldn't take her to the breast any more because of her biting. Rhodri had never paid much attention to babies; back in Pencarith he was too young, and children did not feature in the life of the King's Third. But he was sure that back in the Kingdom women nursed their own babes, rather than passing them around. It seemed everyone in the tribe had an equal hand in bringing up children. Nasira could often be found with other people's children latched on to her while someone else fed her own daughter. She never seemed worried about where Asta was, or who she was with. She assumed Asta was safe within the embrace of the tribe. Perhaps it was a better way to live.

Rhodri stretched out his legs, watching Nasira tend the fire. These were the best times, when it was just the three of them, not worrying about what lay over the next horizon. He wished things could always be this peaceful.

His musing was disturbed by the rumble of cantering hooves. Sudak approached at a furious pace, the chestnut gelding he rode lathered and panting. He pulled the exhausted horse up in front of the wagon, overturning the cooking pot in his haste.

"Rhodri! Rhodri, we found them!"

Rhodri tightened his grip on Asta, feeling a surge of excitement. "Where?" he demanded. "What did you find?"

Sudak struggled for breath. "A trail. Broken bushes and iron-shod hooves, hundreds of them, not a mile from here."

"Fresh?"

"I'd say a quarter-moon old."

"Fuck! We must have just missed them. Where's the rest of your patrol?"

Nasira pressed a cup into Sudak's hand, and he wet his throat before replying. "Following the trail," he said. "Don't worry, I told them to stay out of sight, and run rather than fight. I thought you'd need a full report, but I wanted to let you know as soon as I could. Did I do right?"

Rhodri smiled, but he felt the tension building. "Rouse the warriors and gather them outside the camp. Wagons in a circle, women and children in the middle. Nasira, will you take care of that?"

She frowned. "Not likely. I ride with you!"

"I'll organise it." Sudak backed off hastily, running to do his leader's bidding.

Rhodri glared at his wife. Her eyes flashed with a gleam of gold. He waited, his lips pressed tight, until the young warrior was out of earshot. "Nasira, we talked about this—"

"You talked. I listened. I heed my own counsel."

"I don't want you anywhere near those men! What if something goes wrong? What about Asta?"

She flashed her teeth. "Don't use Asta against me! I would walk in shame if I didn't fight to defend her future, and avenge Odval's honour. Would you deny me that right? My blade thirsts for short-hair blood, and if you don't let me ride, the blood it tastes will be yours!"

He took a step back, not sure how much of what she said was genuine threat. "I would deny you nothing . . ."

"Then let me fight!"

Asta screwed up her face at her mother's raised voice, and Rhodri joggled her against his shoulder to soothe her. "Not in the front line," he said, relenting. "Stay back with the archers. And if I give you an order, you follow it. This isn't like hunting deer."

"I know that. You act like I've never ridden on patrol. I'll tell the other women to make ready. What?"

He drew in a breath to steady himself, thinking of the women who had ridden with him to hunt down the men who had taken Odval. Thinking of Astan, who would have, should have, been a hero in the front line. "I know things are different here. I know women ride on patrol. But I can't lead them into battle. In my culture, the women stay behind while the men fight."

"*Your* culture? The culture that thinks it an acceptable act of war to capture me? To abuse my sister?"

Rhodri shook his head and narrowed his eyes. "No. That was never acceptable. I've seen you hunt, so why shouldn't you ride to war? But I won't watch you die, Nasira, and I can't give you mercy. Don't ever ask me to do that."

170

She took hold of him, long fingers curling round his upper arms. "I promise never to ask," she said, planting a tender kiss on his forehead, "and I hope you never regret that promise."

*

By noon, the camp was ready. The wagons were pulled into a tight circle, protecting the children, the women who had offered to stay behind armed with bows and blades and grim faces. Kilujen stayed with them. The shaman refused to join the preparations for battle, sitting with his arms folded and a black look on his face. Rhodri made a last attempt to appeal to him, to break through the wall of shadow the shaman swathed himself in.

"You don't fight with us, Kilujen?"

Kilujen glared at him. "My skills aren't suited to fighting."

"We could use a healer."

That blank, implacable stare. "Those who fight under you need healing in their minds, not their bodies."

"Fucking hells, Kilujen!" The anxiety and frustration of the day spilled over. "What's the matter with you? You're not the only person who's lost someone they loved!"

Kilujen bristled. "You know nothing about it."

"My best friend bled to death in my arms. I couldn't save him. I live with that every day. So I know something about it. If you can't support me, fine, but don't hinder what I'm trying to do, or I'll see you shackled." He clanged the metal bands around his ankles together to emphasise the threat.

"You wouldn't do that!"

"Try me." Rhodri turned away, shaking his head in disgust. Bristling from the confrontation, he saddled Liberty and headed out to see his troops, massing between the camp and the spot where Sudak had found the trail. They were a fearsome sight, the gathered tribes painted for war, human and horse alike. Every inch of harness was dulled with soot, but horsehair and braids were brushed until they shone. Looking at them lined up in neat rows the way he had drilled them, Rhodri felt a surge of pride. They were his army, they rode to his will. If he couldn't have his kingdom, at least he had his followers.

Temion's long braids were fastened in a lattice across the top of his head, battle-style, his cheeks patterned with sooty fingerprints. He grinned, teeth flashing white. "What do you think of your army, brother?"

"I'm impressed." Rhodri let his voice carry, and his words were met with a cheer. "Let's destroy those short-haired bastards!"

As a speech, it lacked gravitas. But as a battle cry, it did the job. This time the cheer was louder, punctuated by war whoops and the rattle of drawn sabres. Liberty tossed her head and flicked her tail in excitement. Her ears were pricked and her front hooves pawed the ground. She was as ready as he was for the fight.

He bent low over her neck. "Let's go, my girl. Dance for me!"

With a long whinny, she reared, spinning in a full circle on her hind legs. Keir had taught Rhodri some impressive moves, some of them on horseback, and this was one. The Atrathenes cheered and clapped as he crashed back to earth and nudged his little mare into a canter. With a rumble of hooves that set the ground trembling, the tribes moved out, tracking their quarry.

*

On the fourth morning, Rhodri saw smoke on the horizon, and called his troops to halt. He had spent too much time thinking what would happen when they caught up, but he had focused on bloody detail, rather than tactics. It was time to change that.

He called Temion and Nasira to him, and they rode towards the brown clouds that puffed up in the distance. He had forbidden his own men to light fires. They rode as close as he judged safe, looking out for patrols. Beron's death was still sharp, and painful.

"You chose me as a leader," he said to Temion. "I can't lead alone. Let's talk tactics."

"Do you want to kill them all, or drive them away?"

"I want to push them back towards the mountains, to their own land. But at the same time, I want to give them such a beating Serren will be utterly humiliated, so she'll never be able to send such a force again. We can't do that without killing. But I don't want to see blood spilt for the sake of it."

Nasira chuckled. "You want to herd them, like mustangs for breaking, am I right?"

Temion frowned. "There are a lot of them."

"There are a lot of us," Rhodri said. "Can it be done?"

"If you intend to follow them to the border, you'll need the wagons brought up. You don't want to lose them again."

"I'll get the nursing mothers onto that," Nasira confirmed. "You'll need every riding warrior if you do a sweep— what?" she said as her brother widened his eyes. "You hadn't thought to ride sweep? It makes sense to me."

"Out of the mouths of women comes wisdom." Temion grinned at his sister.

"Out of the mouths of men comes a longing for battle and glory that can only lead to death," she retaliated, pursing her lips in distaste.

"Can one of you please tell me what you're talking about?" Rhodri was baffled. "What does she mean by a sweep?"

Temion laughed. "You've spent too long studying the Spirit Realm, and not enough time hunting." He clapped him on the shoulder. "When we do a big hunt, or herd mustang, we ride out in a crescent. We sweep down on either side of the quarry, and behind it. We close the circle until the beasts are trapped in the middle. There's no reason it wouldn't work on men."

"Short-hairs are brighter than mustangs. Let me think on it." Rhodri walked away from his wife and her brother, staring into the distance, trying to picture the scene. He had been trained as nothing more than a cavalry rider; men of the King's Third learned tactics as they were promoted. He wondered what Dru knew, if Captain Garrod was still with his men. Garrod could out-think Rhodri at every turn when it came to tactics. He couldn't see any reason Nasira's suggestion wouldn't work, but he wanted to avoid a massacre, on both sides. The life of a nation lay in his hands, and it was a heavy burden.

He returned to his trusted lieutenants. "Right," he said. "This is what we're going to do . . ."

*

The sweep began with dawn a ruddy glow beneath the eastern horizon, before the innumerable campfires of the enemy were lit. Rhodri divided his army. This was no killing blow, and he wanted fighters in reserve to protect the wagons, should the sweep fail. "I should have thought of all this earlier," he confessed to Sudak. "I was too intent on the chase. I'm learning as I go along."

The young warrior smiled. "I won't tell anyone."

"You'll be all right?" Command of five thousand souls, with countless wagons and horses, was a massive duty to place on the shoulders of a boy of twenty, but Sudak had proved his worth many times. Loyalty was a valuable commodity, and Rhodri prized and rewarded it where he found it.

"I'll follow with your wagons, have no fear. I'll keep your little girl safe."

"You'd better, or I'll have your eyes for dice." Rhodri forced a laugh, but he missed Asta terribly. And if he suffered, how much worse must it be for Nasira? She said nothing, but he caught her sighing and looking glum more often than usual, and he knew her heart was pained.

He wondered about his own mother. Valery had snatched Rhodri from Lydia's arms when he was so young he couldn't even remember her. She must have gone through all kinds of hell, if

174

she loved him the way he loved Asta. At least he knew where his daughter was, knew she was safe. Lydia had been told he was dead.

Curse you, Valery Northpoint!

Like a stone flung into a lake, the ripples caused by Valery's actions were still felt a generation later, long after his parents had gone North. He couldn't break free of them, and he wondered if Serren felt the same. How much did she know about her lost brother?

As Sudak led his smaller force back to the wagons, Rhodri inspected his depleted army with a grim smile. Serren would learn who he was soon enough, and she wouldn't welcome the knowledge.

He split his forces still further into three long lines, one to sweep either flank of the enemy camp, and the last, the one he led himself, to take the centre. He checked his bow, watching the sun, waiting for a signal from Temion on the left flank and his opposite number, one of the sons of the leader of the Yellow Snake tribe, on the right.

Nasira trotted up to him, war paint banded across her tan cheeks. She trembled as she leant in her saddle to kiss him. He seized his final chance to ask her. "Are you sure you want to do this?"

"I don't want you to face it without me."

"I won't be alone. I've got five thousand men at my back."

She smiled. "There's a filthy joke there, but now isn't the time. You will be careful, won't you?"

"Trust me."

She narrowed her eyes as Liberty pranced before her, eager to be away. "You and the little mare have the same look in your eyes," she said. "You're both begging for a fight!"

"This is what we trained for. Not burning settlements and killing women and children. These men need reminding of that."

"Teach them well, my love." She kissed him again, more lingering, ignoring the whoops and jibes of the men nearby. "Stay safe. I'll see you when our work is done."

As she parted from him, he pushed away the thought that he might not see her again. If let fear rule him, he would not be able to fight. He raised his arm in silent salute to his troops, and nudged Liberty into a canter. Behind him, the line spread out, curving away on either flank. The tribes of Atrath rode to hunt.

It was a long time since Rhodri had felt such exhilaration in the saddle, the rushing wind and the thrill of blood pulsing in his veins. Battle madness. Master Tay had warned against the red mist that clouded your eyes and infected your mind. Rhodri could see how it happened, but the sheer, unfettered joy of riding, and riding with purpose, doing what he had trained over a decade for, overrode his fears. Serren's army must be able to hear the rumble of hooves sweeping down upon them.

As the Western camp came into view, Rhodri increased the pace to a gallop. Liberty's ears were flat against her head, her teeth bared. The steppe flashed by. The tents near the edge of the camp drew near at a terrifying rate. He had the vague impression of shouting, men running for swords and horses.

The tribes, moving as one, hit the camp with the force of a hurricane, dragging down tents and scattering the campfires beneath their hooves. Liberty's iron-shod front hoof clanged against a cooking pot, sending it spinning away. She bucked, a lashing hind foot ripping a hole in a nearby tent, and kicked free of the fabric.

Her speed had carried Rhodri further into the camp than he planned. He pulled up and swung her around, looking for his men. He was alone, exposed and unarmoured, surrounded by the army he had betrayed. For a heartbeat, he was paralysed, frozen with fear.

"Tribes, to me!"

His urgent cry caught the attention of a thick-set Kingdom soldier, running through the ruins, drawing his sword from the sheath across his back. He lunged towards Rhodri, and the instant of adrenaline drove out the paralysis, the fear, everything but the vital impulse to stay alive.

Rhodri swung his sword in a low arc, glancing off his enemy's shoulder as Liberty reared to dodge a clumsy blow. A flailing hoof caught the attacker in the shoulder and he fell back, cursing, sword falling from numbed fingers. Liberty crashed back to earth and Rhodri tasted blood in his mouth, warm and coppery. He spat.

A running man cannoned into the mare's hip, bounced off, and kept going. All round, soldiers scattered in panic, like ants whose hill had been kicked open. Rhodri heard shouted commands, issued from some distance. Time to regroup. His mouth filled with blood, and he spat again. "Fall back! Archers!"

He didn't know if anyone was listening. As he spun around, sounding a retreat, Liberty was buffeted by a band of tribesmen, charging past into the melee, loose braids whipping at their faces.

"I said fall back!"

They were young, the battle-madness was on them, the red urge to kill. Rhodri charged after him, his way barred by collapsing tents, loose horses, and armed men. He heard, too clearly, an Atrathene war cry end in a sharp scream, but he had lost sight of his followers in the confusion of battle.

Someone, at least, was listening, or acting on the commands he had already given. Rhodri saw gaps in the front line, opening to let through his mounted archers, their shots arcing over his head like a swarm of deadly, stinging insects. The shouting around him turned to screams.

Holding his round shield over his head for protection from the murderous rain, Rhodri dodged back through the line of archers. On the stiff breeze, he could hear distant sounds of hard fighting. His flanks were closing in. They had pushed far enough for the day, and it was time to retreat. The raid had lasted less than a bell, but it had achieved his aim.

As he saw the soldiers of the kingdom forming into organised lines, prepared to meet the onslaught head on, Rhodri gave the signal to fall back and scatter. The tribes were outnumbered four to one. In a direct confrontation, they stood little chance. They had made themselves known to Serren's men, and that would do. For now.

Chapter Nine

THE RAID WAS a modest success, only thirty-seven warriors lost, but Rhodri mourned for those wasted lives. He could not join in the celebration, knowing they had died doing his will. The men of the Kingdom would be planning their reprisal. He tried to out-think them, to work out what they would do next, but it was hard, lying on the sodden ground with the rain trickling down his neck and into his eyes. A hand's reach away, the next man in the line cursed the weather spirits. This eagle's watch on the enemy camp lasted all night, and on into the following day. Rhodri's tongue throbbed where he had bitten it, and he rubbed it against his teeth, toying with an ulcer the size of a berry. Liberty flopped her head across his legs and snuffled, grumbling at being forced to lie out in the downpour that engulfed them. He nudged her with his foot.

"Be grateful for the rest," he said. "It might be the last you get for a while."

The rain pooled around his elbows, and gathered in the hollow at the small of his back. Rhodri wondered if anyone had ever drowned lying on the open steppe. He was grateful for the deluge, if it stopped Serren's army from launching a counterattack. No one went looking for a fight in weather like this. But he was reluctant to withdraw. He needed to see what happened next.

As the rain thinned, cautious, shadowed figures moved through the mist. Rhodri tensed, nerves stretched tight as the string of his bow. Moving silently, he shifted into a crouch, a warning hand on Liberty's neck.

There was a yell, a scuffle further down the line, and he sprang to his feet. Liberty heaved up behind him with a snort of surprise as he raced towards the disruption, tugging his sword free.

One of the enemy patrol lay dead, another rolled on the ground clutching his leg and moaning as the others fled. Throwing down the blade in a fluid movement, Rhodri drew his bow and loosed an arrow. He was rewarded with a scream as the slowest of the patrol caught the missile between the shoulder blades and pitched forward on his belly. A brief shower of arrows followed, but Rhodri didn't look to see if they hit. He dropped to his knees beside the wounded man and pressed a hand to the deep slash on his thigh.

"Stop moaning!" he ordered, in his native tongue. "You'll live, but only if you keep quiet!"

The soldier's eyes widened, and he opened his mouth to speak, then snapped it shut at Rhodri's warning glare. He turned to his archers. "Call a retreat," he ordered. "We'll follow Sudak to the wagons, get treatment for the wounded, then we press forward again. You hear me?" He shook the injured man, slipping easily between languages. "We press forward, and we don't stop until you leave our land. I want you to take a message to your commanding officer from me."

"You're letting me go?" The gleam of hope shone in the stranger's eyes.

"Not yet." Rhodri took off his belt and strapped his prisoner's hands together. "Get to your feet. Can you walk?"

The captured soldier tested the weight on his wounded leg. "I think so," he said.

"What's your name and regiment?"

"Mairwas of Beritha. Kings Sixth Foot, under Captain Collis."

"I'm surprised an Estmarcher would fight a war like this."

Mairwas glowered at him. "We don't all follow the Red Tree. Who are you, anyway?"

"I'm the man who decides whether you live or die." Rhodri jerked the belt, and clucked Liberty over to him. She came with head high and a dancing trot, pleased to have something to do. He lashed Mairwas's hands to her saddle with a length of bridle leather. "You're a soldier of the Foot," he said, bluntly. "Let's see you walk."

*

The rumbling wagons made steady progress across the steppe, and it took two days of relaxed riding to join up with them. Sudak had done a good job. Rhodri's riders were met by a patrol long before they sighted the convoy. Mairwas did his best to keep up, dragged along by the leather that bound him, but his boots lay in shreds around his ankles, his feet stinking and raw with blisters. Rhodri stitched the wound on his thigh with clumsy hands. It would leave an evil scar, but Mairwas would live, and Rhodri had a use for him. He threw Liberty's reins to Temion as he dismounted.

"Look after her," he said, "and him. Hitch him somewhere."

"What will you do with him?" Temion asked.

"I have an idea. There's something I must do first. Where's Nasira?"

Temion pointed, and Rhodri saw his wife running into the camp with her hair flying out behind her. "She's ahead of you, brother! Now, where are my little ones?" As he swung down from his own ride, he was leapt upon by his two daughters, who squealed with joy at his safe return. Siralane followed more sedately, carrying their son. Nasira walked with her, Asta wriggling in her arms and stretching out for her father. She was laughing, and he felt a rush of love for her. "Asta! There you are!"

"She missed you," Siralane said with a smile. "They always miss their fathers."

"Let me hold her." Nasira released her daughter with reluctance, and Rhodri held her above his head and spun her round. She squealed and chortled, legs and arms waving gleefully. "Did you grow again while I was away?" he asked her. "What will I do when you're too big to throw around?"

She squirmed, straining towards Liberty. "Hss!"

"Did you just say 'horse'? Nasira, she said 'horse'!"

"She just made a noise. She needs her dinner. Give her back and go be a great war leader, terrible boy." She leant over to kiss him. "I'll be warming our bed for you when you're done."

"Promise?"

"On my name." She smiled. "But I might not be awake . . ."

"I'll wake you up."

She replied with a mocking slap. "If you want to sleep with the horses for the next moon—"

"You couldn't keep your hands off me for that long! All right," he sighed as Sudak hailed him. "I'd trade being a war leader to spend the night with you. I hope you appreciate that."

She frowned, suddenly serious. "Rhodri, I wish you would."

He kissed her forehead. "One day," he promised. "When all this is over." Sudak called him again, and he felt a surge of irritation. "I'm coming!" He tickled Nasira behind the ear. "A few moons, little patchcat, and I'll be all yours."

Her eyes were deeply hooded as they looked into his, but all she said was, "I hope so."

*

Rhodri called council the following night. He kept a close eye on Mairwas, who was lashed to a heavy wagon wheel under armed guard. The prisoner seemed well, if sullen, as Rhodri squatted down to check his wounded leg. His head hung down to his chest.

"Do you need anything? Food or water?"

"Not from you." The leg was healing well, with no sign of infection.

"We have a council tonight. You'll be free by morning."

No reply. Rhodri rose to leave, but the prisoner's words stopped him dead: "I know who you are now." He spoke with venom, and spat towards Rhodri's boots.

Rhodri remained frozen. "Why does it matter who I am?"

"You're the Northpoint bastard! I heard rumours, but didn't credit them. Yet here you are, a fucking traitor to your country. Just like your father—"

Rhodri was on him at once, dagger pressed against his ribs, hearing the prisoner's breath catch in his lungs. "Don't mention me in the same breath as that man. What rumours? What have you heard?" He jabbed the blade. Mairwas flinched, edging away as far as his bonds allowed.

"What I said! You're Valery Northpoint's bastard, and you want to finish what he started. So you took up with a tribe of savages to wage war on the Queen. Everybody knows it."

Rhodri sat back on his heels. "Shit! Is that what they're saying?" He shook his head. "You're lucky I need you alive, Mairwas of Beritha, or you'd die for speaking that rumour."

"Do you deny it?"

"I deny everything Northpoint stood for. Hells! Why should I discuss my past with you? You're nothing to me." He slammed his dagger into the sheath. "You start another rumour for me. Drusain of Austover. Tell every man you meet that I'm coming for him. His life is mine, and I won't rest until I've watered the steppes with his blood. I swear it on the spirit of my mother, and the life of my daughter."

Mairwas curled his lip. "Who was your mother? Some kitchen maid? Some whore?"

Rhodri's backhanded slap cracked his prisoner across the jaw. He stood, nursing his stinging knuckles and looking down in contempt. "You don't talk about my mother. Mention her again, and I'll cut out your tongue. You don't need to talk to deliver my message." Before Mairwas could utter another word, Rhodri stalked away, fuming over Drusain's duplicity, and the half-truth blown up into a rumour to set every man in the Kingdom against him.

He was still raging as the council assembled to decide the prisoner's fate. Mairwas was carried out, strapped to the wheel that took four men to lift. They propped him against a rock, where he glared at the assembled Atrathenes; the tribal leaders, their shamans and trusted lieutenants, and Rhodri, leader of them all, who paced back and forth, unsettled, itching for violence. The bruise on the prisoner's cheek had darkened to purple, but it wasn't enough. It was Drusain he wanted to kill. Drusain, and Valery.

"Do you want to kill this short-hair?" Temion asked. "You have the look of blood in your eyes. What troubles you, my brother?"

Rhodri glared at Mairwas. "Something was said. Something untrue, and painful. It sullies my name to all who hear it."

Kilujen cleared his throat. "What does your name matter, in the vastness of the plains? You're Western—I hear you don't put much value on your names."

Rhodri bristled at the calculated insult. Temion caught his arm. "It's spite," he said in a hushed voice. Louder, to the assembly, he added, "Whatever insults the shaman throws, fighting amongst ourselves won't help. Rhodri is Western, true. He is also our leader. I bow to his judgement, whatever he decides will be the prisoner's fate."

"I don't want to kill him," Rhodri said. "He likes to spread stories—I want him to spread *our* story, the story of the tribes of Atrath." He slipped back into the language of the Kingdom, speaking solely for Mairwas. "I want you to go back and strike terror into the heart of every man. I want that whole army,"—he waved his arm into the darkness beyond the guttering torchlight—"to know we're coming after them, that we'll fight to the last man to defend our home. We won't stop until they're gone, or we're all dead. Every man who raises sword or bow against Atrath is a corpse from this day forward. We will hunt, we will kill, and we will win."

He repeated the speech in Atrathene, to cheers and applause. "And we'll prove we're serious. Sudak! Fetch the irons, and the forge."

He crouched down before Mairwas. "Do you see these bands?" He flicked one with a finger to create a metallic ringing sound, echoing in the silence between them.

"When I first met my tribe, they bound my feet with iron rings. I hated them for it. But I grew to know their ways, to love them despite my scars. The burns they gave me are part of our story. I want to make my tribe part of yours. You forget too easily. Every time you look down, I want you to remember the people you're trying to destroy. Remember what we're capable of if you push us, and know real fear."

"What are you talking about?" Mairwas thrashed in his bonds, eyes wide with terror. "You want to put rings round my feet? I won't let you, you bastard! Let me go!"

"I don't want to put rings around your feet." Sudak stoked the mobile forge. Rhodri felt the heat lapping the back of his neck, making the fine hair that grew there crackle.

"Do you want me to do it?" Temion asked.

Rhodri shook his head, not taking his eyes from Mairwas. The colour drained from the prisoner's face, leaving him pale as moonlight. "I'll do it," he said. "It's my duty. Put the Plains Hawk brand in the fire."

He reached out with deft fingers and unlaced the Kingdom soldier's ragged, filthy shirt, pulling it open to reveal the curling hair on his chest. He laid his hand over his heart. "Do you see where my hand is? Do you see it clearly?"

"I see it." Mairwas's voice was a croak.

"Make sure you don't forget. Temion?"

"The brand is ready, little brother."

The handle of the brand was wrapped in damp leather, but the heat radiated through it as Rhodri took hold. "Pin him down," he ordered. "I don't want to make a mess of it."

"No! Let me go!"

185

As Temion and Sudak moved in, Mairwas struggled, arching his back to try and break free of the ropes. Rhodri tightened his grip on the brand, the metal glowing red-hot. He stood over Mairwas, took a deep breath, and pressed the glowing tip of the brand hard against the skin above his heart.

The soldier screamed, head thrashing from side to side. There was a sickening smell of burned hair and scorched flesh. Rhodri let the brand fall and turned away, gorge rising at the scent, and his own painful memories. He struggled to compose himself.

The screaming broke off.

"Is he all right?"

"He fainted," Temion said. "What do we do with him?"

"Untie him and give him healing. I won't give Serren's men more reason to call us savages."

He forced himself to watch as Mairwas's limp body was carried away into the darkness. He nodded to Sudak. "Go with him. Guard him against careless healing, or any other accidents that might befall him. I don't want anyone taking revenge into their own hands."

"As you wish." Sudak hurried away, and Rhodri turned to his people, hoping he didn't look as sick and tremulous as he felt. "The message will be sent," he said. "The seed is sown. We will grow fear in the hearts of our enemies. Tomorrow we return the prisoner to his own people to spread our story. We'll ride after them, panting on their heels like dogs at the chase, and we won't let up until they scuttle back over the mountains like the vermin they are! The time for speeches is past. It's time for action. Are you still with me, my brothers?"

The cheer was resounding. Only Kilujen sat silent and brooding. But his quiet condemnation rang louder than all the salutations, and while Rhodri found himself at the centre of congratulation, the shaman rose and walked away.

*

Sudak and Rhodri rode out at dawn. The young warrior insisted on accompanying him, for protection, though Rhodri didn't feel he needed guarding. They trotted slowly, the extra weight of Mairwas over the back of Sudak's gelding slowing them down. The Estmarcher was gagged, trussed hand and foot like a hog bound for slaughter. The jolting motion of the horse against the fresh burn sent tears of pain rolling down his face.

"Shall we take him up to the camp?" Sudak asked.

Rhodri scanned the area. They were probably within range of the patrols, but they were as yet unchallenged. "No," he said. "Let's dump him here. I want to make sure his men find him."

Sudak moved to push the prisoner off his horse, but Rhodri dismounted. "Make him comfortable, at least," he remonstrated. "He's suffered enough at our hands."

Between them, they manipulated Mairwas into a sitting position on the grass, no easy task, for he was a hefty man, and a dead weight as he resisted them. Above the gag, his grey eyes blazed with rage and hurt.

Rhodri untied the bandage that swathed his chest to take a final look at last night's gory work. Around the edges of the mark, his skin was red and blistered, but the heart of the scar was black, the stylised image of a hawk seared into his breast. The brand was as big as Rhodri's palm, and Mairwas flinched as Rhodri examined it.

"It'll heal. Let it remind you of my warning. I'll free your mouth now. You can yell as loudly as you like and hope your friends find you before the patchcats do." He sliced through the rag over Mairwas's mouth and, as an afterthought, cut his feet free. He jerked his hand aside before the man could land a kick, stepping back while Sudak covered Mairwas with his bow.

"Run back to your unit," he said. "Show them your scar. Tell them we were merciful."

"Merciful? You bastard!" Mairwas massaged the feeling back into his feet, keeping a watchful eye on the arrow levelled at his heart.

"Not me. I know my heritage, and you'll come to know it too, I promise." Rhodri turned his back in contempt, swinging up onto Liberty's back. "I hope the feeling comes back to your legs soon, before the wild cats scent you."

Mairwas rubbed his legs with renewed vigour, and Rhodri took a last glance towards the enemy camp. No one rode their way yet, but it wouldn't be long. He nodded to Sudak. "Let's get out of here." He aimed his own bow at Mairwas as his companion mounted.

His final shot was to Mairwas: "Tell your friends we're coming back. Maybe tomorrow, maybe the day after. In the dawn, or the dead of night. Tell Drusain to keep looking over his shoulder, because I'm coming for him, and when I catch up with him, he's a dead man. Now go!"

He pulled back on his bow. With a strangled cry, Mairwas scrambled to his feet and stumbled back to the uncertain safety of his own camp.

*

The retaliation, when it came, was swift and brutal. The first Rhodri knew of it was when an alarm went up through the convoy shortly before noon. Sudak, on foot, limped towards the wagons, supporting a boy from the Black Horse tribe on his arm. The boy bled from a dozen slashes; his shaman whisked him away before Rhodri had a chance to question him.

He caught Sudak as his knees buckled, and forced a drink into his hand. "What happened to the rest of your patrol?"

"Gone!" Sudak sank to the ground, and the hand around the flagon tightened until his knuckles were white. "There were two women patrolling with us. We fought, my leader, we fought to the last man, but the short-hairs took them . . ." He tried to rise, confused, spilling his ale on the barren ground. Rhodri held him down. "We need to get them back!"

"Hold, my friend. How many died?"

"Six cut down where they stood, and Jaycho of the Yellow Snake died in my arms on the way back. I should have fought harder . . . let me go after them, Rhodri! I will walk in shame if I do nothing—"

"You're going nowhere." A heavy sense of defeat pressed down on Rhodri. The commander at Northpoint had been right in his assessment, made so long ago, that battle was much harder on women. "There's nothing we can do."

"At last, some sense from our glorious leader." Kilujen's voice grated on Rhodri's raw nerves. He squatted beside Sudak and opened his healing chest. "Where are you hurt?"

Sudak ignored him. "What do you mean?" he asked Rhodri. "We can't leave them with the short-hairs. You know what they do!"

"What do you want me to do? Go after them?"

"Yes!" Sudak slapped away Kilujen's hand as he tried to dress his wounds. "Bring the fight to the short-hairs! I'm sick of sneaking around."

Rhodri hunkered down in front of his friend. "Sudak, I'd love to bring the fight to the Westerners. But there are too many of them, and we're not ready. They'd cut us down like grass before their blades."

"You should have thought of that before you dragged us into your madness," Kilujen crowed.

"Fuck off, Kilujen. I'm trying to think."

The shaman bristled. "You can curse me in the tongue of my enemy as much as you like. It just reminds me you're no different from them."

Rhodri's face burned at the insult, but he held his tongue. "We can't help our women," he said, speaking to Sudak alone, "I wish we could, and it burns me up to think of them . . ." He shuddered. "Serren's army is too strong for a frontal assault, but there are other ways to attack them. Can I ask you to fight like a thief a while longer?"

Sudak frowned, and grunted in pain. "Tell me of these ways to fight. If I don't like them, I'll take on the whole army myself—"

"I don't doubt it, my friend. But a thousand small cuts can kill a man, as surely as one massive blow. We'll bleed her army to death, a little at a time. Take their food, their horses. Steal their signal flags and burn their tents, drive them back over the mountains. We'll be such a burr under their saddle, they won't be able to go on. Can you live with that compromise?"

Sudak nodded, after a moment's hesitation. "I can live with that. If you let me lead the raids."

*

Sudak took his duties seriously. Every few days, a raid would produce a few horses, a captured signal flag, tales of burned tents and spoiled food. The Atrathenes stung like insects, striking fast and veering off before they could be caught, and Rhodri knew the tactic must be driving his former allies wild with frustration. He kept the wagons back from the front lines, ready to scatter at the first sign of assault. Again and again they scattered and regrouped, leaving the Western army striking at phantoms. And, despite the losses, he had to confess to himself that this game of cat-and-mouse was secretly thrilling.

Like hounds on a quarry, the tribes of Atrath pressed westwards, driving the invading force before them, harrying them with every stride. The push towards the mountains was slow, but inevitable. Rumours flew, wild as the little birds skipping from bush to bush across the plains. To his followers, Rhodri was a hero, the man who would drive the enemy from their land. At the head of every battle, his little grey mare was a potent symbol to the tribes. To the soldiers of the New Kingdom, he was a traitor born of a line of traitors, despised and feared. He knew the order had been given to execute him on sight, and the price on his head could buy a string of warhorses.

The truth, as always, lay somewhere in between.

"Rhodri? I saw the mountains today while I was on patrol. What happens when we reach them?"

Rhodri felt a prickle up his spine at Nasira's question. Unexpected in the darkness, it carried more weight than her casual tone suggested.

He played for time. "What do you mean?"

She leaned one elbow and looked down at his face, her eyes as dark as the surrounding night. "You said we'd chase them over the mountains, out of Atrath. Do you hold to that? Are we going to chase them into the mountains and just . . . stop?"

He said nothing.

"I know you, Rhodri short-hair. You don't want to stop, do you?"

His fingers danced along her spine. "Don't think about it now. It's the middle of the night. We'll talk in the morning, I promise."

"Promises made in the moonlight are always forgotten by dawn. Tell me, have you thought about this?"

"No," he lied. In the back of his mind, the fantasy hovered, airy and fragile as butterfly wings beating against the inside of his skull.

"I can tell when you're lying. You won't look me in the eye." She sat up, glaring at him. "I ask you again, have you been thinking about this?" Her unsheathed claws drummed a tattoo against the bare skin of his chest, signalling suppressed anger.

"And I can tell when you're annoyed with me. Put your talons away, Nasira. I want to talk to my wife, not the cat inside."

Her brow furrowed with concentration, and slowly the claws retracted, leaving only blunt nails and her fingertips, calloused from the reins of her horse. "You don't know how hard it is to keep control sometimes," she said.

"I've lost my temper enough times. I might not have a raging patchcat inside me, but I've got a good idea what it feels like."

"You haven't answered my question."

Rhodri folded his arms behind his head and stared up at the roof of the tent. The moons, fat and cream-hued, shone through the branches of a tree outside and cast eerie shadows against the canvas. On the steppe, a night bird shrieked, answered by the distant rumbling cough of a patchcat. All around were the small noises of the camp at night, over ten thousand people crammed together, living and working as one tribe, looking to him for guidance. Could he, should he, lead them where his heart wanted to go?

"Rhodri? Talk to me."

He thought of the Kingdom. *His* kingdom, by right of blood. He thought of her dense forests, low rolling hills, decorated with compact homesteads. He missed buildings. He even missed the sombre granite streets of Northpoint, with their beggars and hawkers, and the pervading smell of the sea.

"I want to go home." In his head, he spoke like a little boy. Nasira hugged him tighter in wordless sympathy. "My home was taken from me, and it hurts, Nasira. I want to go back, I want to force Serren to look into my eyes and see that I'm her brother. I want my birthright, for Asta. She deserves it."

"Asta doesn't care about your birthright, my love. She cares about ponies and toys."

Rhodri returned her embrace. "But *I* care. Asta will never be pushed out in the cold like I was. I promised when she was born I would keep her safe, give her the home and family I lost. I owe it to her to make Serren acknowledge the blood they share."

Nasira's voice was soft in the stillness. "If you go back to your stone fortress alone, they'll execute you as a traitor."

"I know."

"But you can't ask the tribes to follow you into a private war. The mountains are so dangerous . . ." Her voice drifted away.

"Some of the younger warriors want to go on. I've heard talk . . ."

"Men without families seeking glory and adventure. They're reckless, Rhodri. Don't take advantage of their youth and inexperience just to get your own way." Nasira sighed. "It's early yet, but I think I should tell you. You're to be a father again."

"I am?" His hand slid to her stomach, flat and well muscled. There was a trace of swelling under his palm, but he wouldn't have noticed if she hadn't told him. "When?"

"Seven moons. In the Spring. Are you . . ." Her eyes dropped to his hand. "Are you *happy* with that?"

He chuckled. "You mean, am I going to panic and run, like last time?"

She joined in with his laughter. "My grandmother isn't here to carry you back by the scruff of your neck this time. You'd better not run, or I'll send Temion after you!"

"I won't run." He stroked his fingers across the warm skin of her belly. "But it limits our options. No more fighting for you."

"Rhodri! I can fight as well as anyone. I'm having a baby, I'm not sick."

"I know, but—"

She huffed and rolled away from him. "We can argue about *this* in the morning. Never mind your foolish mountains!"

Rhodri lay back, a slow smile spreading across his face as Asta, disturbed by their voices, burbled and chattered in her crib. He picked her up, cradling her against his shoulder. Warm and sleepy, she slurped on her fingers as he carried her outside.

"Let's not disturb Mummy, princess. You're going to have a little brother or sister. What do you think of that?"

Asta removed her fingers, drool making her chin shine in the moonlight. "Hss?"

"Not a horse, a baby. Like you!" He prodded her tummy and hugged her close to his chest; she giggled. He wanted to give her everything, all the love and security denied to him. If that meant risking his own life, he would gladly take that chance.

*

The tribes edged closer to the mountains, until they dominated the skyline ahead. Hounded on every side, with no escape from the constant bee-sting of Atrathene arrows and blades, to Serren's troops they must have appeared like water to a man crossing a desert.

The afternoon they reached the foothills, the roots of the high peaks pushing long tendrils out onto the plains, Rhodri led a party hunting for game. The local wildlife was scarce, depleted by the demands of two armies, and all they caught were a couple of goats who had survived by being, as Temion put it, "real bastards to pin down". For Rhodri, food was becoming a worry. There were usually horses to eat, older steeds who struggled to maintain the fast pace, but even their numbers were running low. The wild plants harvested from the plains would not last forever, and most of the fish had vanished from the rivers. On the far side of the mountains, he knew, grain ripened in the fields, and the fruits of autumn grew fat on the trees. There was plenty there, just a few miles away, but with the peaks of the range blocking their path, it might as well be on the moons.

As the hunters returned to camp, bounty slung over their saddles, Rhodri was hailed by Sudak, waving his arms and yelling in excitement as he approached. He reined in with a flash of his large, horsey teeth. "They're gone!" he declared. "We won!"

"What are you talking about?" Rhodri asked.

"The short-hairs!" Sudak waved his hand in the direction he came from. "There's no sign of them!"

"It could be a trap." Temion's voice was sharp.

Rhodri cut loose the goat he carried and tossed it to Nasira's brother. "Unlikely," he said. "I want to see for myself. Sudak, you show me."

At a leisurely canter, Sudak led the way back to the spot where Serren's army last camped. Rhodri kept a watch out for patrols, but it seemed his worry was unfounded. The campsite was deserted, although the smells—human waste, horses and old camp fires—lingered in the air, the ash thick underfoot. Rhodri stirred it with the toe of his boot, unearthing scorched scraps of canvas that might once have been a tent. He frowned. "Let's see if they left anything useful."

A search of the site dug up a few knives, scraps of mail and armour, a couple of damp but functional bedrolls, and a broken betrothal chain, trampled into the mud. Rhodri prised it free with the tip of his dagger, and called Sudak. "I've found something for your woman."

"I've found something for you," came the answering cry from a clump of bushes. Rhodri stuffed the gold chain in his pocket as Sudak emerged, leading a string of eight horses. Even from a distance, Rhodri saw they were no cavalry steeds, but older pack horses, broken down and wheezing. Pushed too hard, they would never make it over the mountains, but he assumed whoever cared for them didn't have the heart to put them down.

"Why were they left?" Sudak wondered. "They destroyed everything else, it seems."

Rhodri nodded. "Burned what they couldn't carry. Westerners are sentimental about horses. Let's have a look at them."

He ran his hand down the forelegs of the first mare, listened to the rattle in her chest and opened her mouth to check her teeth. Her smooth incisors told him she was old, older than Liberty, and hadn't been treated as well. The rest of the string was in a similar state, well-groomed but worn out. Rhodri shook his head, and sighed. "I hate to say it, but they're more use to us as food than rides. Take them away and butcher them. There's not much else useful here."

Sudak shrugged. "What does it matter? They're gone! Now we head back to Kharikan for winter, am I right?"

Rhodri looked at the mountains, their towering heads wreathed in cloud, and thought about the land beyond.

"Rhodri?"

"I need to think on it. Tell the tribal leaders to meet me at my wagon tonight. And find Temion."

Sudak rode off, leading the doomed pack horses behind him. Rhodri followed more slowly, with many a longing glance at the mountains. His heart was set. He would make the crossing, for good or ill, no matter how many of his people followed him. He hoped he wouldn't be making it alone.

*

"I knew this would happen." Frown lines creased Nasira's brow. "As soon as I saw those mountains, I knew I'd lose you to them."

"You haven't lost me," Rhodri protested, taking a gentle grip on her upper arms.

"So I have to follow you, even in your last madness?" Tears glimmered in her eyes.

"You don't have to follow me. You could go back to Kharikan, with Asta. I won't be gone forever."

"You will if you die!" She pushed his hands away and turned her back, shoulders quivering with suppressed sobs.

Rhodri slipped his arms around her waist, pulling her against him. "I'm not going to die. I've crossed the mountains before."

"I'm not worried about the crossing. I'm worried about the gold-price Serren put on your head. You're a wanted man, you know that."

"I'll be careful," he promised.

"You'll be dead! You'll leave me alone with two children because you've killed yourself chasing a dream—" Her lips snapped shut at the sound of a tread on the steps outside, and she wiped her eyes on her sleeve. "Do you want me to leave?"

Rhodri caught her hand between both of his. "Stay. Hear me out."

"I've heard enough!" Her voice dropped to a whisper as she drew back the canvas door to reveal Kilujen, dour as ever. The shaman honoured her with a polite nod, but said nothing to Rhodri as he sat down on one of the folding benches that ran down the sides of the wagon, hands knotted in his lap. Nasira slipped out, and Rhodri could see her through the doorway, head bent low over the fire. He wished she had stayed at his side; the tension crackled in the humid air. He hoped the other leaders would arrive soon.

Kilujen broke the silence first. "You want to take us over the mountains, don't you?"

"I haven't decided yet."

"I didn't ask what you'd decided. I asked what you want."

"I want what's best for the tribe."

Kilujen's hands knit tighter, knuckles showing white through his skin. "You think a dangerous mountain crossing into a hostile land is the best thing for the tribe? Or the best thing for you, to bring peace to your troubled spirit?"

"You lost the right to worry about my spirit long ago, Kilujen. Let me take care of it now." He heard Nasira call a greeting as the other leaders approached, her voice artificially bright, and he smelled milk warming in the pot. "We'll discuss this as a tribe, the way it should be done."

Rhodri turned his back on Kilujen to welcome the remaining elders. The crowd made the wagon stuffy, and the flagon of hot milk Nasira pressed into his hand brought uncomfortable warmth to Rhodri's cheeks. Her thigh pressed against his, and he hoped the squeeze she gave his hand meant he had her support, in public at least.

The milk coated his throat, made speaking easier. "I've asked you here," he said, "because of what Sudak discovered this morning. The Westerners have fled. For the moment, we've won."

There was a smattering of congratulation at this, but Rhodri held up his hand to cut off the praise.

"I said for the moment. This battle is won. There will be other battles on the road ahead. The army have left, but they'll be back, in greater numbers. This isn't over."

A couple of the more hidebound leaders exchanged surprised glances. In the tribes, when you took a beating, you stayed beaten.

"How do we make a lasting peace, my husband?" Nasira asked. "It strikes me someone will have to talk with their leader, this Serren, and make a trade."

He could have kissed her, but Nasira wasn't looking at him. She stared down the elders one by one, calm and confident. "Can we make a good trade with this leader woman, from where we stand?"

Feet shuffled, heads shook. Kilujen cleared his throat. "I say we trade Rhodri."

Nasira drew in her breath with a little hiss. "What do you speak of, Kilujen?"

"She wants his head. She offers gold and jewels for him. I say we hand him over, and demand peace in return. What do you think, Rhodri? Your sacrifice would be very . . . *noble*."

Temion caught Rhodri's arm before he could rise to the bait. "No man is being traded, Kilujen. Least of all Rhodri. He led us to victory. If you want to trade him to this woman, you do so over my grave!"

"It's not our way to sell people to their enemies, Kilujen," Rhodri reminded him with all the patience he could muster.

"What is *your* way, Rhodri? Please, share it with us!"

Ignoring the sarcasm, Rhodri turned to the rest of his followers. "We have a stark choice," he said. "Summer is nearly over. We can return to Kharikan, wait out the winter, and carry on as we always have. But if we do that, I promise you Serren's men will return, in great waves. One defeat doesn't mean they'll leave us alone. A conflict that has endured for generations won't end in a day."

Nasira shuddered theatrically. "You say a return to Kharikan bodes ill for us all. What's the other choice?"

"To keep going, over the mountains." Rhodri had to raise his voice over anxious muttering. "I know it's a hard road, but there are dwellings on the far side, food and shelter . . . And it would prove our intent to Serren, take the fight to her!"

More muttering. One of the older leaders wrung his hands. "Would we all go? The wounded, and the children? Your woman,

I hear,"—with an apologetic nod to Nasira—"is breeding. Surely she'd be safer in Kharikan?"

"For a few moons, yes. But I want to make a peace that lasts years, not moons."

Nasira laid a hand on his upper arm. "Let me speak, Rhodri."

He fell silent at her quiet insistence. "It's true, I'm breeding," she said. "I would much rather deliver my child at Kharikan, not on some foreign grassland. But how safe will he be, if we don't finish the fight that started on the plains? I trust Rhodri. He rides a dark path, but I ride at his side."

"And me," Temion added. "The Plains Hawk follow you, Rhodri, whatever the other tribes decide."

Rhodri shook his head. "We're one tribe," he said, "but many spirits. I want every man to make up his own mind. It's too much to ask anyone to follow me just because his leader asks him to."

This was a radical concept, and he watched the leaders faces contort as they tried to come to terms with it. He pressed home the thought while they were off balance: "We've done many things these past moons that break with ancient tradition, and it's served us well in battle. This is one more step." He turned to the man who had noted Nasira's condition. "Joychi, what do you think? I can see it worries you . . ."

Joychi sighed, rubbing his hands across his face, skin like cracked brown leather. "Will things go back to the way they were when this is over?" he asked, a plaintive note in his voice. "Rhodri, you've brought so much change, and I'm an old man. I doubt I can cope with much more."

"Everything will be as it was," Rhodri assured him, knowing it to be a lie, for how could so many new ideas not leave their mark on this conservative society? He was about to take them where few had ventured before, for only the boldest warriors crossed the mountains to raid in the Estmarch. The journey would expose them to a different way of life, to farming, living in one place all year round. He didn't know what they would bring back with them

199

when they returned from the New Kingdom. If they returned at all. He could be leading the tribes of Atrath to their doom.

Kilujen, as always, read the conflict behind Rhodri's eyes. He sprang to his feet. "How can that be true?" he demanded. "You want to change everything. You could kill us all, destroy our world in your pursuit of glory!"

Rhodri raised a sardonic eyebrow. "This is usually the part of the conversation where you storm out, Kilujen. Are you going to finish your drink before you go?"

Caught off guard, the shaman sat down with a thump. He stared hard into his mug, the tips of his ears flaming scarlet.

"It's every man's choice, to follow me or stay behind. If I go alone, peace may never be secured."

There was a long silence. "It will take a sacrifice," one of the shamans muttered. "The fire-lizards in the mountains are not easily appeased."

"I know." Rhodri remembered the flap of wings above the glacier, the blood spilling over his hands, Drusain's hard breath at his shoulder. He shuddered. Nasira gave him a sidelong glance, but said nothing. "Can you arrange it? I leave two days from now."

This provoked her to speech. "Two days, Rhodri? So soon?"

"Every day we waste is a day for Serren's army to regroup, and a day closer to winter. If we're to cross, let's do it before the nights draw in." He laid a protective hand on her belly, felt her stance soften at the gesture.

"I understand," she said quietly.

Rhodri looked around at the tribal leaders, confident of his wife's support, but not theirs. "Two mornings from now," he said, "I leave with the dawn, with any who choose to join me. Does that give you enough time to make your sacrifice?"

To his surprise, Kilujen spoke for the shamans: "It does," he said. "We'll do as you ask, and pray to the spirits this is not a terrible mistake."

*

The sacrifice to appease the dragon was deemed so important only a horse would suffice as an offering, rather than the usual goat or wildfowl. It cut Rhodri to the heart to watch a horse die, especially a fine young stallion like the one Kilujen led up to the hastily-constructed altar, eyes rolling and nostrils flaring. Nasira tightened her grip on Rhodri's hand.

"Sorry you have to watch this," she whispered.

He squeezed in return, never taking his eyes from the fretful stallion. "It's my duty, even if it sickens me."

"Do you think it will help?"

"It won't help *me*. But it might give some of the others the courage to follow . . ." He fell silent as Kilujen picked up the curving sacrificial blade and beckoned him forward with it. Between them, the other shamans forced the bucking, struggling stallion to his knees, neck stretched out across the altar. Only the whites of his eyes were visible, and Rhodri felt a deep pang of sympathy for the poor beast. He hoped Kilujen's strike would be swift, and merciful.

There were two sounds that could rip Rhodri's heart from his body: Asta's crying when she was in pain, and a horse's scream. He twitched, fighting the urge to cover his ears and run, as the stallion's dark blood pumped out over the offering stone and pooled around Kilujen's feet, splashing his robes with fresh crimson.

Stepping carefully to avoid the puddles, Kilujen walked towards him, carrying a bowl of blood in his outstretched hands. Rhodri closed his eyes as the shaman smeared the warm liquid across his cheeks and forehead, and held the dish to his lips. "Drink," he urged in a low voice. "Everyone is watching."

"Are you enjoying this?" Rhodri swallowed a mouthful, trying not to gag, and failing.

"This is my duty as much as yours. Keep drinking."

Somehow Rhodri forced half the liquid down his throat without vomiting. "Will that do?" he gasped, feeling it dribble down his chin.

"It's enough. You have a strong stomach." For a second, there was a flash of humour in Kilujen's sorrowful eyes.

"I got it from cleaning up my daughter." Rhodri forced a smile, feeling the drying blood crack on his cheeks. "Will you join us for the feast, Kilujen? It would be good to celebrate together."

"Maybe. I hope this sacrifice brings you luck in the mountains, Rhodri. I fear you'll need every ounce for your chosen road." He clapped him on the shoulder, a friendly gesture that made Rhodri mourn what was lost between them, but the shaman's eyes were dark with sorrow.

"We'll eat well on the other side, Kilujen. I hope when we do you'll join me in a drink."

"You might eat well. Food from the Western earth won't touch my lips." Kilujen turned away, leaving Rhodri to wonder at this last pronouncement as he turned to the other shamans to order the butchery of the horse. The sacrificial victim would fill a lot of bellies tonight.

The ale flowed freely at the feast. Rhodri, relieved to have cracked Kilujen's wall of reserve, and boosted by Nasira's support, threw off the heavy mantle of responsibility for a few hours and downed a few flagons. The night was cloudy, both moons shrouded from view and only a few stars gleaming, but he decided it was worth the risk to light the torches, even if he still kept a guard on the perimeter of the camp. With ale in his belly and his woman at his side, the danger of the mountain crossing didn't seem so bad, and he could blot out, for the moment, the thought of what awaited him on the far side.

Rising to empty his bladder, Rhodri noticed that Kilujen had vanished from his spot near the fire. The shaman had been sitting quietly, speaking only when addressed and nursing a small flagon.

Now his drink, untouched, stood alone, and Kilujen was nowhere in sight.

Ambling into the darkness, Rhodri took a leak against the wheel of a nearby wagon. He was pleasantly drunk, well-disposed to everyone around him. Now, he decided, was the time to blow away the clouds that lay between him and Kilujen. He realised he was nodding to himself and smiling at nothing as he fumbled with the lacings of his breeches, awkward fingers tangling them in a hopeless knot. Abandoning the enterprise, he pulled his shirt down as far as he could, just in case, and headed off though the silent ranks of wagons in search of his former friend. In the blackness, with his muzzy head, everything looked the same. Getting lost was a novel experience for Rhodri, and not one he enjoyed.

"Can't be lost," he muttered, retracing his steps and stumbling over a pile of abandoned kindling. "I *never* get lost. Too smart for that. Kilujen!"

There was no reply to his shout. Finding a barrel of water, Rhodri sluiced his head and face, hoping the chill would clear the fog in his mind. It seemed to help; he regained his bearings and headed in the direction of Kilujen's tent. Since Ginamor died, the shaman had chosen to isolate himself from cousins and siblings who would have taken him in without question.

The tent was empty, impossibly tidy for a man who lived alone, mattress rolled and neatly stacked against the back wall. Stumbling in the darkness, Rhodri stubbed his foot against Kilujen's healing chest, boot bouncing off it with a hollow sound. It was unlocked, and empty, just a dusting of powder and a few dried herbs in the bottom.

That's strange. With increasing anxiety, Rhodri let the lid fall. He left the tent and stood outside, breathing in the night air and staring into the darkness, wondering where the shaman had gone with all his equipment.

Far to the left, something flickered. Fireflies, maybe, or candles. Certainly not a camp fire, and only a shaman would light candles alone in the dark when there was warmth and companionship a short walk away. Treading carefully, sobered by his impromptu bath, Rhodri headed for the guttering lights.

Kilujen lay on his back, inside a rough circle scratched in the dirt, the tools of his profession arranged neatly around his recumbent form. In the candlelight, his skin was waxy. His lips stirred faintly, as if he whispered to someone who wasn't there.

Rhodri looked for the rope that tethered the shaman to the world of the living. There wasn't one, no lead rein to bring him back.

"Shit!" The expletive burst from Rhodri's lips as he sank to his knees, hands on Kilujen's cold skin. If Kilujen had abandoned himself to the Spirit Realm, only Rhodri could bring him back, and the last time he had made that perilous journey, it had cost him more than anyone knew.

Chapter Ten

"**A**RE YOU READY?" The Yellow Snake shaman frowned, though whether in disapproval or anxiety, Rhodri wasn't sure.

He checked the binding round his waist for the tenth time. "No," he said, "but I'll never be ready, so let's get on with it."

"Rhodri, I wish you wouldn't." Nasira chewed her lip. "If he hasn't taken a rope, he doesn't want to come back. Why does it have to be you?"

"I'm shaman-trained, and we share memories. More than Kilujen shares with any other shaman. I've got the best chance of retrieving him." Her chin wobbled. "Don't look like that. I know what I'm doing, I swear."

"What if Valery—?"

"Don't talk about Valery!" Rhodri had the queasy notion that saying his adopted father's name would summon him, the way staring in a looking glass and chanting the name of a demon was meant to bring it into the realm of the living. He had never told Nasira how Valery had shown him a glimpse of his mother's memories, a confused blur of pain and horror so powerful it still woke him sweating and trembling in the night. He knew the full impact of her memories would have driven him to his knees and broken his mind, and that was what Valery wanted. He dreaded the thought of seeing him again, and had avoided the Spirit Realm for fear of encountering him. But now he had no choice.

He lay down in the circle. As he closed his eyes, he felt Nasira's lips stroke his forehead. "Something good to hold on to," she whispered. "Come back safe to me."

Her voice faded as he plunged down through grey, gauzy layers of memory, searching for Kilujen. He opened his eyes to the flat, artificial landscape of Spirit. Before him, Kharikan looked like the painted backdrop to a theatre performance. The river curled across the plain like a sheet of ribbon, flat, still and silent. It was so smooth he wondered if he could walk on the surface of the water.

Kilujen sat on the rock where he used to watch the maindy run, legs curled under him, pipes dangling from his right hand. He raised his head as Rhodri approached, but offered no greeting.

Rhodri joined him on the rock and they sat in silence, Rhodri staring at the false river, Kilujen gazing into the distance with a faintly hopeful expression on his face.

"Why don't you play your pipes?" Rhodri asked eventually, determined to break the quiet but unsure where to start.

Kilujen shrugged. "I don't have the breath to play them here."

"That's a shame."

"Yes."

Another long silence. Kilujen seemed to be wrestling with an internal dilemma. Several times he licked his lips and cleared his throat as if about to speak, before changing his mind. Rhodri drummed his fingers on the rock, wondering how time was passing for Nasira. Worrying about him wouldn't be good for her, or the baby.

Eventually Kilujen sighed, dragging his attention from the distant horizon back to Rhodri. "What made you look for me here?" he asked.

Rhodri shrugged. "You were happy here. If I was going to cut myself off in the Spirit Realm, I'd go somewhere I was happy."

"Why did you come after me? To save me?" The shaman's fists clenched. "You can't make me go back."

"I didn't come here to save you." Rhodri was surprised by the truth of this. "I thought I did. But . . . I came to make peace with you, before we say goodbye."

"Really?" Kilujen relaxed, sprawling on the rock as if he was basking in the sunshine, although no real sun shone in the Spirit Realm. "I don't deserve it. I might not agree with everything you do, but I treated you badly. I should tell you why, to ease my spirit."

"You were grieving. If I lost Nasira,"—Rhodri shuddered at the prospect—"I'd be looking for someone to blame."

"I should have been there," Kilujen spoke to the sky.

"I've told myself that a thousand times. It's likely we would have met the same fate as Trogir. Sometimes evil happens for no reason. There's nothing you can do to prevent it, only make sure it doesn't happen again. That's what I'm trying to do." Rhodri sighed. "And you've fought me at every stride, you bastard."

"Only for your own good, and the safety of the tribe." Kilujen sat up and extended his hand, warm and solid as Rhodri shook it. He still lived, back in the real world. "I'm sorry for the hardship I caused you. I thought you were reckless. Still do. It's true, I was grieving. But my grief should never have been allowed to harm the tribe. The tribe is everything, Rhodri, you know that. There had to be harmony between you and Temion. Whatever I had to sacrifice to bring that about was worth it."

"Sacrifice?" He recalled the taste of horse blood on his tongue, hot and metallic. "What did you sacrifice, Kilujen?"

"I was fond of you, you know that. And Temion . . ."

"Temion wasn't. But he came around, in the end."

"I sat up, long into the night, for many nights, whispering to his spirit. I gave his spirit all the affection I felt for you, and night by night it drained out of me, flowing into him. As you gave your blood for Nasira, so I gave my love for you to Temion, for the tribe. To keep our peace. I didn't realise it would lead us to fight your war."

Rhodri felt a cold lump settle at the base of his stomach. "So Temion hates me? It was all a lie?"

"Not a lie. His affection for you is as real and true as mine was. There's no point watering the ground if the seed isn't planted, and the seed of Temion's love for his brother was always there. I just made it grow."

He laughed, that old, familiar chuckle. "I can tell you, now the burden of flesh is lifted from me. I never hated you, Rhodri. But Temion needed to love you more than I. Don't tell him—it would undo all the good I did. I still fear for you, and for all the tribes of Atrath."

Rhodri seized the opportunity. "I won't tell him. Come back with me! I need your help."

Kilujen shook his head, genuinely sorrowful. "Your compulsion drives you back to the place from which you came, you can't fight it. Mine brings me here." He looked towards Kharikan. "There she is. Everything I want in the world."

Rhodri stared into the grey haze that marked the fringes of the world. A figure, a lone rider, trotted slowly towards them, more defined with every stride. Even at this distance, he knew it was Ginamor. Kilujen jumped down from the boulder, moving with more enthusiasm than Rhodri had seen in many moons. He followed more slowly, reluctant to interrupt their reunion. Dismounting, Ginamor raised her hands to Kilujen's face, her spectral fingertips brushing, but not touching, his skin. His hand slipped through hers with a glassy ripple, and Rhodri had to turn away at the pain on the shaman's face. Kilujen was right, Ginamor was everything he needed. He could see and speak to her, but he could no longer hold her in his arms, feel the soft crush of her lips against his. He was condemned to a life held in a cage, hating all that he had once cared about, all that he had sacrificed for Temion, and for Rhodri. A worse loss, because the shaman could torture himself with visions of his lost wife every time he felt the desire, but never feel the closeness of her love. It was a cruel fate. No wonder it had driven him to despair. He had given enough, more than enough, and Rhodri would not see him suffer any more. An act of mercy did not always have to be delivered at the tip of a blade.

He felt a tug on the rope around his waist, reminding him of Nasira's presence at the far end of it. How long had he been here? She must be worried, to call him back. "Kilujen, I have to leave." The shaman looked at him anxiously. "Don't worry, I won't let them drag you back with me."

"You're a good friend to grant me that kindness after the way I treated you. I can see how you win men's loyalty. I hope you don't abuse their trust."

To hear the shaman voice Nasira's doubts sent a chill through Rhodri. "It was for the best, for the good of us all. It's hard to balance on this knife blade. Your wisdom could have helped me . . ."

"You want my advice? I know you won't turn back, you're too stubborn for that." Kilujen's face darkened. "Stay away from the castle. If you walk into those halls, you'll be leaving behind everything that's precious to you. You might not walk out again, and if you do, you won't be the same man. You're being tempted down a path that can only lead others to ruin." He tightened his grip on Rhodri's shoulder. "Don't become like the man who raised you. It's not always easy to tell if the trail you lead people down is the right one."

Rhodri shuddered, battling to stifle his memories. To think about Valery here could be fatal. He raised a hand in salute to Kilujen as the rope jerked with increased urgency. "I wish you good hunting on your chosen trail."

"And you on yours." Kilujen clapped both hands to Rhodri's upper arms in farewell. "Be careful, Rhodri. I'd hate to see you join us here."

"So would I."

The Spirit Realm dropped away below him as he was tugged upwards, the sickening jolt of flying as the air thickened around him. He closed his eyes, fighting down nausea and the embarrassing urge to cry for what was lost, for the time he had wasted fighting with his teacher.

His back smacked against the ground with a thump that left him gasping. For a moment, Rhodri lay still, gathering himself together. His tingling skin was warm, and he screwed his eyes shut to ward off the painful glare of sunlight. He must have been gone over half a day.

"Rhodri? Are you back?" Nasira's voice wavered, and the hand she laid on his wrist shook feverishly.

"I'm back." His mouth was dry and gritty. He coughed.

"Thank the spirits!" Nasira sagged. Rhodri caught her in his arms, alarmed at the black hollows below her eyes.

"Nasira? Have you been here all night? When did you last eat?"

"I don't remember . . . Kilujen?"

A considerable crowd had gathered, despite the efforts of the other shamans to keep them back. Temion was at the forefront, face dark with frustration, and Rhodri gestured to him.

"Let my brother through," he commanded, "and fetch my wife a drink!" He bundled Nasira into Temion's arms and took a gulp from the water skin held out to him, choking on the fiery brew.

"Does the shaman live?" Temion asked, in a low voice. Rhodri shook his head, and reached out to Kilujen to confirm his fears. The shaman's pulse was weak and erratic, and it faltered and failed under his fingers. His eyes were open, staring unblinking into the sun, and the corners of his mouth turned up in a slight smile.

Rhodri closed his master's eyes. "Ride in peace, my friend," he whispered.

At his gesture, Nasira uttered a muted sob, turning her face to her brother's shoulder. "Look after her," Rhodri told Temion, staggering to his feet, trying not to breathe in too far to combat the sharp pain in his ribs. The crowd parted as he walked away from the circle of enchantment, falling back before him in silence.

Sudak waited by the wagons. He held Liberty, saddled and bridled, the two of them as quiet and still as statues.

"I thought you'd need her," he said, simply, handing over the reins.

Not trusting his voice, Rhodri said nothing. He mounted, and Liberty responded to the lightest touch, trotting through the camp with her head high. Rhodri didn't need to direct her; she carried him out to the open steppe, stretched out her legs, and threw him an enquiring look.

"Go!"

Liberty needed no more prompting. Neck stretched to the full, she galloped across the plains, hooves thundering on the dusty ground, not as fast as she was in her youth, but still with a speed that snatched the breath from Rhodri's battered lungs. He lost himself in the sensation, the pounding of her hooves, the breeze that whipped away the tears, the scents of sweat and horse. There was nothing else in the world, no Kilujen, no Serren, not even Temion. Just man and horse, running for the sake of running. Running from Kilujen's warning, running from a dark destiny.

*

Kilujen was buried according to the customs of his people, wrapped in a blanket in an unmarked grave. Rhodri found it hard to watch his friend's body lowered into the chill, crumbling earth. He turned away as the hole was filled in, a scattering of mud showering Kilujen's upturned face, and swallowed the bile rising in his throat. It seemed so cold to treat a fallen hero like this, without the glory of a death pyre. Kilujen might not have fought on horseback, but he had sacrificed more than anyone knew to help them in their struggle.

Nasira wrapped her arm around his waist. "You must be our shaman now," she said.

"Me?"

"Unless the Plains Hawk can trade a shaman from another tribe, who else is there?"

He shook his head. "I don't know enough. I don't have the time."

"Who will do it, if not you? Kilujen wanted you to succeed him—"

"Then he should have trained me properly!" His raised voice drew attention. Clamping Nasira's arm under his, he led her away from the grave. "I can't do it," he said, in a lower tone. "You can't ask me."

Her brow creased. "What will we do without a shaman?"

"We're one tribe, for now. Would the other shamans mind performing rituals for the Plains Hawk?"

Nasira shrugged. "We could ask them."

"Persuade them. You're good at that." He offered her a smile, which she returned. "That's better. Let's not worry about this until we've crossed the mountains, at least."

His gaze wandered to the path ahead. Under a high, late-summer sky, the pass looked deceptively tranquil. He wished he could fool himself into believing the crossing would be easy. Perhaps it would have been simpler to make the journey alone? "How many do you think will follow us?"

Nasira nudged him, and pointed. "Bektaran might know," she said.

The man approaching to speak to Rhodri had a left leg several inches shorter than his right, giving him a curious, lop-sided gait. He nodded to Nasira, but didn't waste his breath on excess words.

"Six wagons," he said, arms folded.

"Six wagons what?" Rhodri asked.

"Your woman asked my woman, and I've come to tell you. Six wagons."

Rhodri glanced at Nasira, who looked as baffled as he felt. "Do you mean six wagons to cross over the mountains?" It was less than he'd hoped, but more than he'd dreaded.

Bektaran snorted. "The opposite!"

"Meaning—?" Rhodri's patience was on a short rein.

"Six wagons going back to Kharikan. The wounded, the breeding, and those with tiny babes. Cripples like me." He looked down at his feet with a rueful shrug. "Some fool needs to take care of everyone. I suppose it's me."

Rhodri's eyes swept the vista of the camp. Only six wagons returning to the rock. "How many people are you taking with you, my friend?"

"Forty-seven. Some are going with you who should be with me." He looked Nasira up and down, boldly. She ignored the implication.

"That's good news. Isn't it, Rhodri? Rhodri?"

He shook his head, staggered by the enormity of the task that lay before him. He had expected a few hundred, a large raiding party. What he had now was an army, ready to spill over Serren's eastern border on his command. If he could get them there alive.

*

The weather was warm when Rhodri's army left the foothills for the barren slopes of the mountainside, but the nights closed in earlier, and the wind held a sharp nip. It would be colder on the heights. The ground was rough and stony, treacherous for riding, and when one of Sudak's cartwheels shattered on a boulder, Rhodri called a halt. It was time to continue on foot. Horses and humans, loaded down with everything vital they could carry, pressed on into the mountains.

The air grew colder. Rhodri struggled to catch his breath. This pass was higher than the route he had taken into Atrath with the King's Third, where Jime had fallen and Rhodri had lost part of his soul in a dark tent on a blizzard-lashed mountainside. He walked beside Nasira, head down, mile after endless mile. Asta, strapped to his chest, barely protested, and the warmth of her body against his heart was a comfort.

"We're not the only ones who walk a hard route." Nasira pointed. His senses dulled by fatigue and hunger, Rhodri had to stare hard to make out what she had spotted. Abandoned on the side of the trail, two New Kingdom soldiers sprawled in death, their faces grey, lips and nostrils choked with ice. They could have been there for days in this cold.

Rhodri sighed, and coughed, breath steaming in front of him. Some of his followers had suffered the same fate, dropping on the path to be buried without ceremony under rough cairns of pebbles. But this was the first time they had passed the corpses of hardened troops.

"Are you having doubts?" Only Nasira's eyes were visible under her thick hooded cloak of patchcat fur, and they were large in her thin face, full of concern.

Sometimes Rhodri cursed his wife for being so perceptive. He nodded. In the thin air, he didn't want to waste his breath on talking.

"It would be a harder road back, now we've come so far." She slipped her arm through his. "Tell me about your country again."

"I can't," Rhodri admitted, "I don't have the breath." But the thought of the rich land far below, plump autumn fruits and fattened livestock grazing in the fields, spurred him on. It was an easier life on the far side of the range. He threaded his numb fingers through Liberty's reins and led her on. Everything they owned, their dwindling supply of food, was piled on the little mare's back. She plodded onwards with an air of resignation mirrored in Rhodri's own heart. Cold and exhaustion numbed him to the core, and all he could do was keep walking, day after day, on sore, blistered feet. Encouraging his people, urging them on when all he wanted to do was lie down on the rocks and let the snow claim him, as it had taken Jime. Until now, he hadn't appreciated the courage and fortitude of his late friend, who had led them through far harsher conditions in Dragon Pass with unfaltering good humour and patience. Drusain was right; Jime had been

214

rare, the shining star of his generation. Beside him, Rhodri was less than nothing, a traitor to blood and country. He wondered anxiously what kind of welcome awaited him in the Estmarch.

Sunk deep into these gloomy thoughts, Sudak had to hail him several times before Rhodri found the energy to respond. The young warrior had taken it on himself to roam ahead, spying out the land, and Rhodri was happy to let him. Now Sudak clambered over the rocks towards him, heedless of the cuts to his hands and knees, gesticulating wildly.

"What is it, Sudak?"

"Trees! More than I've ever seen in my life!"

"Show me." Rhodri followed Sudak down the slope and around a jutting outcrop of boulders. At their feet, the hillside dropped away in a steep slope. A few stunted, twisted trees sprouted between the rocks, and for a moment Rhodri thought Sudak was referring to them. But looking down, he could see an ocean of waving fronds, green and restless in the gusty winds whirling down from the peaks. A forest of wintergreens blanketed the lower slopes of the range, marking the eastern border of the Estmarch. He was home. The thought made the breath catch hard in his throat. He had always been willing to die for this country . . .

"Are you all right?" Sudak sounded concerned. "You've gone grey . . ."

"Give me a moment." Rhodri sank to the ground, his back against a boulder, and stared out over the hills of the Estmarch. In the distance, the sunlight glittered off water. Beyond the trees, smoke rose from a campsite or homestead.

Asta stirred against his chest, slurping on her thumb. He lifted her from the sling and turned her to face the Kingdom.

"Can you see it, little one?" he whispered in her ear. "This is your kingdom. Everything you see belongs to you, by right of blood. What do you think?"

Asta yawned, unimpressed by her inheritance.

"I'm tired, too. Let's find your mother and tell her what we've seen. It will be yours before long, I promise. You'll sleep in a big bed behind castle walls, and you'll never go hungry."

"Din!" Asta pointed to her mouth.

"That's right, lots of dinner." He scrambled to his feet, feeling less overwhelmed as the practical concern of feeding his daughter took priority. "Come on! We eat under Western skies tonight!"

*

The forest was crowded with bodies. Most of Rhodri's army slept where they dropped, bundled in their cloaks to protect them from the light, misty rain drifting down from the sky. The night was as black as the grave, no moon or star pierced the thick blanket of cloud, but at least it was warm. The humidity made Rhodri restless. As the night paled to the dull grey of dawn, he rose, careful not to disturb Nasira. She slept curled up on her side, one arm wrapped protectively around her swollen belly, the other holding Asta to her chest. He looked down at his family as the morning light crept over them, highlighting the dark hollows under Nasira's eyes, the fine bones of her cheeks marred with smudges of dirt. She deserved better than this life he had given her.

She sighed, eyelids fluttering as she twitched in her sleep, and Rhodri crept away. Craving solitude, he took Liberty from her picket and led her through the forest, inhaling the spicy tang of tree needles as he crept past the sleepers, who were beginning to stir as the light increased.

Further down the slope, the wintergreens gave way to deciduous trees. The edges of their leaves curled, tinted with the bronze and russet of early autumn. The ground was spongy with rain and the mulch of fallen leaves. Brambles snagged in the rings round Rhodri's ankles, and after the third stop to free his legs, he decided it was time to ride.

The grey, silky light grew as the trees thinned. Every branch Rhodri brushed under dumped a shower of cold water down his neck. Liberty's hooves made no sound as she picked her way with high, delicate steps across the forest floor. It was an eerie place, devoid of all the little sounds he expected to hear in a forest, no buzzing insects or warbling birds. Even the rustle of leaves was muted by the damp, only the constant drip of water serving to break the silence.

He emerged from the woods on the southern edge of a lake. Liberty snorted in alarm, backing up as the oily water lapped her front hooves. The lake was covered in thick green slime, and as Rhodri watched, a bubble like a massive blister rose to the surface and burst with a faint wet pop. The smell it released left him gagging, and he pulled the collar of his shirt up to cover his nose.

"I'm no shaman, but I can tell this is an evil place."

Startled, Rhodri swallowed a curse. He hadn't heard Temion approach over the soggy ground. Nasira's brother stood at his shoulder, surveying the ruined lake. The flaring nostrils of his gelding indicated the horse's fear.

"Did you follow me?"

"I saw you leave. Can you imagine what Nasira would do to me if I let you get hurt?" He grinned, and screwed up his nose at the smell. "Let's go back. This place stinks of death."

Rhodri shook his head. "I want to ride on for a way. We might find fresh water."

"There's nothing fresh around here," Temion said, with a gesture of disdain.

"It's worth a try."

They rode on around the lake in silence. The oppressive atmosphere made the hairs on the back of Rhodri's neck prickle. On the north shore, the desolation was harsher, a scar on the ground sweeping in a broad crescent away from the edge of the water. Nothing grew here, not even grass. Temion dismounted and tasted a handful of the bare, dead earth with the tip of his tongue. He spat.

"Salt," he said.

"From the lake?"

"No. I'll wager this was done deliberately. What's wrong?"

A scar in the earth a mile wide . . . the ground sown with salt . . . hundreds dead . . .

Rhodri slipped from the saddle, wrapping his arms tight around his belly to quell the hideous gnawing there. He leant against Liberty's shoulder, seeking comfort in her warmth, but his legs wouldn't hold him and he slithered to the ground. Temion loomed above him, brow creased with concern. "Are you all right?"

Rhodri's words died in his throat. He groped for his water skin to wash away the sickly taste. The piles of an abandoned jetty emerged from the water like a row of broken teeth. People had lived here, once.

Temion dug his toe into the poisoned earth. "What manner of man salts good grazing land?" he wondered aloud.

The kind of man who betrays his best friend, steals a babe from his mother's arms . . .

Rhodri found his voice: "The man who raised me."

"What?"

"This was my mother's village, but there's nothing left of her here. Let's go. The stench makes me sick."

"Are you sure?" Temion took a few steps towards the shack. "There might be something . . ."

"There's nothing!" Rhodri scrambled into the saddle and Liberty turned her back on the lake and trotted away, as eager to put the place behind her as he was. He didn't look to see if Temion followed. His hands clenched tight on the reins, blood pounding in his ears. He had not expected to see evidence of Valery's blackest deed with his own eyes, but now he had witnessed it, it carved a scar on his heart as deep as the scar in the earth. Whatever good had once been here was razed to the ground and utterly destroyed. His mother may have walked these shores, but now her memory

218

danced on the ashes of the dead. He didn't want to remember any more than he had to of Lydyce.

*

The path Rhodri followed with his army swung out in a wide loop, skirting the contaminated lake and the dead shore. He pushed his people north. Winter was coming, and they needed rest and shelter before the worst of the weather descended from the high peaks. He knew where he was going, but it would be a hard ride, and a harder fight at the end of it.

The countryside around Lydyce was abandoned, miles beyond the scar in the earth and the poisoned lake. No one wanted to live with the shadow of death hanging over them. It was almost noon when Rhodri's scouts reported the first signs of habitation, a small farm huddled in a dip between two hills. Woolbeasts and cattle roamed the slopes, but as Rhodri scanned it he could see no sign of humans.

"We should take some cattle," he told Sudak. "Keep them for their milk, and some woolbeasts for food and skin. The men who own this place need never know we were here . . ."

"Tell them that." Temion, who rode with them, jerked his head at the army, which had halted half a mile behind. "Your men itch for blood, Rhodri. Did you bring them all this way to sneak around like thieves?" His decorated braids rattled together as he tossed his head. "We are warriors, short-hair. Let us be what we are!"

"We should raid the buildings," Sudak added. "It's not just food we're low on. We need blankets, tents, wagons, fresh horses—"

Rhodri's frustration boiled over. "All right!" He knew Sudak spoke the truth. "Raid, if you must. But no killing. The men down there aren't soldiers, and they haven't raised a hand against the tribes."

"As Trogir never raised a hand against the short-hairs?" Temion arched an eyebrow. "What about Odval? And Nasira never loosed an arrow against your sister's men, but they beat her and tried to make sport with her—"

"Do you think I've forgotten that? That I can't see every bruise on her skin, every time I think about it?"

Temion's ride bucked as he raised his voice. "Then let us do to them what they've done to us. Let your sister be on the sharp end of the blade, for once!" Before Rhodri could protest, Temion wheeled his horse around and galloped back to the waiting army.

By the time Rhodri caught up with him, the camp was buzzing with rumour. Behind the excited chatter that greeted him, he heard the sound of weapons being sharpened, and harness jingling. A woman grabbed him by the leg as he slowed Liberty to a walk.

"Is it true?" she asked. "Are there short-hairs over the hill?"

He looked down into her face, painted for war, her braids pinned up battle-fashion.

"I haven't seen any," he answered, honestly.

Her eyes were bright. "I hope there are. The short-hairs took my husband just before we crossed the mountains. They need to feel the bite of my arrows!"

Rhodri shook his head and turned away. How could he say anything, when this woman's husband had died following him on the war trail? She was entitled to take her revenge. Every tribe had lost someone. *Serren brought this on herself.* But his justification sounded hollow in his mind, and he hung back as Temion led the raiding party over the hill and into the valley.

The attack was a hammer blow from the sky. The owners of the farm barely had time to run for their weapons before the tribes were on them, running for shelter only to be cut down in their own yard. He saw a man fall, dropped face-down with an arrow in his kidneys. Screams and howls, the clash of metal and the smell of smoke. This was not a raid, it was slaughter. Killing and burning, wanton destruction. The tribes took their long-awaited revenge in the manner the Kingdom army had taught them, and all Rhodri could do was watch, and hope this violent outburst of energy would be enough to calm his followers, at least for a while.

*

In the following days, the Atrathene horde spread out across the hills of the Estmarch like a swarm of voracious insects, consuming everything in their path. Farms, hamlets, nameless villages, all were swallowed up, every morsel of food consumed, everything that could not be used put to the torch. Rhodri counselled restraint, but he knew his more hot-headed warriors were not so concerned, and his words were forgotten in the exhilarating rush of violence and revenge. Sweeping north, they encountered more and more empty towns, abandoned before the crushing tide. Sudak reported that the roads ahead were clogged with fleeing refugees.

"Is this what you wanted?" Nasira asked, as she stood with Rhodri on a rise watching another farm burn. Atrathene warriors danced in the light of the flames, gorging themselves on the spoils of victory. "If your sister lives in a stingflies nest, you've just prodded it with a stick."

"I pushed the cart to the top of the hill. It's rolling away now, and I don't think I can stop it."

"Pull it back before we crash, Rhodri," Nasira warned. "This is just raiding. What happens when we reach a city? Will it become another Lydyce?"

Rhodri shuddered. "Not that. Never that."

"Then rein in your men!" Her lips snapped shut, and she folded her arms across her stomach and turned her face away, staring into the gathering dusk.

It was a hard thing to discipline the free-spirited Atrathenes, unaccustomed to taking orders, and the latest test of Rhodri's leadership came sooner than he wanted. The town—he remembered from his schooling it was probably Terinth—lay in a hollow surrounded by hills. It was protected by a square stone wall, with a stout watchtower at each corner. The gates were firmly closed, and the walls bristled with archers. Terinth would not fall without a fight.

Beside him, Temion offered a shrug. *What do we do now?* the gesture asked.

Rhodri sighed. "We take the town, but it's time to do things my way. I've let the men have their fun, but none of the tribes know anything about fighting in cities. I do. Tell your men to do exactly as I say, and we'll come out of this with a victory, and hopefully without many losses." He scanned the landscape. "See the road coming down from the north? I want that cut off. No one leaves to send for help, and no one comes in. I expect they've already sent out a messenger hawk, so let's not drag this out. Let them know they're surrounded, but stay back from the walls. We'll leave them to chew it over for a day or two before we attack." He watched a speculative arrow whizz from one of the watchtowers, falling to earth just short of where they stood. "No one goes closer than this, is that clear?"

Temion nodded. Sudak stared at the arrow, quivering in the ground where it stuck fast.

"Let them know we're here. Scare them as much as you like. If we're lucky, they'll surrender without a fight."

"And if we're unlucky?" Sudak asked, unable to tear his eyes from the arrow.

"We'll make them see reason." Rhodri spoke with more confidence than he felt.

"Or we'll torch the town!" Temion added.

"It won't come to that." Rhodri's nails dug into his palms. It would *not*, he swore. He knew he danced on the cliff's edge. It was only a matter of time before he slipped and fell.

He spent a restless night. Nasira was uncomfortable, rising several times to empty her bladder, but even if she had slept, the noise from the camp would have disturbed him. Temion heeded his order to let the town know the Atrathenes were there. Constant drumming, war whoops and shouted threats reverberated off the implacable stone walls. Their noise set Asta crying, and eventually Rhodri picked her up and took her outside, pacing up and down. He bounced her in his arms and watched the sun rise behind the distant mountains, turning the sky to pale blue flecked with gold and crimson.

The frenzied drumming and chanting grew louder. The Atrathenes often drummed in celebration, but the war drums had a different tone, heavy with menace, like the rumble of thunder in the hills. If it unnerved him, what must it be doing to the minds of the Estmarchers trapped in the besieged city?

Asta pressed her hands to her ears and screwed up her face in protest, but there was nothing he could do except wrap her inside his cloak and hope the noise stopped soon. There was no escape from it, but he headed towards the picket lines, where it was a little quieter.

Liberty lay sleeping, nose flat on the ground, and Rhodri leant against her as he had done at Northpoint when he was a boy. He held Asta in his lap as her thumb crept to her mouth and her eyes closed. If he was lucky, she would sleep for a few hours, and so could he.

He was drifting off when a hand pressed against his neck brought him back to startled life. By instinct honed through long training, he did not cry out, but one hand flashed up to seize the wrist of his assailant, while the other groped for his dagger. The sudden movement spilt Asta out of his lap, and she burst into tears.

"Sudak! Look what you've done!" Rhodri beat his follower's hand away and scooped up his daughter. Her wails rivalled the war drums in their volume. "What's the matter?"

Sudak would not look him in the eye. "It's my fault," he admitted. "I was talked into it . . . We were too eager—"

"What are you talking about?" Rhodri had to raise his voice over Asta's cries.

"Some of the younger warriors tried to raid the city, and I went with them." Sudak stared at his boots.

Rhodri tightened his arms around Asta, still protesting. "They did what? Didn't I tell you—?"

"I know! I should have discouraged them, it was my fault!" When he looked up, Sudak's eyes were wide with fear.

Rhodri's heart sank. "Tell me what happened."

"Six of us tried to scale the west wall. I was keeping watch. I warned them to be careful. But they went over the top and they didn't come back. I heard fighting . . ."

"When was this?"

"Before sunrise. I came straight to find you. Rhodri, there were women with them—"

"Fucking hells!" Rhodri thrust Asta into Sudak's arms and grabbed Liberty, not bothering with saddle or bridle, and ignoring her snort of protest. "Take her back to her mother, fetch Temion, and meet me where we studied the town yesterday. Quick as you can!"

He cantered to the overlook, unleashing a string of curses under his breath. Racing clouds cast dark shadows over the town, and he saw people swarming like insects on the walls and in the streets below. Looking down the road, blocked with his own troops, he saw no one trying to leave. Most of the activity centred around the nearest watchtower. He had been spotted, he knew, from the arrows that whizzed towards him, but he had no fear of them reaching him. The shots were just a whispered threat, but the catapult being assembled on the walls spoke more loudly, and he urged Liberty back a dozen yards.

Temion arrived, breathless, Sudak trailing at his heels. The younger man looked abashed, and Rhodri didn't bother to question the bruise darkening on his cheek. Let Temion mete out discipline as he saw fit. Rhodri was more concerned with the fate of his missing warriors. Were they hostages? Should he leave the town alone in exchange for their freedom, or fight to save them?

"What's happening?" Temion asked. "Have you decided what to do?"

"They've brought up a catapult. I want to see if they use it. I'd give up the town to see our people returned safely, but how do I tell them that?"

"I could take a message," Sudak said, eagerly. "Let me help, my leader. I've been a fool."

The catapult fired. Rhodri ducked as Liberty skittered backwards. The missile slammed into the base of the hill with a dull thump. He had expected rocks to be hurled, but looking down he saw the sprawling body of a man, broken and twisted from the impact. He bit his lip, swallowed against nausea. "Sudak? Fetch him, but be careful."

Silent, holding a shield above his head for protection, Sudak picked his way down the hill on foot to collect the body, lifting it over his broad shoulders. The peppering of arrows stopped as he made his journey, cementing Rhodri's fears.

Sudak dumped the body at his feet. The dead man was no Atrathene, but a Westerner. His throat was slashed open, so deep his tongue drooped through the bloody gash, and he was shirtless. On his left breast, the outline blurred but unmistakable, was the stylized brand of the Plains Hawk.

"Why do they throw over their own people?" Temion asked. "It shows no respect."

"It's a message," Rhodri said, softly. "They want us to see it." He cradled his head in his hands, a chill creeping over his skin. This man was not Mairwas. He was much younger and more lightly built, yet he bore the same scar. What did it mean?

Temion cleared his throat. "Rhodri? They're sending another one. Should I—?"

Rhodri nodded. "Do it."

The second body was dressed identically to the first, military breeches but no shirt. This man was older, his grizzled beard suggesting Telesian ancestry, and he had been killed by a knife wound through the small of the back, piercing his kidney. As Temion rolled him over, Rhodri caught a glimpse of the brand, and groaned.

"Rhodri?" Temion sounded worried. "Why do these short-hairs wear our brand?"

"I don't know," Rhodri admitted, "but it bodes ill. I want to talk to the city."

"I don't think that's a good idea—" "—Let me do it!" Temion and Sudak spoke at the same time.

Rhodri straightened. "I'll go," he said. "You two stay here. That's an order, Sudak, and I expect you to obey me this time!" Before his companions could argue, he urged Liberty down the slope, shield held in front of him, heading for the massive wooden gates of the city and trying to ignore the erratic drumming of his heart.

He approached to within hailing distance, feeling small, exposed and alone. He wasn't about to show that to the defenders as he sucked in a deep breath. "I speak to Terinth. Who answers for the city?"

There was a disturbance on the walls above, and a bass voice rumbled down. "I speak for the city. What do you want, Atrathene?"

"I want my warriors back."

There was a moment of agitation. Rhodri sensed shock that the leader of this tribe of savages should come in person to plead for his men's lives. That he should be a Westerner.

"*Your* warriors?"

Wishing he had a more imposing steed, Rhodri made the most of his five-and-a-half feet. "Do you know who I am, men of Terinth?"

The reply was spat back at him, in a voice thick with scorn and loathing. "We know who you are, Northpoint bastard! Terinth will never surrender to a traitor. The city would rather burn!"

Rhodri shrugged, keeping his voice deliberately casual, while inside he seethed with fury. "If that's how you want it . . . ?"

"Here's your answer, Northpoint!" The catapult sprang into life, hurling an object the size of a melon high over the walls to land a

226

few yards from Rhodri. Liberty started at the movement, and he pressed a hand to her neck to soothe her. High above, the guardians on the walls rained down catcalls and abuse, but to Rhodri they were nothing but a muffled blur. He stared down at the severed head rolling in the dirt beneath Liberty's hooves.

He knew the boy by name. Karook, of the Running Goat tribe. He had seen eighteen summers and his woman was expecting their first child. The head weighed heavy in his hands as he leaned down and lifted it by what remained of the hair. Karook's warrior's braids were hacked short in a gesture of final insult. Disgusted, he backed away from the gate until he was beyond the range of all but the luckiest arrows, then turned and trotted for the hill where Temion and Sudak waited, keeping his movements calm and deliberate, cradling Karook's head in his arms as he was accustomed to cradle Asta. He held out the head towards Sudak, who recoiled in horror.

"Take it!" Rhodri thrust it at him. "You're to blame for this, so you can tell his woman. Be a man about it."

Sudak took Karook's head gingerly, wrapping it in his shirt. "What about the city, brother?" Temion asked.

Rhodri turned back to look at the town. Spikes were being raised along the battlements. Six spikes, for six limp bodies, one without a head. He closed his eyes in pain. "Burn it to the ground," he said.

*

The order to destroy the city, wrung from Rhodri's lips by bitter circumstance, was easier to say than to achieve. The Atrathenes had no experience of sieges, and all Rhodri knew was remembered from books, and book learning was far removed from real life. Every day he expected a relieving army to flood down the northern road, to rescue the beleaguered city and spill his tribe's blood on the red hills of the Estmarch.

Day and night, the tribes harried the town, arrows and sling-shot stones bouncing off the high walls, sometimes finding a target among the defenders above. Those inside the city replied with their own arrows, but the scene was nothing more than small boys throwing pebbles at each other. It was frustrating, and all the while Rhodri was aware of the passage of time, the threat from the north and the chill of approaching winter.

"We need to get into the city," Rhodri declared after several days of back-and-forth. "It's taking too long to starve them out, and we need shelter. Real shelter, not this." He slapped the canvas wall of his tent.

"How do we fight, surrounded by houses?" Temion asked. "On the grasslands, everything was simple, but here?" He made a wry face. "The horizon is too close. I feel smothered, little brother. I want to stretch my limbs, to ride under endless skies. Don't you feel the same?"

"Let's worry about breaching the walls first." Rhodri ignored Temion's wistful question. This was his home, his kingdom. He belonged here. He shouldn't feel this cramped and confined, and waiting added to the pressure. The sooner Terinth was brought to its knees, the happier he would be. "Once we're in, we fight the way we did in the Spires, after the short-hairs took Odval."

Temion's face cleared. "That was a fine day, and a worthy victory."

"The Telesians have a fighting style they call the Horned Frog," Rhodri went on. "I've seen pictures. This Horned Frog has overlapping plates on its back that make it hard to bite. If we overlap our shields above our heads, we can get a body of men close to the walls."

Temion rasped his thumb along his jaw. "It won't protect us from fire," he pointed out. "Or boiling water. Scaling the walls worked out ill for Sudak . . ."

Rhodri shook his head. "I want to bring down the gate with a ram. A tree trunk, maybe, tipped with iron. If I draw it, can you build it?" He tapped his ankle with a rueful shrug. "You're good with metal, after all."

"I can make anything you want. Trust me, brother, I won't let you down."

Temion, happier with a task to keep him busy, kept his promise with robust enthusiasm, bullying and cajoling anyone he could find to help him. Content to give him his head, Rhodri watched the city, and the road beyond. The bodies of his followers hung rotting from the battlements, a constant thorn under his saddle. Every time he saw them, his ire was inflamed afresh.

It wouldn't happen under my rule. Did Serren know or care that barbaric acts were being committed in her name? "When I rule here—"

"Rhodri!" He started. He had not heard Nasira ride up behind him. Her ears were cat-sharp, and her eyes flashed dangerous amber.

"What?"

"You know I don't like that talk. Or the look in your eye when you think about it."

"Think about what? Have you seen Temion? How's he getting on?"

"Don't change the subject," she snapped. "My brother is right. The skies are too narrow here. When do we go home?"

"If you want to go home, the mountains are that way." He pointed. "Go on. Take Temion with you. I'm staying until I achieve what I came for."

"Which is what? Peace for the tribes? Or a kingdom for yourself?" She turned away in disgust before he could reply. "Temion has finished his work. He wants you to see it."

"Nasira, wait!" Rhodri trotted to catch up with her, pulling Liberty round in front of the taller mare his wife rode, forcing them to stop. "I'm doing this for you, you know. For Asta, and the babe. I want to give you what I never had."

"I'd rather you gave me what I want, not what you think I need."

"You want peace, don't you? That's what I'm trying to give—"

"Leave me alone, Rhodri!" She delivered a hefty kick to the sides of her mount and cantered away, leaving him clenching his fists in frustration. The baby-madness must be on her, even though the child was still a few moons away. He would be glad when it was born, when he would be able to help her. All he could do now was tolerate her ill temper.

Temion met him at the bottom of the hill with a broad smile that made Rhodri feel better at once. He was standing beside an object draped in canvas, longer than a man was tall. Rhodri rubbed his hands together in anticipation.

"Let's see it, brother!" Temion whipped back the canvas. The tree trunk, smoothed and polished, was reinforced with wide steel bands. It hung suspended from stout ropes, in a cradle on wheels. Rhodri gave it an experimental push, and it swung back and forth easily under his hands. "A fine job," he declared.

"You haven't seen the best part," Temion said. He pulled away the draped fabric that concealed the tip of the ram to reveal an iron point, fashioned in the style of a horse's head, with two long, vicious spikes jutting out from the forehead, above the eyes.

"We can splinter the wood in the door. No man will be able to stand before it. I call it the Scourge. What do you think?"

Rhodri grinned. "Terinth won't know what it's up against until it's too late to stop it! Well done, my brother!"

Temion looked eagerly at the walled town. "Do you want to test it out?"

"Wait until it rains," Rhodri said. "Then they can't fight back with fire. Have your men practiced the Horned Frog?"

Temion frowned. "Fighting on foot isn't natural to them. There has been resistance."

"The Horned Frog relies on every man moving as one. If any man won't do it, replace him. If we get this wrong, we could be here for moons, and your sister will take my ears for a necklace!"

*

It didn't take long for the gloomy skies of the Kingdom to provide Rhodri with the weather he wanted. He awoke to the steady patter of rain beating against the roof of the tent, and hugged himself in silent glee, anticipating the day ahead. Adrenaline surged through his limbs. He felt ready to take on a dozen cities, ride into the Midlands and lay claim to Hierath, shout his proud lineage from the highest tower. If he stretched, he could touch the glowering sky. Tingling all over, he reached for Nasira, turned away from him on her side. He traced a finger up the curve of her spine, and she shuddered.

"Busy day ahead," he whispered in her ear, his breath lifting the fine hairs on the back of her neck. "How are you feeling?"

She fended off his roaming hands. "Fat, sick, and not in the mood."

"You're not fat." He pulled her towards him, stroking his palms over the curve of her stomach. "This little one doesn't kick as much as Asta."

"I praise the spirits for that." Nasira pushed her hair out of her eyes and fixed him with a steady gaze. "This is what you live for, isn't it? The excitement, the fighting . . ."

"I live for you." He kissed her, mouth lingering on hers, and felt her breath quicken. "You and Asta, and the babe when it comes."

"So the fighting is honey on top of that?" She pushed his head away as he sought her nipples with his tongue.

"I spent years training for days like this. How can I not feel a thrill?"

"I'd rather you kept your thrills between the blankets, safe with me."

He crept his arms round her back, massaging the tension from her shoulders, feeling her relax into his embrace. "Nasira, there's nothing more thrilling than you, you know that."

She smiled. "Do you have to hurry away?"

"We can make time . . ."

By the time Rhodri left the tent, his nerves sang a high, feverish note. Taking his pleasure with Nasira had not relieved his tension. The trampled ground was oily and treacherous underfoot, and Temion frowned over the Scourge. "Today?" he asked.

Rhodri nodded.

"It'll be slippery under the gate. Dangerous."

"As dangerous as fire falling from above?"

Temion shrugged. "I've never fought under a rain of fire, so I don't know. But I have fought in the mud. I'd rather deal with what I'm used to."

Rhodri watched as Temion gathered the strongest warriors, those who would push the battering ram, and the tallest, to protect them with a shield wall that overlapped above their heads as he had envisioned. Being neither tall nor burly, Rhodri found himself redundant to the operation. He roamed the front ranks behind the Scourge, encouraging his army, leading them in war chants and vibrant drumming. By the time Temion passed word that the team around the ram were ready to move, the front ranks of Rhodri's army were wound tight, quivering with as much anticipation as their young leader. It would take only a word to see them hurl themselves against the walls of the city.

Rhodri made them wait, drawing them tighter and tighter, playing on the tension of his men like a harper tuning a string. The rain lashed down, plastering his hair to his forehead and dripping in his eyes. The Scourge strained through the mud, wheels clogging in the mire, inching forward while falling arrows bounced harmlessly off the shield wall.

There was a disturbance, far away to the north of the city, the sound muffled by wind and howling rain. The storm of arrows faltered, and with an effort almost beyond human strength, Temion's men heaved the Scourge forward until its long, pointed horns rested against the gate.

Over the wind, Rhodri heard the distant sounds of chaos. Liberty could hear it too. Her ears flattened against her head and she danced on the spot, muscles straining towards the sound of battle as he struggled to hold her.

There was a dull thump, the sound of wood cracking, louder than the violent elements. A cheer rose from his men's throats. The drumming rose to a frenzy, and Liberty's eyes rolled. The Scourge crashed against the wood of the city gate three more times. The final blow, and the metal horse's head with its spiteful horns ripped through the aged wood as if it were thinner than a sheet of parchment.

That was the moment Rhodri had waited for. With a whoop of victory, he gave Liberty a slight nudge to send her down the hill, the tribes of Atrath thundering in his wake. They streamed past the Scourge, abandoned in its cradle, and flooded through the shattered gate into the narrow, winding streets of Terinth. A murderous tide; every Atrathene had seen the bodies of their comrades degraded and skewered on the walls of the city, and every man wanted his revenge.

As the initial exhilarating rush faded, the Atrathenes spread through the town, determined to extinguish any resistance and let the terrified inhabitants know who their new masters were. Rhodri led a small group through the wealthy quarter of the city, where the merchants' houses stood in their own grounds and the streets were broad, swept clean of dirt and mud. Beside him, Sudak clapped his hands in delight as they rode down an alley between high walls, metal gates revealing glimpses of the luxurious houses beyond. "Rich pickings here!"

"We take what we need," Rhodri reminded him. "Remember, we're better than Serren's attack dogs—"

He broke off at the sound of a sharp scream from the far side of the wall. Without thinking, heedless of his own safety, Rhodri vaulted from Liberty's back onto the broad top of the wall and scrambled down the other side, Sudak in breathless pursuit. He landed, cat-like, on smooth wet grass, and sprang up with bared sword in hand. He took in his surroundings with a sweeping glance, committing them to everlasting memory.

The house, two storeys of stone and timber, had a wide lawn sloping down to the wall where he crouched in the shadows. The lower windows of the house were shattered, and the back door hung open, bashing back and forth in the wind.

A group of Atrathene warriors crowded near the door. They hadn't noticed his arrival. Their attention was focused on the man twisting and struggling in their midst as they forced him to the ground.

"Stop!" As the ringleader dropped his breeches, Rhodri lashed out with a blade, carving a red line across his buttocks. "What are you, animals? Let him go!"

The man spun around as if stung by an insect, lashing out with his stout war axe, the metal striking sparks off Rhodri's sabre. As he registered Rhodri's Atrathene clothing and pale, Western face, he let the blade fall. They didn't know each other by sight, but the thug retreated a pace before his fury.

"Leader? It's the spoils of conquest . . ."

"Not this conquest." Sudak came up behind him. Rhodri was reassured by his lanky presence, though he was so enraged he would have taken on all five of the would-be rapists himself. "If I catch any man in my army abusing any woman, or man, for sport, I'll make sure he joins his brothers who are spiked on the city walls! Is that clear?"

The miscreants mumbled their agreement, backing off from the blade he brandished.

"Let him go." As he caught the man by his arm and dragged him to his feet, Rhodri staggered at the flash of memory, the vision Valery had tried to force into his head. "Now leave us. Spread my word. Any man I catch in the act of rape or attempted rape will lose his balls first, then his life. I won't have it, you hear me?"

As they hurried away, chastened, he turned the kneeling man's face upwards and wiped the blood from his temple with the ball of his thumb. He was a few years older than Rhodri, fair hair curling around his shoulders. His face was delicate, with high cheekbones, attractive under the dirt and blood. His eyes were red-rimmed and his arms reddened with bruises. He regarded Rhodri in dull incomprehension.

"Are you hurt?"

His eyes widened, and the colour drained from his face, leaving him grey and wraithlike. "Northpoint!" He slumped in submission, bowing his head. "I'll do what you say, only don't burn me! Anything but that!"

"What are you talking about?" Rhodri struggled to pull him up, but he was a dead weight, sagging in his grip as he passed out.

"Let me." Sudak scooped up the unconscious man and draped him over his shoulder, legs and arms hanging loose. "What was he babbling about? He seemed more scared of you than the men you drove off."

"He asked me not to burn him." Rhodri shrugged, confused. "He knew who I was . . ."

"Your story has spread far beyond the steppes, my leader." Sudak beamed.

"I'm not sure that's a good thing."

Sudak hefted the man into a more comfortable position. "What should I do with him?"

"Take him out of the city. Stay with him until he comes to. Don't let anyone touch him." He frowned. "I'm not the demon he thinks I am."

Abandoning the pretty youth to his friend's care, Rhodri rode on, troubled by what he had seen and heard.

*

By the following morning the gales gave way to glorious, if chilly, autumn sunshine. The city was under Atrathene control. There were pockets of resistance, but most of the inhabitants had pulled

235

their heads in after a night of bloodshed and horror. The garrison had resisted valiantly, but the Atrathene incursion coursed through the streets like blood through a man's veins, savage, red and raw. The tired soldiers, reeling with shock, were no match for them, and before dawn the last man threw down his arms and surrendered. It was left to the civilians to try and hold on to what was theirs.

High on the walls of the city, above the gore that ran like water in the streets, Rhodri stood alone. He watched a trio of men belonging to the Running Goat tribe take down the spikes that pierced their slaughtered comrades. The carrion birds had snatched their eyes, pecked their flesh, and the stench of decomposition made him gag, but they were his tribe. He would not leave them as a grisly trophy. There were plenty of dead littering the streets, too many to treat every individual with the respect he deserved, but these five boys and their blood-sister would be honoured according to the traditions of their people.

He helped wrap the bodies in blankets, uttering a hollow shamanic blessing over each one, and hating the fact that he had to ask their names. He should know everyone who died under his command, and it shamed him that he didn't.

He straightened over Karook's body, back aching, eyes gritty with fatigue. He hoped he could catch a little sleep, in a doorway or here on the battlements. Nasira liked to joke that he was the cat, who could sleep in any patch of sunlight or on any awkward ledge. He rubbed his eyes, thinking of Nasira, how much he needed her arms around him now. He hoped she was safe.

"Rhodri!" Temion hailed him from below. *No chance for sleep then.* Rhodri leant over the edge of the battlements and looked down at his brother-in-law, standing with his broad arms resting on Liberty's back. "Are you busy?"

Looking at the shrouded bodies, Rhodri sighed. "There's nothing more I can do here, so I suppose not. What's wrong?"

"We need you. Come down!"

They rode together through the silent streets, hooves splashing through spilt blood. Rhodri kept his sword drawn, wary of ambush, but it seemed the people of Terinth had retreated to lick their wounds. Or maybe they were too afraid to face him.

"There's resistance in the northern city," Temion told him. "People trying to get out of the gate. We let some go, the women and children. That was what you wanted?"

Rhodri nodded. "What do you need me for? You seem to have everything under control."

"Not quite." They rode into the main square. On a normal day, it would have been packed with traders, hawking wares from every corner of the kingdom. Now the stalls lay in ruins, smashed pottery and trampled fruit mixing with the fresh blood that stained the flattened earth. A baby boy, crusted with filth, wailed beside the body of his mother, and Rhodri turned his face away.

"How long has he been there?" he demanded. "Take care of it. Where are our women?"

"They didn't want to touch him in case he was diseased." At Rhodri's glare, Temion held up a placating hand. "I'll have it dealt with. That's not why I brought you here." He pointed to a tower that buttressed the north-eastern corner of the square. It was the highest building Rhodri had seen in the city, stretching to five stories. There were no windows on the ground floor, and the only visible entrance was a small door at the height of the second floor, reached by a slender stone stair. It was surrounded by baying Atrathenes, shields up to ward off from the arrows that dropped from above.

"We think it's where they store their weapons. There's a group inside, men and women. They won't come out, and we can't get in. The prisoners translated for us; they say they have food to last a moon, and enough weapons to hold us off long into winter. What shall we do about them?"

"I'll talk to them," Rhodri said. "Maybe I can bring them to their senses." He dismounted and pushed through the crowds.

The prisoners, shackled, formed a human wall between his men and the armoury tower. As he approached, one man turned his head and spat at him.

Rhodri's eyes narrowed. "Are you looking for special attention, my friend? You've just earned it. Walk in front of me." He jabbed at him with his dagger to emphasise his point.

The man spat again. "I'd sooner die in chains, you fucking traitor!"

"If dying in chains is what you want, I can arrange that." Rhodri seized his arm as the prisoner stumbled over his manacles, breath tight with fear. "You don't want to die, or why would you surrender? Do you want to get out of the city alive? Then do exactly as I say, or stars help me I'll open your throat myself. Walk!"

Having no choice, the man shuffled in front of him, shielding him from missiles hurled from above, Rhodri's dagger pressed close into the small of his back. He could hear his prisoner cursing him for the "bastard son of a rapist" under his breath.

"You're bold, for a man with a knife in his back. I suggest you keep your breath in your lungs, while you still have it." Rhodri's voice was clipped, as he struggled to contain his anger. "Hail the tower," he added as an arrow skimmed past his hand. "Tell them I'll start killing prisoners if they don't stop firing, and you'll be first."

"The city is lost! Surrender, and you will not be harmed!"

The flights of arrows stopped abruptly.

There was a stirring at one of the highest windows. He couldn't see anyone, but a man's voice called down, dripping with scorn. "You lie, Northpoint! I'd trust you as far as I'd trust your father!"

"I'm not Valery, damn him to the hells!"

"We don't surrender to Atrathenes or Northpoints. Go back to your tent. Mourn the blood that fashioned you."

Rhodri's fist tightened on the hilt of his dagger. "Are there women and children with you?"

A scuffle, no reply.

"If there are, let them leave—"

"Into your custody? Not likely."

The sun was still ascending, the clouds light and streaky. "You have until noon."

"Before what, Northpoint? You can't get in here. We could hold you off until Winterfest, and help will arrive long before then."

"Really? I've seen no aid coming so far. Could it be your friends at Whitewood have abandoned you to my cruelty?"

Another silence. This was good. The unseen man wasn't as confident as he sounded.

"Let the women and children go. If you want to sacrifice yourself, go ahead. Remember, noon." Dragging his human shield with him, he returned to his own men.

Temion shot him an enquiring look. "What do we do now, my brother?"

"They won't come out. Have the prisoners gather wood, anything that will burn. Pile it round the base of the tower, and lay the dead on it. We'll light such a death pyre Serren will see the flames in Hierath."

By the time the sun reached its zenith, the wood heaped around the base of the tower reached to the door. Corpses were piled on it with little respect, and less regard for whether they were Atrathene or men of the Kingdom. Rhodri, hanging back out of arrow range, kept an eye on the windows. The armoury tower was quiet, had been eerily so since the first wood was thrown on the pyre. He hoped for a sign of surrender, but none was forthcoming. If he had to smoke them out, so be it. He would have his victory by the end of the day. He felt a grudging admiration for the obstinacy of those inside. He doubted he would have the courage to hold still in the face of such odds.

Temion handed him a burning brand. The heat licked at his face. The last time he had put flame to a death pyre was back in Northpoint, saying goodbye to Astan. He wondered if his friend saw what he did now, and condemned him for it.

I'm sorry, Astan. I wish I could live up to what you thought of me.

239

The path he rode was overgrown, and it was impossible to tell the right direction. All he had were his instincts, and the blistering determination not to be like Valery. He hoped the men in the tower would surrender quickly, when the smoke crept up the stairs and into their lungs.

"Last chance," he called. "Come out, or burn with the dead!"

There was no reply, no movement. He hurled the brand, twisting end over end, trailing smoke in the noon sunlight. It struck the pyre, and caught.

The damp wood threw up clouds of smoke as it burned. Rhodri's eyes watered as he gestured his men to retreat to where the air was clearer. He watched the door, almost lost under billowing clouds, waiting for movement that didn't come.

Where are they?

Temion, a cloth held tightly over his mouth, patted him on the shoulder and pointed up. On the pinnacle of the tower, almost lost in the drifting smoke and hazy heat, figures moved.

"What are they doing?" Rhodri shouted over the roar and crackle of the flames. "There's no way out up there."

"Come away." Temion plucked his elbow. "They don't seek a way out, not the way you mean."

"What are you talking about?"

The shifting smoke parted, pierced by a shaft of sunlight. A willowy figure teetered on the edge of the roof, her floating dress billowing like a silky refection of the roaring flames below. She held a bundle tight against her breast.

"No!" Rhodri struggled against Temion as the woman, head high, stepped off the roof and tumbled like a rag doll into the consuming flames. "No! Put the fire out! Put it out!"

"Come away, brother." Temion's voice was muffled by the cloth. "The flames have taken hold. There's nothing you can do."

"I never meant it to happen! They were supposed to surrender!"

"Listen," Nasira's brother said, seizing his shoulders, "*I* know that, but your men don't. Don't show them your sorrow, or they'll

240

take it for weakness. They came here for revenge, to burn and destroy. They follow you because we are of one heart, my little brother and the tribes. You must rejoice in their victory, or you'll lose them. I may be no leader, but I know a good leader must swallow his emotion for the sake of the unity of his men. Dry your eyes, and listen to the cheering."

Rhodri was dimly aware of the sounds of celebration as the stone of the tower cracked and the falling bodies thudded to earth. He shuddered, and rubbed his face clean. "Let's leave before the whole city goes up," he muttered. "Temion, have the men follow me to the north gate. We ride for Estmarch Castle now."

He turned his back on the burning tower, pulling his shirt over his mouth. If he could, he would have covered his whole face, so that none may know him as he rode through the abandoned, smoke-filled streets, unshed tears burning his eyes.

Chapter Eleven

R HODRI RODE IN silence, alone with his thoughts, as the tribes of Atrath streamed out of the ruined city of Terinth on the road that led north to Whitewood and Estmarch Castle. In the wake of the fire at the armoury tower, they had burned everything that could be burned. A column of smoke stretched a mile into the sky, its head lost in the dull grey clouds of autumn. On the road, they overtook crowds of fleeing refugees, who scattered in fear before them. The tribes were jubilant, buoyed by their first substantial victory. Every man had words of praise for him, but Rhodri had rarely felt so hollow and isolated. He wished he could talk to someone who understood what he was going through, and knew how much the decision to fire the tower cost him. Nasira was loyal, never complaining at his black moods, but she had never been forced to make a soldier's choice. He would not expose her to the evil of his troubled heritage.

At Rhodri's order, the army bypassed Whitewood, the more headstrong warriors chafing at the restriction. He had had enough of cities, of fire and destruction, and he wanted his men fresh for the long siege he anticipated at Estmarch Castle, a mere day's ride away. They might need to raid the city for supplies, and it was senseless to reduce it to a smoking ruin before winter set in.

Halfway between Whitewood and the castle, Temion trotted up beside him, lips tight with worry. "The scouting party you sent out this morning . . . they haven't come back."

Hells! "How many?"

"Nine."

It was an unexpected blow, and Rhodri ordered his troops to halt. It might be nothing; maybe they'd found a farm to raid or simply wandered too far. But he doubted it.

"Sudak, take some men and check out the road ahead," Rhodri ordered. "If you find trouble, run from it!"

Sudak bristled. "I'm no coward, my leader."

"I'm not saying you are, but you're more use to me alive. Get going!"

As he watched his young friend gallop away, leading a small party of warriors, Rhodri pushed down the feeling that he might not see him again. Instead he fell to organising his followers into a defensive stance. If there was a fight coming, he wanted to be ready to meet it the way he chose. He watched the sun and waited for his scouts to return.

He judged over a bell had passed, and still no sign of them. Liberty trotted up and down the front line, flicking her ears and jingling her harness. Rhodri could feel her quivering beneath his hand. Several times he started a few paces down the road, then thought better of it and came back. Temion sat stoic, arms folded, but his eyes were fixed on the point where the road ahead disappeared, and beads of moisture gathered at his temples.

"There they are!" he cried. Rhodri's eyes couldn't pick out the returning men at this distance, but he rode to greet them, pulling an arrow from his quiver as a precaution. Temion caught his bridle. "There are less of them now. Be careful."

Sudak drooped in the saddle. His gelding's nose almost touched the ground, flanks heaving and white with foam. The other horses were equally blown, and the broken bodies over their pommels told the story Sudak was too exhausted to relate. Only four of the search party had returned alive.

Rhodri took Sudak's rein and spoke to him in a low tone. "What happened, my friend?"

Sudak ran a trembling hand over his face, wiping away the sweat and blood. "An army," he said. "Five miles east, riding hard towards us. We barely escaped with our lives, and—" He broke off with a shudder.

Rhodri cursed. "They must be from the castle," he said. "How many?"

"Fewer than us, maybe three thousand, but they fought like patchcats in mating season." He rubbed his upper arm. Blood seeped through his tough jerkin.

"Get sewn up. We can take three thousand, now we're not caught by surprise. I'll spread the word."

Rhodri cantered back to his followers. Nasira threw him an enquiring glance. "Trouble?"

"Nothing we can't deal with. Men!" He clattered his sword against his shield to attract their attention. "We face an army ahead, approaching with speed. Archers to the front!"

The moons of drill, in Kharikan and on the road, paid off. The Atrathene force moved with the seamless elegance of a flock of migrating birds, assuming their battle positions by instinct. It made Rhodri's heart swell to watch them move with such fluidity. They served him well, the ranks of hawk-eyed archers, and behind them the bristling wall of mounted spearmen to punch holes in any cavalry charge. Line after line of cavalry, not highly trained as he was, but skilled and passionate, ready to lay down their lives for a fight they believed in. He hoped it wouldn't come to that. They were a fearsome sight. If Sudak was right and the approaching army was only a third of their size, a sensible commander would turn tail and flee to the mountains rather than face them. His men dug in, and waited.

Waiting was the hardest part of any fight. When blades clashed, and horse and rider moved with one mind, Rhodri could lose himself in the moment. There was no time to think about what lay ahead, be it victory, death, or crippling injury that was worse than dying. Mercy; he tried never to think of mercy, but in the drawn-out time before battle, it crept into his mind, sending a cold shaft down his spine.

Liberty snorted and tossed her head up and down. She knew when he was tense, and his nervous excitement transferred to her. He patted her neck to calm her as she bucked like a colt, making light of her fifteen years. For all her skittishness, she wasn't as fast as she had once been, and she didn't have the stamina of her youth. This would be her last campaign, he decided. She deserved a lazy retirement in a grassy paddock, if they both survived.

Thinking about Liberty's future distracted him from his own fears as he checked his bowstring, his arrows, his harness. All the things that meant the difference between life and death were they to fail in battle. He was so preoccupied that the thunder of Sudak's hooves racing up to him made him startle and curse.

"What is it?"

"They're coming! They've sent a rider ahead—I think he wants to talk. Will you speak with them?"

The army at his back thirsted for a fight, but if there was a way to avoid bloodshed Rhodri wanted to seize it with both hands. "I'll talk," he said. "Temion, will you cover me?"

"Have you lost the taste for blood, little brother?" A disdainful expression flashed across Temion's face. He was as worked up as any of them.

"I never had much taste for blood. You can choose to believe that, or not. Are you coming with me?"

Temion snorted with laughter. "You call yourself a war leader! I'll come with you, to put an arrow in the throat of any man who draws blade against you. I'll not have my sister left a widow!"

Reassured by Temion's presence, and with the tall figure of Sudak flanking him on the other side, Rhodri slung his bow over his back and drew his sword, taking comfort in the weight of the hilt in his palm. Gesturing for his men to hold their position, he trotted ahead towards the small party approaching from the east. They were helmed and mailed, and although his comrades were

246

watchful, their leader seemed relaxed. His sword was sheathed, and he held out open palms to show he carried no dagger. He rode a sturdy mare Rhodri didn't recognise, but his gait was familiar as he dismounted. He removed his helm, and Rhodri felt his spirit soar. The skinny man with his ironed-flat hair drooping in his eyes was no threat.

"Niklaus! What in all hells are you doing here?"

"Not causing as much trouble as you, I hear."

Liberty whickered in joyful recognition of his voice. Nik fondled her nose as Rhodri swung down from the saddle and embraced him, thumping him on the back.

"I have to ask, Rhodri," Nik said, half-serious, "are we going to have a battle? I'm very busy, and I'm not sure I have the time."

"Busy? Or scared my army will squash yours like a bug on a window pane? What are your orders regarding me?"

Nik shrugged. "I don't take orders from any man at the moment."

"What are you talking about?"

"It's a long story." Niklaus glanced at the threatening sky. "I'd rather tell it indoors, as it's about to piss down. Tell your men they're welcome in my base, if they want to follow us. We've got food and shelter."

"Enough for all of us?" Nik nodded, and Rhodri fell back to pass the message to Temion. Nasira's brother glowered at the lithe Kingdom soldier, and his lip curled.

"Food and shelter for all of us? It smells like a trap to me. Is he just a warrior who walks with the rest, or one of your leaders?"

"He's a warrior who walks, like I was. I've known him since I was a boy."

"You trust him?"

"As much as any man."

Temion snorted. "I'm sure he trusted you once too, before you left your people to join ours."

Rhodri cast a doubtful look back at Nik, standing in the road open-handed and open-faced as the first drops of rain dashed cold against his cheeks. Nik had risked a whipping to cover for Rhodri in the past, kept his secrets and covered his backside. Surely not . . . But Astan had trusted Rhodri, and been betrayed. Captain Garrod had promoted him, and Rhodri had returned the favour by stabbing the King's Third in the back the moment his feet hit the grassland. There were too many miles between himself and Nik for them to trust each other the way they had once done.

"Be careful," he said to Temion, "but try not to look as if you're being careful. If we hit trouble run, don't fight. And,"—he held a hand up to forestall another protestation against coward-ice—"watch out for trouble in the ranks. We ride this path with care. Sudak, you go back and tell the tribal leaders we may have shelter. Temion, with me."

They trotted back towards Nik. The rain was lashing down now, and Liberty flicked her ears in irritation. Shelter, even if it was in a trap, was an appealing thought.

"If you think you can shelter ten thousand men, we'll take it," he said.

Nik grinned. "It might be cosy."

"Better than standing out here in this piss. How did you get a base of your own? What are you, the fucking Queen?"

"You couldn't be further from the truth," Nik told him with a chuckle. "I want to hear what you've been doing to get this terrible reputation!"

Rhodri sighed. "You've heard what they say about me, then?"

"Rapist, murderer, bastard son of a traitor and a whore? If it was anyone else, I might believe it."

"Rapist?" Rhodri shuddered. "That's a new one. I thought I'd heard everything."

"There's much you haven't heard, my friend." The rain spattered harder across Rhodri's shoulders. "Ride with me. It's not far, and we can talk when we get there."

"I'll follow," Rhodri told him. "If I don't lead my men, they tend to make their own entertainment. Where are you based?"

"Estmarch Castle. I'll be waiting for you."

*

With no walls to restrict it, the town sprawling around the base of Estmarch castle spread like lichen, away from the looming walls. The last time he passed this way, Rhodri was with the King's Third. He had felt a hostile atmosphere in the town at the time, but, preoccupied with the campaign ahead, he paid little attention. This time, the difference in their reception was marked, and surprising. People lined the streets to witness their passing. Some waved flags, or applauded, not with enthusiasm, but at least with politeness.

Riding at his side, Nasira looked around with bright-eyed interest. She pointed. "What does that symbol mean? I see it everywhere."

The whitewashed wall of a nearby house was decorated with a mural which stretched from the foundations to the eaves. He recognised the design as the flag of the Estmarch, a white tree standing alone and proud on a green hill, beneath a solitary star. But on this mural, star and hill were painted deep blood red, and the tree, bare of leaves, thrust striking black fingers into the painted sky.

"I don't know," he admitted. "I'll ask Nik about it."

The castle stood on a hill overlooking the town, and the gate was flung open in welcome. Nicklaus waited in the paved courtyard. He had changed from his mail to a simple woollen jerkin, with a patch on the breast identical to the mural on the side of the house. He was brushing down his horse with long strokes, but as Rhodri and Nasira rode through the gate he abandoned his task and hurried to greet them.

"Your men can sleep here, as long as they need," he said. "It might be a bit tight, but my home is yours."

Rhodri laughed out loud. "Your home? Have you been keeping secrets from me, that you're really the son of a lord?"

Niklaus did not join in his laughter. "You're one to talk about keeping secrets, Rhodri. Come on, we've food and shelter here. Let's stable the horses, then we'll talk. You haven't introduced me to your woman, either."

Rhodri took Asta from his wife's arms and helped her dismount, the bulge of her pregnancy making her movements awkward. "This is my friend Niklaus," he said to her, in Atrathene. "He's a good man, for a short-hair. We should be safe here."

She tightened her arms around Asta, who squirmed at the pressure and kicked to be set down. "Are you sure?"

"Sure as I can be. I told Temion to stay alert, just in case. What's troubling you?"

She nodded at the boxy walls of the keep. "We sleep here? I've never slept between walls . . ."

"It's no different to Kharikan. I'll be at your side." He kissed her on the forehead and turned back to Niklaus, who watched the exchange with a bemused expression. "Nik, this is Nasira, my wife."

"Your *wife?* She wears your chain?"

In reply, Rhodri reached out to Nasira's throat and caught his finger in the chain that held the locket, pulling it free.

Nik chuckled. "I didn't think you were the marrying kind!"

"Nor did I, until I met her."

"Is the little one yours too?"

"I fear so. This is Asta."

"After . . . ?"

"Yes."

"Good choice." Nik turned abruptly back to his horse. "Give a hand here, my friend. Tell your woman to make herself at home. There's food in the hall."

Rhodri passed the message on, sending Nasira on her way with a pat to the shoulder. Leading Liberty, he followed Nik to the stables. "You got a new ride then," he observed.

"This is Rebecca." Nik slapped the mare affectionately on the shoulder.

"What happened to Ghost?"

"I lost her. She broke a leg, about a year ago." Nik stared into the middle distance, and blinked hard.

"Shit, Nik, I'm sorry!"

Nik shrugged, and turned his back. "What can you do?" His voice wavered slightly. "These things happen. Your Lib's looking well."

"She's all right." Rhodri changed the subject. If he lost Liberty, he didn't know how he'd cope. "You haven't told me how you ended up here."

"That's a long story. I want to hear your tale too. Come on!" Nik gave Rebecca a final rub down. "Let's leave these girls to their feed and find some of our own."

The hall in Estmarch Castle was reached by a flight of wooden steps up to the second floor entrance, then down several passages and further flights to the heart of the keep. The only light in the room, apart from the roaring fireplace, came from arched windows high up near the roof. A galleried landing ran around three sides of the hall. It was dim inside, but cosy, and Nik grabbed two seats at the nearest table. Nasira stood near the fire, looking lost and confused amid the hubbub of the busy hall. Rhodri beckoned her over.

"Is this too much for you?" he asked. She nodded. "Would you like to go somewhere quiet?" Rhodri turned to Nik. "Is there somewhere for Nasira to lie down?"

"You can have my rooms," Nik said at once. "I'll get someone to show her the way." He snapped his fingers at a maid as she scurried past. "Show my friend's wife to my suite. They'll be sleeping there from now on."

"Go with her," Rhodri told Nasira as the girl dumped her tray with ill humour. "Nik has given us his rooms. I'll be up later."

Nik pressed a flagon of ale into his hand. "When's the babe due?" he asked.

"Beginning of spring, I think. What?"

Nik shook his head and smiled. "You're the last person I'd expect to see settled with a wife and babies. Strange how things turn out. How did you end up with her?"

Rhodri told the story, from the day the avalanche had set them along different paths, skipping over the shameful details of the deaths that came afterwards, embellishing the best bits. It took a long time to tell, and his ale was empty by the time he stopped talking and realised he had gathered a curious audience. Men and women, simply dressed, but all wearing the same emblem as Nik, hung on his every word. They surrounded him, a blade on every hip, but if the jaws of the trap were closing he didn't sense it. They were curious, interested, even warm. There was more going on here than he had realised, and his old friend was at the heart of it. He seemed to be their leader. Rhodri thought back to when they'd parted; Nik couldn't have led a tavern sing-along.

"Tell me your story," he said. "You're not here with the King's Third. Why did you leave them? I thought it was your life?"

"As much as it was yours, my friend. After the avalanche, Dragon Pass was blocked. Captain Garrod said we should try to break through further south where there might be less snow. But riding down through the Estmarch, I saw the same things you did. The army is sworn to protect, not respect. That's what they kept telling me, so I bit my tongue. It wasn't until we crossed the pass into Atrath that I realised we weren't there to fight, but to slaughter."

He sighed, and took up his flagon with a shaking hand. "I was like you," he said. "I didn't sign up for that. So I deserted. I went home."

"You went home?" Rhodri's eyes widened. "Across the mountains? On your own?"

"Not alone. There were three of us."

"Even so, Nik, that's a hellish thing to do."

Nik shrugged. "It was that, or stay in Atrath and kill women and children. I'd rather risk death on a mountain pass."

Rhodri regarded his skinny friend with renewed respect. "Then what happened?"

Niklaus grinned. "I fell in with this band of criminals and reprobates. They were badly in need of military advice, and I offered it. We took Estmarch Castle, and here we are."

"And we're not going anywhere!" A short, heavy-set woman joined them at the table, resting a hand possessively on Nik's forearm. The design on the patch they all wore was inked into the skin of her wrist, and she reminded Rhodri of some of the women at the Golden Orbs. Not the whores, but their female clientele.

Nik squeezed her tattooed wrist. "My woman, Jilly," he said as an introduction. "Jilly, this is Rhodri."

She scanned him up and down, unimpressed. "The man who cast me out of my bedchamber?"

"I'm afraid so." Rhodri looked round at the ring of faces, some hopeful, others wary. "Who are you?" he asked, although he had already formed a suspicion.

Nik smiled, stretching his legs out under the table and folding his arms behind his head. "We represent the interests of the Estmarch, and the Estmarch alone," he said, eyes twinkling.

"Estmarch Freedom? Bloody hells, Nik, you're as big a traitor as I am!"

There was a gale of laughter at this. Nik sprang to his feet and threw a mocking punch that glanced off Rhodri's upper arm. "Hardly! Come on, I need to piss."

"You don't need me to hold your cock, do you?"

"You'd love that, wouldn't you? And you a married man!" His smile faded for an instant. "Seriously. We need to talk."

Rhodri downed the last drops of his ale and followed Nik out into the courtyard. A biting wind whistled around the keep. Bladders emptied, they sat on the stair in companionable silence. He wished he'd brought his cloak.

"I know who you are, you know."

Rhodri couldn't see Nik's face, but he groaned at the words. "I don't want to hear it, Nik. Not from you. I'm sick of people speaking my name in the same breath as that of Valery Northpoint."

"You don't understand. I know who you *really* are . . ."

His words fell away into the darkness of the courtyard. There was a long silence.

"How do you . . . ?" Rhodri's voice trailed off.

"I always suspected. There was something about you from the start. If any of us was a prince in disguise, it wasn't going to be Dru! Jime, maybe . . . My father was a jeweller."

"I remember you telling me. What's that got to do with it?"

"Not much, on its own. Remember that blonde you fucked at Hierath? I heard you talking to her."

"I thought you were asleep," Rhodri said bitterly.

"And the chain your woman wears, with the pictures of your parents. No peasant farmer could afford that. I knew you were keeping something from me. I didn't want to pry, but I did some digging." He sounded hurt. "You could have trusted me."

Rhodri sighed, and shivered in his shirt sleeves. "I only found out that day. I was trying to wrap my mind around it."

"And now?"

Rhodri dug his dagger into the wood of the steps, prying up long splinters. "Serren is my sister. My *younger* sister. By blood and law, the throne is mine."

"Do you want it? I can help you get it . . ."

Another splinter came free, jabbing him in the wrist. "Keep talking."

Niklaus spoke fast now, breathless. "I have three thousand men here, more scattered through the Estmarch. Serren is no queen. She lets her soldiers abuse her own people, and sends them to kill children in Atrath. I might persuade my men to ride with you, on one condition . . ."

"Freedom for the Estmarch?"

"It's the only thing we ask for, from the Kingdom. Your father wouldn't grant it. Will you?"

Rhodri flicked a sliver of wood away into the darkness. "Nasira doesn't want me to fight for the Kingdom."

Nik's voice was soft. "If you go for the throne, Estmarch Freedom goes with you. You'll have a better chance. We both will, to get what we want out of Serren. Think about it." He rose, boots ringing hollow on the stairs.

"I've thought of nothing else." Rhodri scrambled up after him, eager for the stuffy warmth of the hall. "Do you think your men will follow me?"

"Not if they think you're Northpoint's heir. That puts your life in danger here. We still mourn for Lydyce. Come on, my friend,"—Nik slapped him on the shoulder—"time to confess. Let Serren know her brother's coming for her!"

*

Rhodri's hand, moving independently of his sozzled brain, traced lazy circles in the air as he tried to articulate his point. "It's easier," he slurred, "for men to believe a sordid truth than a mundane lie . . . that's not right, is it? Am I making sense?"

Nik yawned. "After seven pints, not much does!" He sprawled across the table, regarding Rhodri from beneath a drooping lock of hair, and hiccuped. "Do you know what I'm going to do for you, my friend? I'm going to fix your feet!"

"You can't fix his feet." Rhodri hadn't seen Temion approach. The Atrathene rested his supple hands flat on the table in front of him. "No one can." His Western speech was halting, but clear.

Niklaus blinked at him as he tried to focus. "What makes you so sure, Atrathene?"

"I put the shackles there. Nothing will get them off."

Nik staggered to his feet, fumbling for his dagger. Rhodri caught his arm. "Leave him, Nik. He's Nasira's brother. And my friend."

"A friend wouldn't do that," Nik mumbled, sitting down with a thump.

Temion glared down at them. "You've had a skinful, little brother. Why don't you go to bed?" He seized Rhodri by the elbow and dragged him upright.

Nik rubbed his eyes. "I can fix them," he promised, in a sleepy voice. "King's Third can do *anything*."

"Not the bloody King's Third any more, are we?"

With Temion's hand gripping his bicep, Rhodri allowed himself to be steered across the room and up the stairs to one of the rooms off the galleried landing. He found himself in a short corridor, which ended in a door with scratched and pitted woodwork, as if someone had forcibly removed the decoration with a chisel.

Temion gave him a little push. "Sleep it off, brother," he urged as he lifted the catch. Rhodri stumbled across the threshold into a sobering blast of cold air. The moons were choked with cloud, and the room was dark. He dug out his candlestones and lit the torch that stood in a sconce beside the door. The light flared, falling across the low bed, stark white and empty.

Fear drove out the last shreds of drunkenness; Nik had warned his life was in danger, and now Nasira and Asta were missing . . .

He swung the torch. The light flickered over a heap of blankets beside the bed, and one long, outflung leg, and his heart leapt in relief. He dropped to his knees and rested a hand on Nasira's bare ankle. She stirred with a sleepy grumble.

"Nasira? Why are you on the floor? And why are the shutters open?"

She sat up, pushing her hair out of her eyes. Asta fidgeted against her shoulder. "I couldn't sleep in the bed." She yawned. "It was too soft. There's not enough air in here."

"There's too much air," he chided. "You'll get a chill."

"I didn't get a chill when you dragged me over the mountains."

Rhodri closed the shutters against the night breeze. "Even so, Nik and Jilly gave up their bed for us. Do you really want to sleep on the floor?"

He helped her into bed, Asta curled up between them. It was softer than Rhodri was used to, and he sank gratefully into the yielding mound of furs. Nasira rested her head on his chest. "You smell of ale," she grumbled as her eyes closed, long lashes sweeping her cheeks. "What did you and your friend talk about?"

"He wants to help us."

"Why?"

Rhodri was surprised at her question. "What do you mean, why? He's my friend."

Nasira sighed. "No short-hair ever helped an Atrathene except for profit. What does your friend hope to gain?"

He tapped her on the shoulder. "I helped you, remember?"

"And what you gained was me. You got a good deal there, terrible boy!"

"But—"

She laid a hand across his lips to cut him off. "Go to sleep, Rhodri. Wake in the morning, soothe your ale-head, and then think about what your friend wants, and what you're prepared to give him."

*

The breeze that had chilled Rhodri's skin the night before brought the first flurries of snow whirling down from the mountains. Winter arrived with an icy blast, and that helped Rhodri's decision. Nik was willing to let the Atrathenes hole up in Estmarch Castle all winter, to recover from the trials of their long journey and plan for the spring. Nasira looked wistfully east, but as the midwinter festival approached and her child grew inside her, she conceded that staying put made good sense.

Winterfest at Northpoint had been a rowdy celebration, characterised by drunkenness, whoring, and frequent brawls. The festival Nik hosted was more sedate, mainly because, with so many extra mouths to feed, ale and meat were in short supply. Nasira sat at the table, pushing food around her plate and fidgeting.

"Is something wrong?" Rhodri asked. "You don't look as if you're having fun. Do you want to dance?"

"I'm not hungry." She pushed to her feet, wincing. "There are lots of less fat girls around. Boys too!" She winked. "Why don't you dance with one of them?"

"There's more of you to love, fat girl!"

She delivered him a hefty slap on the upper arm, and flinched again.

"Are you sure you're all right?"

"Dance with me, you wicked short-hair who made me fat. Before I decide I don't want you any more. Nik will dance, if I ask him . . ."

"You'll have to get through Jilly first!" Nik and his woman made an awkward, unlikely couple, shuffling around the floor in a dance that was more endurance than elegance.

"She would dance with me too. She likes girls, the same way you like boys. I'm willing to try something new." She giggled.

"Dance with me first, before you abandon me for a new adventure." Rhodri took his wife's hand and led her onto the dance floor. "I'm not very good," he warned her. "I might tread on your toes."

"Is that why the women of your kingdom wear such thick boots?" Her eyes gleamed. "To protect them from your clumsy feet?"

"Come here and say that." He whirled her round the dance floor, letting the music carry them in stately parade, watching the other dancers over her shoulder. The women who followed Nik were thin, for the most part, washed out and tired, but some of the
258

men were handsome in a rugged, weather-hewn way. One caught his eyes, flashed a smile, and winked, and Rhodri stumbled over Nasira's feet. She cursed, and kicked him in the shin.

"Stop watching the boys!"

"I'm not," he lied.

"At least look where your feet are going." She smiled, and he grinned back, grateful for her indulgence, and tried to slip back into the rhythm of the dance, burdened by his shackles, and the curve of her kindling belly. Nasira was panting for breath as the tune ended.

"Do you want to go again?"

"Drink first," she gasped.

Rhodri laughed, twirling her round and pulling her close. She whimpered in sudden pain, biting her lip. "There *is* something wrong! Why did you lie about it?"

She hung her head. "I didn't want to miss the party. I knew if I told you . . ."

"Told me what?"

"I lost my baby-water this afternoon."

He stared at her in confusion. "Lost . . . what does that mean?"

"Our new babe is on the way."

Taking her arm, he led her to the side of the room, where she wouldn't be bumped and hustled by other dancers. "Surely it's early yet?"

"By a moon. I might have counted wrong . . ."

"Can it be stopped?"

She laughed, a touch hysterical. "If you know any shaman skills to stop a baby coming early, you'd best use them now!"

"None at all, I'm afraid."

"Then I'm going to dance again." Nasira took a stride back towards the dance floor, and he caught her by the hand.

"You're bloody not. Let's find Nik."

"What good will he be?"

"He might know where we can find a birthing woman. Don't cry!" He kissed her on the cheek. "Everything will be fine."

"It's not fair!" Tears clouded Nasira's eyes. "I've been looking forward to this festival, and now I have to miss it because the babe doesn't know when he's meant to be born!"

"Nasira, you're being unreasonable . . ." She would not be consoled, sinking onto a bench and burying her head in her arms. Her shoulders heaved. Rhodri patted her on the back, unsure what to say beyond a repeated promise to find Nik.

Niklaus took one look at Nasira and nodded. "Come with me," he said, leading them across the hall, past the musicians, to a small door. Rhodri assumed it led to the kitchens, but behind it was a private audience chamber, richly carpeted, with upholstered sofas against the walls. Even with the door closed, he could hear the band. "Ask her if this will do," Nik said. "She might not be able to dance, but at least she can listen."

Rhodri relayed the message. His wife's grateful smile twisted into a grimace of pain. "Tell him he's a kind man. Can he fetch Siralane? I don't want to be alone with strangers . . ."

"You won't be alone." Rhodri stroked her hair as she sank down on one of the couches. "I'll stay with you as long as you need me."

"The cat . . . These Westerners might not understand . . ."

"We can fight the cat together." He turned to Niklaus. "There's an Atrathene woman, her brother's wife. Nasira asks for her. And a trained birthing woman, if you have one. She'll need leather gauntlets, or vambraces. Something to protect her arms and throat."

"Why will she need that?"

"It's better you don't know. Trust me."

Niklaus looked from Rhodri to Nasira and nodded. "I'll send Jilly up to take care of Asta," he said. "I'll be as quick as I can."

Left alone, Nasira clutched Rhodri's hand tightly, her ill temper replaced by fear. Her nails scored the back of his hand. "I'm scared, Rhodri. What if I hurt someone?"

He took her face between his hands, staring deep into eyes that were turning from black to amber. "When you had Asta, when I saw you tied up on the floor like a victim for sacrifice, I swore I'd never let that happen again. I'll be with you the whole time. No one will get hurt. Least of all you."

A spasm of pain crossed her face. "I love you, Rhodri. I wanted to tell you, in case—"

"In case nothing. Come on, on your feet!" He helped her pace the room. "I don't want to hear that sort of talk. Nothing bad is happening today."

There was a knock at the door, brisk and business-like. It opened to admit a waft of music and the smell of roast meats, and a tiny, bustling woman, rotund, and laden with towels. Her look swept Rhodri up and down with scepticism.

"I'm Bronnagh," she said. "Time for you to leave."

Rhodri shook his head. "My wife doesn't speak our tongue," he said. "She wants me here to translate. And there's something else." He glanced anxiously at Nasira and switched into Atrathene. "Should I tell her?"

"Go ahead." She doubled up, in the grip of another contraction. He waited until it passed, massaging her lower back.

"Nasira has,"—he searched for the expression—"a *demon* in her, an angry spirit that comes out when she's afraid or hurt. Or wild at me." He grinned. "She might try and fight you, not realising what she's doing. She wants me to stay, to calm her down."

"Is that why you asked for leathers?" Bronnagh shrugged. "Fine with me."

"You're not worried?"

"You see everything in this job. Except men in the birthing room, that's new. If you faint, I'm going to step over you or kick you out of the way. Is that clear?"

"As glass."

"Let's have a look. Tell her to lie down."

261

Rhodri cradled Nasira's head as the midwife bundled her skirts around her waist and looked between her legs. "Baby's well on his way," she said.

"It's early." Rhodri translated Nasira's words. "It wasn't due for another moon. Although she said she might have counted wrong, whatever that means . . ."

"If you don't know that, I despair of you. The babe may be small . . ."

"I don't want her cut open," Rhodri said firmly. "Only as a last resort."

Bronnagh scowled. "I'm not a bloody butcher!"

"I'm sorry, I meant no insult."

"When I tell you, tell her to push. Will she listen to you with this demon in her?"

"I hope so."

"Just to be sure . . ." Bronnagh slipped on the leather gauntlets with a determined air. "Give her this to bite down on. It might help."

She handed him a flat piece of smoothed wood. "Are you ready? Tell her to push!"

Nasira screamed, hips arching off the sofa, body twisting. Her claws raked down the inside of Rhodri's arm as he struggled to hold her. She snarled, lashing her head from side to side.

"Bite this!" He pushed the wooden paddle into her mouth and she bit down. There was a cracking sound.

Bronnagh wiped sweat out of her eyes with her shoulder. "Well," she said, "that's never happened before."

"You said you'd seen everything."

"I've never seen a woman bite through half an inch of solid whitebeam. She must have powerful teeth."

"You're not wrong." Pulling on his own gloves, Rhodri extracted the splintered wood from Nasira's mouth, wary of her savage canines. She lay back, panting, and snapped at him weakly. "Enough of that," he told her. "I'm trying to help."

"Hurts!"

The cat had not entirely taken over. That was a good sign. "Not long," he promised. "Bronnagh? How long?"

"As long as it takes. Get ready to push again."

Nasira tightened her fierce grip on Rhodri's hand, and pushed, sinking her teeth into her bottom lip, fighting the pain. It made him sick to see her suffer. He took his dagger from his belt.

"No knives while I'm delivering." Bronnagh protested. "This is dangerous enough for her."

"It's all right." Tearing a strip of cloth from his shirt, he wrapped it round the blade. "Bite down on this, little cat. I'd like to see you put a dent in Northpoint steel."

She bit down on the dagger, eyes blazing. Rhodri looked at Bronnagh. "How is she doing?"

"Not long now. I'm impressed you're still upright. Another big push. Tell her she's doing well."

Nasira spat out the dagger and bared her teeth. It was not a smile. "Doing . . . well?"

"I'm proud of you."

She responded with a stream of cursing, punctuated with snarls. Her lashing claws ripped open the cloth of his shirt, and the skin of his chest. "Proud of me? You stay away from me! This is your fault, you horse-fucking bastard!"

Bronnagh raised an eyebrow. "What was that? It sounded so loving . . ."

"Not really."

The midwife chuckled. "That's another reason we tell the fathers to stay away. Even the most sedate women turn the air blue when they're having a baby. She still loves you."

He shrugged. "I'd rather hear her swearing than growling."

"Tell her I can see the baby's head. One more should do it. She can make a noise, it might help."

Nasira needed no encouragement. She let out a scream, a primal roar, called out for her mother, and cursed Rhodri with every name under the sun. The bones in his fingers cracked under the pressure of her hand. In a blur of pain and blood and swift, decisive movement, the babe slithered out into Bronnagh's arms. It was purple, covered in blood and slime, and Rhodri recoiled at the sight.

"Don't be such a feeblewit." Bronnagh slapped the babe on the backside, splattering the birthing mess, and it replied with a lusty wail. "Hand me a towel."

"Is it supposed to look like that?"

"He. And yes." She made a quick inventory of fingers and toes. "He's fine. On the small side, but healthy. Listen to those lungs!"

"I want to see." Nasira struggled to sit up. Every trace of the patchcat was gone from her eyes. "Give me my baby!"

"Are you all right to hold him?" Rhodri asked.

"It's the worst pain in the world, but when you hold your babe, it all goes away. Give him to me!"

Bronnagh had cleared most of the mess and blood away with a towel. "Here you go." She placed the baby in Nasira's eager arms and pulled a blanket around her to give her some dignity. "I'll give you two a moment."

Rhodri perched on the edge of the couch, and stared down at his son. Cleaned up, he looked more human. His skin was lighter than Asta's. She had been born with a shock of dark hair, but he had only the palest wisp on the crown of his head. He yawned, showing pink gums.

"What shall we call him?" Nasira asked.

"You get to name him. I named Asta."

She yawned in turn. "I'm too tired to think. You come up with something, and I'll tell you if I like it. A name with meaning, mark you. Not a nonsense name like yours!"

He thought of the names he knew that had meaning in Atrathene, as well as his native tongue, and curled his son's wispy blond hair around his finger, marvelling at its softness.

"Finn," he said at length. "In ancient language, it means 'fair'. How does it sound to you?"

Nasira smiled. "Fair in colouring, or in outlook?"

"Either. Both, I hope."

She nodded. "In my tongue, it means swift, a fast runner. I like that. What do you think of your name, Finn?"

Finn's eyelids drooped. "Do you want me to take him while you rest?" Rhodri asked.

"Please. But don't be long, he'll be hungry. Make sure you hold his head up . . ."

"I know. Shall I send the woman back to clean you up?"

Nasira nodded, covering her mouth with an elegant hand as she yawned again. "Bring Asta here too. This is a moment for our family. We don't get enough of those."

Rhodri let Bronnagh back in. The birthing woman was ready to smile now the drama was over, but she caught his arm as he headed towards the hall. "Be careful with him," she warned.

"I have a daughter. I know how to handle a baby."

"That's not what I meant. Sons are different, especially yours. Think about it." She vanished into the chamber before he could reply, closing the door with a soft, firm click that excluded him from this women's business.

The band still played a cheerful tune, and people danced, unaware that a small, everyday miracle had taken place only a few feet away. Rhodri moved through the crowd, hardly aware of them, of the music, his spirit poured into the bundle cradled in his arms. He felt dizzy with euphoria and relief. He wanted to shout Finn's birth from the roof. He was eager to introduce Asta to her brother, his son . . .

A hand under his elbow. Nik steered him across the floor, almost quicker than he could walk. "Boy or girl?" he asked, under his breath.

"Boy."

"That's what I feared. Keep walking, don't make a fuss. Nod and smile."

Two women, noticing Finn in Rhodri's arms, headed in their direction with eager smiles. Nik picked up the pace, fending them off with a genial wave. "You get to see the babe later, I promise!" he called as he hustled Rhodri up the stairs and into the privacy of the gallery.

"Nik? What's going on?"

"Not here." Niklaus pushed him into the room with the scarred door, and barred it behind them. He blew out his cheeks and sank down on the bed. "Let's see him, then. What have you called him?"

"Finn." Rhodri held him out to Nik, who looked at the baby as if he was about to explode. "Do you want to hold him?"

"Me? Stars no, I'd bounce him on his head and your woman would gut me! Is she well?"

"Well enough. Tired, I think. Nik, what's this about?"

Nik was interrupted as the door to the inner chamber crashed open. Asta ran into the room waving her doll. "Daddy!"

Jilly followed on hands and knees, playing a game, but straightened as she saw the two men. Rhodri noticed she wore a dagger on each hip, and the hilt of a third protruded from her boot. She nodded at Nik. "It went well then? Is it a boy?"

She showed no desire to hold him, but Rhodri's arms tightened around his son. "Why do you need so many knives to look after Asta, Jilly?"

"Just being cautious." She sat down on the bed, and Asta clambered determinedly into her lap.

"You can trust Jilly," Nik said. "I asked her to protect Asta."

"Why does Asta need an armed guard?" Rhodri's daughter noticed Finn for the first time and climbed, with a lot of awkward grunting, across the bed to get a better look. Rhodri caught her in his other arm and spoke over her head. "Who does she need protection from?"

"Be smart, Rhodri. You have a son now."

"Baby!" Rhodri caught Asta's hand as she poked her finger in Finn's mouth.

"Whatever threat you were to Serren before, it just doubled," Nik went on. "Finn has a better claim to the throne than her. If she finds out about him . . . It's easier to get rid of a baby than a fighting man."

"You think she'd have him killed?" Rhodri hugged his children closer. Asta seized on his distraction to stick her finger up her baby brother's nose, and he kicked in protest.

"Maybe not herself, but there's no shortage of men who might act on her behalf. Dru, for one . . ."

"I'd kill him before he got within a mile of my children. Serren too, if I had to."

"You can't be with them all the time. Who do you trust?"

"Temion," Rhodri said at once. The loyalty Temion had to him was stronger than magic, as strong as blood.

"The one who shackled you?"

"He's Nasira's brother. He loves these little ones like I do. And Sudak. And . . ." Rhodri trailed off. Who, of the horde he led, did he really trust with the lives of his children? Suddenly his options seemed very limited.

Asta lunged across his arm, making a grab for Finn. He held her back. "There's no one else," he admitted. "Not to trust with their lives. Do you have anyone?"

"He has me," Jilly said. Nik smiled at her.

"You," he said, "and you alone. I'm in a worse position than you, Rhodri. I'm not sure I can trust any man who follows me, and that makes my skin itch."

"I didn't realise. You should have told me sooner."

"You were busy getting ready for that one." Nik stroked Finn's head with a quick, nervous gesture. Asta, frustrated in her efforts, climbed into his lap, bouncing up and down. Nik jogged her on his knee. "Is this right? I won't drop her?"

"I've dropped her a few times," Rhodri confessed. "She seems to bounce." Finn grumbled in his arms and he got to his feet, pacing, trying to settle himself as well as his son. No harm would come to his children while he lived. It was all the more reason to confront Serren, as soon as spring arrived.

Chapter Twelve

Winterfest lay two moons behind, and the snow had given way to rain and breezes that carried the tang of fresh greenery. The weather was still unpredictable, and Rhodri waited impatiently for it to settle into a steady pattern before he let his men off the leash, chafing at the wait as much as they were. He suspected Nasira would be happy to stay in Estmarch Castle forever. Finn was a demanding baby and, no matter how much Rhodri tried to help, she was constantly exhausted.

He lay with Nasira and his children on the bed. Both of the little ones were asleep, and they were enjoying a rare moment of tranquillity, when Jilly arrived with a message that they were to meet Nik in the hall without delay. Leaving Finn and Asta in her care, they hurried to meet him.

Nik wore a mischievous smile. He had something hidden behind his back, and he presented it to Nasira with a flourish.

"A gift for you," he said in hesitant Atrathene. "You like?"

"Thank you," she replied, equally halting and with an anxious glance at Rhodri. She looked puzzled as she showed the gift to her husband and slipped back into her native tongue. "What is it for?"

Nik's gift was a rose, intricately crafted from glass, every thorn and petal perfectly rendered and detailed. Rhodri could even see drops of dew, and the veins on the leaves. The time and craftsmanship put into it was astounding.

"I think it's just to look pretty," he told her.

"It is pretty, but I don't understand. What use is it?"

"Doesn't she like it?" Nik sounded anxious.

"Of course she likes it. She's surprised to receive such a fine gift. I hope it wasn't expensive . . ."

Nik laughed. "It cost me nothing! Come on, I want you to meet someone."

He led them into the yard. A woman waited there, middle aged and busty, adorned with too much cheap jewellery, her cloak tight across her shoulders. She had her arm around a dark-haired boy of about fifteen summers, pinning him to her side with her embrace. He shuffled his feet in the snow, bored.

Nik introduced them. "Rhodri, this is Brunhild and Yestin. They've walked two days to see you."

"Is this him?" Brunhild peered at Rhodri from beneath her thick fringe. "Doesn't look much, does he? I've seen fatter skeletons!"

"Did you really walk two days through the snow to throw insults at me?" Rhodri flicked his hand in a dismissive gesture. "I've got better things to do than stand in the cold listening to this."

"Brunhild," Nik butted in, "do you want the reward or not?"

"Of course I want the bloody reward! Just making conversation, wasn't I?"

"Nik, what reward is she talking about?" All Rhodri's initial doubts returned in a rush. Niklaus wouldn't sell him out, surely?

Brunhild elbowed Yestin in the back, pushing him forward. "Go on, son," she urged. "Show him what you can do."

Yestin scowled. He was attractive, with deep brown eyes and coal-black hair falling across his forehead, his lips curled in a sulky pout. "Why? I've done it once already."

"Because the lord,"—she simpered at Niklaus—"will give us good silver for it."

"Like I'm going to see any of that," Yestin snapped, his patience as thin as Rhodri's.

He stared them down. "If you two don't mind, my wife is getting cold. Tell me why you came, or go home with no reward from anyone."

270

Brunhild gave Yestin another prod. "Show him."

He glared at her. "Give me something, then. Your bracelet."

The bangle his mother handed him was fashioned from cheap copper beads and little bells that jingled as she swung her arm. Yestin held the trinket at arm's length, crushing it between his palms. His brow furrowed with concentration, sweat streaming down his face despite the chill. Red streaks, like lines of fire running along his veins, pulsed across his hands, forming a glowing ball between his palms. He gasped and shuddered convulsively; the fire flared, then faded.

"There!" Yestin dragged an arm across his brow, and gasped triumphantly. "Is this what you wanted to see?" He dropped the bangle into Rhodri's palm. It was no longer gilded copper, flaking and tinged with green, but glass, delicate and translucent as ice.

"Impressive," Rhodri said. "You did the rose too?"

Yestin smiled sardonically. "A sample of my talents." He was panting, and Nik called for a drink.

"You're talented, but glass trinkets are no use to me." Rhodri turned to leave. Nik caught his arm.

"Wait," he said. "You haven't heard why they came here yet. I offered thirty silvers to anyone who could take the irons from your legs. Will you let him try?"

"I thought you'd forgotten about that." Rhodri looked down at the metal bands that clasped his ankles, weighing him down. His riding boots were cut off just below them. He could twist them around like a ring on a maiden's finger, but they would not move up or down more than an inch. "Is there a risk he could turn my ankles to glass along with them?"

Nik looked inquiringly at Yestin, who shrugged.

"I don't think so," he said. "I've taken rings from women's fingers before, with no harm done."

"Let's try it." Rhodri brushed the snow from the steps and sat, stretching his legs out in front of him. Yestin knelt before him, dark head bent over his feet as he studied the shackles. He peeped up through long lashes, and Rhodri stared straight ahead, avoiding his gaze.

"It shouldn't be too hard," Yestin said. "It might burn a little."

By now a small crowd had gathered. Rhodri heard bets being exchanged. Estmarchers would gamble on anything, even the prospect of his feet turning to glass. He felt a light touch against his shoulder, and looked up to see Nasira leaning on the banister rail. She took his hand and threaded her fingers through his in a silent gesture of support.

Yestin placed his hands on the ring that clasped Rhodri's right ankle, an unexpectedly tender touch. He felt a quiver in his thigh, and silently urged himself to concentrate on what the boy was doing, not on how it made him feel. He winced as the metal grew hot, energy pulsing through Yestin's hands into the iron band. His skin crackled with heat, and he twitched, trying not to pull away.

"Keep still!" Yestin spoke through clenched teeth. Nasira rested her free hand on the back of Rhodri's neck and muttered in a soothing voice, but he couldn't hear her words over the drumming of his heart. The pain flared like fire and he closed his eyes against it, head spinning, fighting the memories of the delirium he had endured when Temion first bound him to the tribe.

"There!" Yestin sounded triumphant. The burning faded to a dull, throbbing ache as he let go. Rhodri drew in a long, shuddering breath, trying to calm his fears, and opened his eyes.

Where once there had been metal, now there was glass. He could see the flesh of his ankle through it, hazy, pale as the snow blanketing the courtyard. White, maybe, but living, human flesh and blood. He groaned in pained relief.

"Do you want me to do the other one?" Yestin asked. His face was scarlet, and he took a deep swig of ale and rubbed the bottom of his shirt across his cheeks. "It's hot work."

""Give me a moment." Rhodri could not hide his trembling hands as he took a drink for himself.

"Did it hurt?" Yestin asked.

"It's nothing compared to when I had them put on. The memory . . ." Rhodri shuddered. "Let's get on with it, if you're ready."

This time he knew what to expect, biting his lip against the burning, holding his leg steady with both hands. He barely twitched as the fire spread across his ankles, trying to catch the moment when everything changed, when the band became cold and slippery, brittle as frost on a window pane.

"All done." Yestin sat back, breathing heavily. "What you do with them now is your choice."

Nasira massaged his scalp. Rhodri leant back against the pressure of her fingers, letting her ease his tension.

"Tell your friend Nik," she said, "that we need a hammer, and a blanket or old sheet. Best get some bandages too, just in case."

Rhodri tapped the solid glass round his left ankle with a fingernail. It was unlikely he could get the rings off without cutting himself, but the relief of being free made it a small price to pay.

Temion pushed through the crowd, wielding a hammer with gleeful intent. Rhodri wrapped his hands protectively around his ankles. "Last time you did this, you took pleasure in trying to cripple me. I'm not sure I trust you!"

"I set you free, and you leapt into bed with my sister!" Temion grinned. "I should have brought the hammer down on your balls. Hold still."

He made a few experimental taps against the seamless glass, looking for a weak spot. "I'll have to smash it," he said. "Are you ready?"

"No."

"Hard leather!" Temion swung the hammer, a blow that spilled shattered glass across the courtyard at Rhodri's feet. He moved swiftly, freeing both feet, leaving behind nothing but debris and a few dark spots of blood on the snow.

"How does it feel?" Nasira asked.

Blood trickled down pale, soft flesh over the scars of long-healed burns to drip into the trampled, melting snow at the foot of the steps. He twisted his foot to either side. It felt light, and he hoped it was strong enough to bear his weight. "Really strange," he said, "but good. Nik, help me up."

He shifted his weight from foot to foot, holding the railing for support. Walking was going to be awkward for a while, but he rarely walked when he could ride. He grinned. "Thanks for this, Nik. I didn't get you anything for Winterfest!"

Nik clapped him on the shoulder, and he wobbled, clutching the rail and trying to disguise his weakness. "There's always next year," the Estmarcher joked. "Look at you. You're as wobbly as a foal. Why don't you go and lie down?"

*

Stairs were a challenge. It took the combined effort of Temion and Nik to get Rhodri back to his rooms, and he was exhausted by the time he sank onto the bed. He unlaced his boots and pulled them free, rolling up his trousers and inspecting the full extent of the damage for the first time in years.

Asta, escaping Jilly's restraint as Nik steered his woman out of the room, toddled up to him and prodded his scars with a forefinger. "Daddy ow!"

"Daddy's all right, kitten." He lifted her onto his lap and cuddled her. "It's an old hurt."

Not strictly true, blood dripped from the fresh cuts to pool on the wooden floor. Around the pallid flesh, hidden for so long, the burn scars radiated out like flames, red, ragged weals, hairless and shiny. Branded for life. He rarely looked at his legs, to do so brought back the horror of that night. He could still smell the scorched flesh, hear his own screams echo in his mind . . .

Asta caught hold of his shirt and drew it into her mouth with her thumb. She mumbled something, and he hugged her tighter, cradling her to his chest and struggling not to cry.

Nasira's touch was soft against his neck. "I thought you'd be happy," she said.

"I thought so too."

"So what's wrong?"

"Look at me, Nasira!" He extended his legs, brandishing the scars. "I'm fucking raw! And not just on my skin . . ."

She took Asta from his arms as the little girl grumbled about being disturbed, and carried her to the adjoining room where Finn was sleeping. Returning, she sat at his feet and took one of his abused ankles between her hands, tracing deft fingers over his scars.

"Don't . . ."

"Why not?" She kissed the marked skin, lips fluttering like moths. "You did the same for me once."

"It's not the same."

"Of course it's the same." Nasira wore a dress Nik had given her, in the style of the ladies of the Kingdom. It fastened with ribbons at the bodice. As she released them, the fabric slumped and pooled around her hips, leaving her torso bare. Rhodri could see the edges of the patchcat scars, and the marks where her skin had stretched to accommodate his children. He ran a hand across them.

"Our story . . ."

"Our story is written on our skin." She climbed onto the bed beside him and took off his shirt, fingers massaging the hard knots on his collarbone. "How did you get these?"

"Falling off a horse." Keir had borne the same scars. He lay back, enjoying the pressure of her hands. "I broke my left collarbone twice, and my right three times. And my right arm, but there's no scar there."

"What's this then?" She brushed an old mark, three parallel white lines scored from elbow to wrist.

"You did that, little patchcat."

"Was that me? I didn't mean to." She kissed the white patch on the inside of his wrist. "What about here?"

"Weapons training. Dru said it was an accident."

"I don't like this Dru." Her hands slid over the prominent bones on his hips, and her mouth followed. He groaned, reaching down for her as she slid from the bed on to her knees. "And this one?"

"My father did that, with a belt."

A quick intake of breath indicated her disapproval. "Valery?"

"Dallow. Valery never raised a hand to me."

"The only thing he has to his credit." Her mouth rested on the old scar as she slipped her hand between his thighs. "Lie back now." Lips and tongue danced over his delicate skin as, with hands and warm, gentle mouth, she brought him to shuddering climax.

Chapter Thirteen

TEMION BLOCKED THE chamber door, arms folded across his broad chest, as stubborn and immobile as a mountain. "You asked me to take care of your son," he repeated. "I offered my blood to defend him, and I'll defend him from you if I have to, brother!"

"Go on then." Rhodri's fists balled. "I don't want to fight you, Temion, but I will over this."

"Stop it, both of you!" Nasira lay on the bed, Finn latched on to her breast, enjoying his dinner. "I won't have you fighting over my children in front of them. Talk about it like men. If you want to scrap like puppies, go outside!"

Temion lowered his fists, turning his wrists outward so Rhodri could see the parallel scars below his left thumb, one for each of Rhodri's children, marking the blood he had shed, the oath sworn to defend them.

"They're my children," Rhodri pleaded. "I won't be separated from them."

Temion looked beyond Rhodri to Nasira as she sat up and brought Finn to her shoulder. "Sister, you can't agree with this?"

"Listen to Rhodri, Temion." She was calm, reasonable as ever. Only Rhodri knew how conflicted she was. She hid it like a mage performing a trick.

"I'm asking what *you* think, Nasira. Not the short-hair. Do you want to place them in danger?"

"They won't be in danger. They'll be far back in the train. If the choice is between taking them, and leaving them here with strangers . . . Tell him, Rhodri."

"My parents left me with strangers. They never came back, and then Valery . . . I don't want my children to carry the scars I do."

"They won't, will they?" Temion snapped. "They're not like you, they have normal minds—"

The anger, which had been fading, rushed back. Rhodri brandished his dagger at the door. "Get out."

"Rhodri, I—"

"Out!"

Temion backed away. "At least think about it, brother . . ."

"Get away from me, and my children!" Rhodri kicked the door closed behind Temion with venom.

"He didn't mean it," Nasira told him, wiping Finn's mouth with a cloth. "He takes his duties seriously."

"And I don't?" Rhodri sank beside her on the bed and took his son from her arms. He was warm, and smelled of milk. "Do you think I'm abnormal?"

"I think you're unique." She massaged his scalp, fingers playing over the crown of his head, toying with his hair the way he loved. "Unique, and damaged. My messed-up boy."

"I don't want the little ones to grow up knowing we abandoned them. Is that wrong?"

Nasira was silent for a long moment. "Your poor mother," she murmured after a time.

"What about my mother?"

"If I left Finn here, I would leave part of my spirit behind. Your mother must have felt that, but she had to leave you. She had more courage than I can imagine, and she must have suffered every day. You condemn her for abandoning you, but you don't know what happened. It must have shattered her spirit to ride away without you."

"What about my spirit? She left me, Nasira! Even Valery was a better parent to me than she was . . . I won't repeat the mistakes my parents made. I can't." He rose. "The children ride with us, wherever we go. I'll fight Temion, or any other man who tries to take them from me."

Nasira reached out, and took his hand. "I'll fight at your side," she promised.

*

The first shoots of new grass were budding as Rhodri's army gathered to leave Estmarch Castle and advance on Hierath, on horseback and on foot. There were even a few Atrathene wagons in the convoy, although Nik was cagey about how he had acquired them, and Rhodri didn't want to know. They were a rowdy, excited rabble, and he sent Nik's Estmarchers ahead, hoping to ease their passage through unfamiliar country. He was about to mount when Yestin trotted up to him, riding a grey gelding so skinny he could count its ribs. Rhodri was surprised, he hadn't seen the boy and his mother since his rings were removed, and had assumed they'd taken their reward and returned to their village.

"How are the feet?" Yestin asked. On the rare occasions he smiled, it lit up his face like the sun breaking over the horizon.

Rhodri stuck out an ankle for inspection. "I'm getting used to it." He grinned. "I'm looking forward to summer, when I can swim again."

"Good." The boy twisted his reins, but made no move to leave.

"I thought you'd be riding with Estmarch Freedom?" Rhodri wondered what he wanted.

"Estmarch Freedom means nothing to me. You watch, we'll swap one lot of distant overlords for another, and nothing will get better for the poor." He shrugged. "I hoped I could ride with you. I hear your tribe is looking for a new shaman."

"You fancy yourself a shaman?" Rhodri suppressed a snort of derision. "How old are you? Fifteen summers?"

"Fifteen's not that young. What were you doing when you were fifteen?"

"I was—" Riding in the army, defending a port city from its own internal divisions, feeling Keir's summer-light touch on his thighs and chest . . . "I was a lot older than you are now. It was a different world then."

Yestin's face clouded over. "I'd like to be trained. What's wrong with that? Plenty of apprentices start at twelve. You've seen my skills. I've had interest from the green-eyes . . ."

"Magic users?" Rhodri was intrigued.

"They came sniffing around last summer. I told them I wasn't interested, and sent them on their way."

He puffed up as he spoke. Rhodri thought it more likely that Brunhild had sent the green-eyed mages packing, with no help from her son.

"Why not take the green?" he asked. "I've heard mages live a thousand years. Don't you want to live that long?"

Yestin shrugged. "I don't trust them," he said. "They want me for their own agenda. They have too many rules for my liking. Besides,"—he grinned—"I've heard that for the first five hundred years they lock you in a cottage with some old woman for training. I want to see the world!"

Yestin's low opinion of mages echoed Rhodri's own. "If you want to be a shaman, it would mean living with the Atrathenes, and winning their trust. Believe me, it's not easy."

"I have an advantage over you." Yestin tilted his head proudly. "My father was an Atrathene."

The black hair, eyes as dark as two coals, the smooth tan skin . . . Rhodri should have seen it earlier. He nodded. "Now you say that, it's obvious. You have the same colouring as my daughter."

"You'll train me then?"

Rhodri laughed. "Not me! My training ended a little too abruptly. You speak Atrathene?"

"Enough to get by."

"Talk to the Yellow Snake shaman. Tell her I order your training. It's a hard road you ride, but you seem confident enough to take it on." *Or arrogant enough*, he thought to himself. The Yellow Snake shaman would have her hands full dealing with Yestin, and the boy roused feelings Rhodri was trying to bury, for Nasira's sake. He would rather Yestin stayed where the tribes could keep an eye on him, than roam the Estmarch performing parlour tricks for coin.

He directed the boy towards the rear of the army, mounted, and raised his arm, giving the signal to move off. There was no need for a rousing speech; every man and woman who followed him knew why they were here. He wished he could be so certain himself.

*

Rhodri's strategy of sending Nik and the soldiers pledged to Estmarch Freedom ahead on the road proved a success. The inhabitants of the Estmarch, even those loyal to the Crown, were reluctant to open fire on their own people, and they assumed, as he hoped, that Rhodri's greater force were more Estmarchers, especially as he harried them past towns at such speed that all anyone witnessed was a cloud of dust and a prolonged rumble of hooves. But he had no doubt Serren knew he was coming, and he anxiously awaited her response.

The border of the Estmarch was marked by the banks of the Ferrybane, running south, dividing the town of Beritha in both geography and attitude. Rhodri decided it was wise for the army to rest here a few days, before they entered hostile territory. While the bulk of his men made camp outside the town, he took Nik and Nasira, accompanied by the inevitable brooding presence of Temion, to discover more about what lay ahead.

The Flying Falcon tavern stood on the river, only a strip of grass separating it from the water. Painted tide lines on the wall indicated the depth of former floods. Some were higher than Rhodri's head, but at the moment the river, though high, showed no signs of inviting itself in for a flagon of ale. Rhodri glanced at Nik, who nodded. "I've been here before," he said. "It's a good place. The landlord is sympathetic to our cause."

"*Your* cause, maybe." Rhodri snorted. "I'm not sure what he'd think of mine."

As they entered the tavern, Nasira slipped her arm through Rhodri's. "I've heard your stories of these places," she said, in an undertone. "Are you sure it's safe to bring the children here?"

"Safer than leaving them in the camp." He squeezed her arm and offered a grin. "Sometimes tavern tales get exaggerated. I've been for many an evening's drinking that hasn't ended in a brawl or murder."

She shook her head. "It's strange you have buildings just to drink in. We have the whole of the plains. No wonder you fight, crammed together like this."

To Rhodri's eyes, the Flying Falcon wasn't crowded. There were plenty of free tables, and room at the bar. Their entrance attracted a few curious glances, but the drinkers were more interested in chatting amongst themselves than causing trouble for strangers.

The landlord, a burly man in late middle age who looked as if he would be handy in a fight, caught Nik's eye, and they exchanged nods. He directed the party to a table in the corner away from the other customers, and brought their drinks to the table himself, pulling up a seat without waiting for an invitation. He had thick, dark eyebrows, overlapping in the middle to form one alarming tuft of hair. He rolled up his sleeve to expose the Estmarch Freedom tattoo on the inside of his wrist, and winked at Nik. "Legend tells me you're on the warpath," he said.

"Legend is not always fact, as my friend here will tell you. Everyone, this is Owain. You can speak freely before him."

"Can we trust him?" Nasira asked Rhodri, in a low voice. "He has the look of a fighter."

"A fighter, a trader, and a traveller in exotic lands, lady of Atrath," Owain replied in flawless Atrathene. "Do I surprise you? You should never make rash assumptions that people won't understand you. Otherwise you might betray more than you intend!"

Nasira hung her head, and Rhodri bristled. "I didn't come here to have you speak to my wife that way," he said in a dangerous tone.

Owain raised his hands to placate him. "Your woman doubted my honesty. She's wise and cautious, but perhaps not cautious enough. Other men may not be so candid. I'm sorry, woman of the steppes," he said, switching to Atrathene, "I meant no offence. Will you drink with me?"

She drank from the flagon, quick gulps to mask her confusion. Asta slipped from her lap and hid under the table, playing a private game in the forest of chair legs and lower limbs.

Owain fixed his eyes on Rhodri. "I know Niklaus well," he said. "I don't know you at all, but I have a healthy mistrust of rumour and reputation. If Nik vouches for you, I don't doubt him, but you'll forgive me if I'm wary. Old habits die hard, even when a man retires to run a quiet tavern by the river."

Nik chuckled at this. "Retired my arse! You'd die of boredom if you were forced to retire!"

Owain roared with laughter. "Very true! But what brings you to my humble inn, and why is there an army of Atrathene warriors camped outside the town? You've made an interesting alliance, Niklaus. I want to know more about it, and what part you want me to play."

"We came looking for shelter for a few nights. And some information, if you have any," Nik said.

"News from the Midlands? Oh, come on! It's obvious where you're headed. I'll side with you on one condition, but it's a serious one. No more branding. It's barbaric, and it wins you no friends."

"Branding?" Rhodri shuffled in his seat. "There was one incident, true, but . . ."

Nik stared at his fingers, resting on the table top. "I didn't like to bring it up," he admitted.

"Bring what up?" Rhodri looked from his friend to Owain's heavy-browed, disapproving face. "What are you talking about?"

"Don't pretend you don't know," Owain said. "I've seen it with my own eyes, when the King's Third last passed this way. You brand your prisoners as a warning. It's sickening, and it has to stop."

Rhodri licked his lips and drummed his fingers on the table. "How many?" he asked.

"How many men have I seen branded?" Owain shrugged. "Nine or ten. I suspect there are more. You tell me!"

"Where were these brands? Did they show them to you?"

"Some on their chests, some on their arms where I wear my tattoo. They didn't trouble to hide them, and when I asked they were willing to talk."

"To say what? That the Atrathenes burned them? Shit!" Rhodri sat back, and blew out his cheeks in a hefty sigh, ignoring Nasira's anxious query. "I met a man in Terinth. He was terrified I would burn him. Now I know why . . ." He shook his head. "One man. I branded one man with the badge of the Plains Hawk. I was angry. Nasira's sister . . . well, it doesn't matter now. I made a mistake, and now it's turned around to bite me. I guess I deserve it." He sighed again. Asta tugged at his knee, and he lifted her onto his lap.

"Rhodri, what in hells are you talking about?" Nik asked.

"It's not Atrathenes branding those men. I should have realised at Terinth. Serren's army are branding themselves, and claiming it was my people."

"Why would they do that?" Owain asked.

"To demonise the tribes. To discredit me." Rhodri thought of Drusain. "Hells, some of them might be doing it for fun."

"They wouldn't," Nik said at once. "Not the King's Third."

"The King's Third have done a lot of things I never imagined they'd do."

A heavy silence fell at Rhodri's words. Owain clicked his fingers at the barmaid to bring fresh ales, even though the ones on the table were only half drunk. Asta yawned, her head lolling against Rhodri's shoulder, and he caught Nasira's eye.

"I'll tell you everything," he promised. "Do you want to take the cubs up to bed?"

Temion rose. "I'll go with you," he said. "I'm learning nothing here. Give me my niece."

Asta's eyelids fluttered as she was transferred to Temion's arms, but she was already limp. Owain ordered the barmaid to show them to their rooms and provide everything they needed. He finished his first pint in one gulp, wiped his mouth with the back of his hand, and started on the second flagon before the first could settle.

"I may have misjudged you," he admitted to Rhodri. "You seem a decent man who cares about his family. And the things done in Serren's name . . ." He shuddered. "I don't want to be involved in waging war on a slip of a girl, mark you. I'll find out what I can. Use it as you see fit, but if it all turns to crap, I don't know who you are. Is that clear?"

Rhodri nodded. "Thanks, Owain. I appreciate it."

"I'll tell you this for nothing." He drained his pint and looked around for the barmaid. "The Aged Ones have been in, asking questions about you. If you're smart, you'll keep your head down."

"Aged Ones? Are you talking about witches? I thought they were all dead?" Rhodri's spine tingled. Valery had told him many lies, but he had no doubt that what he told him about witches was true.

"Not witches. Older than witches, and more powerful. They have their own schemes, those green-eyes, but they'll be out to protect Serren and her family. Her mother was close to the mages, I've heard. You'd be smart to stay out of their way!"

*

"Who is he, Nik?" Rhodri had watched Owain for a few nights, trying to figure him out. The innkeeper seemed to know everyone, and everything, and he changed his personality according to whom he spoke with. The real man was as elusive as a fluttering moth, and Rhodri wasn't sure he had seen him yet.

Niklaus shrugged. "Poet, spy, mercenary . . . it depends who you talk to. The tales he spins are so tangled it's hard to tell where the truth ends and fantasy begins. But he's a good man. I've known him a while and I've never had cause to doubt him."

"I hope you're right." Nik was a good judge of character, and his loyalty was unquestionable, but Rhodri worried that it made him think highly of people who didn't deserve it, himself included. He fell silent as Owain strode over to their table, exchanging bawdy chat with his regulars, and dumped two brimming flagons they hadn't ordered down in front of them.

"Kingsmere," he muttered, not letting his smile of bonhomie drop for a second.

"What?"

"Serren's army gathers at Kingsmere. It's a long swing south over rough country if you want to avoid them. Best place to get an army across the Lam if you're intending to march on—" He broke into spontaneous laughter as a customer passed a little too close. "She didn't! Those Whitewood whores will do anything, won't they? I can't tell you more than that, my woman would kill me!"

He moved away. Rhodri drained his drink and rose abruptly. "Let's take a walk," he said.

Turning their backs on the river, Rhodri and Nik ventured into the dark streets of the town. It was late, and few lights burned in the windows. Finding a stone bench in the open town square, Rhodri sat and watched the scantily-clad whores hustle for business on the steps of the mayor's house. "Tempted?" he asked Nik.

"Jilly would kill me. Besides, you didn't drag me out of a warm tavern for a tumble with a whore. You want to talk about Kingsmere. I don't know any more about it than you do."

"It's like Pencarith," Rhodri said. "One of those little villages you ride through without noticing. We came through on our way from Hierath. It's on the left bank of a ford in the Lam. If I were Serren, I'd want to stop us crossing the river at all. The ground rises up sharply from there, and the trees are thick on the right bank, so it's a good place for an ambush— what?"

Nik laughed and shook his head. "I wish I could do that!"

"Trust me, you don't." Rhodri shuddered. "If I could wash it all out of my mind with drink or chewing herb, I'd leap at the chance."

"It must be handy, though. I'll wager you never forget to buy a Winterfest gift for your woman!"

"Oh, I don't forget that." Rhodri laughed, a bitter, humourless chuckle. "I don't forget that any more than I can forget the smell of Astan's blood soaking through my shirt, or Nasira's sister crying after the King's Third held her down and fucked her. She was a child, Nik! And I remember every detail. Other people tell me hurts fade with time, but everything that was done—to me, to my family and friends—is a fresh wound on my brain. It won't fucking heal! It doesn't get better with time; everything hurts as much as it did when it was new, and I don't know how to make it go away!"

His outburst attracted the attention of the whores. One, a haggard girl with sunken cheeks, sashayed over to him. She moved in a way that would have been sexy if she'd had some flesh on her bones, but was closer to the jerky movements of a skeleton. "Whatever's troubling you, honey," she purred, "I can make it go away. Three silvers, and I'll make you feel much better!"

"Three silvers?" Nik stepped in. "Last time I took a whore it was only two, and she had more to get hold of than you do—"

"Leave her, Nik." Rhodri turned to the whore. "I appreciate the offer, but I have a wife waiting for me. Take this as a gift." He pressed a coin into her hand. "Buy yourself a meal. You look like you could use it. But you and your friends have to leave us alone."

The prostitute looked from one to the other, and a grin stretched across her sallow face. "Oh, I see! In that case, I'll leave you and your 'wife' to get on with it. Have fun!"

She retreated to join her cohorts. Nik stared after her. "Did she think we—?" A gale of laughter rose from the gaggle of whores. "She bloody did! She thought we were together!"

"Your face! You look like you've bitten a stingfly!"

"I can't believe she thought I was that way! You I can understand, but me?" Nik lapsed into indignant incoherence. Rhodri couldn't contain his laughter.

"Hells, Nik, thanks for that. I needed a good laugh!"

"I'm glad it amused you, at least." But a warm grin spread over Nik's face. "It is funny, I suppose . . ."

"It's hilarious! Your reaction!" Rhodri wiped his eyes. "I feel better now."

"So." Nik grew serious once more. "Kingsmere?"

Rhodri nodded. "Kingsmere is the place. Let's test my sister's steel."

*

The west bank of the Ferrybane marked the beginning of hostile country, the border between the rebellious Estmarch and the Lambury Plains, where Serren's authority went unquestioned. Rhodri pulled the riders from Estmarch Freedom back into the main body of the army, knowing they would not help smooth the journey here. The road between the Ferrybane and the Lam was well-travelled and swift, dotted with farmsteads and nameless hamlets. Rhodri's army swept along like a ship through water, diverting neither left nor right, slowing for no one. Travellers on the road learned to get out of the way at the rumble of their hooves, or risk being ridden into the dusty ruts of the track. Everyone knew a storm was brewing, and nobody wanted to be caught by the clash of the lightning.

Barely a moon from Beritha, and spring was edging into summer. The winds were shrill, pushing frequent showers that came from nowhere and passed quickly. It was raining, dark clouds forming a patchwork against the dawn, as Rhodri and Temion followed Sudak in single file towards the river Lam. On foot, crouched low, they moved silently. It would have taken a highly alert sentry to spot them. The man on guard, staring stoically ahead with the low morning sun in his eyes and rain dripping from his helm, may not have noticed the trio if they stood before him and bared their backsides.

"They've been here a while," Temion whispered, looking down at the camp. It sprawled along the riverbank and extended into the trees. "They've got women there. I hope they've become lazy with waiting."

"Not too lazy." Rhodri pointed. Weapons were racked, horses saddled in readiness for the forthcoming battle. "They know we're close." Anticipation sent a tingle through him, a rush of adrenaline and nervous energy. "I want to drive them back across the river. Flank them left and right, and hit them hard in the middle. If we can break their shield wall, they might scatter without much of a fight." It was a slim chance, but one worth taking.

"What about the guard?" Sudak asked in a low tone. His fingers brushed his belt dagger.

"Leave him, unless he raises the alarm. Stay here and watch. It won't be long."

Rhodri's army spread out, forming the massive arc so effective for hunting game, and Western soldiers. Temion took the right flank. Rhodri rode left and put Estmarch Freedom in the centre under Nik's command. His friend was anxious.

"I'm not sure about this," he confessed as they were about to part.

"Not sure about what?" Rhodri swung Liberty round to face him. "You've got three thousand men under your command. I've seen you lead them, so don't tell me you can't do this. Not now."

"I've led them on guerrilla raids against small bands of soldiers—"

"You took Estmarch Castle!"

"We had inside help. I've never asked them to go up against the entire New Kingdom Army before! What if things go wrong?"

"Then we'll be too busy trying to stay alive to worry about anything else!" But the doubt in Nik's eyes left him with a dilemma. "Can I trust you not to bail?"

"What's wrong?" Nasira watched the exchange with keen interest. "Has your friend lost his spine?"

"A little." Rhodri kicked his heels in frustration. They were wasting time.

"I can help. Give me the left flank to command."

Rhodri shook his head. "Out of the question."

"Why? Don't tell me it's too dangerous. We've had this fight before, and you never win."

"You're a woman. The men won't follow you."

She tossed her braids and laughed at this. "Foolish little short-hair! After all this time, the ways of your homeland still rule your head. I thought better of you, Rhodri."

"What about the children?" he countered. "Where are they, while you play the heroine?"

"Safe in the vanguard with Siralane. Where they are every time I ride into battle, no matter what position I take." Her eyes flashed a warning. "Do you think I would risk our children, Rhodri?"

"Of course not, but—"

"Yes, I'm a mother. I'm also a hunter, and a fighter. So is every woman who rides with you. Let me take the left flank. The men will listen to me, and I know how to lead them. I've been with you long enough!"

290

She flashed a sharp-toothed smile, and he relented. "Stay safe, then."

"And you, my husband. See you on the far side of the river!"

She raised a hand in salute and trotted away. Niklaus raised his eyebrows. "You two having a fight?"

"There's no point fighting a woman who's always right." Rhodri sighed. "She's taking my command on the left flank. I'll ride beside you, my friend."

"A woman in charge? Will the men follow her?"

"Yours might not, but mine will." Rhodri shrugged. "Atrathene ways. You wouldn't understand, and I'm not sure I do, but let her have her head. We've got a battle to win."

Nik handed his Estmarch Freedom flag to Rhodri to adorn his standard. "It's your show, my friend," he said. "I never thought it would come to this."

"Nor did I." But it was a lie. In his heart, ever since he discovered the young woman who ruled in Hierath was his younger sister, Rhodri had known their paths were set for conflict. It was as inevitable as the changing of the seasons. He wondered if Serren felt it too, the crushing destiny driving them to war. He waved the banner high, and a cheer erupted around him, Estmarchers hailing their flag, Atrathenes their courageous leader. Boosted by their support, with the blood surging through his veins and Liberty prancing beneath him, champing and foaming in her eagerness to be off, Rhodri led his army towards the river, and the battle he had waited years to fight.

Only a mile down the road, Sudak crossed the front ranks to fall into stride beside him, his lanky gelding easily outpacing Liberty. "They're coming in fast!" he called. "Brace yourselves!"

"Nik, take this!" Rhodri tossed the standard to his friend, drew his bow, and urged Liberty forward into the front rank of archers. The mare tossed her head and squealed, scenting battle, muscles straining to keep pace with the larger, younger horses.

On the road ahead, a dust-cloud rose. Over the thunder in his ears Rhodri could hear the war cries of Serren's army, galloping into range of the deadly Atrathene bows.

"Loose!" Rhodri couldn't make out his own voice over the chaos, but his men heard. A volley of arrows arced high, to slice like a deadly shower into the ranks of the Queen's army. Sheets of arrows rained down, but the enemy barely faltered, replying with shots of their own. And then they were on them. Too late for shooting.

Rhodri stashed his bow and drew his sword, plunging into the fray. Instinct took over, made him its instrument. Ducking and weaving from side to side, horse and rider moved as one. Noise and movement, sweat and chaos, red mist drifting from the sky. Metal meeting metal, flesh, bone.

He felt blood spray across his eyes, and blinked it away. A hand seized his leg, and he kicked, booted foot crunching against bone. He felt a searing pain in his calf, but he couldn't look down at the wound. Intent on dodging the next blow, fending off the next attack, Rhodri fought for his life. For the lives of his family.

One on one now. The disciplined lines broke down. Men grappled, on foot and horseback, slipping and sliding in the churned-up mud that was once a grassy road. Showers of blood mixed with the rain, dripping from Rhodri's hair into his eyes. Every limb ached. The adrenaline spurring him on was gone. He moved like a machine, no thought but to evade the hits, dodge the tumbling arrows, stay alive a little longer. The idea of reaching the river faded. There was nothing, had never been anything, but the fight, eternal and exhausting.

Liberty stumbled, hooves skidding in the mud and gore, slammed by another horse barging into her side. She slipped, flinging Rhodri from the saddle. As the ground rushed up to meet him he twisted and rolled. Over the sounds of battle, he heard a sickening snap in his right shoulder.

He staggered to his feet, quivering at the shock. Liberty had vanished, carried away by the storm. He was alone.

The horse that ploughed into them lay on its side, screaming, flailing hooves throwing up gobbets of mud. Splintered fragments of bone ruptured the skin of its left foreleg.

The rider sprawled on his face, one arm flung out, fingers twitching towards the wounded horse's bridle. There was a chilling familiarity about horse and rider. Rhodri tightened his hand around his hilt, and tried to shift the weight of the shield on his left arm. The movement sent a hot lance of pain along his shoulder into his neck, and he hissed at the flare.

The injured rider sat up, and dragged his horse's head into his lap. A warrior stumbled between them. Rhodri didn't see the moment of death, but the screaming stopped abruptly, leaving behind an aching, silent void. A cloud darkened the sun, and the rain returned.

The rider raised his head. One blue eye glittered. The other was a dark slit, unreadable. He thrust the horse aside and leapt to his feet, sword waving. Rhodri stepped back, testing the uncertain ground beneath him. He tried to keep his weak arm steady. Without Liberty, he felt vulnerable and exposed.

Drusain advanced, wiping his eyes. "I thought it was you," he said. His voice was soft, full of menace. "I've been looking for you. I want the honour of killing you myself."

Rhodri's muscles tensed as he sized up his opponent. The carnage of the battle faded away. It was just the two of them now. "It won't be me that dies today, Drusain."

They circled, slow and cautious, boots dragging in the mud. Two old adversaries, looking for an opening, a weak spot. Rhodri knew his left arm wasn't up to the fight. He just hoped he could disguise it for long enough.

"You fucking traitor, you make me sick," Dru goaded him. Rhodri tried to stay calm, not to rise to the taunts. If he lost his head, Dru would strike like a snake.

"At least your father only betrayed his friends. You've turned against your country!"

"I've heard the lies you spread, Dru. You have no idea . . ." He narrowed his eyes. "I should thank you. You've made me a legend!"

"I'll make you a fucking corpse!" Dru charged in, sword raised, spittle flying from his lips. Rhodri barely had time to bring up his shield. The jarring clash buckled his knees. He gasped.

"Was it your idea to brand your own men, Dru?"

Rhodri ducked the blow whistling past his ear. He rolled to the side, crying out in pain as he brought up the blade. His two-handed strike crunched into the mail of Dru's thigh. He stumbled, grunting. "Did you do it yourself? I bet it made your cock hard . . ."

"Not as hard as your little sister did!" Dru flung up his arm to block Rhodri's furious blade as he recovered his balance, panting. "I love how those savage whores moan. I'll try out your woman too, when I'm done with you!"

Blind anger triumphed over the pain, lent strength to his exhausted limbs. Dru staggered under the onslaught, blows crashing against his shoulders and limbs.

He dropped into a crouch, shield up to protect his face, sword lashing wildly. A lucky strike against Rhodri's shield split it down the middle, Dru's blade wedged in the severed wood.

He tried to jerk it loose as they circled each other in a morbid dance. Dru thrust, the tip of his blade lacerating Rhodri's forearm, blood trickling towards the hilt. Every movement wrought fresh hell in his injured shoulder as he struggled to wrench free.

He pushed against Dru with all his strength, broken bone screaming under the strain. His mouth was full of blood, and darkness gathered at the edge of his vision as his feet scrabbled for purchase in the mud.

Dru's wide eye brightened. He drew back his mailed fist, powered by the weight of his shield, and slammed it into Rhodri's collar. There was a crack, a scream, an explosion of pain in his skull. His vision blurred. He had the distant sensation of falling, and then nothing.

The sunlight stabbed through Rhodri's skull, and he screwed shut his fluttering eyelids. He lay still, wondering if he was in the Spirit Realm. Anger surged through him for all he had lost, for his children: Finn, who would never remember his father, and Asta, who he would miss most of all.

Tears gathered at the corners of his eyes as he thought of his daughter, but he blinked them away, letting in the harsh sunlight. He was aware of a cold, creeping sensation, damp soaking through to his skin, cold rings of metal from his mail pressed into his ribs. He shifted to ease his discomfort, and pain lanced through him, pinning him to the ground. His guts twisted, and he vomited, barely able to turn his neck so most of his sick splashed on the ground beside his head.

Maybe this wasn't the Spirit Realm? There was no pain there, Kilujen always told him. Maybe this was one of the hells. Stars knew, he deserved no better. The demons would come for him with brands, to scorch the skin from his flesh . . .

Rhodri shuddered. "Fuck that," he muttered. He wasn't going to lie here and take his punishment. Even in the worst hell, there must be somewhere to hide. He opened his eyes, slowly, getting used to the light, and carefully sat up.

The movement disturbed the crows feasting nearby and they took off shrieking into the cloudy sky. The showers had passed, and golden shafts of afternoon sunlight shone down on fragments of mail and sticky pools of blood. The gleam made Rhodri's eyes sting. He was surrounded by blood and death, twisted, broken bodies sinking into the mud, but this was no hell. The battle had tumbled over him and left him behind, alone with the dead and dying.

Why wasn't he dead?

He should be dead. Dru should have hacked open his throat, sliced his head from his body and left his staring eyes open for the crows to pluck out. He must have known he was still alive. Where had he gone?

There was a blankness in his memory, darker and more unsettling than any hell.

He used his dagger to cut away the straps that held his broken shield and let it fall, whimpering at the torment in his shoulder. The flesh beneath hung in dirty ribbons, snarled with dirt and splinters. When he moved his arm, he could feel the shattered ends of bone scraping over each other, and it made him retch. He retrieved his sword, wiping it automatically on his shirt before he returned it to its sheath. The shirt was caked with mud and blood, and cleaning the blade there achieved nothing.

His feet itched with cold and damp. Some bastard had stolen his boots. Lucky he didn't wear rings, or they would have had his fingers off too. The crows circled above his head, cawing, furious at being disturbed as he forced himself to his feet. There had to be somewhere to go.

He stumbled across the battlefield towards the distant clash of arms. His limbs felt heavy and dull, and every step jarred his shoulder. Senses battered by the fight, by exhaustion, he stared at the ruins of the field, seeing everything, remembering it all, but taking nothing in. He needed Nasira and his children to make him feel human. He needed his horse.

"Liberty!"

Only the screech of crows, the groans of the dying, the slop of his feet through the chilly mire. It was like slogging through tar. He was so numb, he wasn't even sure he had shouted. His voice might be confined to his mind.

"Where are you? Liberty!"

"Freedom!" A man in soldier's garb floundered on his elbows in the mud. "Help a fellow Estmarcher, friend!"

"I wasn't—it doesn't matter. Take my arm." Rhodri extended a hand and helped the burly man to his feet. His face was grey, and blood seeped from a wound on his hip.

"Where are you going?"

"I'm looking for my horse," Rhodri said. "I lost her. I've lost everybody." Grief crushed him, and he sagged.

"Sounds like you're in a bad state. We should find the baggage train. Can you help me walk?"

Having someone depend on him gave fresh purpose to Rhodri's shattered spirit, something he could focus his attention on, to try and force the horrors of the day to the back of his mind. "Let's stick together," he said.

The Estmarcher nodded, wincing as he took a limping step. "My name's Elay," he said. "You dress like an Atrathene, but you're not, are you?"

"Midlander." There didn't seem much harm in admitting it now. "I'm Rhodri."

"Same as . . . ? Oh . . ." Elay twitched, in pain or fear.

"Forget it. Let's keep walking. And talking." It helped to talk, to blot out the carnage around them. "Tell me about yourself."

Elay was from Tashk Mill, on the southern border of the Estmarch, and passionate about his cause. He had left a wife and four children to follow Niklaus into battle. "Do you have any little ones yourself?" he asked.

"Two." Rhodri felt a pang. "I don't know where my wife is . . ."

"She won't be far. Maybe with the vanguard?"

Rhodri shook his head. "She was fighting. She insisted. She's a fine shot, but . . ." He trailed off. The baggage wagons lay ahead, drawn into a circle. They seemed quiet, but he drew his sword, his movements awkward with Elay leaning on his arm.

There was movement from one of the wagons. A little figure, a tumble of waving arms and legs, running towards them, falling over and scrambling back up. "Daddy!"

"Asta!" Disentangling his arm from Elay's, Rhodri ran to his daughter and scooped her up, pressing her close to his chest. She struggled to get away, protesting at the dirt and the smell. "Is Mummy here?"

She shook her head and wrinkled her nose.

"Siralane, then. Can you get Sira?"

Asta nodded, sliding down his legs as he lowered her to the ground. "Your daughter?" Elay asked as Rhodri took his arm once more. "She's dark. Pretty though!" he added hastily. "Is your woman Atrathene? I wouldn't have expected that . . ."

"Why not?"

"I don't know." Elay shrugged. "Your father had an Atrathene mistress. I suppose it makes sense."

"He wasn't my father." Rhodri broke off as Siralane ran towards them, wringing her hands. "Where's Finn?" he demanded.

"Asleep. You're hurt! Where's Temion? Nasira?"

"They're not here? I don't know . . ." He slumped, exhausted, his companion's weight too much to bear. "Fetch shamans, and Western healers. This is Elay. He's hurt his leg."

"What about you? Your arm . . ." She caught hold of him as he collapsed, leaving Elay to stumble along behind them.

"I came off Liberty and snapped my collarbone. It's no matter, I've done it before . . ." He sank on to the wagon steps as Siralane fussed over him. Asta snuggled under his good arm. "If they're not here, I need to find them."

"You're going nowhere! You look like the dead, and your friend's not much better. We have a healing tent set up, although it's packed full. Go there."

"I'm staying here. As soon as you set my collar I'm going to find Nasira."

Siralane stamped her foot, like Asta throwing a tantrum. "You impossible short-hair! What good are you to anyone dead? You stay right here, I'll fetch you a drink."

She bustled off. Elay sank to the ground at the foot of the steps. "Trouble?" he asked.

"Family dispute."

"I see." The Estmarcher stared into the distance. "All the things I've heard . . . I didn't think I'd like you, Rhodri. But you're all right, I suppose."

"Half the things you've heard are lies. The rest is exaggeration. I know what people say about me."

"You said Northpoint wasn't your father?"

Rhodri rested his head against the side of the wagon, trying to ease the ache in his shoulder. "That's the biggest lie of all," he said. "The one I've spent my life trying to escape."

Siralane returned with bandages, and a brimming flagon which she pressed into his hand. Ale, strangely spiced, that spread a warm lassitude over his limbs. Even his collarbone didn't hurt as much as he drank, but the mug felt heavy in his grip. He needed to rest for a moment. Then he would find Nasira. He would find Temion and Nik, and bring them all home . . .

*

It was evening when Rhodri woke. He lay on his back in a tent, and when he tried to move, he discovered his left arm was strapped against his body. His chest was bare, but his hair was crusted with blood, sharp little spikes that stung his eyes when he shook his head to clear the vestiges of sleep.

Asta curled up beside him, thumb in her mouth. He slipped out of bed, careful not to disturb her, clutching at the tent poles for support as his head swam. There was a bitter taste in his mouth, like crushed autumn leaves. He spat.

"Rhodri!" Someone called his name, insistent, as if they had been calling a while with no response.

"Coming!"

The evening air was cold. It hit his bare skin like a slap as he lifted the tent flap and looked out, rubbing his free hand over his face. Why couldn't he wake up? Normally he slept and woke like a cat. "What's going on?"

"The little mare! You have to come and catch her."

"Liberty?" This roused him. He spat again to rid himself of the taste. "Siralane, did you *drug* me?"

"To keep you from killing yourself. And I'd do it again. Nasira and your friend are here, and safe. Finn is with them."

"And Temion?"

A shadow crossed her face. "The little mare is wild. No one can get near her."

"What does that have to do with Temion?"

Siralane took his hand, her fingers cool and trembling. "Come," she said.

A crowd had gathered outside the camp, circling the anxious mare, but staying well back. One of the young warriors of the Running Goat nursed a broken arm. Liberty was skittish, bucking, lashing out with her hooves. A man slumped on her back, one arm around her neck. Rhodri marvelled that he was able to hang on.

"Hey, Lib! Stop that!"

At the sound of his voice she snorted, hooves dancing. He approached her from the side, hand out, wary of her teeth. Her eyes rolled, and lather gathered on her neck and flanks.

"No need to be scared, girl. You're with me now. I'm right here."

Another few steps. Liberty tossed her head and flashed her teeth. Her bridle was missing, but he reached out and caught a handful of her mane, blowing in her ear and down her flaring nostrils to calm her. She nuzzled against him, snuffling at the unfamiliar sling.

"Hand me a rope." Rhodri spoke in a soft voice, keeping his eyes fixed on his horse. "Move slowly."

Liberty tried to shy at the approach of a stranger, but she allowed Rhodri to drop a loop of rope over her head and lead her to a nearby tree, where he hitched her, and turned his attention to Temion. Nasira's brother had clung on, not through a superb feat of horsemanship, but by lashing himself to her saddle. His eyelids flickered as Rhodri cut her free, one-handed and awkward.

300

"Little brother?" His voice was hoarse. "Do you ride the Spirit Trail too?"

"No, and nor do you. Some help here!" Temion slithered to the ground, leaving a crimson smear on Liberty's hide. No wonder she was terrified. With only one free arm, Rhodri couldn't lift him. He huddled on the ground, arms wrapped around his stomach.

"Not yet, brother, but I hear my mother calling me . . ."

"Don't talk crap, Temion! We'll patch you up and you'll be fine."

Nasira's firm hands pushed him aside as she helped her brother to her feet. "Come to our tent," she said. "We'll get a healer."

He gripped her arm. "I need to see the sunset, sister. Can you help me?"

"Whatever you need." She waved away offers of help, supporting her brother on her arm. Rhodri followed, feeling redundant, with no idea what to do.

Siralane dragged blankets out of the tent to create a nest in the grass. The sun was low, bathing the camp in a ruddy glow, and Adeamus, rising, was full and milk-pale. Temion nodded as he sank into the blankets. "It's a fine night," he said. "Sit with me, little brother. I'd rather not travel alone." He winced.

"What happened?"

"I don't know. I lost my horse, and I was hurt. I thought I was leaving the world right there on the battlefield, but the little mare found me. She seemed as lost and scared as I was. I couldn't ride, so I strapped myself to her back and trusted her to carry me home. I knew wherever she was, you wouldn't be far away."

"I thought I'd lost everyone," Rhodri confessed.

"Ah, little brother, it would take more than that to lose us all! Where's my woman?"

"She's coming now, with healers." Rhodri made room for Siralane in the nest of blankets, and she huddled close to her husband, soothing his wounds with soft hands while the healers inspected him.

Nasira sat on the steps of the wagon, head in her hands, shoulders slumped. Asta clung to her arm, frowning and solemn. Rhodri drew her hands down and cradled them in his. "Temion will be fine," he promised. "He's had a bad time, but Siralane is with him. The healers . . ."

"I know." She wrapped her hands around his neck and pulled him close, until their foreheads rested together. "Keep telling me that. I believe it when you say it." Her eyes were two black pools, glittering with tears, as Asta pushed between them demanding a hug.

The Yellow Snake shaman cleared her throat to break up the family embrace. Her face was sombre, and she shook her head.

Rhodri felt numb. His throat was tight, and he struggled to force his words out. "How long?"

"Before dawn. Spend time with your brother. He needs you."

"No!" Nasira crumpled into Rhodri's arms. Asta, bewildered by her mother's distress, burst into tears.

"Go to him," Rhodri urged. "I'll get Finn. I know he'll want to . . . want to . . ."

"Fetch him. I need him." The kiss she gave him was fierce, broken off with a sob as she snatched Asta into her arms and hugged her protectively.

By the time Rhodri returned with Finn, Temion's family were gathered. His wife and children gathered around, hugging him, tears flowing. He lay on his back, staring into the darkening sky, cradling his young son to his chest. Rhodri stood apart, feeling like an outsider, ravaged by memories of Astan's lingering death. He should have had his family with him, should have known how much he was loved.

"Where's my little brother?" Temion's voice was weak, and a spasm of pain crossed his face. "I would see Rhodri, before it gets dark. Make room for him."

Rhodri sat beside him, cross-legged, with Finn in his lap. Temion looked up at him. His smile was strained. "He's a fine boy," he said. "He'll grow up to look like you."

"Don't tell your sister that," Rhodri tried to joke, knowing the humour was forced. "Nasira wants at least one of our children to take after her."

"Strong blood." Temion coughed and rolled onto his side. His skin glistened with sweat, and his lips quivered. "You're not much to look at, but your blood is fierce. I'm proud . . ."

"I shouldn't have made you follow me," Rhodri said bitterly.

"It's not the sky I would choose to die under, but it's not so bad. I can see why you love this funny little country. You'll look after it well when it's yours. I'm glad I could help you win it, for Finn."

He raised a shaking hand to caress his nephew's head, toying with a wisp of blond hair. His eyes closed, and his hand dropped to his chest. "I'm glad you were my brother."

The tears rolled unchecked down Rhodri's face. "I will always be your brother, Temion."

The last of the sun slipped below the horizon. There was no reply.

Chapter Fourteen

TEMION WAS BURIED at dawn, his face turned towards his distant homeland. Rhodri moved mechanically now; there were children to feed, an army to direct, a war to fight, but he could only manage one thing at a time, and his family came first. Asta was confused, clinging close to him, tripping him up every time he turned around until he yelled at her and drove her into the sanctuary of her mother's arms. Nasira told her Temion had gone away and wasn't coming back, and she was red-faced with fury that she wasn't allowed to visit him.

"Rhodri, she's upset. Shouting at her won't help."

"Keep her out from under my feet, then," he retorted. "Why can't she cling to *your* leg if she's scared?"

Nasira drew in a deep breath. Her eyes were dry, flashing with anger and hurt. She was trying to be brave, for the children, but her own grief gnawed at her. "Couldn't you take her to . . . ?"

"No." He shook his head in flat refusal. Nasira had already broached the subject, but he'd put her down then, and he wouldn't change his mind.

"But if you were there, she'd be safe! It might help—"

"Walking the Spirit Realm isn't safe. Not for me, and certainly not for her. You've been there, you know how it is!"

"I was a patchcat then." She sighed. "It's so different. I can't explain . . ."

"Then don't. I'm not taking her, and nor will any shaman. You don't know what you're asking."

"Is it because you're afraid of Valery?"

"What's that got to do with anything?"

There was a gentle but pronounced throat-clearing outside the entrance to the wagon.

"Rhodri?" Sudak's voice was tentative. "I hate to interrupt, but I need to see you. I can come back later . . . ?"

"I'm coming." Rhodri threw a warning glare at his wife and daughter, then jumped down the steps. The movement jarred his broken collarbone, and he swallowed a curse.

"Are you sure? One of the prisoners is asking for you. If you're not ready—"

"I said I was fine!" Rhodri rubbed a hand over his face, trying to organise his thoughts. "What prisoners? No one told me we had prisoners."

"There was no time yesterday, and after Temion . . ." Sudak shrugged, a mournful expression on his face. "Niklaus said you weren't to be bothered. He didn't know what to do with them."

"Let them go, I suppose. They're no use to us now it's over."

Sudak blinked. "Now what's over, leader?"

"The war. We've lost, so there's no point in keeping prisoners, is there?"

"What are you talking about?"

"This!" He gestured angrily around him, at the camp. "If this is all that's left of us, we might as well try and get home. Accept it, Sudak, I've failed you. I've let you all down, and I'm sorry."

His taller companion caught his shoulders, ignoring the way he flinched. "What happened to you yesterday?" he demanded. "Did you hit your head? We won, you stupid short-hair!" He gave him a little shake. "Do you hear me? We *won* the battle!"

"Then where is everybody? What happened?"

"We drove your sister's army back to the river and beyond." Sudak grinned, a flash of genuine joy. "They scattered like straw in the wind. Our army is camped over the river, half a day's ride from here. I came back to find you, but you were busy." His face fell. "Your Estmarcher friend set me to guard the prisoners until you were ready to lead again. He's a fine man."

"I didn't realise . . . why did nobody tell me?"

"You were asleep most of the afternoon. Then Temion came back. I didn't think anyone was in the mind to celebrate."

The heavy sense of defeat pressing down on Rhodri's heart lifted. Temion was dead, but since his passing Rhodri had been convinced his sacrifice was in vain. Now it seemed it might not be.

He hurried after Sudak, trying to keep up with his stride. "Who's this prisoner asking after me?"

Sudak shrugged. "He asked for you by name. Rhodri of Pencarith, he called you. He said,"—his brow furrowed—"the boy he saved from his father's beating was always courageous, but sometimes foolish. Does that mean anything to you?"

Rhodri's step faltered. "The Captain? Here?"

"I don't know what you mean, but there he is." Sudak nodded. The prisoners, around twenty men, were tied to stakes driven into the ground, like sacrificial victims ready for burning. Most of them drooped in defeat, but one man held his grey head high. The look he directed at Rhodri was defiant.

"Do you need a bodyguard to approach me, Rhodri of Pencarith?"

Rhodri glanced at Sudak. "Leave us," he said.

"Are you sure, leader?" At his nod, Sudak retreated, watchful eyes fixed on the prisoner.

"You wanted to see me, Captain?" The respect for Garrod was ingrained so deeply in Rhodri's psyche he found himself straightening as he addressed him, conscious of his grubby shirt and unkempt hair.

"I asked for you. I wondered if you'd have the balls to face me." Garrod shifted in his bonds to ease his discomfort. "Is that courage, or stupidity, I wonder?"

"A little of both." Rhodri drummed his fingers on the hilt of his dagger, feeling awkward. "Are you wounded? I can send for a healer . . ."

"Uncomfortable, but not hurt." The creases in Garrod's face deepened. "Let's not shit about, Rhodri. You've made your point. When are you going to put a stop to this?"

"Put a stop to what, Captain?"

"All this!" Garrod twitched, the ropes that bound him preventing him from gesturing. "Don't play games with me. You know you can't win."

"Then why are you tied to a post while I walk free? Serren's army is scattered and broken—"

"You won't take Hierath." Garrod cut him off with a snort of contempt. "Northpoint only managed it by treachery and witchcraft. You're twice the man he was, and the castle still won't fall to you. Why did you turn against your own men, Rhodri? Because of him?"

"I turned against the King's Third because I was sick of their ways! The murders, the rapes, the burning villages . . . Those people did nothing to us, but we torched their homes and put their women and children to the sword. I didn't join the King's Third to kill maids and babies, and I'm damn sure you didn't either. How can you defend what we did?"

A cloud crossed Garrod's eyes. "I'm not defending it," he said. "But that's war, Rhodri. Every man has to do things that make him uncomfortable. If a woman with a babe strapped to her back comes at you with a knife, you don't have time to think about anything beyond the blade in her hand. Surely Master Tay taught you that?"

Rhodri scowled. "He taught me to fight with honour, not to slaughter innocents as they sleep."

Garrod's lip curled. "No," he said, "I suppose that's more your father's fighting style . . ."

"Don't talk about my father! You don't know me, or my family. My father—" His voice faltered. "Valery Northpoint wasn't my father."

"Thank you for confirming it. I suspected as much."

"You did? For how long?"

"As you grew. I spent a long time in the service of the King. There's more of his manner about you than you realise, but by the time I was sure of it, you were a man grown. The political trouble it would cause wasn't worth my hide, or yours. I liked you once, Rhodri of Pencarith." His voice held no affection now, just bitter disappointment. "I would have protected you, if I could. It's too late for that now." Garrod's eyes darkened. "I know you have a son. I intend to make sure Serren knows it too."

Rhodri's fist closed around his dagger. "Are you threatening my family?"

"I'm offering you a chance to save them."

"Save them from you, you mean?"

"Listen to me, Rhodri." There was a note of pleading in Garrod's voice. "You were a good soldier. Call this off and I'll talk to Serren. I'll make sure your execution is quick and painless."

"And my wife and children?"

"Your wife and daughter will be imprisoned, of course, but at least they'll be safe. That's all the mercy I can get you, and it's more than you deserve. What happened to you, Rhodri?"

"I saw a different sunrise." His hand shook on the knife. "What if I don't call my men off?"

"How does having your entrails ripped out with red-hot hooks grab you? Or being buried alive? Northpoint revived some interesting punishments once used for traitors. I'm sure Serren would find it appropriate to try one of them on you."

Rhodri's voice was a whisper. "And my son?"

"He is as great a threat to the kingdom as you are. He'll share your fate. Think about it."

"I don't need to think about it. I'm sorry, Captain." The knife slid up, his hand moving without conscious thought, under the Captain's ribs, twisting into his heart.

Garrod sagged as far as his bonds allowed. Rhodri jerked the blade free, blood gushing over his wrist and down his sleeve. He stepped back, dagger falling from cold, numb fingers.

I'm sorry, Captain . . .

He turned to see Nik staring at him in horror. "Rhodri? What have you done?"

Rhodri pushed past him without replying. Nik snatched at his arm. "Rhodri?"

"Kill the prisoners!"

"Rhodri, the Captain! What did you—?"

"Kill them all, or I will!" He could hardly see, his vision blurred as he stumbled away.

"Rhodri? Where are you going?" Nik's voice was a despairing wail.

"I need to be with my son! Leave me alone!"

*

Riding was awkward with a broken collarbone, but not impossible. Rhodri had done it often in the past, although never with a baby strapped to his chest. Since Garrod's threat, he was reluctant to let Finn out of his sight. Whatever happened, Serren and her followers would get nowhere near his children.

The baggage train met up with the bulk of the army two days later, on the far bank of the river. They skirted the bloodiest horrors of the battlefield, but as she rode beside him Rhodri heard Nasira playing a morbid game with Asta, persuading her to cover her eyes and sing loudly as they passed torn and twisted corpses. Nothing could hide the stench rising from the dead. All he could do was pull his shirt up around his mouth and try not to inhale too deeply.

Nearer the river, efforts had been made to clear the bodies by burning or burying. The water here ran swift and shallow over gravel shoals. The camp lay on the far bank, a sprawling, stinking, jubilant army keen to help the trailing wagons across the border into the region known as the Heart of the Kingdom. The land they stood on now looked to Hierath for protection, and it was Hierath Rhodri's heart turned towards. A few days ride would bring the army within sight of the brooding walls of his childhood home, the seat of his ancestors. He was tempted to ride ahead, to see it for himself, alone. The celebratory atmosphere of the camp unsettled him. The victory had been hard won. Temion was dead, but it was the memory of Garrod, the disappointment written across his face as Rhodri plunged the knife in, that drove him from his bed at night to stalk the picket lines like a brooding ghost.

Returning to his wagon after another round of futile midnight wandering, Rhodri found Nasira. She was not sleeping as he had left her, but searching frantically, pulling up the bedclothes and shaking them, rummaging in bags, dragging the cooking pots down from their hooks on the ceiling and peering inside them. She seemed unaware of his presence, and he watched her desperate hunt until he could no longer contain his curiosity.

"What are you looking for?"

She started and cursed, clashing the pots together. Rhodri held his breath, anticipating a wail from Finn, but the baby merely stirred and settled into deeper slumber.

"Nasira?"

Her chin trembled. "I can't tell you. You'll be so angry with me!"

"I won't, I swear. Don't look at me like you're scared of me!" He hated the fear in her dark eyes. "It can't be that bad."

She sank down on the side of the bed and buried her head in her hands. "I've looked everywhere," she wailed. "I've been looking for days. I might have lost it in the battle, I don't know!"

"What have you lost? It can't be that important." He took her hand. "Tell me."

"The necklace. The one you gave me when we were bonded, with the image of your parents in it. I've looked everywhere, Rhodri. I didn't want to tell you . . ."

He laid his hand against the bare skin at the back of her neck, where the clasp of the chain had rested for so long, and closed his eyes. Gone. His proof, and with it the faces of his parents. Fallen by the wayside or trampled into the mud of the battlefield. He struggled to keep his voice light.

"I'll buy you another chain."

"But it was your only proof!" She burst into heaving sobs. "Your parents . . ."

"I can remember their image. That's not going to leave me. My face is my proof. Everyone says I look like my father . . ."

"I'm so sorry!" As she clutched his shirt and he pulled her close, it dawned on Rhodri that this was the first time she had cried since Temion's death. She wept for more than the loss of his gift.

He stroked her hair. "Tell me what to do," he murmured. "How can I make things better?"

"Hold on to me."

He held her against his chest, rocking her until her breathing slowed and the tears dried on her eyelashes. She slept, and he pried her clutching fingers from his shirt and pulled the blankets around her until she was warm and safe, cradled in their bed. Then he went outside, rested his head against one of the high wheels of their wagon, and kicked and punched against it in impotent, silent frustration, until his knuckles were raw and bleeding.

*

Rhodri's army followed the path of the River Lam as the banks rose to high, rocky bluffs and the waters dropped away beneath them. Hierath came into sight at sunset, towering above the highest point of the gorge, the dying rays of the sun staining her walls

312

blood-red. Rhodri called a halt and rode on ahead with his wife, wanting to take in the moment alone.

As they slowed, he reached across and took her hand. He had abandoned the sling, but his shoulder was still tender and inflexible. They stood on a hillock looking up at the castle, shaded and protected by a small grove of trees that the racing wind contorted into bizarre hunched shapes.

"Look at it, Nasira!" Her lips were thin as she took in her first view of Hierath. "We'll live there, you and me, and the little ones. There's our future."

Nasira scowled, squinting in the slanting sunlight. "I thought it would be bigger."

"It's much bigger when you get up close," Rhodri promised.

She shuddered. "I don't want to get close. I don't like that place. I don't like the look that comes into your eyes when you see it."

"What look?"

"Like you want to fight and fuck and burn the plains, all at the same time." She deliberately turned her back on the castle. "I don't want to see it."

"You can live as a great leader, a queen, with everything you desire. You'll love it!"

"And if I desire to go home? What then?" He had no reply to that. "I thought so. I've given up my home, willingly, to help bring you back to yours. But I can't pretend it will make me happy, and I won't lie to you."

"I don't want you to. It's not about me. The children deserve their inheritance."

"You keep saying that," she said, a chill in her voice. "Maybe one day it will be true. Come on, the wind blows cold and Finn will be hungry. I want to get back to feed him."

"You ride on," Rhodri said. "Give me a moment."

She shook her head. "Don't go thinking you can be king so easily. There's a long ride ahead of us, my Rhodri." She turned her horse around and trotted away through the broken, twisted trees.

313

Above Hierath, the first few stars glittered in the darkening sky. Rhodri wrapped the loose folds of his cloak around him to ward off the growing chill.

"I might not be a king, but Finn will." He would fight to his dying breath to make sure his son received the inheritance he deserved. Hierath was his children's rightful home, and they would never be cast out of it as Rhodri had been.

Below him, he saw Nasira stiffen. Her head tilted back, scenting. Liberty's nostrils quivered, and she flicked her ears. Rhodri felt a tremor run through the mare.

"Nasira! What do you smell?"

"Smoke." Her talons closed over the reins as he caught up with her.

"It's just the camp fires." He caught her bridle. "Rein it in. You're unsettling your ride."

"More than camp fires." She shook her head. "Let's hurry back. I miss our cubs!" She nudged her mount into a canter with her heels, and Rhodri had no choice but to pursue her.

The air thickened as they approached the hollow. The camp was in uproar. It was hard to tell where the roiling smoke originated from; it seemed to be everywhere.

Rhodri leant out of the saddle and grabbed a man as he ran past, sloshing water from a bucket. "What's going on?" he demanded.

"Fire! The baggage train!"

"The wagons? No!" Rhodri could see his wagon ahead of him, smoke billowing from the entrance, wood cracking in the heat. Siralane staggered away from the steps, face blackened with ash. He hurled himself from the saddle and grabbed hold of her.

"Sira! Where's Finn? Asta?"

"I only left them for a moment!" She dropped to her knees, choking. Behind him, as if from a great distance, Rhodri heard Nasira screaming over the roar of the flames.

Chapter Fifteen

HE STEPS CRACKED and splintered beneath Rhodri's feet. The heat of the flames was like a punch to the face. He staggered, gasping, the embers scorching his lungs. The smoke in the wagon was as black as tar. He tried to shout, but it forced inky fingers down his throat and choked off his voice. The wood crackled around him, greedy, ready to swallow his children if he didn't get them out.

A hammer blow to his back sent him stumbling forward, threw him to his knees. Rolling over, he had a vision of white teeth and soft fur.

Nasira, get out!

His words were stifled by the suffocating smoke. He caught the lash of her tail across his face as she turned and vaulted his body before he could struggle to his feet, a dark shape clamped between her jaws. With a muffled snarl, she was gone, taking Asta with her.

Where was Finn?

The crib was at the far end of the wagon, where the smoke was thickest. The floor buckled in the heat. Rhodri stumbled towards it, and cannoned into someone he couldn't see in the darkness, someone tall and well-muscled, leaning over the cradle.

"Sudak?" he croaked.

"Take him!" Elay's voice was distorted as he thrust a bundle of blankets into Rhodri's arms. "Run!"

The roof above their heads split open, a beam of light severing the darkness. The tortured wood screamed, metal rivets cannoning from the walls. Rhodri clutched his son to his chest and ran through the debris as the wagon collapsed around them, showering sparks and red hot splinters. A burning spar from the door frame caught him across the back as he leapt over the space where the steps had been, and he crumpled onto the soaking wet grass. Behind him, the roof of the wagon crashed in, releasing a cloud of dust and sparks that washed over him like a hot, dry wave.

Finn's face was black with soot. His lips were blue. Rhodri cleared the grime from his mouth and blew gently into his lungs. His own throat was on fire. "I need a healer!" he croaked.

Siralane staggered towards him, tears streaking her soot-smeared cheeks. "Let me take him." She held out her arms. In her embrace, he looked so small.

Nasira lay panting on the grass, curled around Asta, a protective circle of limbs. Someone had been smart enough to slip a collar on her and leash her to a post. Her tail lashed as he staggered towards them, and Asta offered a quivering smile. "Mummy's a cat now!"

"Are you hurt, kitten?"

She extended her arms, bottom lip trembling. They were red and blistered. "Sore!"

"Like Daddy's!" He tried to smile, but the joke felt hollow, and he felt sick as he sank into the grass beside them and rested his head on Nasira's soft flank, longing for her to change back, to hold him with human arms. Would she ever change back, if Finn . . . ?

He couldn't bring himself to finish the thought. Asta clambered over the tangle of Nasira's legs into his arms, thumb in her mouth. Over her head, he could see Siralane and two shamans treating Finn.

Siralane caught his eye as she looked up, pushing the hair that had escaped her braids out of her eyes. She looked away quickly, but not before he saw the slight shake of her head.

"Stay here with Mummy." Rhodri wrapped Nasira's tail around Asta, and she smiled as the fur brushed her nose. He walked towards Siralane, every step dragging, and she came to meet him. Her eyes were red.

"Rhodri, I'm so sorry. The smoke . . ."

"Give him to me."

"There's nothing you can—"

"Siralane, give me my son!"

He shoved her aside and snatched Finn from the arms of the Yellow Snake shaman. His arms and legs dangled limp, his head was heavy in the crook of Rhodri's elbow. His eyes were closed, his skin warm. He could be asleep. There must be a way to reach him, somewhere in Rhodri's memory . . .

There was no time to draw a circle, or fetch a lead rein. He hoped the other shamans would realise where he was going, as he lay flat on his back, holding Finn on his chest. He closed his eyes and let the memories consume him, carry him to where his son had gone.

The Spirit Realm, always hazy, was flatter and more grey than Rhodri had ever seen it. He stood on a high plain, like the plateau of Kharikan, but vast and empty. The sky was the same dull steel hue as the rock beneath his feet, and he was alone.

"Finn!"

His voice sounded muffled, pressed down by the sky. In the distance there was movement, white against the grey. He ran towards it, his movements as stifled as his voice. It was like running through tar.

Finn was not crawling yet, but he had recently discovered he could propel himself across the floor of the wagon on his belly, using his arms. He was wriggling across the barren rock, away from Rhodri, heading for the sheer cliff edge. For now, he lay somewhere between life and death. Rhodri knew if he went over, they would lose him forever.

Fighting the lassitude that clogged his limbs, Rhodri threw himself into a last, desperate burst of speed. He snatched Finn up, feet skidding on the loose pebbles at the edge of the cliff. He was real, solid in his arms, in the little bunched fist that smacked

317

him on the nose. Not dead, not yet. He could bring him back. There was still a chance.

Looking down, the bottom of the drop was lost in roiling mist the colour of smoke. Shadows moved there, blurred shapes, climbing over one another, slowly ascending the sheer face of the cliff. It wasn't the drop that caused the cold twisting in his gut, but what emerged from the fog. The figures of men, more than he could count, scrambling towards him faster than any man could climb. The closest looked up, straight into his eyes. He was dressed in military uniform, his face leached of all colour, and ash dribbled from the gaping hole just below his jaw. It was Luk, with Beron and Tomas clambering behind him. The spirits of the dead, the men whose deaths he had caused, come to take their revenge. Somewhere in that colourless horde would be Garrod, Temion, maybe even Astan. Rhodri backed off, arm tightening around Finn as he groped for his dagger with his free hand. How could he fight the dead?

The plateau seemed to have shrunk. The dead poured over the edge from every side, surrounding him. He felt the chill rising off them, the scent of old bones. Atrathenes and Kingdom soldiers, some in modern dress, some wearing clothes dating from the civil war, over two decades ago. They must have died fighting for his mother and father, against Valery. He could not be blamed for their deaths, could he?

"That's not fair!" He clutched Finn closer, and brandished the useless dagger. "I was a fucking *child!* You can't blame me!"

The knife dropped from his hand. The spirits of the dead surrounded him, closing in on all sides, reaching out as Valery had done, to fill him with their memories, to drive him past the brink of madness. But his hand was still full, and looking down, he saw the end of a rope materialise in his palm. On the far side, in the world of the living, someone was trying to bring him back.

He seized the rope and gave it a furious tug, tightening his grip as he felt it slip through his hands. No time to loop it round his waist, as the spirits closed in on him; the rough hemp scalded his palms as he was lifted up, away from the vengeful horde, more sinister for their silence. He felt his hands slithering, and clung on tighter. Finn, squealing, was clamped under his arm.

Cold fingers closed around his ankle, light as the brush of insect's wings, but the chill pierced through to the bone beneath. Rhodri looked down into Luk's grey face, expressionless, without malice, as the cold, the pain, travelled up through his body and erupted like a freezing jet, just below his jaw. The spot where he had punctured Luk's skin and driven the mercy blade into his life vein. He screamed, fumbling his desperate grip on the rope, mouth full of blood and wet ash. Lashing out, his foot passed through Luk's face, insubstantial as fog, and the Spirit Realm spun away beneath him.

Rhodri screwed his eyes shut. There was only Finn, warm and living, kicking under his arm, and the rope, burning in his hands. He felt his back slam into the ground, his son flung from his arms, and he clutched his throat, choking on Luk's memories. They called it mercy, but he understood now, knew the pain and desperate loneliness of death. There was no mercy there, and he would not forget.

Finn howled at the rough landing, red faced, fists waving. As Rhodri rolled over to comfort him, he saw Nasira, naked, running towards them. She had thrown off the collar and resumed human form. She dropped to her knees, trying to hug them both at once, tears streaming down her face.

"I thought I'd lost you both! You . . . you brought him back to me. My baby boy!"

Rhodri couldn't speak, his throat clogged with the taste of death, but he wrapped his arms around her and burrowed his head into her shoulder. She tasted of soot, of sweat and fear, and feline musk; he never wanted to let her go.

*

The fire that ripped through the wagon had spread to the rest of the baggage train before it could be brought under control, destroying food, tents, medicine, and fodder for the horses. Sudak tallied up the losses with a grim expression.

"Any deaths?" Rhodri asked.

"Seven. Two healers."

Rhodri frowned. Healers were rare, and precious. But it was the loss of the food that threw his plans awry. "Do you feel like a raid on the town?"

Sudak's eyes brightened at the prospect of action. Hierath Town was at the bottom of the gorge. It was two days' ride back to a spot low enough to access it on horseback. "Always willing, my leader. What will you do?"

"Press on to the castle, I suppose. What else can we do?" He didn't like to voice his doubt, but the cold fact hung in the air between them. Without supplies, the army could not go on, and it could not go back. They had to take Hierath, or face starvation. And take it before the ribs started showing through their skin.

"Do you know how the fire started?" he asked.

"We think it was in your wagon. Siralane might have left a lantern burning—"

"Not Siralane. She's too smart for that."

"Asta, maybe . . . ?"

Rhodri looked at his little girl playing on the grass. She looked up at the mention of her name, and toddled over to him, holding up her arms to be picked up. He didn't like to think of her playing with candlestones, but he had to concede it was possible. "I'll talk to her," he promised, "though I might not get much out of her."

He spotted Elay nearby, and hailed him as Asta buried her head in his neck. "I didn't get a chance to thank you yesterday, for saving my son. My sword is yours, should you ever need it."

The burly Estmarcher shrugged. "I didn't do much. I was passing and saw the smoke. You were right on my heels. That trance thing you did . . . I think that saved him, not me. Do you know how it started?"

"Not yet. How would you like to go on a raid, with Sudak?"

Elay tapped his sword. "Point me in the right direction!"

*

Legend said Hierath castle had never been taken by force, only treachery. Valery's treachery, and Rhodri was sick of hearing about that. Serren, her army broken, pulled her defenders back inside the keep, abandoning the outer wall that enclosed the castle grounds. Here at least were abandoned village huts, the barracks, cottages in the mews for his men to take shelter in. The Estmarchers seized them willingly, but Nasira baulked at the sight of the barracks.

"I'd rather not sleep in there, Rhodri. I felt squashed small all the time we were in the last place. I know most of the tribes will feel the same. Do you mind if we stay in a tent?"

He slipped an arm around her slender waist. "If that's what you want. I don't intend to stay here too long."

"You think your sister will lay down her weapons quickly? What if she doesn't?"

"She will. When she realises we aren't going anywhere, she'll give up."

Nasira stared into the middle distance. "Unless," she said, "she realises that we're not leaving because we have nowhere to run. What if you can't bring down her walls, Rhodri?"

The walls of Hierath were high and strong, and the Atrathene army ringed around it, looking for a way in, a breach in Serren's defence. It was hard to even get close to the castle, as Rhodri discovered to his cost.

The attack began at dawn, and Serren was ready for it. The approach to the castle lay over open ground, already churned into mud. There was only one gate, a massive, impregnable structure of wood and iron, but if his men could grapple over the south wall, even just a few of them, they might be able to get it open, and after that there would be nowhere for Serren to hide.

It took thirty paces for Rhodri to realise he had underestimated his sister. That was the moment his cavalry came within range of her arrows.

Estmarch Freedom had taken the front rank at Nik's pleading. His men were desperate to show Serren they were more than a band of terrorists fighting a hopeless cause, and they wore heavier armour than the fast-moving Atrathenes.

It wasn't enough.

Arrows sleeted from the sky, shearing into the front line of Estmarchers. They fell like hay before the scythe, the frontrunners mown down before those following them could react and defend themselves. Rhodri pulled up in alarm, ducking as an arrow whizzed past his head. Something was wrong here.

The rider beside him uttered a strangled cry and slumped in his saddle, an arrow through his lungs. He was wearing plate armour. It should have bounced harmlessly off his chest. He should not be gurgling and twitching as his horse reared and bolted.

"Retreat! *Retreat, now!*"

His call was taken up, echoed by the throats around him. He dragged Liberty round, her haunches slipping in the mud, eyes rolling in fear. All round, men were fleeing, falling, dying in the mud at the foot of the wall, under that deadly, piercing storm.

Chapter Sixteen

"**S**O THIS IS what we're fighting." Rhodri twisted one of the arrows that had fallen short of its target between his fingers. It had a savage cross-head that had punched through leather and mail like sun-warmed butter. Serren's arrows had taken hundreds of his men in the dozen heartbeats before he realised what they fought against. "Nik, why don't we have anything like this?"

Nik shrugged. He had been quiet since Captain Garrod's death, uncomfortable with his friend's unexpected violence. "I don't know," he admitted. "I heard King Alex increased the defences after your—after Northpoint, I mean—" He broke off in confusion.

"Hierath was a hard shell to crack before. It's going to be impossible now. Unless we have a man on the inside . . ." Rhodri mused for a moment. "I don't want to go down that route. If I take Hierath, I want to do it with what little honour I have left intact." He sprang to his feet. "Walk with me, I need to think. You too, Nasira."

The trio walked around the castle, striking a rough path between besiegers and besieged. Serren's forces were pinned down. They could not send for help as every messenger hawk was shot down by keen-eyed Atrathene archers, but the tribes could not get near the castle without coming under those vicious arrows.

"We don't have the provisions for a siege, and we can't eat messenger hawks forever. What can we do?"

Nik smiled bitterly. "Whatever state we're in, I'll wager conditions inside are worse. We can hunt in the forests. Serren can't have had much time to stockpile food after Kingsmere. We might be able to starve her out in a moon."

"The men don't want a siege," Nasira said in her native tongue. She understood Rhodri's language better than she spoke it. "They grow tired of this narrow sky. They talk of returning to the plains before the snow comes. They're proud to follow you, but they say they've shown Serren their teeth. Now it's time to use our mouths for talking, not snarling."

Rhodri translated for Nik's benefit. His friend nodded. "She's right. Nobody wants to be here until winter. Let's try talking to Serren."

"Saying what? That I want her out of Atrath and the Estmarch? Out of Hierath? She'd laugh in my face."

"You could tell her you're her brother. That seems a good place to start."

Rhodri snorted. "You think she'd believe me?"

"If she could see you and talk to you, she might be convinced. It's a long arrow . . ."

"She'd hardly fall on my neck and embrace me! She's more likely to drag me straight to the gallows!"

Nik sighed. "Do you want me to bargain with her under a flag of truce? I'd be happy to act as your emissary, if it means we can resolve this."

"You'd be willing to do that? It could be a way forward . . ." The more Rhodri considered it, the more he saw the benefits in talking. He'd like a glimpse at the cards Serren held. "Let me think on it. Come to me in the morning. I'll have your message then."

Rhodri spend most of a restless night up with a cranky Finn, thinking about what he would like to say to his sister. By the time Nik arrived, he was black-eyed and in ill humour. Nik, ever resourceful, was armed with parchment and writing sticks. They sat together on the floor of the tent to draft a message to Serren that was part entreaty, part threat.

Rhodri stared down at the rough draft of the note while Nik painstakingly copied it out in his small, curling script. It was only a page long, and didn't seem enough. If he couldn't talk to Serren, he felt he should write her a sprawling missive explaining how he had ended up standing at her gates with an army of hostile foreigners. He sighed, the paper fluttering under his breath.

"If you ask me to start again, you can fuck off." Nik didn't even look up from the parchment. "We agreed this was the final draft, and we don't have the paper to start again. Do you have a seal?"

Rhodri scowled. "I don't even have my own name, do I?" He dripped candle wax on the parchment to seal it, and pressed his thumb into the hardening wax, leaving an imprint of the loops and whorls of his skin. It would have to do. "Are you ready?"

"No time like now." It was Nik's turn to sigh. "It shames me to walk up to Hierath under a white flag, my friend. Jilly keeps telling me no Estmarcher should have to endure that, and I agree."

"You're not surrendering," Rhodri assured him. "You're an emissary, a representative of a free and independent nation. Serren can chew on that until she chokes!"

"She'd bloody better." Niklaus tucked the letter in his jerkin and took up the white flag, a square Nasira had cut from an old crib blanket. "Walk with me? I want you to see me spit in her eye!"

"As far as I can." Rhodri tried to make light of it, but he saw the tremor in Nik's hand holding the flag. He walked into the unknown, without sword or shield, for his own people and for Rhodri, as he had once risked his own hide in these grounds to protect his friend. And Rhodri had repaid his loyalty with lies and deception. It was beyond time to make things right.

As they walked through the camp, a curious crowd trailed behind them. Rhodri had spread the news that he wanted to sue for peace, to spare as many lives as he could so they could go home before winter, and everyone had words of praise and encouragement for Nik. Their fate lay, for the moment, in his elegant hands.

Rhodri fell back as they neared the range of those lethal cross-headed arrows, and ordered his followers to go no further, but he let Jilly push past him to kiss her man goodbye. Nik brandished the flag, a brave little flourish that did nothing to disguise his anxiety. "Here I go then!" His voice was high, falsely chipper. "See you before sunset!"

"Get Serren to hand over a few barrels of ale," Jilly said. "We're all bored out here with nothing to do but hunt hawks!" She turned away from him, skewering Rhodri with a glare that made a lie of her humour. *You shame us*, it said.

"I'll tell her." Niklaus flashed a grin, then turned and walked towards the castle, waving the white flag from side to side. Within range of the arrows, he stopped, and placed his sword and dagger on the ground, making sure both sides could see he travelled unarmed.

As he neared the gate, unchallenged, Rhodri sensed the men behind him twitching. A foolish rush on the keep would undo everything Nik was trying to achieve, and probably mean his friend's death. He held up a warning hand. "Any man who steps closer to the castle than *this*,"—he drew a line in the dirt with the toe of his boot—"before Nik returns, will find his head decorating the outside of my tent before sunset. Spread my word!"

His men fell back with a little grumbling. He would ask Sudak to keep them in order; the young man was more aware than most of the perils of disobeying a direct command. There was nothing to do now but wait, sharpen swords and spears and hope they would not have to use them.

*

"Rhodri, what happens if Niklaus doesn't come back?"

Rhodri sat outside the tent, staring blankly into the gathering dusk, a grey day fading into murky twilight. Asta sang to herself while Nasira nursed Finn. He was glad they couldn't see his face.

"He'll come back," he said, sounding more confident than he felt.

"How can you be sure?"

"Apart from you, he's the only person who's never let me down."

She snorted. "Have you been eating bitter roots, my Rhodri? Six thousand men behind you, but you feel let down and disappointed? What will it take to make you content?"

"I don't know. Giving my children the life they deserve, being able to provide for my family . . ."

"Your sister recognising your claim and giving up her leader's robes?"

"Maybe." He shrugged. "Nik coming back would be a start. I—"

He was interrupted by shouting, pounding feet racing towards him across the muddy grass. Sudak appeared through the dusk, gasping for breath. "You're here, praise the spirits! We need you, my leader!" He doubled over, hands on his knees, sucking in air. Rhodri offered his hip flask and he gulped greedily.

"Slow down and talk. Has Nik come back? Where is he?"

"Siralane and the shamans are with him. It's not good . . ." He swallowed again, wiping his mouth. "He asks for you."

"What did that fucking bitch to do him?" Rhodri sprang to his feet, gesturing for Nasira to stay behind. "If she's killed him . . ."

"He'll live. You have to come now!" Sudak seized him by the arm and they ran through the camp, every jarring step sending pain through the fresh-knit bone in Rhodri's shoulder. Visions of the tortures Garrod had described raced through his horrified mind.

The healing tent was lit up like the sun, strung inside and out with brass lanterns. Rhodri smacked his head on one as he pushed his way through the entrance, and the shamans fell back in respect.

Nik lay on the floor, Jilly cradling his head. His heels beat a drumroll of pain against the floor, and he scrunched the blanket between his fingers like a child. He was bandaged from the bottom of his ribs to his armpits, and patches of blood oozed through the linen.

Rhodri dropped to his knees and took hold of his wrist. His skin was hot and fevered. "Nik! Nik, talk to me! What happened?"

"You should leave him," Siralane warned, hovering over him with a mug. The smell wafting from it was that of bitter leaves. "He's not fit for your questions. That woman . . ." She looked like she tasted poison.

Nik opened his eyes. They were bloodshot, haunted with pain, but he managed a faint smile for Rhodri. "Got your note," he said, voice cracking. "I hope you appreciate the shit I go through for you!"

"Hells, Nik, I didn't expect you to go this far to get your head in a woman's lap!"

"It's not fucking funny." Jilly touched her dagger, and Sudak drew a hissing intake of breath. Nik patted her wrist.

"Rhodri means no offence, my love. He knows I'd do anything for a piece of cunny. Do you want this letter or not?"

"I want to know what happened. Can you talk?"

"I can talk." A shadow crossed Nik's face. He reached for the drink Siralane offered him, and Rhodri twitched it out of reach. "Can't I drink now?"

"Siralane's a witch. She'll drug your drink so she can have her way with your woman while you're passed out!" He winked. Jilly scowled.

"I'd rather be awake to see that." Nik coughed, and groaned in pain. "I'm tired, Rhodri. What do you want to know?"

"Did you see Serren?"

"Not a chance." The blood from his wounds spread, joining at the edges. Glaring at Rhodri, Siralane unrolled fresh bandages. "I got as far as Lord Caythen. He seems to be her anointed protector.

He wrote the note. I don't know—" He broke off to cough. "I don't know if the words came from Serren, or from him. I didn't read it to find out."

"Did he do this?" Rhodri touched the bloody patchwork, appalled.

"Not him." Nik shook his head. "He seemed a decent man. Hand me that drink, Rhodri. I'm gasping!"

Rhodri relented, and pressed the cup into his hands. "Who did it?" he urged. "Tell me, so I can kill him myself, if Jilly doesn't beat me to it."

Nik sipped from the cup. "Serren's goons decided to have some fun. It wasn't too bad until they saw my tattoo . . ."

"Your tattoo? Oh Nik, you haven't . . . ?"

Nik closed his eyes. "She's a powerful witch, all right," he whispered. "I didn't think I'd feel better . . ."

His head dropped to one side, resting on Jilly's sturdy thigh. Siralane snapped her fingers at Rhodri. "Look at what they did," she said. "Maybe then you'll stop talking of peace! Temion doesn't ride the Spirit Trail so you can make an easy peace with this demon-woman."

"She's no demon-woman. She's my sister."

"Would a good sister do this to your friend?" Siralane stripped back the blood-soaked bandages. Jilly winced.

Three whip-scores slashed open Nik's chest, long, shallow cuts that bled freely. On his left pectoral muscle, just above his heart, there had once been an Estmarch Freedom tattoo. Rhodri had never seen it before, didn't know it was there until now. The flesh around it was slashed, as if someone had tried to hack away the decorated skin in one piece, as a grotesque trophy.

"They couldn't cut it off." Nik's lips twitched, his words low and slurred. Rhodri had assumed he was asleep. "I don't know if they got bored, or . . ." He shuddered, and fell silent once more.

Fearful of hurting his friend, Rhodri ran light, darting fingers across the fresh brand. Beneath it, the red edges of the tattoo were visible, but seared across the picture was a curling letter *H*, black and mocking, pressed deep into Nik's skin. Stamping Hierath's authority on the Estmarch for all time.

Siralane bundled Rhodri aside to apply healing salve to Nik's abused skin.

"Did you find a note in his shirt, Sira? Some parchment with wax on it?"

"I tossed it over there." She nodded towards the corner of the tent. "Writings and parchments won't solve this, my leader. They won't heal his wounds, or bring an end to the violence in our hearts. Only your demon-sister can do that, by surrendering, and by giving back our lands."

Rhodri took a final look at Nik's scarred chest as she covered it up. "I hope you're wrong," he said, softly, "but I've got a nasty feeling you're right."

Jilly caught up with him outside the tent, Nik's blood staining her shirt. Her eyes were dry, and her hands twitched above her twin blades.

"Are you going to kill her?" she demanded.

"I don't know . . ."

"Because if you don't, I will. I'll march up to that gate myself—"

"You won't get ten yards, Jilly."

Her eyebrows drew together. "You're not *my* leader. I don't have any loyalty to you. Bloody well find a way in, or I'll make sure you lose Estmarch Freedom. You get me?"

"I get you. I'll find a way in."

Rhodri waited until he was back in the sanctuary of his own tent, and the familiar scent of milk and cooking, before he broke the seal on the parchment. The letter was squashed and smudged, stained with mud and blood on the plain side, but easy enough to read. His eyes raked it, taking in the contents with one sweep, committing them to memory. He read it again, more slowly, some lines over and over as he took them in. Nasira watched him in silence, and it wasn't until he screwed up the note and cast it aside with a curse that she moved in to caress the back of his neck. "Ill news?" she asked.

"She won't see me. That's ill news for her, not for anyone else." Rhodri glared at the crumpled paper, heedless of his wife's hands smoothing over his scalp and tense, knotted shoulder blades. "She didn't even write it! Lord Caythen signed it; he called me 'the claimant'. As if I was nothing, as if I don't even have a name!"

"What else did it say?" Her touch was soft, soothing.

"It said I was cruel."

"Cruel? How so?"

"To claim to be someone I'm not, and bringing sorrow and distress to the family." Lord Caythen's words had been far harsher, but he didn't want to voice them.

"If they think you're cruel, that proves how little they know you. Did she give you terms for her surrender?"

"Not a chance." Rhodri sighed. "She'd rather starve to death in Hierath than give up her claim to the Estmarch, and she spoke of pacifying Atrath. Pacifying!" He spat in contempt. "The peace she brings to the tribes is the peace of the grave. I wonder if she even realises that."

"She's a stubborn one." Nasira's kiss was feather light against the skin of his throat. "Like her older brother."

"She's nothing like me." But the scar on Nik's chest told a different story. Serren may not have wielded the brand, but the parallels were too close for comfort. No matter how much he tried to deny it, the fact was there. They shared the same blood, and it wasn't Valery's influence alone that made him the way he was.

"And Niklaus?" It was as if she knew his thoughts. "Will he live?"

Rhodri's breath came hot through his nostrils. "He'll live. They have some balls to call *me* cruel! Serren should look in a mirror if she wants to see cruelty. This ends now, Nasira. I've come to the end of my rope."

"How will you finish it? It would take powerful magic to make her change her mind, it seems . . ." Her restless hands stilled on his back.

"We don't have any powerful magic, Nasira. I doubt the spirits will help us."

"We need to use the resources we have. I have an idea. I don't know if it will work, I need to ask around the camp. But this won't end without bloodshed on both sides, Rhodri. I can't see any way to prevent that."

*

Nasira disappeared into the camp early the following morning, and was gone until lunchtime, when she found Rhodri sitting with Niklaus, rolling dice and reminiscing about Northpoint. Rhodri was recounting the time he had seen Starshine bolt after an apple while Astan was mounting, dragging him right across the yard and out into the street before he could free his leg. Starshine's greed was legendary.

Nik laughed softly. It hurt him to move too much or laugh too hard, but Siralane's drugs held back the worst of the pain. He looked up as Nasira's shadow fell across them. "Your woman tracked you down," he observed, in a low, raw voice.

Nasira's hands twisted anxiously. "May I join you?"

"Have you been plotting?" Rhodri stowed the dice and shuffled up so she sit next to him.

"I've been talking to people, if that's what you mean. He's coming here to see you. He doesn't know if it's possible, but he's willing to try."

"Who?" Rhodri asked, frustrated by her Atrathene habit of refusing to use the names of people she didn't know well.

"The boy who fixed your ankles. The boy who can change things into glass."

"Yestin?" She nodded. "How can he help us? He's only a boy. I'm not denying his talent, but it seems more useful for creating ornaments and trifles. What good can it be in war?"

"It wasn't a trifle when I fixed your feet, leader." Yestin spoke from the entrance, his voice thick with sarcasm. "If all I'm useful for is making trinkets, maybe I should see if Queen Serren needs me more."

Nasira sprang up and caught his arm, pleading with him to stay. Nik looked at them in confusion. "What's going on?"

"I'll translate for you," Rhodri said, following the quickfire barrage of argument between his wife and the young magic user. "You don't need to hear this, though. Yestin, come here and sit down."

His commanding tone left no room for dissent, even from the intractable boy. Yestin sat, cross-legged, holding himself proudly upright. His dark eyes scanned Nik as if he regarded convalescence as an indulgence for the weak.

Rhodri glared at him. "You told Nasira you were willing to try something to help us. What is it?"

"Your woman asked me if there were any limits to my talent. I told her there were none that I was aware of, but I hadn't pushed it as far as I can." In a rare moment of humility, he added, "It's very tiring, sometimes exhausting. I don't know how far I could go before I passed out. An object of that size . . ."

Rhodri swallowed his irritation. "What object, Yestin?"

"You and your wife don't talk much, it seems." Yestin's lip curled. "She asked if I thought I could turn the main gate of the castle, or at least part of it, into glass."

Rhodri raised his eyebrows. "It would be easier to break through than wood and iron," he said. "Even if you took out a few crucial points, it might weaken the whole gate enough. Do you need to look at it first?"

Yestin nodded. "After dark," he said. "I'm not risking an arrow in the eye for you or anyone!"

It was a long wait for night, and Rhodri spent much of it with his mind on Hierath, even while he went through the thousand routine tasks needed to keep his men happy and alert. If the gate fell, six thousand warriors were poised to descend on Serren like a surging tide. He didn't know how many men she had at her disposal, but if legend held true, his parents had fought like angry patchcats for possession of Hierath. He doubted Serren would put up any less resistance.

"Maybe there's still a chance," he muttered as he and Yestin picked their way towards the gate under cover of darkness, crouched low, a few steps at a time. Sudak covered them, the tall man moving like a phantom, but Rhodri's own footsteps sounded loud in the silence, and Yestin blundered about like a horse with colic. Any moment a light would flare on the walls, and a piercing arrow would put an end to their ambitions.

The solid wall loomed ahead, the ground gave way, and he found himself slithering in four inches of muddy water at the bottom of the deep ditch that circled the walls. He gulped back a curse and held as still as a corpse, cold water seeping over the tops of his boots and down his calves like trickling, icy fingers.

Still no burst of flame to expose them, no sharp query. Maybe Serren felt safe behind her impregnable walls, or maybe her guards slept, hungry and exhausted. Either way, he had been lucky. He didn't trust his luck to hold if he stumbled again.

Sudak slipped into the water beside him, and hauled him up the far bank. A narrow strip of dry earth and gravel separated the moat from the massive walls, heavily buttressed. The stone scratched his palms as he felt his way along them, one careful sideways step at a time. He almost wished there were lights on the walls. At least then he could see where he was going.

Stone gave way to wood beneath his groping fingers. The gate, barred and studded with iron rivets the size of Rhodri's fist. Even the Scourge would have struggled to make an impact on it. The enormity of what they were trying to do was overwhelming.

"Move aside!" Yestin's lips brushed his ear, his voice barely audible, sending a tingle down Rhodri's spine. "I need space to work."

Rhodri edged sideways. Yestin's hands were pale, fluttering shapes in the dark, flickering over the gate, massaging the rivets and hunting for any weak spot.

"Rivets," Yestin murmured. "The rivets hold the bars, strengthen the wood. Not as bad as I feared . . ."

From the wall above came the thud of boots, a soft cough and a muttered exchange as the guards switched shifts. Rhodri held himself so close against the wall he felt the cold stone digging through his shirt. Yestin was pressed against the gate. Out of the corner of his eye, Rhodri saw a red glow seeping between the boy's fingers. He hoped the overhanging wall would hide it from the men above.

Silence fell, thick and heavy as a winter blanket. Painfully aware of the guard standing mere feet above their heads, Rhodri watched Yestin work his magic. In the dark, he couldn't see any change to the gate, but he heard his companion's laboured breathing, loud as the rustle of leaves in autumn.

It dawned on him that Yestin had stopped moving; leaning against the gate with his fingers splayed against the wood, his forehead dropped forward as if the effort to hold his head up was overwhelming. Alarmed, unable to call out, Rhodri edged over to him. He could feel a plank beneath his hands, but now it was smooth and cold to the touch.

He brushed Yestin's wrist. The boy's skin was hot. Not the heat of a burn, but that of freshly-worked iron. It took all his will not to snatch his hand away. "Yestin?" he whispered. "Are you all right?"

"Get me away from here!" The boy sagged against his shoulder. Rhodri struggled to hold him up as his feet slipped towards the moat. It took a moment of silent, sweating panic to steady him.

Above, the guard stirred. "Did you hear something?" he asked an unknown companion. "Bring a light over here."

Rhodri pushed his mouth close to Yestin's ear. "Can you run?"

"I doubt it."

"Try!"

Rhodri dragged the boy into the moat, abandoning the effort at silence, not looking back at the lantern that cast a swathe of light across the killing ground in front of the gate. Hauling Yestin along with him, Rhodri dodged from side to side, stumbling. An arrow whirred past his elbow and plunged point-first into the ground in front of him. He knew at any moment another would find its deadly mark in his back. All he could do was run, get away from that sweeping light and hide in the shadows of the camp. He heard Nasira screaming his name, urging him on until he collapsed into the safety of her arms. Yestin flung himself to the ground, trembling like a sapling caught in the wind. Under the moonlight, the grass beneath him darkened and charred, wisp of smoke rising from it. As Siralane bent to help him, he yelled at her.

"Don't touch me! Bring water!"

She looked at Rhodri in confusion. "Water," he told her. "Buckets of water. He's burning like a falling star."

Siralane and Nasira ran to do his bidding. Rhodri dropped to his knees beside the stricken boy, careful not to touch him. "Are you in pain? Did it work?"

"Shit, Rhodri!" Yestin struggled to sit up, and collapsed. His skin was smoking, pale tendrils rising into the darkness. "I think you killed me!" His eyes were huge in his sallow face, and, for once, they reflected his youth.

"Do you want me to send for your mother?"

Yestin gulped. "Please. I did it, though. Not the whole gate, but it should be enough. Water!" He snatched the bucket from Siralane's hands and poured it all over himself with a faint sizzling sound. He slumped back on the burned grass and closed his eyes. "I hope you get what you want, Rhodri. You're certainly making us suffer for it."

336

*

"You're thinking about what he said, aren't you? About how we're all suffering to get you what you want?" Nasira picked at the grass in front of her with long, elegant fingers. "It's not true. They were bitter words from a child in pain."

"It's not just Yestin. Jilly thinks so too."

"What you do here, you do for the benefit of all of us. I may not like it, but I understand you well enough. Your sister makes a poor leader, always sending her men out to fight and kill. I think you would have a kinder hand."

They lay on their bellies in the long grass near the edge of the camp, hands on bows, watching the activity around the gate. There was a postern next to the main gate just wide enough to let two men pass through it at once. Serren's men came and went, bows levelled towards the besieging army in an uneasy moment of truce. Rhodri could see the gleam of sunshine on glass, glistening bands of white light. Not the whole gate, but three wooden planks, each a foot high and as long as Rhodri was tall, had been transformed. Weak points in Serren's armour. The only chance they had.

He trained his bow on the men at the gate, far out of range, and toyed with the idea of firing a warning shot to scare them. Nasira caught his wrist. "Are you listening to me?"

"Always." The Scourge could shatter that glass, burst open the gate, allowing his men to pour through. If they lay down planks to carry it across the moat . . . His force might carry the day, but it would be messy, and there was no getting past that.

"You're not, are you?" Nasira rolled onto her back with sigh of discontent. "You're trying on your sister's robes in your head. That benefits no-one while we wait out here and she hides behind her walls."

"I'm not trying on her robes."

"Then tell me what you're thinking."

There was no evading her sharp tone. He had wondered how to broach the subject, but now it came to it, the blunt knife was the one to use.

"How would you feel," he asked, "if I went in there to talk to her?"

Her eyes were fixed on the sky, but he heard her intake of breath. "Rhodri, you can't! You saw what happened to Niklaus."

"I did, and it's my fault. If I'd never taken up that brand . . . I can't let that happen to anyone else, or ask anyone to go in my stead. Maybe Serren will listen to me. If she sees our father in my face—"

"If she sees her father in your face, your face will be your death."

"If we take the gate, hundreds will die, our men and hers. There's a chance I can prevent that, and I have to take it."

Nasira's fists clenched at her sides, claws raking the grass. "If she hurts you, I'll have her eyes!"

The postern gate closed. Rhodri risked sitting up, so he could see his wife's eyes glowing with ferocious amber light. "That sounds like you won't fight me if I decide to go."

Sharp nails raked his wrist. "You say 'if', but you've already made up your mind. I know you, Rhodri." Her lips trembled. "What will I do if you don't come back?"

"You'll lead the men. If I don't come back, if she won't listen to reason, she will have brought the storm down on her own head. Can you do that for me?"

She drummed her fingers. "If I must. Make sure everyone knows your plan. Will you go today?"

He looked at the gate, glass panels gleaming in the early summer sun. "Tomorrow, at dawn. There's a lot to prepare. I want to spend one last night with you. Serren won't deprive me of that."

"Come on then!" She pushed him away as he tried to kiss her, and sprang to her feet. "If it has to be done, let's do it. We have much to organise, and no time."

338

*

It was after midnight when Rhodri collapsed into bed. Everything was ready, every man in his army knew what they were meant to do. Except him.

Nasira shifted in her sleep, nose twitching, hand clenching around the blanket. Her eyelids fluttered. "What was that?"

"I didn't wake you up, did I?" Secretly, he was glad she was awake. "If you're not too tired, maybe we could—?"

"Someone's outside."

"Probably Sudak." He reached for her. "We can be really quiet—"

"Shut up!" Her teeth flashed. "It doesn't smell like Sudak."

He groped for his candlestones. "Should I fire up the lantern?"

"No. If we lie still, he might go away." He felt her beside him, quivering, tense, and carefully reached for his breeches.

"I might have a look—" There was a rustle on the far side of the tent where the children slept. A change in the light, and a slow, cautious tearing, the canvas parting under the blade of a knife.

"Fuck!"

Finn screamed as the shadowy figure snatched him from his crib. Rhodri lunged, too slow, legs tangled in his breeches. Nasira vaulted him with an animal snarl, bursting through the torn canvas and vanishing into the darkness.

Rhodri scrambled after her, shirtless, snatching up his sword and yelling to the guards. "He took my son! Where did he go?"

"Towards the gorge!" Sudak yelled. "I think he had a wolf chasing him, or—"

Rhodri didn't wait to hear the rest. His feet crunched on the gravel as he ran under the arch that marked the exit to the castle grounds. Adeamus bathed the landscape in bone-coloured light. He couldn't see anyone. "Nasira!"

Finn screamed again, loud enough to raise a corpse, and Rhodri veered to the left, slowing as he forced his way through bushes and trees broken by recent violent passage. Pushing clear of the last branches, he stumbled into a semicircle of open ground, bordered by a crescent of trees and, directly ahead of him, the rocky lip of the gorge.

Finn sat on the grass, wailing and beating his fists against the ground. He was the first thing Rhodri saw, and he snatched him up. He didn't appear hurt, but his cries were piercing, and he would not be comforted.

The kidnapper sprawled on the ground, Nasira's weight holding him down. Her front paws kneaded his chest, and her teeth snapped, an inch from his throat. Her tail lashed as she saw Rhodri, and her tongue flashed across her incisors.

"Call it off! Call it off, I'll tell you everything!"

"Elay?" His voice was hard to make out over Finn's howling, but that Estmarch burr was unmistakable. "What in hells is going on?"

"Call off your beast, and I'll talk! Why the fuck do you keep a wild cat in your tent?"

"What were you doing? What do you want with my son?"

Nasira snarled low in her throat as he shouldered her aside; she swiped at him, a stinging slash across his chest. He caught her by the scruff of the neck and dragged her heavy head round so he could look in her eyes, trying to reach the woman inside.

"The cub needs you. Go to him. I'll handle this."

She growled, but slunk away, letting Rhodri's sword take the place of her teeth. "Talk, then," he said, twitching the blade to let the Estmarcher know he was serious. "Talk, or I'll set her loose on you."

"What are you, a fucking wizard?" Elay spat.

"I'm the man with the knife at your throat. Why did you take my son? Did Serren offer you gold?"

"Not gold, no . . ."

"But you are loyal to my sister, am I right?"

"I am *loyal* to the Crown. The Queen sent me to infiltrate Estmarch Freedom, and report back to her. To sabotage them if I could—"

"A fucking spy, then." Rhodri jabbed the sword. "Keep going."

"Better a spy than a traitor, Rhodri Northpoint! Yes, I was with Estmarch Freedom, and then I heard about you. Estmarch Freedom was an undisciplined band of fundamentalists and glory-hunters, until you showed up and turned it into a bloody army! I exchanged hawks with Serren, she knows all about you, and your children. She told me to get rid of the boy. I tried to make it look like an accident . . ."

"The fire." Rhodri shook his head. "You bastard, I thought you were trying to save him!"

Elay choked at the pressure against his throat. "Are you going to let me talk? When I heard you were going after Serren tomorrow, I knew it was my last chance. I thought if I took the baby, I could buy her some time. Maybe you'd change your mind. But I wasn't going to hurt him."

"You expect me to believe that, you lying piece of shit?"

"No. I have nothing against you. You seem like a decent man. I was following the Queen's orders."

Rhodri sucked in a deep breath to steady his hand. "And you think that because I'm a *decent* man, and you're a good little soldier of the realm, that I'm not going to kill you?"

"Are you going to kill me?"

Rhodri let the blade drop a fraction. "No," he said, "I'm not."

Elay sighed with relief.

"I'm going to let my wife kill you."

"Your . . . wife? The savage?"

"Nasira!"

She looked up. She had Finn held between her front paws, cleansing his tears with her rough tongue. Rhodri stepped back. "I suggest you run," he said to Elay.

The spy needed no second warning. He leapt to his feet and took off like a hart chased by hounds. With a savage roar, Nasira bounded after him, tail lashing as he blundered into the trees and was lost to the night.

*

Nasira returned before dawn, her lithe, naked, human form slipping under the blanket beside Rhodri. She shivered. "Are you awake?" she whispered.

"I couldn't sleep without you. Is Elay—?"

"Dead." She yawned, licking her lips. A horrible suspicion grew in the pit of Rhodri's stomach.

"Nasira? You didn't . . . *eat* him, did you?"

She frowned. "How can you think that? I'm no cannibal. Besides,"—she ran her tongue over sharp incisors—"he would have tasted awful." She twitched her braids over her ear and wrinkled her nose in distaste.

Rhodri smothered a grin. "What happened, then?"

"The edge of the cliff gave way. He fell. I'm not sorry, but I don't want to think about it. Not when I have so little time left with you. The Estmarch man has stolen enough of our night. How's Finn?"

"Sleeping soundly. Asta too, I don't think she even woke up. You should get an hour in, it's going to be a long day."

"How can I sleep with this wire tangled around my heart?"

He brushed the loose hair from her forehead. "I'm sorry. I hate what this is doing to you . . ."

Nasira's voice was calm. "You can't stop it now, can you? I wouldn't ask you to. But I need you, Rhodri. It won't be light for a while."

"True." He moved over her, mouth on hers, on her throat, tongue darting across her nipples, breathing in the musky scent of her hollows. Her hips shifted beneath his, moving with the urgency
342

of desire. Her hands curled around his backside, and he felt her sharp claws drag against his bare skin as she pressed him to her.

Her warm lips brushed his ear. "Come inside me, Rhodri. I need you."

He slid inside her, deep and slow, taking his time and savouring every quiver and soft sigh she uttered. She arched her back as he took her breast in his mouth, her muscles clenching and unclenching around him, drawing him in. A tremor ran through him as she raked her talons across his back, crying out in desire, calling his name, taking him with her over the edge until they came together, one body, one heart. For a time, there was no Serren, no Hierath, no dawn.

But it was over too quickly for Rhodri. He wanted to stay inside her forever, making her cry out, hearing her whisper his name as she pressed against him. But dawn crept through the torn canvas, and Finn stirred and fretted.

"You have to go." Still she held him close, her breathing slowing. "Don't make it more difficult by dragging it out."

"It couldn't be more difficult." He dressed slowly, fiddling with his boot laces while Nasira nursed Finn and raised Asta from her slumber.

"Give Daddy a hug," she urged. "He has important work to do today."

Asta threw her arms around his neck and rested her head on his shoulder. He carried her outside, into the dawn, kissed the top of her rumpled dark head, then Finn's, and gave his daughter back to Nasira. He checked his sword and dagger, although he would need neither.

"I suppose this is it." He thought of Kilujen's warning, given from beyond the living world, that if he walked into Hierath he would not come out, and his movements grew sluggish. If that was what it took, he would offer his life to save his chosen people. But he would not hurry towards that fate. He would savour the last of the sunlight, as Temion had done.

Nasira put Asta down and took his hand, lacing his fingers through hers. "Do one thing for me," she said. "Make sure you come back."

Still he lingered. "Can you remember what you have to do?"

She nodded. "Trust me. I've stood by you every mile of this journey. Even when I thought you were wrong, or mad, my heart never questioned you. If you don't come back, I will walk out as the light of tomorrow's noon hits the highest tower, and I will command your men to throw themselves against the walls of Hierath. I will command them because I love you, and they will obey me, because they love you too. Your name will be written across the sky. It will live on their lips and in their hearts for all time. Your followers want a legend, but I,"—she smiled—"I need my husband, and the cubs need their father. You can be both, legend and father, but only if you come back. Can you promise me that?"

He swallowed. "If I don't, remember my last thought was of you."

"If you don't, I'm coming in there to get you out!" She forced a grin. "Here's Sudak with the little mare. I asked him to bring her."

Liberty trotted towards them. Sudak had brushed her until her grey coat gleamed, and braided her mane like an Atrathene warrior. It must have taken most of the night, if the hollows under his eyes were an indication of his toil. He had even woven in bells, which jingled as Rhodri pressed his face to her mane and inhaled. She nudged him hard with her nose, questing for treats as he rubbed a hand along the curve of her neck.

"Are you ready?" Nasira's voice was soft and urgent.

"No." But there was nothing left to delay him. It was only a short walk through the camp and up to the gate, but it felt right that he rode this last distance. As he mounted, Asta broke free of her mother's loose grip and ran towards him, arms aloft, begging for a ride.

"Daddy, up!"

"Not this morning, kitten. I'm sorry."

"Daddy, up now! Want Libby!" She stamped her foot, face scarlet.

"Take her," Nasira said. "Take her as far as you dare. I'll follow and bring her back."

Rhodri lifted his daughter up in front of him and trotted through the camp. He knew hundreds of eyes were on him, but he kept his face straight ahead, watching Asta play with the braids in Liberty's mane.

At the edge of the camp, he stopped. "Time to get down, kitten."

Asta pouted. "More horse!"

"Maybe later. Daddy has to go. Look after Libby for me." He lifted her down, wrapped her little hand around the reins, and kissed her goodbye. "Be good."

Taking in a deep breath, he turned his back on her and stepped out in full view of the castle walls, walking slowly with his head high. Behind him, he heard his daughter's thin wail of distress. *"Daddy! Daddy, come back!"*

If he looked back at her, he knew he could not go on.

"Daddy! Come back!"

His heart cracked, but he kept walking. There was a stir on the walls, and he knew he was seen. He stopped, took off his sword and dagger, and laid them both on the grass, keeping his movements slow and deliberate. If he took an arrow in the heart now, Asta would see everything. Would she be able to forget?

The arrows didn't fall, although Rhodri knew his steps were being tracked by dozens of crossbows. He reached the postern gate. In the dark, he hadn't noticed it was accessed by the narrowest causeway, barely wide enough for a man to cross without vertigo. A new addition since his childhood. The small gate swung open at his approach, not an invitation, but a yawning mouth ready to swallow him up.

Rhodri closed his eyes, clenched his fists, and stepped across the threshold into Hierath.

He was surrounded by a ring of steel. Half a dozen blades, levelled at his chest and throat by men with wolfish hunger in their eyes. He wondered if they were the thugs who had burned Nik, and he tried to swallow his loathing. Dying here would achieve nothing. He spread his hands to confirm he went unarmed.

"Who are you? What do you want?" A tall man with a haggard face shouldered two of the swordsmen aside. He wore a captain's insignia, and his eyes were bloodshot and bruised, two red and scarlet holes bored into his face. "Are you an Estmarcher, or an Atrathene?"

"Neither and both." Rhodri drew himself up to his full height, and looked up into the captain's face without flinching. "My name is Rhodri of Hierath. I'm here to see my sister."

*

The cell Serren's men bundled him into was small, but clean, with fresh straw and a wooden bench to sit on. Not that Rhodri intended to stay long. He hollered and banged on the bars until he attracted the attention of the warden, who stormed down the passage to see what the fuss was about. He was an older man, loose skin hanging in heavy dewlaps around his throat where he had rapidly lost weight. Rhodri cursed the fact that he didn't know him.

"What do you want?" he demanded. "Keep it down!"

"I want to speak to my sister." Rhodri reached through the bars and seized him by the shirt. "It's life or death."

"Your death, maybe. The last false Rhodri we had, his parents were only in here a few days before they cracked and admitted their deception. You don't look like you've got much substance."

"I've got more than you know. I've got my father's blood."

The warden's eyes narrowed. "Your father's blood? You're the Northpoint boy. How dare you mention your blood and that of King Alex in the same breath? You disgust me."

He tried to move off, but Rhodri had a tight grip on him. "Listen to me," he said, urgently. "I lead six thousand Atrathene warriors who want to bathe in the Queen's blood, and I'm the only one who can call them off. If I don't get back by noon tomorrow, all the hells are going to descend on Hierath. I *have* to see Serren."

The warden shook his head, sagging skin flapping. "She won't see you. Why should I believe you?" But an element of doubt crept into his tone.

There was one person in all Hierath who might back up his story, and speak for his defence. "Not Serren, then," he said. "But one favour, that's all I ask. One favour to save hundreds."

The guard hesitated, reluctant to trust him. "What?" he said.

"There's a girl. Amerie of Hierath. Her mother is Celandine who used to work in the kitchens, and her father was Padraig. You remember Padraig?"

"I remember he was murdered. By your father."

"Never mind that. Amerie. Will you get her for me? I need to see her. I swear I'll ask nothing else of you."

The warden scanned Rhodri up and down. "I shouldn't listen to you," he said at length. "But I suppose it can't do any harm. I'll ask her. Doesn't mean she'll see you, mind!"

Rhodri let him go. "Thank you so much. You don't know what that means to me."

"If it's the only way to stop you yelling and banging, I'll do it gladly. You wait here." He broke into a wheezy chuckle. "Like you've got a choice!"

The warden departed, taking his lantern with him, leaving Rhodri alone in the dark. Rhodri groped his way to the bench and sat down, listening to the rats scuffling and fighting in the blackness. It was impossible to tell how quickly time passed, staring at nothing with his head sunk into his hands, dabbing his bleeding lip with his shirt while anxiety gnawed away at his belly. It could have been noon, or midnight, when the grate of a steel door opening and the warm, friendly lantern light announced the warden's return.

Rhodri started up, rushing to the bars and peering out as best he could. At first he could see nothing but the light, painful after so long spent in darkness. The shape of the warden formed behind it. "Here he is," he said over his shoulder. "He says he knows you."

Her hair, gathered into a rough plait that hung over her left shoulder, was golden in the lamplight, and her blue eyes were hooded as she stared at him, unblinking.

"Amerie? Amerie, it's me, Rhodri! You remember me, don't you? Tell him who I am, so I can get out of here!"

"I'm sorry." She took a step back and shook her head at the warden. "I've never seen him before in my life. Can I go now?"

"Amerie!" Rhodri threw himself against the unyielding metal bars, jarring his injured shoulder with a gasp of pain. "Amerie, you know who I am. Don't do this to me!"

"I'm sorry," she repeated.

"Amerie!" He beat his fists against the door of his cell in rage and frustration, as she followed the warden away from him, without looking back, leaving him alone in the dark.

"Amerie, come back! *Amerie!*"

Chapter Seventeen

AMERIE WAS GONE, leaving Rhodri in darkness and despair. He slumped to the floor, head pressed against the bars. Only the steady drip of water nearby measured the passage of time. He lay so still, a bold rat, emerging from its hole, ran right across his feet. He yelled and kicked out, scrambling up onto the bench, huddling there with a sickened shudder. There was nothing to do but await his fate. Life in the King's Third had taught him to take advantage of any chance to sleep, no matter how uncomfortable the circumstances, but the chatter and rustle of rats disturbed the silence. And then there was Finn.

If Rhodri died, Finn would never know his father. Rhodri's remarkable memory had come to him by accident, if what Valery had said was true; it wasn't in his blood. Asta forgot things all the time. Maybe she wouldn't remember him either . . . They would both be deprived of a father, as he had been. The thought of his children growing up without him brought bitter tears to his eyes. They were his world, and they would never know what happened to him. All they would know was that he didn't come back.

He lay staring into the darkness, eyes stinging, listening to the rats dance. Outside, the world turned, and his family waited for him. The fate of a nation twisted on Amerie's whim, and she had turned away.

Cursing her did not make him feel any better. He fidgeted on the cold, hard bench, trying, and failing, to think of a way out of this mess that wouldn't result in his death, the red-hot hooks

Garrod had described tearing into his abdomen and ripping him apart. The thought made him clutch his belly in terror, lying on his side with his knees drawn up to his chest. He hoped he would die before it came to that.

The iron door at the far end of the passage rattled. Rhodri didn't stir; probably the warden doing his rounds. He'd made a promise to the old man that he would cause no more trouble, and he didn't have the strength even if he'd wanted to break it. The lantern light was welcome, though, bobbing and weaving, and sending the rats scurrying back to their nests. It made his eyes water as it paused outside his cell, and it dawned on him that the heavy stamp of the warden had been replaced by a softer tread.

He raised a hand to shield his eyes. "Who's there? Amerie, is that you?"

"Are you sure you want do to this?"

It took a moment for Rhodri to realise Amerie wasn't speaking to him, but to a shadowed figure who hung back beyond the circle of light. The girl beckoned him towards the bars, holding the lamp high. She was pale, and her eyes were red. He didn't move.

"We can go back, my lady." She spoke over her shoulder again, her voice full of tender concern. "If it's too much for you—"

"No, I'll see him." A woman's voice, well spoken, with a faint trace of an Estmarch accent. She sighed. "Only because you seem so convinced, Amerie. Let's get it over with."

Lady Meganne Caythen stepped up to the bars of the cell. Even in the lamp light, which leached the colour from her porcelain face, she was beautiful, but her eyes were dark hollows, and her silver-shot hair was dragged into loose bun. She wore a heavy night robe clutched around her as if for protection rather than warmth.

"Come into the light." Her voice was chilly. "Let me see you for myself, then I can go back to bed and end this nonsense."

Rhodri ran his hands through his unruly hair, brushed the straw from his jerkin, and stepped up to the bars. His eyes locked with Meganne's.

She took a step back, hand pressed to her mouth, muffling her exclamation of surprise. A shudder ran through her, and when she spoke, her voice was less steady than before. "I can see why he convinced you, Amerie. There's certainly a resemblance . . ."

"More than that, my lady." Amerie laid a daring hand on Meganne's arm as she turned away. "Listen to him. He knows things only someone who lived here would know."

"A talented spy could tell me what colour the tapestries in the hall are, or how many steps up to the dais. It proves nothing."

Rhodri was distressed to see tears glittering on her lower lashes, but he had to make her believe. "Red and green," he said, "and three steps. The third tapestry on the left in the great hall is a hunting scene, with three white harts. The one in the middle has a wine stain on his back. I was never allowed in the laundry, but it's out past the kitchen door. On the staircase leading to the third floor, there's a stain on the wall that won't wash off. There are eighteen steps in that staircase, and the bottom one is bigger than the rest, because there's a secret compartment in it for storing gold." He tightened his fists around the bars. "Do you want me to go on, Lady Caythen?"

"So you lived here!" she snapped back, an angry flush of colour in her cheeks. "That still doesn't mean anything, Alex! It—oh!"

In the sudden hush, the dripping of water was magnified tenfold.

"You called me Alex."

"My tongue slipped. I—" She turned away, flustered. Rhodri snaked his arm out between the bars and caught her sleeve.

"Horseshit, Lady Caythen. You lost your temper, and you called me Alex. *That* means something. Look at me again. Look at me!"

"I don't know!" Meganne wailed. Her tears shone streaks on her skin. "You look so like him, it hurts! I can't take the chance . . ."

Rhodri rested his head against the bars. "You have to," he said in a low voice. "I have to talk to Serren before noon tomorrow. Shit, I don't even know if it's daylight yet! Let me see her. Look

351

at me in real light. What can I do? I'm unarmed, Serren has her guards. I just want to talk to her."

Meganne dashed an angry hand across her eyes. "I don't know," she said again, "but my husband might. Swear you won't try and escape?"

He shrugged. "Where would I go?"

Meganne turned to Amerie. "Run and fetch the keys," she said. "Quietly now!" As the girl scurried off down the passage, she held the lantern closer to Rhodri's face. "So many liars . . ." she muttered, eyes mere slits in her face. "They broke Lydia's heart every time. If you hurt my family, I'll kill you myself. Do you understand?"

"Every word."

"I wish I could be sure." She took the keys from Amerie, shaking fingers flicking through them until she found the right one, and opened the cell.

"Don't think you're going anywhere yet!" As Rhodri left the cell, Meganne spun him around with surprising strength, pressing his face to the bars and jerking his hands behind his back. She bound them tightly with the cord of her robe, and jabbed him in the back. "Walk in front of me. Not too fast. Amerie, go ahead and make sure there's no one about."

It was uncomfortable to walk through the deserted night-time halls of the castle, Meganne's eyes boring into his back. Amerie led them through a warren of little-used corridors and passages, up narrow flights of servants' stairs. Even at this late hour there was a faint hum of noise. Hierath was on high alert. Now the gate was breached, the Atrathene attack could come at any time. Only Rhodri knew how close it was, and only he could prevent it. If Meganne didn't kill him first.

Amerie ushered them through a small door into a suite of rooms on the second floor. Meganne turned to her. "Fetch Bale," she said. "He'll be down in the hall with the men. And then go to bed, you look fit to drop. I'll handle this from here."

"But Rhodri—?"

"If he is Rhodri . . . Go to bed, Amerie. This is none of your business."

"Yes, my lady." Amerie inclined her head as Meganne turned her back on her. Over her shoulder, Rhodri saw her mouth the words *Good luck!* He smiled, grateful she had not abandoned him.

"Sit down!" Meganne snatched up a small dagger from the sideboard and brandished it at Rhodri. He sat, slow and cautious, eyes fixed on her. The chair was padded with red velvet, and he was grateful for the unexpected comfort, even with his wrists bound awkwardly behind him.

Meganne remained standing, poised on the balls of her feet like a runner. She was in her early fifties, but, judging by the speed and strength with which she had spun him round earlier, she was fit. Rhodri didn't want to test her by running, or trying to disarm her. She seemed willing to listen to him, and that would be a sure way to lose her trust and get himself killed.

"Do you think Queen Serren—?"

"Don't talk!" She gestured with the knife. "It confuses me when you talk. I don't need to hear your lies. You can talk to Bale when he gets here."

"Is Bale your husband? Lord Caythen?" Nothing Rhodri had heard about Lord Caythen warmed his spirit to the man. Astan had despised him. But Nik said Bale had been devoted to Rhodri's mother. Whether that would serve him for good or ill remained to be seen.

Meganne refused to answer his questions, or rise to his bait, and the knife she levelled against his throat never wavered. He searched her face for traces of himself, his children, but he couldn't see them.

"Stop looking at me like that!"

"Sorry." Rhodri lowered his eyes, and shifted in the chair. He was dirty, itchy and exhausted. His mouth was dry, and his limbs ached from the bruising Serren's guards had inflicted. No wonder Meganne doubted him.

"Meganne?" A man's rich voice sounded from the doorway. Rhodri risked a glance up. "Meganne, is this—? What have you done?"

"I wanted you to see him! I think he might— Bale! Stop it!"

The ominous click of a crossbow, and the tip of a twelve-inch steel tipped bolt pressed hard against Rhodri's breastbone. He didn't move. He barely breathed.

"Tell me why I shouldn't shoot right now." Bale's voice was soft, but his forefinger twitched over the trigger. "Either of you. I'm waiting."

"Look at his eyes, Bale. Then tell me he's a liar, and I say shoot."

The bolt jabbed against him. Pinned into the seat, Rhodri raised his head and looked directly at the man who threatened him.

"On your feet," Bale ordered. "No quick moves, or I stick you."

Up close, Lord Caythen was shorter than he expected, only a few inches taller than Rhodri. His hair was grey, dappled with patches of brown, and his face was tanned and weathered like a battered old hide.

"You were my mother's Champion—"

"Quiet!" Bale cut him off. "You haven't earned the right to talk about her. Let me look at you."

He passed the crossbow to Meganne, who handled it confidently, and took Rhodri's chin in his hand, twisting his face left and right. He muttered a curse. "Meganne! Bring the light closer!"

She obliged, keeping Rhodri covered with the bow. Bale's grey eyes stared deep into Rhodri's, and showed a sudden grief.

"Ah, I don't know!" Bale let go abruptly and turned away. "His eyes are like Alex's, true, but that's not enough. Not for me."

"He has the same nose as Serren, I think," Meganne ventured. "Maybe if we see them together?"

"No. Never." Bale shook his head. "He goes nowhere near her. He shouldn't even be here. What possessed you to let him out?"

"Amerie."

"When did you start taking instruction from Amerie?"

They were ignoring Rhodri, and the dagger lay abandoned on the sideboard. He edged towards it.

"She said they met a few summers ago," Meganne explained. "She tried to persuade me to see him then, but I refused. This time— they're going to execute him, Bale! What if he is Lydia's son? Could you let him go to the scaffold without being sure? And if we hang him, what will the Atrathenes do? We have a horde at our gate, and he claims he can stop them. Whoever he is, we should at least hear him out."

"How can we be sure?" Another few inches. The blade was almost within Rhodri's grasp. "This isn't a child's tale. He won't have a birthmark in the shape of a crown!"

His back against the sideboard, Rhodri twisted the blade in his fingertips, feeling the thin cord of the dressing robe fray and part. "You can't be sure," he said, calmly. "But you can listen to my story, and choose what to believe." He offered the dagger, hilt first, to Meganne. "I trust you. I want you to trust me. Will you listen?"

Bale and Meganne exchanged a long look. "We'll listen," Bale conceded. "Tell us your version of the truth."

*

It was a long story, and by the end Rhodri's throat was so parched he could barely speak. Bale offered him a sip from the bottle of water he carried at his belt. Grey light seeped through the cracks in the shutters. He hadn't slept for over a day, and the creeping light warned him he was running out of time.

He told them everything. About his memory, about being raised by Valery, and his flight to Pencarith. While he talked, Bale sat still, shrinking into himself. Meganne twitched and fidgeted, made the occasional exclamation, but Bale was silent, and it was Bale Rhodri found himself pleading with. He didn't know why, but he needed Lord Caythen on his side, if no one else was.

"That's it," he concluded. "That's all I have. It's up to you to believe it, or not."

Bale glanced at Meganne. "You were lucky, you never met Valery Northpoint," he said. "I did. I knew him well, and this boy did too. I've no doubt of that."

Hope sprang in Rhodri's heart, only to be shattered by Bale's next words.

"But knowing Valery doesn't prove he's who he claims to be. There must have been dozens of boys around Hierath at that time who could tell the same story. I'm sorry."

Rhodri shook his head. He had not expected to be welcomed with an embrace, but this was bitter to hear. His eyes stung, and he rubbed his dirty hands across his face and through his tangled hair. "Then I'm dead," he muttered. "Thank you anyway, for— what?"

Lord and Lady Caythen were both staring at him as if he had sprouted an extra head. "Is something wrong?" he asked.

Bale rose slowly, hanging on to the back of the chair. "Can I talk to you, Meganne?" he said. "In private?"

As soon as the door to the inner chamber clicked shut, Rhodri darted across to it and pressed his ear against the wood. Bale and Meganne's voices were muffled, and he had to concentrate to make out their words.

"You can see it too, I know you can!" Meganne's voice was heated. "His eyes, his gestures, the way he moves . . . He has to be Alex's son!"

"That doesn't mean he's our lost boy." Bale's voice was gentle. "He might not be Lydia's—"

"You think Alex was unfaithful to her? That he would father a bastard, and not tell her? Honestly, does that sound like him?"

Bale evidently shook his head. "I thought not," Meganne went on. "Look at him in the right light, around the jaw. He's got that stubborn look all my family have."

Rhodri heard Bale's boots pace an anxious tread across the room and back. "Following an impossible goal all the way from the far

356

side of Atrath is something your cousin would do, where any sane person would give up," he conceded. "No, he's Lydia's all right, the obstinate little bastard. His face is his father's, but his will is certainly hers!"

"What do we do now?" Meganne asked.

"I don't know." Bale sounded worried. "He stands at our gate with an army. I don't know if he has a valid claim in law, he's been declared dead for years. And I'm not going to hand over whatever he wants, Alex's blood or not! There are the girls to think about. I'm glad we packed them off to Caythen Pass when we had the chance. They'll be safe there. Serren—"

There was a whisper behind Rhodri, the lightest footfall. Before he could react, the lethal blade of a knife pressed hard against his throat.

"Don't move." The female voice carried absolute authority. "Who in all hells are you, and what are you doing in Lord Caythen's chambers?"

*

"Let me get this right." Serren sheathed the knife at Meganne's urging, and sat down, stiff-backed and uncomfortable. "You're saying *he*"—the look she threw Rhodri would have withered grass—"is my brother? That's a lie. My brother is dead. He died before I was born. It says so, in law. He had to be declared dead before I could be crowned. I don't know who you are," she turned to Rhodri, "but you're nothing to me. Nothing but a little soldier boy with his army of Atrathene dogs!"

"If I'm nothing, no threat, then why did you send a man to kill my children?"

"That's enough, both of you!"

Meganne's harsh injunction brought silence, a chance for Rhodri to study his sister up close. Her fair hair was plaited down her back, escaping in wisps around her ears and temples. Her nose was like his, and the jut of her chin, but her eyes were hazel rather than dark brown. Her skin was pale, with a spatter of freckles across her nose, and her lips twisted in a scowl. She looked away before his gaze.

"Bale, if this is a joke, it's a cruel one," she said.

"It's not a joke, little one." Bale spoke more tenderly than Rhodri had yet heard him. "Look at him. Do you think I would have told you this way if I had any doubts? He's your brother."

"I don't want to hear this!" Serren sprang up and marched towards the door. Bale blocked her way, and she tried to push past him. "Let me out! You can't keep me here!"

"Because you're the Queen?" Still that tender voice. "Your authority has just become less than absolute."

"What are you— no!" She pointed at Rhodri. "Not him! He's a liar! Don't choose him over me, Bale."

"It's not a question of choice, but of doing what's right. Rhodri says he came here to make peace. Will you listen to him?" He wrapped an arm around her and steered her gently to the sofa. "I know it's hard, but talk to him. We can solve this."

She frowned. "He's *not* my brother. I won't concede my throne to a traitor!"

"I don't want your fucking throne, Serren!"

"Then what do you want?" she retorted. "Why did you come here, if not to force me out?"

"Because your men were killing my people!"

"*Your* people? Do you want to be King of Atrath too? The security of the Eastern border—"

"What your men are doing in Atrath isn't security, Serren. It's slaughter."

"Rhodri," Meganne interrupted, "what are you talking about?"

Rhodri sighed, struggling with painful memories. "When I joined the King's Third," he said, "I was proud to serve in Atrath, or wherever I was sent. But I didn't take the King's copper to rape women, or kill children. You should be ashamed of what's done in your name, Serren."

358

She shook her head. "You're lying."

"Why would I lie? I saw my own regiment, men I grew up with, slaughtering Atrathenes like dogs. Whole villages, women, children, old men. They were no threat to us! How could I live with that?"

She looked away, biting her lip, and said nothing.

"Did you know?"

"Of course I didn't know, because it's not true! My men wouldn't behave like that."

"You don't know a tenth of what's done in your name. Your army takes boys from towns and villages before they're old enough to think for themselves. They're trained to hate what they don't understand, and then spat out across the border with no clear orders, except to fight and kill. And that's what they do. That's all they do!"

Serren's lower lip quivered. "I don't know anything about what goes on in the military," she admitted. "I see parades, medal ceremonies . . ."

"You don't see the burns, do you? The scars? The men who come back unable to function outside their unit. The men who don't come back at all, and the mess they leave behind . . ."

Serren looked from Meganne to Bale, who looked equally grave. "If this is true, how can I make things better?"

"I'll tell you how," Rhodri said bluntly. "You can stay out of Atrath. And the Estmarch. If you won't agree to that, I can't call my men off. I came here last night to tell you our terms. Agree, and the siege will be lifted." He glanced out of the window at the sun. "You have until noon. If I don't get word to my men by then, my most trusted captain will smash down the gate and take the castle. Atrathenes fight like cornered patchcats. I suggest you consider it."

Her fingernails scraped along the edge of the chair. Rhodri ignored Meganne's sharp inhalation. All his attention was on Serren, watching her muscles tense.

"If you think I'm going to give up the land my parents risked their lives for—"

"Serren" Bale said from the window, his back to the room, "I don't think you have a choice. Look." As he pointed, an urgent hammering sounded against the chamber door. Serren glanced at Meganne, and the older woman rose to answer.

Rhodri couldn't see what Bale was looking at, but he could hear Amerie's breathless report.

"The Atrathenes are massing in front of the gate, my lady! They've got a demon with them! A giant iron horse that breathes fire!"

"Thank you, Amerie. Tell the men to hold their positions." Meganne patted the girl on the arm. "Everything will be fine. We won't let anything happen to you. If they break through, come back here. Do you have a knife?"

Amerie nodded. Her eyes, wide and frightened, met Rhodri's. "What about him?" she asked.

Meganne rubbed her temples. "He's my cousin's son, and he has my protection. That's all anyone needs to know. Now hurry!" She turned on Rhodri. "What's this talk of a demon? Is this a trick?"

"It's not a demon," Bale answered for him. "It's a battering ram shaped like a horse's head. Rhodri, is this what you planned?"

Nasira was moving her troops early. Maybe she hoped a show of force would bring things to a swift conclusion. "How long until the sun crests the highest tower?" he asked.

"Is that your signal to attack? Or is it when that hellish drumming stops?" He shook his head. "It's in your hands, Serren. What will you do?"

Her back was to Rhodri. She stared out of the window, over the high walls at the hostile army that encircled Hierath. He could see the tension in her spine. "I won't give up my mother's country. I won't!" She rounded on him, eyes blazing. "My parents went through the hells to win back this castle. Do you think you can just walk in here and claim it? I won't give it up, you bastard!"

Bale made a grab for her. She evaded his clutch, throwing herself at Rhodri. Sunlight glinted off the blade in her fist.

He flung up his arm to protect his throat. His chair toppled backwards under her impact, sending them crashing to the floor. Serren was quick, and her assault caught him off guard. He rolled as he hit the floor, lashing out with his feet. He caught Serren's hand and twisted the dagger from her grip, pinning her down, one arm pressed across her fragile throat. She kicked, spat in his face, but he held firm.

"Stay back!" A swipe of his fist caught Bale across the jaw, throwing the older man off his feet. Rhodri dragged Serren to her knees, knife pressed to her fluttering life-vein.

"I don't want to kill her," he said, "but I will, if you don't listen. Drop the bow, Lady Meganne."

The crossbow clattered to the floor. Rhodri kicked it out of reach. They would never let him go now. He had nothing to lose.

"On your feet, Serren. You and I are going to take a walk."

"Let her go, Rhodri." Bale dragged a hand across his mouth to wipe away the blood. "This won't help your cause."

"My life is over," Rhodri said. "I know that. But I can still stop the battle. Serren's going to help—"

"I will not!" The Queen struggled in his grip, feet and elbows flying.

"Serren, do as he says!" Meganne's hands were white, clutching the back of her chair in bloodless terror. "Do as he says and he won't hurt you." Her eyes pleaded. "You won't, will you? She's your sister!"

"As long as she does what I say." The thought of hurting a woman, even one as stubborn and intractable as Serren, repelled him, but he couldn't let Meganne see that. He steered his sister towards the door, using her body to shield him in case Bale made a sudden move. A coward's act, and he hated himself for it, but he had no choice.

"Where are you taking me?" Serren demanded. "If I scream, the guards will come running!"

"If you scream, you'll be dead before you hit the ground," Rhodri lied. "Tell them to stay back, or I'll kill you."

He hustled her through corridors and hallways. There was no one about to protect her. He guessed the population of Hierath was defending the walls, or hiding in dark corners. He wished he had that option. The security of his cell was a comfort compared to what lay ahead.

"Do you have a family, Rhodri?" Serren asked out of nowhere as they hesitated at the junction of two corridors. He heard voices raised in fear and anger. "I heard you had a wife, and children. A little boy, maybe?"

He pushed her on. "No family. Your man Elay saw to that. He stabbed my children while they slept."

"Elay? I don't know who you mean. But a traitor always walks alone, Rhodri. Didn't your father teach you that?"

"You know Valery wasn't my father. My blood is as pure as yours."

She sounded thoughtful, as he bundled her round the next corner. "If I lost my family like that, I'd be crippled. I wouldn't be able to walk and talk, much less fight. Maybe you didn't care too much about them?"

"Listen to me!" He slammed her up against the wall, driving the air from her lungs with a sharp gasp. "Don't you *ever* tell me I don't love my children! They were my whole world. There's no point living without them, so there's nothing you can do to hurt me now! Get moving!"

He pushed her down the corridor in front of him, breathing deeply to control his fury. Serren seemed to know every sore spot on his skin, and she relished picking at him.

"Is that why you came here? You lost your family, so you want to push your way into mine? It won't work, Rhodri. No one here wants you."

"Shut up, Serren. You don't know what you're talking about."

"Don't I?" she sneered. "If you are my brother, why do you think my mother gave you up? She never wanted you. Just an unloved bastard child . . ."

"I said shut up!" He shoved her harder than he intended. She stumbled, and he caught her arm before she could fall. "Just . . . stop talking!"

"Hurts, does it?" She rubbed her elbow where she had smashed it on the wall of the narrow corridor.

He ignored her taunt. A door in the curved wall ahead led to the base of one of the towers that jutted out of the corner of the wall above the gate. Through the thickness of stone, he heard the bass rumble of the massive Atrathene war drums, pounding out their threat. When they fell silent, the attack would begin.

"Come on!" Rhodri barged the door open with his shoulder and half dragged, half threw Serren through it. The room beyond was full of weapons, racks of crossbows and savage, hooked spear heads, and a grey-faced man who sprang to his feet at the dramatic entrance.

"Keep back!" Rhodri yelled, as he groped for a weapon. "I'll kill her! I mean it!"

"You won't kill her. You don't have the balls, Rhodri Northpoint."

The last time Rhodri heard that sneering voice, it had been in the thick of battle. He felt a twinge run through his bad shoulder at the memory, and swallowed down his nausea. "You can talk about having no balls, Dru. Why are you hiding in a cupboard when every other man in this castle is up on the walls, ready to die to defend their Queen?"

"Why are you hiding behind a girl? I should have killed you at Kingsmere." Dru levelled his sword. "Come here so I can finish the job."

Rhodri was armed only with the dagger he had stolen from Meganne's chambers. Against thirty-four inches of Northpoint steel, he didn't stand a chance.

"Dru, I can call off the attack. If you kill me, hundreds of people are going to die!"

"Horse shit!" Drusain lunged at him, barging Serren aside. She cried out as she stumbled, her head hitting the stone steps of the staircase with a crack, and lay crumpled.

Dru's sword struck sparks against the wall by Rhodri's head as he ducked under his arm, and snatched a spear from the rack. It was as long as he was tall, and he waved it clumsily, trying to hold Dru off until he found a better weapon.

"Dru, listen to me—" The spear was heavy, and a lucky blow against Dru's hip jerked it out of his hands. Dru winced, sword slipping to score a thin line across Rhodri's thigh. He fumbled his grip as Rhodri staggered back, knocking over a rack of crossbow bolts that clattered down around him. He snatched one and flung it at Dru's face.

The blunt end smashed into Dru's good eye. He cursed, blinking furiously. Rhodri ducked under his waving sword and grappled him round the waist, the momentum sending them both crashing to the floor.

Dru's sword skittered across the flagstones, away from Rhodri's fingers as he made a grab for it. He lashed out with his dagger and Dru's hand caught his wrist, twisting savagely, forcing his fingers apart. The blade tumbled to the floor as Dru's other hand closed around Rhodri's throat.

"Blind me, would you? You little fuck . . ."

"Dru, listen—" Suffocating fingers choked off his words. Black spots gathered at the corners of his eyes.

"What for? You're a lair, a traitor. Always have been . . ."

Shit, the drums were loud! Or maybe that was Rhodri's heartbeat, thundering in his head as he struggled for air.

"You lied about your father. You lied about Keir, Astan, everything!"

"Astan?" His voice was a feeble croak.

"You knew she was a girl. You were fucking her the whole time, weren't you?"

Angry tears gathered at the corners of Rhodri's eyes as he kicked and fought, with fading strength, to break free. Dru, hand still tight around his throat, drew back his fist and punched him in the face.

Rhodri felt his teeth crunch, the metal tang of liquid welling up in his mouth and pouring down his throat. He gagged, tried to spit. Dru's hand was clamped over his mouth, trying to drown him in his own blood. He closed his eyes against the punches, kicking weakly, trying to push him away as the warm blood flooded his throat.

He landed a feeble punch on Dru's upper arm, heard him shriek like a girl, high and scared. His fist smashed into the flagstones next to Rhodri's ear, splitting his knuckles open. He rolled away, clutching his calf and howling. Rhodri rolled over, vomiting blood, lungs rattling as he tried to suck in a breath.

"You fucking bitch!" Dru crawled towards Serren. She had freed her hands and was backed up against the stairs, holding her quivering dagger at arm's length. He tried to get up, legs slipping out from under him like a deer on ice. "You've hamstrung me, you whore!"

"Leave me alone!" She lashed out wildly. "I command you! I'm your Queen!"

Rhodri dragged himself to his feet, using the wall for support, spitting out the blood that filled his mouth. His ears were ringing, and he was so dizzy his vision blurred. He had the dim impression of Serren, pressed against the steps, nowhere to run as Dru dragged himself towards her, screaming and cursing. As his hands closed on her ankle, dragging her to the floor, Rhodri lunged for Dru's abandoned sword. He grabbed it by the blade, heedless of the cuts to his fingers, and swung it around. The pommel, a sphere of metal larger than his fist, crunched into Dru's skull behind his left ear, sending him sprawling on his face. Rhodri kicked him onto his back, and levelled the point of the sword against his throat.

"Goodbye, Drusain."

"No, wait!" Dru squirmed on his back, trying dig through the floor with his shoulder blades. "I spared you at Kingsmere! We've been friends for so long! Doesn't that mean anything to you?"

"*Friends?* After everything you've done?" Rhodri twisted the blade. A spot of blood welled at the tip. "Why did you let me live, at Kingsmere? I wouldn't have shown you any mercy . . ."

To his horror, Dru began to cry, fat tears splashing on to the floor. "Because I couldn't kill you! I can't kill anyone! Every time I fight my hands shake so much I can't even hold a sword, and I get sick to my guts. Every fucking time! Even Astan had more balls than me!"

Rhodri spat in disgust. "I'll say he did! You're a bloody coward, Dru. I should stick you right through the throat for everything you've done . . ."

There was something at the edge of his hearing, a strange absence. He shook his head to clear it.

Serren wiped her nose with her palm. "Rhodri—?"

"Don't kill me! By the stars, Rhodri, you don't have to do this!" Dru writhed in fear, clutching at Rhodri's ankles and pleading. "You don't have to kill me!"

"Rhodri, the drums—"

The war drums had fallen silent. Outside, the attack had started.

"Hells!" Rhodri shook his leg free of Dru's grovelling grip, and kicked him smartly in the face, hearing his nose crunch under the leather. He rolled away, clutching his face and sobbing like a broken man. Rhodri dismissed him from his mind. Dru was no threat; the threat lay outside the walls, from his chosen people.

"Go!" He pushed Serren up the narrow, twisting stair, which ended in a half-landing and a small closed door. As he reached the last step, his knees buckled, and he sagged against the wall, all the hurts of the last few days catching up with him at once.

"Are you all right?" Serren sounded concerned. "Your face looks bad."

"It feels numb." He raised his fingers to the swellings on his jaw, around his eye. One of his molars was loose, he could wobble it with his tongue, taste the blood there. He spat, frothy crimson. "You don't look so good yourself." She had a bump above her eye, a long gash with raised flesh swelling up around it.

"Come on." He pushed open the door a crack, letting in a riot of noise, a shaft of sunlight.

Serren hung back. "Where are you taking me?"

He grabbed her wrist. The moment of truce was over between them. "I'm taking you to surrender, little sister."

"Like hells you are!" She scratched his arm, trying to pull away.

"Why did you bother helping me back there if you're only going to fight me now?"

Serren scowled, said nothing, but let him drag her through the door and onto the battlements above the gate. The wall was in a frenzy, and Rhodri was dazzled for a moment by the bright sunlight striking off swords and spearheads, mail and armour. It took a few seconds for his eyes to adjust, and a few more for the defenders to realise he was there, what he held.

"Get back!" He tightened his arm around Serren's throat and brandished the dagger. "Get back or I kill the Queen! All of you, move!"

From below, above the howls of the Atrathene rabble, came a splintering crash. The solid stone of the wall vibrated through the soles of his feet.

"The gate!" A soldier barged past him down to the armoury, heedless of Serren. "The gate is breached! To arms!"

Rhodri had to drag Serren to one side to avoid being trampled in the rush to the stairs. He glanced over the wall, seeing the Atrathenes pour into the courtyard, through the broken gate. Spreading out, hunting like pack animals. He caught a flash of grey hide in the tumult, and it sent a shudder through him.

Let her be safe, Spirits. I'll give anything you ask, but don't take her away from me . . .

He turned to Serren, who was gaping like a fish. "They didn't stop to help me!"

"They're defending your walls. What more do you want?"

"But if I die—?"

"If you die, they have two more sisters ready to take your place, but there's only one Hierath. The Heart of the Kingdom, remember? It doesn't stop beating just because the Queen is gone." He dragged her away from the wall. "Give me your flag. I can make them stop at any time."

Serren's eyes travelled up to the Eagle standard, flapping in the breeze from the ramparts of the tower opposite the one they had just left. Her bottom lip jutted. "You'll have to kill me first."

"You stupid stubborn bitch!" Rhodri roared, all patience lost; he pushed her along the wall towards the tower. "Can you hear your people screaming, sister? Dying, because of you? My tribe won't back down, and nor will I. Surrender, or watch your men slaughtered in your halls."

The far door was unlocked, swinging open to his touch. Stairs, up and down, and a tiny landing with a trembling teenage soldier guarding it, alone. He levelled his crossbow at Serren.

"I was ordered to defend this stair—"

"Leave us!" Serren's voice was no longer imperious, but high and terrified. "Go, and he'll let me live! If you love your Queen, do as I command!"

A clang of metal hitting stone, and he dropped the bow and scrambled down the stairs. Rhodri dragged Serren up, pushing her through a sloping trapdoor and out onto the highest ramparts of the castle, where the sun had given Nasira the signal to attack. Noon had come and gone, and she had kept her word. She had come in to get him.

"Look!" He dragged Serren to the extreme edge, leaning out over the fortifications so there was nothing below her torso but empty air and unforgiving stone. The courtyard had descended into a hellish melee, every man fighting for himself, on foot,

368

against the battle-maddened ranks of Atrathene cavalry and furious Estmarchers. Men were dying in their hundreds, on both sides. "I wanted to avoid this, but you wouldn't fucking listen, would you? You brought this about, and you can end it. If you don't, every man who fights for you will be dead by nightfall. Your friends. Your lovers. Even Lord Caythen. Give me what I want, and it stops."

Serren stared down in horror at the violence, hands pressed to her ears to try and block out the screams of men and horses in their death agonies. Her lips trembled, and the tears coursed down her cheeks. "Hierath . . . My parents . . ."

"Our parents did what they had to, to save your people from tyranny. Lay aside your sword, Serren. It's too late."

"It's not! We'll fight to the last man—"

"Damn you, Serren, do you want everyone to die? What did you save me for?"

"I saved you,"—she swallowed hard—"I saved you because . . . because I felt sorry for you. Because you reminded me . . . of my . . . of my father . . ."

"Do you think our father would want this to happen?"

"No!" Serren threw herself on her knees before her brother, no longer a queen, but a desperate, terrified young woman. "Stop it! You can have the Estmarch! I'll leave Atrath! Call your men off!"

"Will you give me Hierath? Will you call me your brother, in front of all men? Tell me, Serren! Call me brother, and I can make it stop!"

She buried her head in her hands. Her voice was muffled, rising over the crashing wave of violence and death in her halls. "Yes!" It was a wail of despair, of horror. "Hierath is yours, Rhodri! You are my brother!"

"Take down your flag!" Serren ran across the roof of the tower, tattered dress flying, tearing at the ropes that kept her standard flying. The flag rustled to the floor. Rhodri snatched it from her shaking hands and flapped it urgently from the ramparts.

"Nasira! Nasira, we've won!"

He didn't know if his voice would reach her cat-sharp ears over the chaos. Serren joined him, waving her arms and shrieking. "Men of Hierath, lay down your arms! Lay them down, damn you!"

Gradually, the ripple spread across the bloodbath in the courtyard. Men looked up, saw the empty flagpole, heard the cries. Threw down their weapons, dropped to their knees or prostrated themselves on the ground before their victorious foes, as whoops of victory arose from Atrathene throats. Rhodri sank to the floor, back cradled by the stone breastwork, exhausted beyond thought. The cost had been hideous, too great to count, but he had his home, his children's future. It lay in the stone under his hands, and in the hearts of his people. Tomorrow, when the blood was sluiced away and the bodies burned, it would feel like it had all been worth it.

*

The treaties were drafted in such haste the ink was still wet when Rhodri came to sign them. Up to his ankles in churned mud, resting on the battered wooden body of the Scourge that lay abandoned halfway through the broken shards of the gate. His actions were watched with quiet suspicion by both sides. The setting sun cast a russet wash over the stones of Hierath. He stared at it, squinting through eyes swollen with bruises. The postern gate was wide open, an invitation to walk in and claim his inheritance. He had come here to make a home, find a family, and now he had both. Everything he had ever wanted.

"Here!" Niklaus nudged him in the ribs. He was pale, leaning on Sudak's arm. Jilly hovered at his shoulder like a bodyguard, dour, hands never far from her blades. "Sign this one. This is the one I care about."

Freedom for the Estmarch, under Niklaus. The hilly land of his mother's birth would be an independent state. Estmarch Freedom would have to cope with the responsibility of that, and not everyone who lived there would welcome the change in status, but that was Nik's problem now. The treaty establishing the sanctity of the Atrathene border was less complicated, and as he handed it to Bale to countersign, he recited what it said to his followers in their own tongue, to a cheer of celebration.

He was left with one final document to put his name to. Already signed by Bale, Meganne, Serren and Niklaus, it was left to Rhodri to ratify it. The treaty giving Hierath, and its Kingdom, to him and his heirs for eternity. Finn and Asta's inheritance, Prince and Princess of the Realm. He dipped his quill in the ink and signed it with a flourish.

Behind Meganne, Nasira hung her head. The sky above her was narrow and grey.

Serren glared at him. "I suppose you have everything you want now, *brother?*"

"Not quite." He climbed onto the back of the Scourge, a delicate balancing act, holding the treaty up for his men to see. A witty voice in the crowd called for a speech, but Rhodri was tired of speeches, of fighting over flags and legacies. It was time to put an end to it.

With a flourish to match the one with which he had signed his name, he took the freshly-minted treaty, and, locking his eyes with Serren, took a deep breath. Slowly, deliberately, he ripped it down the middle, crumpled the pieces in his fist, and let the wind take them. Nasira lifted her head to see the fluttering piece of paper whisk above her as it was caught in an updraft, lost against the sky. She caught his eye, then raised one arm in a silent, private salute as she smiled for the first time in days.

"Hierath is yours," he said to his sister. "There's nothing I need here."

*

As Nik and Serren, two sovereign rulers, discussed the finer points of the Estmarch treaty, Rhodri felt a tug on his sleeve. He allowed himself to be drawn away. Lady Meganne Caythen, dressed in her finery, wanted to talk to him. Over her shoulder, she wore a small satchel. In contrast with her delicate silks and linens, it looked shabby, with frayed straps and leather patched so many times that little of the original bag was left.

"I want you to have something," she said.

"Meganne, you don't owe me any gift. Maybe a slap for the way I treated Serren!" He grinned, but her face was serious.

"It's not from me," she said. "I have something that belongs to you."

From the bag, she produced the last thing he expected. A woollen horse, a child's toy. Its eyes were mismatched, the stuffing leaked from its leg joints, and one ear had been worn to shreds.

"You remember everything," Meganne said. "Do you remember this?"

He took the well-loved object, turning it over in his hands. "No," he admitted. "Should I?"

"It was yours. When you were a babe, Lydia left you with Bale's sister. She hoped she could keep you safe from Valery; she knew if he found you he would kill you." She frowned. "What he did to you was little better, I feel."

"She left me." There would always be that heavy finality, the knowledge that she had abandoned him. If not with Valery, then with someone else, people he couldn't remember.

"It broke her heart. You say you don't remember her—how could you? All she wanted was to come back for you, take you somewhere safe. She didn't want the bloody Kingdom, Rhodri! People say she fought for the Kingdom, but she was fighting for you. To get you back. This,"—she shook the little horse—"we found it at the house the day you were taken. They killed Bale's sister, snatched you from her arms, and they wouldn't even let you take your toys! You were a baby, barely walking. Lydia carried this toy next to her heart for the rest of her life. She vowed she would find you and give it back to you. Even when everyone said you were dead, she never gave up hope."

Rhodri felt his hands tighten around the battered toy. His mother must have held it this way, hoping for a miracle she hadn't lived to witness. There was a hot lump of coal in his chest, and it was hard to swallow, much less speak.

Meganne cleared her throat. "I think she'd want you to have it now. So you know that she never stopped looking for you, never stopped loving you." She patted his arm and withdrew, leaving the ragged horse in his hands. When he looked up from it, the sunset was hazy and his cheeks were wet with tears.

*

I have never learned the art of forgetting. Sometimes at night I wake in cold horror, remembering the things I've witnessed, the crimes I've committed. But I have my woman's hand to calm my fears, the laughter of my children to drive out the darkness. Some things, a child's love for a precious toy, a mother's for her son, deserve to be remembered forever. I have my family around me, and wherever we travel across the sweeping steppes of Atrath, we create new, joyful memories. These are the memories I cling to hardest, the ones I will always treasure the most.

About the Author

Joanne Hall lives in Bristol with her partner, and they are owned by the World's Laziest Dog ™ She is a full time writer, part time editor and occasional procrastinator and is happiest when she's making things up and writing them down. She enjoys movies and music, and owns too many books she hasn't got around to reading yet.

Her short stories have featured in a number of anthologies, and she is the co-editor (with Roz Clarke) of *Colinthology* and *Airship Shape and Bristol Fashion*. When she's not writing or editing, Joanne can be found chairing BristolCon, Bristol's annual SF and Fantasy convention, and hanging about on Twitter. Her blog can be found at www.hierath.co.uk and she always likes to hear from readers.

The Art of Forgetting : Nomad, the second half of the *Art of Forgetting* duology, is her fifth published novel.

Acknowledgements

So this is the end. We've ridden a long trail to get here, and it's been entertaining, exasperating and occasionally infuriating, but I hope you'll agree that the end result was worth every second of both swearing and celebration.

I'd like to thank my Tribes : The Kristell Ink Tribe, Sammy, Zoë, Evelinn, and Ken, who between them turned Nomad into a book, and Gilly, Elizabeth, Dean, Paige and Debbie – we have been holding each other's hands for a long time now, and I couldn't work with nicer people.

The Local Tribe : Heather, Claire H, Dolly, Kate (and her own little Tribe), Clare N, Cheryl, Roz, Mark, Gareth, Colin (RIP), Andy, Des, Emma, Pete, and the BristolCon ConCom and Bristol Fantasy and SF Soc, who gave me somewhere to go on Mondays that wasn't deep inside my own head. You guys picked me up, carried me, bashed me round the head when I was being a twit, and turned up in the World's Worst Weather to celebrate the "Rider" launch. Friends are the family we choose for ourselves.

The Online Tribe : Laura Evans, Martha Hubbard, Andy Fairchild, Jen Williams, Emma Pass, Laura Lam, Mark R Hunter, Marc Aplin and the Fantasy Faction Crew, Lor Graham, Danie Ware, Fran Jacobs, and everyone who left reviews or comments, or emailed to tell me what I was doing right (or wrong!). And my readers.

Especially my readers. This would not have happened without you and your support. Thanks for riding with me on the journey.

My Tribe : Mum, Saira, and Nicky and Mark, Jack and Jenny, and Will and Jane.

Extra special thanks and love to Lyra and Chris – you are my family and my home.

Other Titles from Kristell Ink

Strange Tales from the Scriptorian Vaults

A Collection of Steampunk Stories edited by Sammy HK Smith
All profits go to the charity First Story.

Published October 2012

Non-Compliance: The Sector by Paige Daniels

I used to matter . . . but now I'm just a girl in a ghetto, a statistic of the Non-Compliance Sector.

Shea Kelly had a brilliant career in technology, but after refusing to implant an invasive government device in her body she was sent to a modern day reservation: a Non-Compliance Sector, a lawless community run by thugs and organized crime. She's made a life for herself as a resourceful barkeep, and hacks for goods on the black market with her best friend Wynne, a computer genius and part-time stripper. Life is pretty quiet under the reigning Boss, apart from run-ins with his right hand man, the mighty Quinn: until Danny Rose threatens to take over the sector. Pushed to the edge, Shea decides to fight back . . .

Published November 2012

Healer's Touch by Deb E. Howell

A girl who has not only the power to heal through taking life fights for her freedom.

Llew has a gift. Her body heals itself, even from death, but at the cost of those nearby. In a country fearful of magic, freeing yourself from the hangman's noose by wielding forbidden power brings its own dangers. After dying and coming back to life, Llew drops from the gallows into the hands of Jonas: the man carrying a knife with the power to kill her.

Published February 2013

Darkspire Reaches by C.N. Lesley

The wyvern has hunted for the young outcast all her life; a day will come when she must at last face him.

Abandoned as a sacrifice to the wyvern, a young girl is raised to fear the beast her adoptive clan believes meant to kill her. When the Emperor outlaws all magic, Raven is forced to flee from her home with her foster mother, for both are judged as witches. Now an outcast, she lives at the mercy of others, forever pursued by the wyvern as she searches for her rightful place in the world. Soon her life will change forever as she discovers the truth about herself.

A unique and unsettling romantic adventure about rejection and belonging.

Published March 2013

Space Games by Dean Lombardo

The cameras are on and the gloves are off in this battle of the sexes on the new International Space Station.

Say hello to Robin and Joe—contestants in 2034's "Space Games," a new, high-stakes reality TV show from Hollywood producer Sheldon J. Zimmer . . .

Space Games is a compelling story and a biting satire about reality television: those who make and participate in it – and those who watch it.

Published May 2013

The Art of Forgetting: Rider by Joanne Hall

A young boy leaves his village to become a cavalryman with the famous King's Third regiment; in doing so he discovers both his past and his destiny.

Gifted and cursed with a unique memory, the foundling son of a notorious traitor, Rhodri joins an elite cavalry unit stationed in the harbour town of Northpoint. His training reveals his talents and brings him friendship, love and loss, and sexual awakening; struggling with his memories of his father who once ruled there, he begins to discover a sense of belonging. That is, until a face from the past reveals a secret that will change not only Rhodri's life but the fate of a nation. Then, on his first campaign, he is forced to face the extremes of war and his own nature.

This, the first part of The Art of Forgetting, is a gripping story about belonging and identity, set in a superbly imagined and complex world that is both harsh and beautiful.

Published June 2013

The Reluctant Prophet by Gillian O'Rourke

There's none so blind as she who can see . . .

Esther is blessed, and cursed, with a rare gift: the ability to see the fates of those around her. But when she escapes her peasant upbringing to become a priestess of the Order, she begins to realise how valuable her ability is among the power-hungry nobility, and what they are willing to do to possess it.

Haunted by the dark man of her father's warnings, and unable to see her own destiny, Esther is betrayed by those sworn to protect her. With eyes newly open to the harsh realities of her world, she embarks on a path that diverges from the plan the Gods have laid out. Now she must choose between sacrificing her own heart's blood, and risking a future that will turn the lands against each other in bloody war.

The Reluctant Prophet is the story of one woman who holds the fate of the world in her hands, when all she wishes for is a glimpse of her own happiness.

Published August 2013

Shadow Over Avalon by C.N. Lesley

Fortune twists in the strongest hands. This is no repeat; this is what happens next.

A man, once a legend who bound his soul to his sword as he lay dying, is now all but a boy nearing the end of his acolyte training. Stifled by life in the undersea city of Avalon, Arthur wants to fight side by side with the air-breathing Terrans, not spend his life as servant to the incorporeal sentient known as the Archive. Despite the restrictions put on him by Sanctuary, he is determined to help the surface-dwellers defeat the predators whose sole purpose is to ensure their own survival no matter the cost.

Published October 2013

Non-Compliance: The Transition by Paige Daniels

Three months have passed since Shea Kelly and the rest of Boss's crew eliminated Danny Rose from the Non-Compliance Sector, but their troubles are far from over. A new, more dangerous opponent has emerged, causing those once considered enemies to strike a tenuous truce. Secrets about the vaccine, the chip, and the past threaten Shea's budding romance and even the very existence of the crew.

Published December 2013

www.kristell-ink.com

Lightning Source UK Ltd.
Milton Keynes UK
UKOW03f0722270514

232349UK00002B/83/P